chonnel
BLUE

JAY MARTEL is an award-winning
writer and producer. He collaborated
with Michael Moore on the acclaimed
documentary *Farenheit 911* and was
contributing editor at *Rolling Stone*
for six years. This is his first novel.

chonnel BLUE

JAY MARTEL

HEAD
ᵍZEUS

First published in the UK in 2014 by Head of Zeus Ltd

9 7 5 3 1 2 4 6 8

A CIP catalogue record for this book is available from
the British Library.

ISBN (TPBO): 9781781855805
ISBN (E): 9781781855799

Typeset by Palimpsest Book Production Ltd, Falkirk, Stirlingshire

Printed in Germany

Head of Zeus Ltd
Clerkenwell House
45-47 Clerkenwell Green,
London EC1R 0HT

www.headofzeus.com

'God is watching us, God is watching us.
God is watching us from a distance.'

Popular Earth ballad

PROLOGUE

Confidential Memo
From: Gerald O. Davidoff
To: Interplanetary Board Members
Re: Strategies to Maintain Current Prime-Time
Dominance in Western Galaxy

Mankind's greatest quest is no longer for food, or shelter, or freedom, or even to pass his genetic material onto future generations. Today, mankind's greatest challenge is to avoid boredom. Without a steady and cathartic flow of quality entertainment, we know all too well that humanity would soon turn violently on itself and, in time, cease to exist.

That is why our work is so incredibly important.

As you are all aware, we have always taken quite seriously the provision of the very best entertainment to our fellow Edenites. In the last few centuries, we have seen exciting growth as our company has moved into new worlds, establishing planetainments throughout the galaxy. Last year, at the Extra-Planetary Entertainment Awards, we took home Orbys in 217 of 573 categories, and this year we'll do even better. I am presently supervising the construction of *CrazyWorld 67* in the Horsehead Nebula, and I can tell you all right now

1

that it's going to be the craziest world yet. In other encouraging news, *SlutPlanet* is up and running over in Rigel 4 and completely dominating its time slots.

As most of you know, I started out as a travel agent. The two businesses have a lot more similarities than you'd think. In both, we expose our customers to new experiences, immeasurably enriching their lives. And in both businesses it's important to know when it's time to move on. In this case, I'm referring to our planet in the Orion Arm. As you all know, I have a strong attachment to this particular world. It was my very first planet and without it I would never have become part of the Galaxy Entertainment family. But no one can deny that its programming has fallen off quite a bit in the last few seasons, and while I, more than anyone, appreciate the quality shows that have been produced there in the past, I also need to recognise that the storylines have become too bizarre, the cast too unlikable to sustain the ratings we have come to expect. I think we can all agree that this planet 'jumped the shark' a long time ago. Plus, the resources spent on this single world could be used to develop several planetainments in less-expensive solar systems.

As a result of these considerations, I regrettably feel that the time has come to cancel Earth.

CHANNEL 1

GROUNDED IN REALITY

'*Believability.*'

Perry Bunt pronounced the word slowly and solemnly, hoping this would help it sink into the skulls of his screenwriting students.

'Without believability, you have no hope of involving the audience in your story.'

The students in his 10 a.m. class stared back blankly at Perry, their minds occupied, no doubt, with how to argue the believability of a dog with extrasensory powers or a flying baby. On the one hand, Perry couldn't help but admire the courage of their convictions. Once he too had possessed this kind of confidence.

Not so long ago, Perry Bunt had been known as one of the premiere Idea Men in the entertainment business. It seemed like everything he set his eyes on gave him an idea for a movie. One day he picked up his phone and thought, 'What if I could call anyone on this – even dead people?' and in a flash, the entire story unfolded before his eyes (*Guy gets mysterious call on his dead wife's phone telling him who killed her*). Later that week, he optioned 'Dead Call Zone' to a major studio.

There were days when Perry's mind was so full of stories that there wasn't room for anything else. The problems began when he sat down to write them. For while Perry possessed a keen sense of what made a story interesting ('the hook' in the parlance of the movie industry), he was mediocre when it came to actually putting words onto a page ('the writing' in the parlance of the movie industry). Staring at his computer screen, Perry had a terrible realisation: dreaming up a story had almost nothing to do with writing it. Dreaming was inspiring and fun; writing was gruelling and difficult. While dreaming required little follow-through, writing demanded almost nothing but. Perry, it turned out, had very little follow-through.

The executives he worked for were even worse. Jittery at the thought they'd spent hundreds of thousands of dollars in vain, they'd tell Perry they absolutely loved what he'd written and then proceed to pepper him with haphazard notes – 'Consider changing the boy to a dog'; 'Let's talk about changing the dog to a cat'; 'We all agree that the cat isn't working and that a boy would raise the emotional stakes' – the movie-industry equivalent of the panicked screaming you might hear in a burning airplane plummeting towards the ground. When confronted with these contradictory ideas, Perry would further torture his mauled script and then, eventually, give up and chase the next Big Idea. It wasn't that he was a bad writer; if he'd been forced to work exclusively on one of his many stories, a good script would have no doubt resulted. But he was always tempted away by the *next* script, convinced that this would be the one that would prove irresistible to filmmakers and audiences. Ideas, like relationships, are always more exciting when they are new.

'You get six, sometimes seven scripts before they find you out,' his first agent had warned him. Sure enough, after Perry sold his seventh script – and that script, like all the others he'd written, was never made into a movie – his career began a long ride downward. It took a while for him to realise what was happening. The true Hollywood ending is no ending at all; there is no fade to black, no elegiac music, no credits. There is only a phone that doesn't ring. Perry learned that no news wasn't good news, but was instead bad news taking its time. He had once dreaded the phone calls – the phoney banter, the ubiquitous schmoozing, the mendacious puffery – but now he missed them. He wouldn't mind if someone called and lied to him, as long as they called.

For a while, Perry still found work in the entertainment business. On *Hey, Hey Fiancée*, a television show featuring newly engaged couples on a tropical island, he was tasked with devising ways of breaking up the affianced. Sickened by the experience, he quit after two episodes and vowed never to work in the so-called reality TV genre again. Had there ever been a more egregious misnomer than 'reality TV'? In what kind of reality do people routinely become craven animals on display?

His principles came at a high cost: after *Hey, Hey Fiancée*, he could find employment only on a children's show about a talking wombat, which was soon replaced by a cartoon featuring hyper-aggressive koala bears. After scripting an industrial for a juicer, Perry hit the end of the line: teaching.

It was a shock from which he had yet to recover. 'Bunt's a Hit' proclaimed a *Variety* headline that Perry still carried in his wallet. Yellowed and torn, it was a small signifier of his denial that this same Bunt was now teaching eight classes a week of Beginning Screenwriting at the Encino Community College, where he made it a personal mission to break young writers of the delusions he saw as his undoing.

'Ideas are a dime a dozen,' he told his 10 a.m. class. Perry surveyed the students, holding his smallish frame as erect as possible to emphasise his seriousness. Though he had once been considered handsome, with delicate features framed by dark curly hair, that was when a Bush was President, and it wasn't the one who stayed in Iraq. Now in the last gasp of his thirties, balding and a little thick around the middle, Perry's features appeared misplaced on a head that seemed too big for them. 'It's all about follow-through. It's all about execution. It's all about *grounding your scripts in reality.*'

The impetus for his well-worn lecture on believability was a scene written by a large goateed boy–man named Brent Laskey, one of the students Perry referred to as the *Faux*rantinos. Perry's least favourite filmmaker was Quentin Tarantino, not because of his movies *per se*, but because every time he made a movie, a thousand Brent Laskeys bought screenwriting software, convinced that writing a film consisted of nothing more complicated than thinking up new ways for people to die.

Brent's screenplay was about a med-school student who pays his tuition by moonlighting as a hitman for the Mob, then discovers a cure for cancer. It was among the class's more plausible scripts. In the scene up for discussion, the hitman is attempting to assassinate a Colombian drug kingpin. When his sniper rifle jams, he steals a helicopter, flies it upside down, and improbably decapitates the kingpin and his bodyguards.

'Without plausibility, you have no credibility,' Perry said, winding up his all-too-familiar rant. 'And when you lose credibility, you lose your audience. Any questions?' The students' expressions remained resolutely blank, as if their disinterest was all that kept their bodies propped upright. Perry was about to return to the open script on his desk when a hand shot up in the back of the class. Perry was pleased to see that it belonged to an attractive young woman in a blue jacket. This woman's name was Amanda Mundo.

Perry's students generally fell into two categories that he labelled 'the geniuses' and 'the nut-jobs'. The geniuses were laconic, arrogant young men and women who dreamed, like Perry, of being successful writers. This class was a tedious necessity for them, a stepping stone to surpassing their poorly dressed, caffeinated instructor and being recognised for the geniuses they were. When Perry praised, they listened attentively; when he criticised, their eyes glazed over as they travelled in their minds to the ceremonies where they would gratefully gather their Oscars, pausing long enough in their acceptance speeches to attempt to remember, without success, the name of that discontented, sloppy little man who was once their teacher.

Perry disliked these students the most because he had been one of them.

Then there were the nut-jobs. These were students like Doreena Stump, a born-again 52-year-old night nurse who was honing her skills to 'deliver the Good News to Hellywood'. Her 200-page screenplays inevitably involved heroes who were handsome Baptist ministers, villains who were Volvo-driving atheists, and miraculous events: many, many miraculous events. Perry thought about reading them the same way a doctor thought about treating a penicillin-resistant strain of pneumonia.

Finally – or in Perry's mind, ultimately – there was Amanda Mundo. Amanda transcended categorisation. Seeing her stride unselfconsciously into his morning class – her open smile, her freckles seemingly arranged by a mathematical genius for maximum adorableness, her long blonde hair perfectly swept over one shoulder – had become the highlight of his days. She had the daunting beauty of a Teutonic supermodel, but none of the harshness. Her warm hazel eyes crinkled in the corners whenever she smiled or laughed (which was often), and the irises were universes unto themselves: swirling pools of blue, green and grey, the black pupils haloed by coronas of gold. She spoke in a lilting voice with an accent that Perry couldn't place. South Africa? New Zealand? It was just exotic enough to make her even more appealing, if that were possible.

Never had someone so charming and normal taken Perry's class, but this was only the beginning of Amanda Mundo's uniqueness. In his successful years, Perry had met many beautiful women; he'd even dated movie stars (albeit briefly and without getting past first base). There had been stretches of Perry's life when he'd gone *weeks* without seeing a female he didn't want to have sex with – in Hollywood, unattractive women were encouraged to move or hide themselves in basements. And in Hollywood movies, this erasure of the non-beautiful went a step further. Every heroine's name that Perry introduced into his screenplays was followed by a two-word character description: '*Extremely attractive*' – unless the heroine was someone you might have a hard time imagining being extremely attractive, such as an ageing field hand or a crippled fishmonger. In this case Perry would describe them as '*Extremely attractive in a down-to-earth way*'. Had the movie executives read anything else, such as '*Good-looking for her age*' or '*Pretty despite her disability*', their heads might have exploded. '*Extremely attractive in a down-to-earth way*' was the *minimum*.

But for all this, Perry had never met – or dreamt of – anyone like Amanda. If she were to appear in one of his scripts, he wasn't sure he'd even be able to describe her. '*Extremely attractive in a natural* way'? '*Stunningly beautiful but not like any woman you'd see in a movie'?* It took several classes for Perry to figure out what was different about her, but eventually he did: Amanda, for all her beauty, *didn't seem to know she was beautiful.* It was as if she'd been raised on a remote island by the Amish. She never made him feel as if he was lucky to be talking to her, thus removing the self-consciousness that diminished every encounter Perry had experienced with the extremely attractive. He found he could actually talk freely to her and even, shockingly enough, be himself in her presence.

For her part, Amanda seemed genuinely thrilled to be taught by Perry, taking copious notes and laughing whenever he tried to be funny, which was by far the quickest way to his heart. When they began chatting after class, he discovered that she had a skill for revealing little, while simultaneously summoning forth his most personal details. Once he asked her where she was from. She didn't baulk at this terrible cliché, but instead smiled and said, 'Where do you think?'

'I don't know,' he said. 'I can't quite identify your accent. I'm usually pretty good at figuring them out, too.'

'Really?' Amanda said with interest. 'How do you do that? Have you travelled a lot?' And just like that, the focus of the conversation became the summer after Perry's college graduation, when he'd bought a Eurorail pass and managed to vomit in every European capital.

After another class, he opened up to her about the decline of his fortunes. Just when he thought he'd gone too far, that he'd repelled her with the stench of his failure and the musk of his self-pity, she hit him with the most blinding smile he'd ever seen.

'This is just a second-act setback,' she said. 'You know how it works, Mr Bunt. You have over half the movie to come back.' As if this weren't enough, she added, 'And I for one will be watching', affectionately tapping him on the shoulder.

As she tapped him, the sleeve of her jacket pulled slightly up her forearm, revealing a small blue tattoo on the inside of her left wrist. Perry couldn't see what it was exactly, but the mere glimpse of it stirred him in ways about which he felt immediately embarrassed. In his youth, only sailors and hardened criminals acquired tattoos, but now everyone under thirty seemed to have one and, for the first time, Perry understood why. The tap made his whole body feel warm.

'Please,' he said. 'Call me Perry.'

After this, he shared with Amanda his deepest secrets and most fervent hopes. He told her of his undying faith in the life of the mind and the power of creativity, how he knew there was a way to imagine himself out of his current situation.

'I have no doubt you will,' she said.

She became the star of Perry's fantasies. In her smile he saw deliverance from the squalor of his lonely apartment. In her lilting laugh he heard the love that would help him believe again in his writing. In the touch of her hand he felt the confidence that he would one day not have to masturbate quite so often, but also, paradoxically, the need to do so almost immediately.

His fantasies, however, were always tinged with sadness, as he had no doubt that she was out of his league. Though she didn't wear any rings, Perry was certain that a woman like Amanda had to have a boyfriend, and one who probably owned an unstained pair of pants. She never mentioned anyone, though, and the germ of hope that had infected Perry began to cause sleeplessness. He needed to know the bad news as soon as possible to be able to move on with his life. So in the middle of one of their after-class conversations, Perry blurted out, apropos of nothing, 'Do you have a boyfriend?'

To his surprise, Amanda didn't flinch at the Asperger's-like awkwardness of this question.

'Yes,' she said, and Perry's heart plummeted down an elevator shaft. 'But—' His heart shot back up into his chest. 'He lives very far away. We're trying to make it work.'

'Right,' Perry said, feeling the blood returning to his limbs. 'Long-distance relationships can be very challenging.' Just like that, he decided that Amanda's boyfriend was history. Some day, before the term was over, Perry would ask Amanda if she would like to have a cup of coffee and talk more about her screenplay. She would gladly agree, and that coffee would become a date, which she wouldn't even realise was a date until they found themselves in each other's arms. This date would become several dates, a relationship and, eventually, the love that would save Perry from lonely misery.

This, Perry knew, was the Romance Story, one of seven story templates from which all Hollywood movies were constructed. But that didn't stop him from believing it.

There was only one problem with this plan. While the other students routinely assaulted Perry with long and terrible screenplays that demanded his immediate attention, Amanda hadn't turned in a single word. As the term went on, this became a source of anxiety. *Why is she in my class?* he wondered. Was she mocking him? Did she think she could just sit back and watch his degradation without participating in it?

'Excuse me, Mr Bunt?' In the back of the classroom, Amanda patiently continued to hold up her hand. It took Perry a moment to remember the current discussion. How long had he been staring at her? 'I had a question? About Mr Laskey's script?'

'I'm sorry, Amanda. What is it?'

'Was Molina's head cut off by the main blade or that little whirling thing in the back?'

Before Perry could react, Brent Laskey adjusted his backward baseball cap with the cocky confidence of an *auteur*. 'The main rotor. My guy spins the helicopter upside down, flies it six feet off the ground and *whack*, no more head.'

Amanda smiled and made a note on her pad. *Et tu, Amanda?* Perry thought. He glowered at the class. 'The question is really beside the point, since no one in the history of the world has ever used a helicopter to decapitate someone purposely, let alone flown one upside down.'

'That's what made it so awesome,' said Heath Barber, another *Faux*rantino. 'It's completely new. You literally nailed it, dude.'

As Heath and Brent exchanged a high five, Perry fought back extreme annoyance. In addition to encouraging Brent's suspension of logic, Heath had flagrantly engaged in Perry's linguistic pet peeve: the use of 'literally' to mean its opposite. Normally, Perry would have corrected this, but the conversation was already running away from him, devolving into a debate on whether you could fly a helicopter upside down. To his further irritation, this was the liveliest discussion of the term.

'It's physically impossible!' Perry interrupted. 'It breaks every rule of aero-fucking-dynamics, all right? It can't possibly happen!' The students stared at him, and he immediately aware that he was talking too loudly. He cleared his throat and attempted a disarming smile, which came off more like an incongruous grimace. 'It's always fun to speculate, of course, but let's move on.'

Given his certitude on the subject, Perry was more than

a little surprised when Brent Laskey strode into the classroom the next day and dropped a newspaper clipping on his desk.

'I guess that settles it,' the student said.

Perry picked up the clipping and read this headline:

COLOMBIAN DRUG LORD SLAIN
BY HELICOPTER
INVERTED CHOPPER DECAPITATES KINGPIN

CHANNEL 2

THE STRANGE THING ABOUT PERRY BUNT

At the end of the day, Perry gathered up his things and was almost out the door when he noticed the newspaper article. It was still lying on his desk where Brent Laskey had dropped it, transforming his 10 a.m. class into an ordeal. Perry's students couldn't seem to get enough of their teacher eating his words, piling it on to mock his discredited belief in believability. Only Amanda Mundo stood back from the feeding frenzy, looking on with an expression of concern that Perry perceived to be pity, which was somehow worse than if she had joined in his humiliation. Now alone in the classroom, he picked up the offending clipping and, after suppressing the urge to hurl it into the trash, tossed it into his briefcase.

Perry made his way from the college's main building through the ochre air to the faculty parking lot, where he found his Ford Festiva dusted with a thin layer of ash. It was the penultimate day of August. Perry referred to August as *The Apocaugust*, the month that saw Los Angeles shrug off its veils of grass lawns, pleasant gardens and swimming pools and reveal its true nature as a searing, Old Testament desert. Blistering dry summer heat gave way to wildfires that filled the San Fernando Valley with acrid smoke, turning sunlight a sickly yellow and giving every resident – man, woman and child – the phlegmy hack of a chain smoker. Accountants received grim portents of their mortality.

Perry started up the Festiva, used his wipers to clear the ash from his windshield, and wedged himself into rush-hour traffic.

He was eager to get home and write.

Teaching isn't all that bad, he convincingly told himself and the few friends who still returned his calls. Yes, he had lost his girlfriend, his BMW and his home in the Hollywood Hills. Yes, he was more likely to be called by a debt collector than his agent. But Perry Bunt hadn't given up. In his darkest hours, pausing from reading the terrible screenplays of his students to watch a cockroach scuttle over bits of petrified food on the matted grey carpet, he would tell himself that he would find some way to write his way out of this jam. As he'd told Amanda Mundo in one confessional moment, he continued to believe in the limitless power of his imagination and the transcendent powers of creativity. Despite a run of failure that would've made Job switch careers, Perry Bunt was still stalking the Big Idea.

From his first memory, Perry had carried around the feeling that he was destined for greatness, and no amount of failure would disabuse him of this fanciful notion. After reading the news that aerial artist Philippe Petit had walked a tightrope between the towers of the World Trade Center, six-year-old Perry had tied a rope between the chimney and a tree in the garden and started across. He always felt that it was the sound of his mother shrieking his name that had caused him to fall, but it's doubtful that he would have made it in any case, even with the fishing rod as a balancing pole. He broke his right leg, and fractured his skull. Lying in traction in the hospital, two metal plates in his head, Perry was mystified that his daring feat hadn't generated any media attention.

Encouraged by his parents and teachers, Perry gave up the

tightrope for the typewriter and became a prodigy of narrative. For his graduate project in college, he'd written an earnest 612-page novel reimagining Don Quixote as a shell-shocked war veteran on a road trip across America, and it had the distinction of being read nearly all the way through by his faculty advisor.

Subsequently, *Don Hoder* was published by a small college press and nearly read by several critics, who pronounced Perry 'promising' and 'a novelist under the age of thirty to watch'. Since these accolades did little to pay off his student loans, Perry had moved to Hollywood and, by twenty-eight, had become successful enough to acquire debt on a scale that made those loans look like microcredit.

Now he was still in debt but devoid of prospects. Still, Perry Bunt clung even more tenaciously to the belief that he was destined for greatness, unequivocally certain that one day, against all odds, he would regain his confidence and become more successful than ever. This, Perry knew, was the Underdog Story, another of the seven story templates from which all Hollywood movies were constructed. But, again, that didn't stop him from believing it.

The strange thing about all of this was the fact that Perry Bunt *was right*: he was destined for greatness. Stranger still was the fact that the Earth's survival depended on it.

CHANNEL 3

THE LAST DAY OF AUGUST

Perry made his way home to a shoddily built stucco apartment building above Ventura Boulevard named, with unintended hilarity, the Wellington Arms. Temporarily perched on the side of a steep hill overlooking a major earthquake fault, the crumbling Arms was one of many apartment complexes in the area that offered shelter to those who were either down on their luck or too young to know the difference.

In the small studio apartment that served as kitchen, bedroom and study, Perry made himself a sandwich and turned on his laptop. The month before, he'd had what he once would have called a guaranteed sale (back when things sold at all), a Big Idea so commercial that no studio executive would be able to resist its shapely, crowd-pleasing contours. It was an action-thriller entitled *The Last Day of School*, the story of a team of teenaged terrorists who infiltrate the First Daughter's high school to kidnap her. The only man who can stop them? The math teacher, a former Navy Seal, drummed out of the service years before by whom? *The President himself.*

Perry had wanted to be an author, but the public preferred movies to books, so he'd become a screenwriter – just before the public gave up movies for watching videos of cats playing the piano. Yes, he'd succeeded in chasing his culture downhill, always a step behind. In *The Last Day of School*, however, Perry believed that he had found the biggest of all Big Ideas, a story that would not only turn out to be internet-proof but writer-proof as well. First of all, it had teens, oodles of teens, more teens than he could think up good names for. Teens had become very important to the movie business, since they seemed to be the only demographic with the inertia to escape the gravity of their small screens and actually transport themselves to a cinema. *The Last Day of School* would not only bring in the teens, but present them with better-looking versions of themselves screwing and killing each other. How could it fail?

Tonight, however, Perry was having trouble mustering the self-delusional momentum that every obscure writer needs to overcome the fact that no one is interested in reading him. He had made the mistake of mentioning the idea for *The Last Day of School* to his agent, Dana Fulcher of Global Artistic Leadership Limited, and the pause as he waited for her response, which he recognized as the sound of someone looking on their call log for someone more important to talk to, had severely battered his confidence. Her delayed, obligatory 'That's fantastic, Perry, can't wait to read it,' did nothing to soften the blow of that deleterious silence. Perry avoided writing by checking his e-mail repeatedly, marvelling at the technological advances that had turned the once daily disappointment of not receiving mail into thirty or forty disappointments a day. And then there were the numerous phone numbers on which he received no voicemails or texts.

It now seemed like there were infinite ways to not get good news.

As Perry stared once more at his empty mailbox, an ad for swimsuits popped up onto his screen: tanned, handsome surfers and beautiful models lounged on the beach. It was almost like his computer was taunting him.

He turned away from his computer and considered the large stack of unread student screenplays that hovered by his desk. Caught between his own script and those of his students, Perry opted for a different but just as futile activity, the evening masturbation (one of only two daily activities he enjoyed, the other being the wake-up edition). In this he had no lack of encouragement, for the internet was set up like a lawless frontier town where even banks peddle prostitutes and contraband out the back. To this extent, his computer was much more efficient as a portal for pornography than as a screenplay typist. The range of choices, in fact, was paralysing. When Perry finally settled on a website with an acceptable balance of smut and attractiveness, he was interrupted by a knock at his door. Staggering across the room while pulling up his pants, he peered through the peephole at Noah Overton, a young, well-meaning neighbour with the kind of random facial hair that Perry was certain that people in their twenties grew just to bother him.

Noah held a clipboard and stared at the peephole with an air of righteous calm.

Perry tiptoed back to his desk and sat quietly. If he opened the door, his neighbour would request a donation to save the oppressed, the war-torn, the endangered, the globally warmed or all of the above (i.e., a Chechnyan polar bear), brandishing a brochure that declared: 'The Free *Must* Remember the Oppressed' or 'The Earth Has a Fever and We're the Virus', and Perry would once more be forced to face his inadequacy as a human being, not to mention the disappointment in Noah's large brown eyes and the inevitable lecture: *I'm sorry, Per, that you don't think the [name of species or nationality] is worth saving, because I do. I happen to think the whole planet is worth saving. And that's what we're talking about right now – the whole planet is going to die unless all of us start working to save it, one [name of species or nationality] at a time. Will you join me? Starting today? Come on, Per.*

Perry shuddered at the thought of this. How can you save the world when you can't even save yourself?

Searching for something to distract him until Noah gave up and moved on to the next door, Perry's eyes lit on Brent Laskey's newspaper clipping. He picked it up and read it. It was a pretty straightforward news story, though not particularly well written. Perry considered the possibility that Brent Laskey and his goateed, baggie-shorted cohorts had fabricated the clipping as a practical joke on their teacher.

Noah's knocking had ceased. Perry opened his laptop and typed 'death by helicopter' into Google and discovered in .17 seconds that the story was all over the news sites. As far as it was possible to tell, it seemed completely legitimate.

This caused Perry to wonder. While he had admonished his students repeatedly over the absence of reality in their writing, maybe *he* was the one who needed a dose of it. Maybe what he considered to be incredible was in fact happening somewhere on the planet at this very moment.

To test this theory, Perry typed the words 'magic monkey' into Google. One of the worst scripts of the term, written by Heath Barber, involved the discovery by zoologists of an African ape that could grant wishes. Within seconds, Perry was reading news reports about an orangutan in Borneo, who villagers claimed had saved their village from a mudslide. Heath couldn't have copied this idea, either; the news item was dated two days after the script had been read in his class.

Perry proceeded to enter key words from three other scripts: 'murderer clown', 'deranged physicist' and 'breakfast cereal superpowers', and they all retrieved news reports that vaguely mirrored the bizarre events he had criticised his students for conceiving.

The clincher was *Honk If You Hate Jesus*. This was a dreadful screenplay by Doreena Stump, the born-again schoolteacher. It told the story of an evil atheist, who tormented a small Midwestern town by driving his Volvo around with a bumper-sticker that read 'Honk If You Hate Jesus' until, finally, the righteous townspeople rose up, pushed the Volvo into a ditch and, in a scene that would make a slasher film-buff blanche, tore the evil atheist limb from limb. Perry found a related news story from the month before in which the bumper-sticker had read 'Honk If You Love Satan' and the atheist had been merely maimed, not killed.

Perry shut his computer and sighed. It was only a matter of time before all his students came in wielding newspaper articles to justify their awful scripts. He would have to come up with a response before the next morning's class.

* * *

The day that changed Perry Bunt's life, but not, incidentally, the fate of the Earth, began the same as most. Perry rose, showered, dressed and, while brushing his teeth in his filthy, windowless bathroom, did his best to buck himself up, postulating that maybe today would be the day he would ask out Amanda after class. She would not only accept, but carefully lock the classroom door, throw him down on his desk and . . . Perry had orchestrated many different scenarios around this basic premise, but he wasn't picky. Any one of them would do. *Stranger things have happened*, he thought, conveniently forgetting that it's the strange things you want to happen that never do.

He left the Wellington Arms and drove to a nearby convenience store for coffee. It was here Perry had the first of the many uncomfortable encounters that made up his day, with a homeless man named Ralph. Ralph, standing in the searing sunlight next to the convenience-store entrance, wore a large, stained, down-filled jacket and a hat sporting two cup-holders for beer (currently empty). He gripped a handmade cardboard sign that read: 'They're Watching', the jagged scrawl of the penmanship more than adequately reflecting the insanity of the message.

Other than making a left-hand turn at a major intersection, getting past Ralph was the scariest thing Perry would have to do today. He usually succeeded in circumnavigating him while avoiding eye contact, but today was different. Just when Perry seemed to have a clear Ralph-free passage to the door, the homeless man stepped into his path. Perry had no choice but to look into the man's face. His scraggly beard and overgrown eyebrows framed two slate-blue, piercing eyes, the eyeballs of choice for Siberian huskies and visionary lunatics. The heat also made it impossible not to smell Ralph, and this was not a pleasant experience, unless you relished the combination of alcohol, cigarettes, perspiration and faeces.

Ralph spoke, unleashing a froggy voice that seemed to emerge from a giant reservoir of whisky at the centre of the Earth. 'Ralph knows the aliens are watching,' he said. 'How about you, Buddy?'

Perry put a hand to his chin as if to suggest that he was taking the question seriously, all the while wondering why only crazy people and highly paid professional athletes referred to themselves in the third person.

'You don't say,' he said.

Ralph nodded frantically like a dog with a jar of peanut butter stuck on its muzzle.

'I'm telling you, Buddy. They use us! They use us for their own fun!' The hairs that jutted from Ralph's nostrils like mutant whiskers quivered in excitement. 'We have no choice but to play their little games!'

Perry nodded slowly. Then, in a sudden surge, darted around Ralph and through the double glass doors. Once safely in the store, he paused for a moment, basking in the air-conditioned cool. *Made it.* He found his way to the coffee dispenser, filled a cup the size of a small child and stepped into line at the counter. He glimpsed briefly at the tabloid magazines stacked next to the register, one of which boasted the headline: 'Secret Government Films Reveal: Elvis Sighted on the Moon'.

Is it any wonder there are so many crazies? he thought.

Perry peeked out at the parking lot and was relieved to see that Ralph had stepped away from the door to harass a couple walking towards their car. Seizing the moment, he threw down two dollars, scurried out of the store, jumped into the Festiva, and sped away, like a thief fleeing the scene of a crime.

By the time he strode into his 10 a.m. class, Perry had enough caffeine pumping through his bloodstream to pretend that he was happy to be there. Amanda's presence in the front row helped.

He began the day's discussion by quickly recounting his internet discoveries the night before.

'So, from now on,' he said, 'I will no longer tell you that you need to ground your scripts more firmly in reality.' Sardonic applause filled the air. 'Reality has obviously become fluid at this point and is of no use to us. I wouldn't be half-surprised to find out that Elvis really was on the moon.' Out of the corner of his eye, he thought he saw Amanda looking surprised. *She probably doesn't realise I'm joking*, he thought. 'I will, however, continue to ask you to make your scripts more believable to *me*. And that's not going to change.' A few students emitted sarcastically loud moans of disappointment.

'And if anyone out there is searching for an idea for their next screenplay, how about this: God has run out of ideas and is stealing them from a beginner's screenwriting class in Encino.' Perry was pleased to hear laughter, actual laughter, emerge from his normally diffident students. He smiled and looked over at Amanda who, unlike her classmates, stared pensively out the window. *So maybe she doesn't have a great sense of humour*, he thought. *You can't have everything.*

At the end of class, Perry waited with great anticipation for his usual Amanda chat. Bolstered by getting a laugh, he decided that this would be the day he would ask her out. This was as confident as he got in a sober state – it was now or never. To his surprise, Amanda quickly gathered her handbag and notebook and headed for the door.

Perry quickly called to her, 'In a hurry?'

Amanda paused with evident reluctance. 'I'm afraid so, Mr Bunt.'

'Is there anything I can do to get you to call me Perry?' he said, attempting a playful tone that, to his distress, came out of his mouth sounding creepy. Playful had never really been his forte.

'I'm sorry, I really need to go.'

'OK,' Perry cut in, 'I'll cut to the chase. Normally, I don't do things like this, but you've been in my class for a while now, so I wanted to ask you something—'

'I'm sorry, Mr Bunt—' Amanda interrupted.

'Please, call me Perry.'

'Work has been crazy lately. I'm afraid I'm not going to be able to continue your class.'

Perry's stomach clenched as if he'd been punched. 'Is this about what I just said? About reality? Or God stealing ideas? If you were offended, I'm sorry—'

'Please don't take it personally,' Amanda said. 'I'm just too busy. So . . . thank you, Mr Bunt. I had a good time.' She smiled quickly, turned and walked out of the classroom.

Perry watched her go, stunned. He had scripted things differently, using one of his more tasteful scenarios involving laughter and large margaritas overlooking the ocean, followed by a romantic montage involving a tasteful but perfectly toned amount of nudity . . . *Ooh, Mr Bunt, no one's ever touched me like that.* Instead, when Amanda walked from his class, the screen faded quickly to black.

Perry taught the remainder of the day's classes in a depressed fog. At the end of his last class, a student found a blue jacket on the floor behind a computer station, and Perry immediately recognised it as Amanda's. In her haste to escape him and his class, she'd left it behind. Improbable hope filled his heart. He would return the jacket to her personally and prove himself worthy of her love.

This, Perry knew, was the Redemption Story, another of the seven story templates from which all Hollywood movies were constructed. And no, it didn't stop him from believing it.

Not even for a second.

CHANNEL 4

GALAXY ENTERTAINMENT

The secretary in the college's administration office glanced sceptically at Perry Bunt.

'I'm sorry,' she said, in a clearly unapologetic tone. 'I'm not at liberty to give out an address or *any* personal information about *any* currently enrolled student.'

'I just want to return her jacket,' Perry said.

'Leave it in the lost and found, two doors down.'

'Thank you,' Perry said, in a clearly ungrateful tone, and turned towards the door. Then he had an idea. Using Amanda's blue jacket as cover, he reached into his trouser pocket, surreptitiously pulled out his house keys and slipped them into one of the jacket's pockets.

'Oh no,' he said, turning back to the secretary. He pulled his keys out of the jacket. 'Must be her house keys. She's going to need these tonight.'

The secretary reluctantly gave him Amanda's work address. Perry looked at his watch: 4:30. He might still find her there. Clutching the blue jacket under one arm, he ran to the faculty parking lot with an energy he hadn't felt in years outside of a coffee cup.

Minutes later, he pulled up to a large windowless office building on Ventura Boulevard. A large sign in front was already lit, the letters glowing an eerie blue: GALAXY ENTERTAINMENT.

Perry knew Galaxy as the cable monopoly in the area; when he'd moved into his apartment, he had been given two choices for cable provider: Galaxy and none at all. Since he was strapped for cash, he'd chosen the latter.

He wasn't at all surprised that Amanda worked for a company like Galaxy. His students were often from the fringes of the entertainment business, clerks and bean counters desperate to be perceived as creative. Perry stepped out of his car, retrieved Amanda's jacket from the back seat and walked towards the main entrance.

In a neighbourhood that was home to a mind-boggling variety of ugly office buildings, the Galaxy Entertainment building more than held its own. Its concrete bunker-like design (it seemed to have been poured rather than built) was topped with a thick steel roof painted the garish blue of the company's logo. Perry walked to the one opening in the foreboding exterior and through swinging glass doors into a large lobby. Beyond a receptionist's desk and a cluster of low-slung modern furniture was a metal door with a sign on it: 'Employees Only – No Unauthorised Personnel'. The receptionist, a disarmingly clean-cut young man, ate popcorn earnestly from a red-and-white striped paper bag. He wore a blue jacket like the one in Perry's hands and a name tag:

Dennis Perkins
Our Service Is out of This World!

He looked up from his popcorn and noticed Perry. 'No bills here,' he said. 'Please use the entrance on the other side of the building.'

'I'm here to see an employee. Amanda Mundo.'

'I'm sorry. Amanda just went out.'

27

Perry shifted the blue jacket between his hands. He had to deliver it in person. 'I'll come back tomorrow.'

As he turned to go, the glass doors clanked open. Amanda entered the lobby, saw Perry and stopped. He held up her jacket.

She laughed. 'I've been looking all over for that,' she said. 'I thought maybe I'd left it in my car.' She took it from Perry. 'Thank you, Mr Bunt. I hope it wasn't too much trouble.'

As she took the jacket, Perry again noticed the small blue tattoo on the inside of her left wrist. His mind reeled with all the things he wanted to say to her but finally settled for a lame, mumbled, 'No problemo'. Then, before he could follow it up, Amanda was moving again, towards the metal door across the room. She pushed an ID card against a scanner, opened the door, waved back at him and disappeared inside.

Do something, Perry thought. This was it, the moment in the movies when the guy does something dramatic. So Perry did something dramatic. Suddenly possessed with an Olympian speed not accessed since a youthful experimentation with shoplifting, he sprinted towards the closing door. The receptionist jumped up from his desk and shouted something at him, but Perry was already catching the door just before it closed. Without hesitation, he swung it back open and plunged into a long, dimly lit hallway. He vaguely heard footsteps and shouting behind him, but he had Amanda in his sights and wasn't going to stop now. Breathless, he was suddenly next to her.

'Amanda,' he said, 'I wanted to ask if you—'

He didn't finish his sentence because he became aware that he was standing in the strangest place he had ever seen: A huge, dark, cathedral-like space lined with what looked like TV monitors – brightly lit squares dotting the walls as far as he could see until they became nothing more than pinpoints of blue light. Flitting between the monitors, like bees from flower to flower, were red-uniformed men and women in flying armchairs. In the midst of all this was a giant round console festooned with lit-up words and images. On an illuminated image of the Earth glowed the words:

Bizarre
Ludicrous
Unbelievable and always
Entertaining

As Perry's eyes grew accustomed to the dark, he saw what appeared to be a large moving tree in the centre of the console. As he focused in on it, he saw that he was wrong. It was, in fact, a giant green slug-like creature covered with eyeballs the size of ping-pong balls, all of which were beginning, one after another, to ogle him. A great gap-toothed slit below the eyeballs trembled and opened.

'We have a visitor in the central control room,' it groaned.

Perry stood frozen, his mouth agape.

Amanda smiled apologetically. 'Non-employees aren't really allowed in here,' she said. 'Sorry, Mr Bunt.'

Two uniformed security guards, one short and squat, the other tall and muscular with a moustache, appeared out of the darkness. Before Perry had a chance to react, the tall guard grabbed his arms and pulled them behind his back. The clean-cut receptionist appeared in front of them, panting.

'I tried to stop him—' he said, the rest of his words lost in gasps for air.

Perry struggled, but the tall guard's grip felt like iron manacles on his forearms.

'Just relax. OK, friend?' the short guard said. 'Everything's going to be fine.'

The tall guard's head swivelled to his colleague. 'You got your eraser?'

The short guard nodded, took a large brass ring from his belt and slid it halfway down Perry's head to just above his eyes.

Perry, sweating profusely, glanced at Amanda, who still seemed, under the circumstances, ludicrously calm.

'Don't worry, Mr Bunt,' she said, 'They're just going to do something to your brain.' He didn't have much time to panic before everything disappeared.

CHANNEL 5

LEFT HANGING

Perry Bunt opened his eyes. He was sitting in the reception area of the Galaxy Entertainment building. Dennis Perkins, the clean-cut receptionist, stood over him, snapping his fingers in front of his eyes.

'Hey! Mister! Hey there! Are you OK?'

Perry surveyed the room, confused. It took him a moment before he remembered the strange chain of events that led to his loss of consciousness. Meanwhile, Dennis Perkins continued snapping his fingers in front of his eyes. 'Hey! Mister! Can you hear me?'

'Stop that,' Perry said, pushing the receptionist's hand away. 'What the hell's going on here?' He pointed to the metal security door. 'What's going on in that room?'

Dennis Perkins furrowed his brow, puzzled. 'I'm not sure what you're talking about,' he said. 'You came in, asked where Amanda Mundo was, I told you she had just left, and you passed out. Right here.'

For a moment, Perry considered this possibility. The night before, he had taken a Klonopin to get to sleep. Was it possible he was experiencing a delayed side-effect? But what had happened had been so real – the huge room, the giant slug, the annoyed security guards. He looked down at his shirt and saw a faint sweat stain, the result of his sprint after Amanda. He shook his head.

'No,' Perry said. 'I followed Amanda into that room. And there were people flying in chairs and a big . . . I don't know . . . slug monster, like something from a bad science-fiction movie. Then two security guards grabbed me, stuck a metal headband on my head and knocked me out.'

The receptionist laughed in disbelief. 'That is crazy. That is so crazy. Is that really what you think happened?'

Perry nodded.

'You have to do it again,' the receptionist said.

'Do what?' Perry asked. But the receptionist wasn't talking to him. The metal door opened and the same two security guards, one short and squat, one tall and thin, entered the lobby. The tall guard grabbed Perry like an eagle snatching a rabbit. The short guard, smiling apologetically, placed the copper ring over Perry's head.

'Stop it. Why are you doing this?' Perry yelped. 'Leave me alone! Where's Amanda?' He flailed and the room went black.

* * *

This time, when Perry regained consciousness in the empty lobby, Amanda was standing over him. He rubbed his head. His brain felt like a frozen waffle that had been re-toasted too many times. This was because the eraser the security guards had now used twice on Perry's head was supposed to be used only once. Once was all it took to erase the last hour or so from the average human's brain. The problem was, Perry wasn't average. As a result of his childhood tightrope accident, he had two steel plates in his head. So the pulse of energy intended to erase part of Perry's short-term memory had done nothing more than warm the metal in his head a few hundredths of a degree, a definitely unnerving sensation.

'What the hell's going on?' Perry asked Amanda. 'Why do they keep doing that?'

Amanda bent over, placing her mouth next to his ear so that Perry could smell a fragrance like orange blossoms. 'Agree with everything I say,' she whispered. 'I'll explain later.'

While Perry was taking this in, the receptionist walked in with a cup of water. Amanda smiled at him. 'Our patient is awake,' she chirruped.

The receptionist smiled and gave the water to Perry. 'Are you OK?' he asked.

'He's fine,' Amanda said.

Perry nodded warily and took a sip of water.

'Mr Bunt just came in here and passed out, right?' Amanda said loudly, nodding at Perry and smiling as if he were a foreign toddler with a hearing problem.

Perry nodded. The receptionist helped him to his feet and Amanda walked with him out of the building.

'What's happening?' Perry said. Amanda put one finger to her lips. He noticed the tattoo on her wrist again and this time was able to get a better view. It was a tattoo of a blue housefly.

'I'd better drive you home,' she said. 'You might still be a little bleary.' Despite the strangeness of the last hour, Perry's heart raced at the thought of Amanda driving home with him. Then he remembered his car.

They arrived at the Ford Festiva. 'It's just a loaner,' Perry mumbled, avoiding her eyes. Amanda held one finger to her lips and the other hand out. He hesitated, then gave her the keys and his address.

They drove in silence down Ventura Boulevard until Amanda pulled over beneath an underpass and killed the ignition. Above them, the traffic on Highway 101 roared in both directions. Perry looked at her, puzzled. This was the kind of place where no one ever pulled over, where encampments of leathery home-less men propagated in the cement crannies.

'What are we doing here?' Perry asked, then remembered that he wasn't supposed to talk.

'I'll lose my job if anyone sees me talking to you. This is the only spot on the way to your home that's safe. Do you see any flies?' she said.

Perry shook his head, realising that things weren't becoming normal any time soon.

Amanda carefully surveyed the interior of the car. 'Keep your windows up,' she commanded.

Perry couldn't help but feel hurt by Amanda's suddenly officious tone. 'Is it OK to talk now?' he asked, but she didn't seem to hear him.

'That eraser would've wiped the short-term memory of any normal person.'

'Eraser?' Perry said.

'The device they put on your head. For some reason, it didn't work on you. Normally, they would've just taken you off to the Green Room.' Perry had no idea what she was talking about but found himself nodding. 'You seem like a nice guy, so I made sure that didn't happen. But if they should somehow find out that you do remember what you saw, it'll be very bad for you.' Amanda stared intently into Perry's eyes. 'You can't tell anyone what you saw. And you can never come near Galaxy Entertainment again. Do you understand, Mr Bunt?'

She seemed to be back in deaf-and-foreign-toddler mode, but Perry wasn't really listening. His twice-fried brain was still revelling in the fact that she'd said he was 'a nice guy'. Yes, there had been some important-sounding words after that, but how could he be expected to pay attention? Amanda

Mundo, the woman of his dreams, had said that he was 'a nice guy'.

'I said, *Do you understand*?' Amanda repeated.

Perry nodded.

'Good,' she continued. 'We can't be seen together anymore. I'll get out here.' She opened the car door, jarring Perry out of his happy fog.

'Wait,' he said. 'Where are you going? What was going on back there?'

Amanda shook her head incredulously. 'Did you not hear anything I just said?'

Perry hadn't, of course, but he wasn't about to admit it. 'You can't just take off like this,' he said. 'You can't knock me out with a cattle prod a couple times and then leave me on the side of Ventura Boulevard under the 101. I mean, I saw a giant slug watching TV!'

Amanda, taking note of Perry's distress, closed the car door. 'Look, Mr Bunt,' she said. 'I know this all must seem a little odd to you—'

'*Odd* is not the word for it. I can't even think of a word for what this seems like.'

'And I'm sorry if I seem to be in a hurry,' Amanda continued. 'But we don't have much time. If the people I work for find out that I'm talking to you, you could be in terrible trouble.'

Perry grew pale. 'What kind of trouble?'

Amanda searched for a way to explain herself. 'People on Earth who find out about what we're doing have a way of . . . disappearing.'

Perry struggled to take this in. 'I had no idea the cable industry was so powerful.'

Amanda put her hand back on the door handle. 'Are we clear?'

Perry nodded.

'Good.' Amanda opened the door.

'Is this some kind of new show?' Perry blurted out. Despite all his career setbacks, he'd retained the insatiable curiosity that had made him a writer in the first place. 'An incredibly secretive new show? Disney, maybe? Featuring large slug monsters?'

Amanda, irritated, closed the door again.

Perry sensed her impatience. 'Come on. You can't expect someone to see what I just saw and not be curious.'

'Again: I can't tell you anything else. It's for your own good.'

'If they're already going to kill me for what I know, why not tell me more? They can only kill me once.'

Amanda sighed. 'Even if I told you, you wouldn't believe me.'

'Try me.'

Amanda chuckled drily in disbelief. '*I can't tell you.*'

Perry steeled himself and attempted to inject as much menace into his voice as possible. 'If you want me to keep your secret, I think you'd better.'

Amanda laughed again. '*Please.* You have no leverage here. No one would believe you, whatever you told them.'

Perry realised immediately that she was right and dropped any semblance of intimidation. 'All right. Then let me appeal to you as a fellow writer.'

'What are you talking about?'

'I've spent my entire life trying to figure out what happens next. Then *this* happens.' Perry pounded the dashboard adamantly, surprising himself with his conviction. 'I could spend the rest of my life wondering what this was all about. That's *torture.* And it's not like anything I've ever written or even thought about. I'll never figure it out! I'll never know!

That kind of thing could drive a person insane. So you have to tell me. If I'm a bit part in somebody else's crazy story, I *demand* to know how it turns out. It's my right as a writer and as a human being.'

Amanda seemed mildly amused by his diatribe. 'You have no rights whatsoever,' she said. 'And no one's writing this.'

'You know what I'm talking about,' Perry said. 'You were in my class. You know that you can't leave your audience hanging for too long – if you do, you'll make them angry and lose them. You can't end a movie on a cliffhanger, and you can't end our relationship on an unsolved mystery.'

Amanda stared at him blankly. 'Because I'll lose you as an audience member?'

'No,' Perry said, trying his best to sound authoritative. 'Because you have respect for me as a teacher and, most of all, respect for the basics of storytelling. If you don't tell me what's going on, you're consigning me to a fate worse than death. I'll spend the rest of my life wondering. Don't do that to me. I'm begging you, as one writer to another, please don't leave me hanging.'

Amanda smiled and shook her head. She took a deep breath. 'I guess I have always wanted to tell one of you.'

'One of who?'

'You people.'

Perry frowned, confused. 'What people?'

'You know. The people who live here.'

'Los Angeles?'

Amanda shrugged. 'Sure. Why not?'

'OK,' Perry said. 'Then tell me.'

Amanda considered this for a moment. 'OK, I will.' She seemed surprised by her words and shook her head in disbelief. Perry hunched forward in his seat with anticipation, but

Amanda didn't speak for several moments. Her eyes seemed to focus on a distant point miles beyond Perry's dirty windshield. 'I'm not sure why I'm doing this, really,' she said. 'I think it's because . . . *I like you.*' She said these words with amazement, as if each one was an egg plucked from her mouth by a magician. Perry was both thrilled by this revelation and put off by the fact that it came coated in so much disbelief. 'It's very odd, but true nonetheless. I like you and I think you have a right to know.'

'OK, then,' Perry said, prompting her, but she continued to stare out the window. He lay back on his headrest, looking at the roof of his car. 'Jesus. This is like a TV show where they leave you hanging so you'll come back for more.'

Amanda returned her gaze to Perry. 'It's nothing like that,' she said.

CHANNEL 6

THAT'S ENTERTAINMENT

'Our audiences are too sophisticated for that kind of manipulation,' Amanda said. She twirled Perry's car keys on one finger.

'Cable viewers?' Perry guessed. Amanda laughed again. The laugh was starting to get on his nerves. 'Are you going to tell me or not?'

Amanda let the keys fall into her lap. 'To tell you the truth, I don't know where to begin.'

'What's going on in the back room of Galaxy Entertainment?'

'We're producing entertainment.'

'What kind of entertainment?'

'You might call them reality shows.'

'Oh,' said Perry, who couldn't disguise his distaste of the genre. 'I don't know much about that.'

'You know about this show. It's happening right now, all around you.' Perry stared at her blankly. 'We produce Earth.'

'Is that on the Discovery Channel?'

Amanda shook her head. 'We shoot events here on Earth and send them across the galaxy. What you saw was one of our control rooms where we select feeds from millions of different cameras for broadcast. The 'slug monster' you referred to is Guy, one of our directors. Guy is a Nakeeth.'

Perry was looking at Amanda for a while before he realised

that his mouth was hanging open. He closed it and tried to swallow. 'A Nakeeth,' he said.

'Yes,' Amanda said. 'Nakeeths have 462 eyes with independent motion, which make them excellent directors.'

'Makes sense,' Perry said, his mouth completely dry.

She went on to tell him that she, the Nakeeths and her other co-workers were from an advanced human civilisation spread out amongst hundreds of planets that, like most advanced civilisations, enjoyed nothing more than being entertained by those less advanced.

'Everyone who lives on Earth has been in a show at some point,' Amanda explained.

'Comedies or dramas?'

'When you tell stories about yourself, are you the hero or the fool?'

Perry thought about this for a moment. 'The fool.'

'Then you're in a comedy,' Amanda said. Perry stared at her, frowning. He hadn't realised it until this moment, but he'd spent most of his life thinking he was in a drama.

Amanda talked about her civilisation's voracious appetite for comedy, and how there was no place like Earth when it came to producing thousands of laughs per second – more than enough to sate the appetite of even the largest of interstellar empires or, as Amanda referred to it, 'the savviest, richest demographic in the Milky Way'. Galaxy Entertainment, an entertainment conglomerate, used hundreds of high-powered satellite cameras, as well as tiny mobile cameras installed on small self-propelled robots called 'flies', to spy on all kinds of activity on Earth and broadcast it across the galaxy. Perry felt compelled to interrupt.

'Flies?' he said. 'Flies are cameras?'

'Not all of them,' Amanda said. 'Just the blue ones.'

Perry nodded as if this explained everything. 'And we stopped under the freeway because the satellites can't see through it.'

'Right,' Amanda said. 'It takes about three feet of steel or ten feet of concrete to keep them from picking up anything.'

Perry took a deep breath. 'And you all really find the stuff that goes on here interesting?'

'Oh yes,' Amanda replied. She regarded Perry's stunned look with bemusement. 'You really thought no one was watching?'

'I guess I'd never really thought about it.'

'You watch each other. We watch you. Some scientists think *we're* being watched by a more advanced civilisation in another galaxy. Everyone's watching *someone*.'

'But . . . it must be incredibly boring.'

Amanda shook her head emphatically. 'Earth has always been one of our best planetainments. I mean, the events that occur here are so incredible that we used to just shoot them and put them right on the air. We barely had to edit – which is how our viewers like it: raw, unmanipulated footage of terrible and ludicrous behaviour. But then recently—' Amanda paused, as if trying to choose her words precisely. 'Well, the ratings started sagging a bit. There's a lot of competition out there. For a while, we were the only company with a channel devoted to primitive terrestrial life. Now Eden Entertainment has an entire cluster of them in Vega 6, and they're all getting better ratings than we are. Then there are the winged monkeys on Altair 7, which everyone loves. So we've been under pressure to . . . goose things up a little. When I started working here, the channel had a strict non-intervention policy, meaning we couldn't mess with the talent. But lately that's been relaxed, and all the producers have been scrambling for a way to boost ratings. That's why I took your class.'

41

Perry had a realisation. 'The scripts . . . You were stealing ideas from my class.'

Amanda seemed completely unfazed. 'Please, Mr Bunt. Like no one in Hollywood ever stole an idea.'

'Did you use any of mine?' Perry asked, unable to keep a certain hopefulness out of his voice.

'Yours?'

'My scripts.'

'No,' Amanda said. 'We were more interested in your students' work.' Perry's shoulders sagged. His screenplays weren't even good enough for aliens. Still, he thought, she could've gone to any class in the world and she'd chosen *his*.

'Well, you must have liked my class,' he said.

'Definitely,' Amanda said, and Perry's heart tripped. 'We've been monitoring hundreds of screenwriting classes, and yours produce absolutely the worst scripts we've ever read. A drug lord assassinated by helicopter! *That's* the kind of thing that's going to get people watching Earth again. Of course, it took a few million to rig a helicopter to do that, but it was totally worth it.'

Perry tried to hide his disappointment. 'Then why'd you stop coming to class?'

'We thought maybe you were onto us,' Amanda said. 'You talked about God stealing ideas from your students.'

'Well, I certainly knew something weird was going on,' Perry lied.

Amanda unfastened her seat belt. 'I'm going to get back to work. You're going to keep our secret, right?'

Perry shrugged. 'It's no big deal – I hear stuff like this all the time.' Amanda frowned at him. 'I'm kidding,' he said.

Remaining impervious to the joke, Amanda nodded slowly and opened the car door. Watching her step out onto the sidewalk, Perry couldn't help thinking that despite the fact that she was an alien TV producer exploiting the Earth for entertainment, and that she'd threatened him with disappearance, and that she'd stolen ideas from his class without bothering to steal any of his, she still had the nicest smile he'd ever seen.

'Wait,' he blurted.

Amanda paused. 'Yes?'

'Would you like to get a cup of coffee sometime?'

She sighed with exasperation. 'Really?'

'I just thought—'

'*We can't ever see each other again.* We never even had this conversation. Do you understand?'

'Right. I know. I just—' Perry's voice trailed off. 'I've never met anyone as beautiful as you are,' he blurted. Amanda turned down one corner of her mouth sceptically. 'That's a stupid thing to say, but it's true. And I really have enjoyed getting to know you. Granted, you have a very strange job, but does that mean we can never see each other again?'

'*Yes*,' Amanda said. 'That's *exactly* what it means.'

Perry nodded back, trying his best not to appear hurt. 'OK.'

'OK,' Amanda said. She turned to get out of the car, then hesitated. 'Are you sure you understand?'

'Yeah. Just a lot of information to take in.'

Her face softened. 'I'm sorry, Mr Bunt,' she said. 'It must be. Like I said, you seem like a nice guy, especially for an Earthle.'

'A what?'

'An Earthle,' Amanda said. 'That's how we refer to all of you.'

'Earthle?'

'Yes.'

Perry grimaced. 'That makes us sound so lame.'

'Whatever.' She fanned one of her hands impatiently. 'What I'm trying to tell you is that I'm actually very sorry that I can't come to your class anymore. I really did enjoy it.'

'Me too,' Perry said. And then she was gone, the sound of her clicking heels quickly receding into the rush-hour cacophony of Ventura Boulevard.

* * *

That night, Perry ate a Chinese takeaway and watched TV without appreciating the irony. On the screen, a handsome man with a helmet of grey hair was describing a large earthquake that had struck Russia earlier in the day. The late-night news was even more depressing than usual: Food shortages! Fuel shortages! Earth warming! Death imminent! But Perry didn't notice. His mind was somewhere else.

The Earth was being watched by aliens.

Every crazy person in front of every convenience store was right.

Watching what? Perry stared up at the chipped icicle ceiling. They weren't watching now, were they? How could they be? What possible pleasure could be taken in watching a man sitting in a room watching another man? But then why would they want to watch *anything* he did? The only thing more boring than living his life, Perry thought, would be watching it.

He stood and paced like a caged animal. He wiped the grease from his mouth with a paper napkin, opened the sliding glass door and stepped out onto his small balcony for the first time since the year before, when he'd attempted to barbeque a hamburger and set off fire alarms throughout the building.

He walked to the edge and gazed up at the top of the ridge behind the Wellington Arms, taking in the great mansions of movie moguls, the homes of the men and women who had traded successfully on the dreams and aspirations of humanity without knowing that, to the galaxy, their great blockbusters were less entertaining than his students' awful screenplays.

He looked up at the sky. It was free of the usual smoky haze and dotted with twinkling stars. *No*, he thought. *It can't be.*

Back inside, he opened his laptop and clicked from one website to another, as if an explanation to what had happened inside Galaxy Entertainment could be found if he looked hard enough. News sites, porn sites, blogs and gossip flickered before him in a meaningless blur of information. On one site, an ad popped up on his screen for surfboards, featuring attractive, barely dressed men and women on a beach. *What is the deal with surfing?* Perry wondered, before remembering he'd spent a fair amount of time researching surfing on the internet. He'd impulsively made Drake Blakely – the boyfriend of the President's daughter in *The Last Day of School* – a surfer without knowing anything about the sport. But his web server's computers, tracking Perry's activity, had decided that he was a surfer – not just an internet surfer, but on water as well – and was marketing to him accordingly. As Perry was creating a character for his screenplay, the internet was creating a character for him.

Everyone's watching someone.

Perry was about to shut his laptop when a voice spoke to him from his computer. 'What do you want to see?' He looked down at the screen. A woman with skin that seemed too tight for her body lounged on a pink divan in a zebra-print bikini. 'I'll do whatever you want.' A distant man's voice responded, and Perry realised that his visit to one of the porn sites had automatically opened a live video chat for men interested in paying to watch a woman with too-tight skin lounge on a pink divan.

Perry slammed his laptop closed. He stood and stepped back onto the balcony, searching the night sky. *You're crazier that we are*, he thought, *but not by much.* He laughed out loud at the insanity of it all – the idea that both Earth's inhabitants and its aliens had been reduced to nothing more than *watching. Let the country descend into ignorance and apathy, let the Earth burn up in its own emissions, let the universe expand into nothingness, just tell us: What's on TV?*

Perry felt somehow lighter and wasn't sure why. Then it occurred to him: there was no reason to spend time searching for the secret of the universe or contemplating the existence of God. There was someone out there watching all right, but based on their choice of viewing, he was pretty confident that they weren't any more enlightened than him or anyone else.

Not that Perry was religious. While his parents were both devout Presbyterians, Perry had a fickle relationship with the Almighty. When he found a belief in God comforting, such as when he was sitting in the back of a discount-airline jet preparing to land, he believed. (It sometimes occurred to him that the God he occasionally prayed to would be foolish if He trusted the wishy-washy faith of someone like Perry, and thus completely unqualified for the omnipotence that being God no doubt required, but this didn't stop him from issuing such prayers of convenience.) But when Perry wasn't airborne, waiting to find out about an important job or afraid that he might have a sexually transmitted disease, he wasn't religious. In fact, he had often viewed his life as nothing more than a nearly unbroken chain of meaningless humiliations. Now, however, he knew that the humiliations were no longer meaningless. He wasn't a loser; he was an entertainer. They were out there watching.

'I see you,' he said to the night sky, and laughed some more. Laughing felt good so he kept doing it. Then he imagined aliens on the other side of the galaxy watching this man laughing for no perceivable reason and laughed even harder. He was interrupted by murmuring and peered down to see an elderly couple sitting on the balcony below, staring up at him with concern.

'Don't worry,' Perry told them. 'None of this matters.' And he laughed until the couple rose from their chairs and retreated into their apartment.

Was he going crazy? Perry had to seriously consider this. The sidewalks of Hollywood Boulevard were clogged with washed-up screenwriters in stained superhero costumes, posing for tourists and muttering loudly to themselves between sips of gin. Giving into delusions was an all-too-predictable third act for a failed fantasist. And yet Perry had never felt more sane.

Wearing the cleanest boxer shorts he could find, he stood under the fluorescent light in his grey, windowless bathroom, flossing with vigour in case anyone was watching. He was no longer a failure living alone in a cramped dingy apartment; he was a star performing for trillions. He smiled sharply into the mirror. The teeth were a little yellow; he'd have to take care of that.

He lay on his fold-out couch, staring at the chipped-icing ceiling. His evening masturbation was clearly out of the question. But then he thought, *Why not? It's nothing they haven't seen before.* He shrugged and threw himself into it with gusto. Moments later, he had to admit that it had been one of the best ever.

He supposed that he liked being watched.

For the first time in years, Perry slipped happily into the arms of Morpheus. And in vivid colour he dreamt that he and Amanda were on a magnificent movie set, singing and dancing like Fred Astaire and Ginger Rogers. Then it started raining. They ran inside a beautiful mansion, but it was raining in there, too. They danced more desperately as torrents of water cascaded down a marble stairway, bravely strutting against the current until it became too much and washed them away . . .

He woke to find Amanda, the real Amanda, standing over him holding an empty glass. It was empty, he realised one second later, because its contents were on his face. He sputtered and sat up. 'What are you doing here?'

'We picked the lock. I'm sorry, Mr Bunt. I couldn't get you to wake up.' Perry blearily scanned the room. It was still dark outside. A young man he recognised as the Galaxy Entertainment receptionist sat on the couch, paging through an old screenwriting magazine.

'Are you sure about this?' He eyed Perry sceptically. 'He seems a little out of it.'

'This is Dennis,' Amanda said. Dennis smiled uneasily at Perry. 'You met yesterday.'

'You have a funny way of never seeing someone again,' Perry said.

'We need your help.' She sat on the bed next to Perry, who became aware of how foul his breath must be. His mouth was all after-taste, a lethal mixture of noodles, MSG and sleep.

'Couldn't it wait until tomorrow?' he said, covering his mouth.

'Remember when I told you that our ratings have been slipping a little, and that was why I was taking your class?'

'Wait,' Dennis interrupted. 'Should we do this here?' He pointed at the ceiling.

'We don't have time. If they pick up our feed, they pick it up.' Amanda leaned even closer into Perry. 'We received some bad news tonight.' She paused and licked her lips. 'Earth is being cancelled.'

Perry, still groggy, stared at her. 'Cancelled?'

'The gig is over,' Dennis said, tossing the magazine onto the coffee table. 'They're going to start sending us to other planets next week.'

'And the executive producers are determined to get every last viewer they can to tune in,' Amanda continued. 'They're planning a big series finale.'

Perry swivelled his head between the two visitors. 'What's going to happen?'

'Well, no one's getting married,' Dennis said.

'You've heard of a Viking funeral?' Amanda asked.

Perry had. A 'Viking funeral', in the parlance of TV executives, was when you took a show doomed for cancellation and pushed it to extreme spectacle in order to attract as many viewers as possible to its last few episodes. Perry suddenly felt very awake. 'What are they doing?' he asked.

Amanda hesitated. Perry turned to Dennis. 'What's happening?'

'What do you think?' Dennis said. 'They're going to finale it.'

'What?'

'They're going to blow the whole thing up.'

CHANNEL 7

A VIEWERS' GUIDE TO THE END OF THE WORLD

'Earthquakes, terrorist attacks, a stock market crash in China,' Dennis said. Perry stared incredulously at the young man sitting on his couch, blithely ticking off the disasters planned for Earth's finale. 'Then it all ends with this . . . the *coup de grâce*.'

Dennis reached into the pocket of his jacket and produced a pen, which he held in front of Perry's face. On one side of it was a photo of a woman wearing a burka. 'This is going to end the world?' Perry said. Dennis smiled and nodded. 'A pen?'

'Watch,' Dennis said. He turned the pen upside down and the burka vanished, revealing an attractive naked brunette. 'And here's the kicker,' he said, pointing to three small words printed near the tip of the pen. Perry squinted and read: MADE IN ISRAEL.

'We have statistics guys who crunch the numbers on all this stuff,' Dennis continued. 'They've figured out that sending this pen to ten Islamic leaders will cause Earth to destroy itself within three weeks.'

Perry turned the pen right side up, so that the burka slipped back up over the naked woman. 'Just this pen?'

'Well, the pen can't do it *completely* by itself. You need the proper mixture of general chaos to get everyone on edge. Then just add angry mullahs and stir. Before you know it, everyone's being invaded or invading, then the nukes get dusted off, *boom, boom, boom*, it's World War III capped by a post-Armageddon

50

duel-to-the-death in the desert over the last gallon of gas.' Dennis shrugged. 'I know. All very derivative. To tell you the truth, the whole thing sounds like every movie I've seen, but you already know how original our producers are.' He shot a look at Amanda.

'I had nothing to do with this,' Amanda said. 'It's a terrible idea.'

'Wait.' Perry stood, trying to shake off this nightmare. 'Are you saying that all of us are about to be killed . . . for ratings?'

'Not all of us,' clarified Dennis. 'All of *you*. Hey, it was going to happen anyway. The way you guys have been hitting those fossil fuels and warming things up, it's basically over. They just got sick of waiting for it.'

'*Unless* we can show them that the planet can still attract an audience,' Amanda said. 'That's why we're here. I told Dennis all about your class, about all the shows you've worked on and the scripts you've written. If anyone can come up with a good idea, it's you.'

Perry's heart fluttered again, but this time his brain ignored it. 'Me? In case you haven't noticed, I'm not doing that well. Why don't you get someone who's more successful? Steven Spielberg, for example. He saves the Earth all the time.'

'He's right,' Dennis said. 'Didn't I tell you? Spielberg or Lucas.'

Amanda shook her head. 'Famous Earthles are jaded and sceptical by necessity,' she told him. 'No one who's that successful is going to believe we're anything other than kooks.' She turned back to Perry. 'Will you help us or not?'

Perry had terrible doubts. One of the keys to being a professional writer was knowing what you were good at and sticking to it. For this reason, Perry had never written science fiction (he had no idea how people in spacesuits talked), period pieces (or people in tights) or family comedies (he'd actually tried one of these during his long career descent, but for the life of him couldn't come up with anything adorable for a nine-year-old to say while chasing his escaped pet frog).

He'd also never written anything that saved anyone, much less the world. Which is why he knew he wasn't the best person on Earth – or even close to the best person – for the job Amanda had in mind for him.

Amanda must have seen the fear in his eyes. 'Listen to me, Mr Bunt,' she said. 'There must be some reason you're the one. That you came to my job yesterday. That you remembered everything you saw. That you're the only Earthle who knows about what we're doing. This must be your moment, right? The end of the first act, when the story turns and the protagonist sets off on his fateful journey.' She smiled. 'Of course it is. You told me about it after class one day.'

'I did?'

'Yes. You said that despite everything that had happened, you still believed in the power of your imagination, of its power to change your life. If there was ever a need for imagination, this is it. You told me that you keep looking for the Big Idea. Well, they don't get much bigger than this. This is it, Mr Bunt.' She looked him squarely in the eye. 'This is where you get the chance to be the person you always thought you should be.'

After Perry had agreed to save the Earth, Dennis and Amanda waited outside his front door until he put on some clothes, then drove him in a service van to the Galaxy Entertainment building.

'When is this finale supposed to begin?' Perry asked from the back seat.

'It's already started,' Dennis said, steering the van down

dark, empty streets at an annoyingly relaxed speed. 'You hear about the earthquake in Russia?'

It sounded familiar, but Perry had grown desensitised to disasters outside of his own life.

'I'm just mad that I didn't see it all coming sooner,' Amanda said. 'Usually, executives don't want us overtly messing around with Earth's activities – viewers get turned off if they sense we're manipulating events. That all changed in the last few years.' She ticked off the plot developments that the Galaxy Entertainment execs had forced on the producers of Earth, including the instigation of various meaningless wars and the introduction of high-fructose corn syrup. 'It all reeks of desperation,' she said. 'I mean, we knew our ratings were low, but we didn't think it was time to finale the *entire planet*.'

'High-fructose corn syrup?' Perry asked. 'What could possibly be entertaining about high-fructose corn syrup?'

'Fat is funny,' Amanda said. 'Some genius back at headquarters thought that ratings would climb if there were more fat people on Earth. Instead, it worked *too* well. Viewers became disgusted.'

'There are now some crazily large people down here,' Dennis said, chuckling. 'I'm sure we're going to see some of those fatties exploding when this place gets finale-ed. That's going to be *hilarious*.'

Perry listened to this, amazed. 'We're not lab rats! We're human beings!'

'Duh,' Amanda said. 'Rats are boring.'

Perry glared at her. 'You don't even see us as people. We're just little playthings to you.'

'*Very important* playthings,' Amanda said. 'Galaxy Entertainment has spent around twenty quadrillion dollars on this planet. They stand to lose almost half of that.'

'That's all you can think about?' Perry seethed. 'You lost some money? You're all homicidal sociopaths!'

Dennis shook his head. 'You guys are the killers. We never kill anyone – we just watch you.'

Amanda gave Perry a sympathetic smile, as if she were touched by his anger. 'You just don't understand how important entertainment is to us,' she said with a trace of pity in her voice. This response was so unlike anything Perry had expected that his righteous fury quickly dissipated. At a loss, he sat back in his seat and stared out the window.

'I hope you know what you're doing, Manda,' Dennis said. 'I sure would miss my popcorn.'

Perry thought he'd misheard him. 'Your what?'

'Popcorn,' Dennis repeated. 'That's the reason I want to save Earth. It's just so damn good here. All that darn nitrogen in the soil – hard to beat.'

Perry shook his head in disbelief and turned to Amanda. 'What's your reason?'

'I think you know.' She gazed meaningfully at Perry and his heart raced. Then she said: 'Professional pride.'

'What?'

'I've waited all my life to work here, and I know I can put a hit show on this planet if they'd just give me some more time. But they want to pull the plug on the whole thing. I can't let that happen. For one thing, it would look terrible on my resumé.'

Perry felt his fury rekindle. 'A planet of seven billion people is about to destroyed, and the only reason you're against it is because of your *career*?'

'Hey, there're a lot of planets with seven billion people,' Dennis said. 'She only has one career.' He pulled the van in front of the Galaxy Entertainment building and turned off the ignition. From the outside, the building appeared dark and silent, except for the short, squat security guard sitting at the receptionist's desk. 'So what's the planda, Manda?'

'We need to get him into a screening room,' she said.

The receptionist gasped. 'No way.'

'I need to show him Steve at least,' Amanda said.

'Steve?' Perry asked. 'Who's Steve?'

Amanda and the receptionist ignored him.

'You can't do it,' Dennis said. 'First of all, it's a clear violation of the Producers' Code.'

'We don't have a choice,' Amanda responded. 'How's he supposed to come up with something to save the channel if he doesn't know what's on it?'

Dennis remained unconvinced. 'Do you know what they'll do if they catch us? Fire us both on the spot and take writer-boy here straight to the Green Room.'

Something about the urgency of Dennis's argument hit home with Perry. 'Maybe he's right,' he said.

'We're wasting time. We have to go in.' Amanda stepped out of the van, leaving Perry and Dennis no choice but to follow.

CHANNEL 8

LIGHTS! ACTION! ARMAGEDDON!

Amanda Mundo loved Earth. Ever since she was a little girl, all her favourite programmes were on Channel Blue. It was a fixture on her first telescreen and the first channel she watched when she arrived home from school. Like most viewers, she had initially been attracted to the nearly constant stupidity and violence. But she'd seen something more in the Earthles, something that, as a young Edenite growing up in a culture that emphasised rationality, moved her deeply. She loved how Earthles would literally kill themselves climbing tall mountains and diving deep into oceans and walking on wires strung impossibly high. And why would they do these things? Were they being chased by predators? Was there something they needed for their survival on top of the mountain or on the bottom of the ocean? No – there was no reason. They did these things only because they wanted to prove that they could do them.

How could you not love that?

As an adolescent, Amanda learned all about her civilisation, the Edenite Empire, and the Three Rs that had rescued it from its barbaric past: Reason, Rationality and Respect. She learned how her people had managed to transcend millennia of destructive animal-based behaviours to evolve into a society devoid of hunger, killing and ignorance. While she couldn't help but feel proud of her history, Channel Blue remained her guilty pleasure. When not studying the lessons of her elders, she would return home and watch fascinated as the hapless Earthles searched jungles for gold that never existed, went blind writing immense books no one ever read, and starved alone in caves searching for enlightenment that never came. Though Amanda never said this out loud, she found the irrational Earthle instinct for the endless quest, the impossible dream and the unreachable goal heartbreakingly beautiful.

She also loved their sense of duty and honour, the misguided way they would sacrifice themselves for meaningless causes. She even loved their bizarre need to divide themselves up into tribes – 'countries', they called them – and celebrate their tribe as the best of all, even if it meant flinging themselves into terrible battles and certain death to prove it. And most of all, she loved their faith in a higher power to rescue them from those terrible battles and certain death, a power that never manifested itself in any tangible form whatsoever, much less rescued them. They always ended up dying – but incredibly enough (and this, in her mind, was the best part) this fact didn't shake the faith of the surviving Earthles. On the contrary, it strengthened their faith because *the higher power must have wanted it that way*.

Seriously: How could you not love that?

Channel Blue was actually thousands of channels bundled together, but Amanda's favourite channels all originated from the tribe that called itself the United States of America. Because of its relative prosperity, strident religious beliefs, and relaxed restrictions on the use of firearms, the USA was the source of most of Channel Blue's hit shows. This, after all, was where the government murdered people for murdering people and started wars to prevent them. It was a country that took all the madness of the Earthles and distilled it into just a few time zones. And though the citizens of this nation had no way of knowing their amazing exploits were being beamed to billions of viewers on the other side of the galaxy, they seemed to have some innate sense of their primacy.

'America's Number One!' they would chant at patriotic rallies and international sporting events.

'This is the greatest country in the world,' their leaders would often say, and as far as entertainment value went, they were absolutely right.

When asked what she wanted to be when she grew up, Amanda dared to dream big: 'I want to produce Earth.' Adults humoured her, though they knew the chances of this actually happening were remote. In Edenite society, there was no calling higher than the production of entertainment, and producers were revered more than the greatest politicians, businessmen, doctors or scholars. And Channel Blue was one of the most sought-after assignments in all of interplanetary production. But Amanda, according to her genetic profile, was blessed with greater tenacity than her peers. This, more than anything else, drove her to become valedictorian of her graduating class and gain enrolment in the highly selective Academy of Television Arts and Sciences.

She graduated from this hallowed institution in the top percentile and could have had her pick of domestic production jobs. But she kept her eyes on the prize. There were no openings on Earth, so she took the toughest jobs she could find around the galaxy to hone her skills, producing celebrity asteroids and CrazyWorlds. When the opportunity came, she wanted to be ready.

One day, while setting up shots for a mutant fight on Altair 3, she read on her screen that a producer on the USA desk of Channel Blue was retiring. She felt a surge of excitement.

It was not just a job on her favourite planet, but a job producing her favourite tribe on her favourite planet. She knew it was hers even before she interviewed for it.

Unfortunately, dream jobs rarely live up to their hype. It seemed as if Amanda had barely moved into her new office before she started overhearing worried conversations in the elevators. Ratings hadn't been an issue for Channel Blue for years. The channel had made executives rich and shareholders wealthy; it had employed hundreds of thousands of producers, editors and technicians, and was such a reliable fixture of the Edenite culture that 'Earthle' had become an affectionate nickname for someone slow on the uptake. But as the numbers on even its more reliable shows dwindled, the channel seemed vulnerable. Producers forced out of their comfort zones scrambled to come up with new programming, and executives looked the other way while production crews flagrantly manipulated events on Earth in an attempt to increase ratings.

Amanda was the first to borrow ideas from Earthle writers. Unlike most of her colleagues, she was not just a connoisseur of Earthles as entertainment but of Earthle entertainment as well. While her efforts were rewarded with modest spikes in viewership, such was the prejudice against Earthle culture that the practice was not embraced by other producers. The haemorrhaging of viewers continued.

Amanda hadn't dreamed all those years and worked on all those asteroids to give up without a fight. This was still her dream job. And now that she had it, she wasn't going to let them blow it up because of some lousy ratings.

This was why, standing in the dark empty parking lot of Galaxy Entertainment, she talked Dennis out of his jacket and talked Perry into putting it on, along with a Galaxy Entertainment baseball cap she found in the back of the service van. She pulled it down until the brim covered Perry's face.

'Keep your head down and let us hold you up,' Amanda ordered. She and Dennis walked on either side of Perry, steering him through the double glass doors and into the lobby. Under the brim of his cap, Perry could see the security guard look up from his reading.

'It's Tim,' Amanda told the guard. 'He's not feeling well.' The guard waved them on. The three walked together through the security door, which slammed shut behind them.

Keeping his head down, Perry heard distant voices over the hum of electronics. He watched the shadows of the long corridor give way to blurred reflections as they skirted the edge of the huge monitor-filled room. After about twenty feet, he felt a shove from one side and stumbled into a small room. Suddenly, everything was quiet.

Perry lifted his cap and saw that he and Amanda were alone in a room surrounded by white illuminated walls. 'Dennis is keeping an eye out for security,' Amanda said. She approached a smooth black pyramid in the middle of the floor and touched it with the fly tattoo on the inside of her left wrist. The walls came to life with flickering images and the room erupted with a cacophony of sound.

The wall on the right played a series of fast clips that showed men fighting in a bar, rioting soccer fans crushed under a fence and jets colliding in mid-air. These assaulting images were accompanied by a rapid-fire announcement: 'Bar fights! Soccer riots! Air shows! Every fatal Earthle entertainment – catch it right now on *Deadly Fun*! Playing exclusively on Channel Blue 752.'

More clips raced by: a bear chasing a camper, a jogger bitten by a mountain lion and, faster than Perry could keep track, various surfers being attacked by various sharks. 'If you love seeing them in the great outdoors, turn to *Earthles Feed the Animals*, now exclusively on Channel Blue 753!' Then drunks tumbled down stairs, fell out of windows and vomited on themselves: 'Their screwed-up brains just won't let them stop! *Earthles Under the Influence*, now on Channel Blue 754, 755, 756 and 757!' The onslaught of frantic images continued – kitchen spills, naked people shaving their body hair, power-tool accidents, a man setting his hair on fire with a Tiki torch – flickering by faster and faster until Perry, his head aching from trying to keep up, was forced to avert his gaze.

'How many Channel Blues are there?'

'Between 1000 and 2000, depending on the time of day,' Amanda said. 'Our viewers have incredibly sophisticated attention spans. They have hundreds of thousands of channels to choose from and usually watch a dozen at a time. They can switch from one to the other with a mere thought impulse, so we like to give them as many options as we can.'

'Jesus,' Perry said. Nicely dressed men and women were being shot in their faces with corks from champagne bottles. *The Champagne Show* was playing on Channel Blue 769.

'That's nothing,' Amanda said. 'When ratings were good, we had 3000.'

'What's this?' Perry asked. He pointed at the wall opposite the fast-moving clips, where a man on the side of a highway was trying unsuccessfully to change a tyre on his car, cursing to himself. 'Looks a little boring.'

'Oh, that's a series,' Amanda said. 'The guy changing the tyre is Hugh Palmer, the Most Impatient Man in the Galaxy.'

Perry turned his gaze to the floor, where a nun kneeled, praying raptly before a living and breathing Virgin Mary. The Virgin smiled beatifically beneath a halo of blinding light. 'My God,' Perry said. 'That nun is having a vision.'

Amanda briefly raised her eyes from the pyramid. 'Oh yeah. We did a pretty good job on that one.'

Perry blinked. 'You give people visions?'

Amanda nodded. 'It's a great inciting incident.' Perry gaped at the glowing Virgin, then became distracted by a screaming teenage boy running across the ceiling as a volleyball hit him in the head. Two groups of boys in matching shirts and shorts flung balls at each other. Perry quickly recognised this as dodge ball, a routine ritual of humiliation in gym classes.

'Gym class?' Perry said.

'A staple of the channel,' Amanda replied, continuing to push tiles on the pyramid. 'A producer came up with the idea.'

'Of broadcasting gym classes?'

'No. Of gym classes.'

Perry frowned. 'You *invented* gym?'

'Come on,' Amanda said. 'What does gym have to do with education? You didn't think there was any real point to it, did you?'

Perry thought back to his own seventh-grade gym class, in which a squadron of adolescent terrorists-in-training were spurred towards violence by an alcoholic crew-cutted cross between W.C. Fields and Stalin named Coach Rasmussen. 'Now that you mention it,' he said, 'no.'

Amanda threw her hands out as if to say, *There you go.* Perry shook his head, still trying to understand. 'In order to watch boys torture each other, you invented gym class.'

'The girls are also very compelling—'

'How long have you been spying on us?'

'You mean, how long have we been producing Earth?'

'Whatever you want to call it. How long have you been here?'

'About 150 years.'

'What?'

'That's really not that long. We have planets that have been broadcasting for centuries.'

While Perry tried to fathom this, the shots of gym class suddenly gave way to a middle-aged man in a hospital gown lying face down while a medical technician stood nearby. An odd cartoon starfish appeared in the foreground and, in a high-pitched voice, yelled, 'Now let's go *up his ass!*' An unseen audience laughed and applauded as the screen cut to the dark shadowy footage of a colonoscopy.

'This is a *show*?'

'Why else would you put a camera up there?' Amanda said. 'Please. You didn't think there was actually any medical value, did you?'

While Perry considered this, an image of the cloud-shrouded Earth appeared on the wall in front of him, spinning in space as a deep-voiced announcer intoned, 'Sick and tired of Earth? You aren't the only one.' The Earth then exploded in a cloud of fireballs, followed by a graphic: THE END OF EARTH. 'Check it out this Autumn. Exclusively on Channel Blue.'

'Don't pay any attention to that,' Amanda said, tapping away.

Perry continued staring at the screen, which now showed what appeared to be an ad for a flying lawnmower. 'Do people really hate us that much?'

'I think *hate* is too strong a word,' Amanda said. 'It's more like . . . I don't know . . . bored and disgusted.'

'Why? What did we ever do to them?'

'When it first went on the air, people couldn't get enough of Earth. They loved how naïve and stupid and selfish you all were, killing each other, eating your fellow mammals, starting wars over rocks you found in the ground. And every year it seemed like you became even more entertaining, with crazier and more effective ways of killing each other and yourselves: Bombs that could obliterate the world, super-viruses in biological labs, and, of course, the internal combustion engine, which in itself is quite a triumph of self-destruction on so many different levels. Careening around your highways in your metal boxes, poisoning the air, smashing into each other – our audiences had never seen anything like it. But then, they loved *all* the inexplicable behaviours, the ludicrous religious clashes, the constant fornication, the devastating wars over nothing – it all seemed fun and novel. *For a while.* Then, at some point, people grew tired of watching it. It was bound to happen. I mean, you live here, you know what it's like.'

Perry, of course, had issues with some of the people on Earth. Who didn't? In some dark recess of his soul, he probably wouldn't have minded seeing a mass slaughter of religious extremists, political pundits, investment bankers, fraternity boys and figure skaters. But to hate humanity so much that you wanted to see *all of it* destroyed? 'Are we really that bad?' he said.

'You have to understand: in our world, poverty hasn't existed in millennia. Here, in your richest cities, there are people with nothing, who don't have a home, who don't even have enough to eat. That's incredible to us. How can anyone live in a house with twenty rooms while just down the street, a man lives in a cardboard box?'

Perry felt defensive, though he wasn't sure why. He didn't think anyone should live in a box. Hell, he didn't think anyone should have to live in his apartment. But, as Earth's only representative in the discussion at hand, he felt an obligation to defend his planet. 'Well,' Perry said. 'It's complicated. You see, in a free-market system—'

'And the *killing*,' Amanda interrupted. 'In Eden, there hasn't been a murder for 10,000 years. But here, you have complete strangers killing each other in massive numbers just because some guy in a uniform tells them to! It's utterly insane! It's a good thing you're all so ridiculous and funny – otherwise, they would've started turning you off a long time ago. Here we are.'

Amanda made a final tap on the pyramid and the wall in front of them filled with the image of a man in sunglasses driving a sports car through traffic while talking on an earpiece. His bright golf shirt was unbuttoned enough to reveal a tanned, shaved chest and a crucifix on a shiny gold chain. 'Yeah, I banged her,' he said. 'Hold on.' He accelerated and cut off another car attempting to merge into his lane. 'Nice try, asshole!' he yelled to the other car. Smiling, he continued his phone call. 'Yeah, she was totally hot. I might even take her out again.'

Perry turned to Amanda, who was watching the man in the car with unmistakable pride. 'That,' Amanda said, 'is the most famous man on Earth.'

On the wall, the man in the car turned into a parking lot, leaned on his horn, and cut off a minivan to slip into the parking lot's last open space.

Perry watched this, perplexed. 'Who is he?'

'Steve Santiago,' Amanda said. 'He's incredible. Watch.' Steve jumped out of the sports car – the vanity licence plates read LVE MY RDE – trotted into a Starbucks and walked past a line of waiting customers to the counter.

'I need a latte pronto,' he shouted at a barista. When one of the waiting customers dared protest, Steve froze him with a glare and said, 'I've got a medical condition, I can't stand in line.' Mumbling 'asshole' under his breath, Steve conspicuously dropped a five-dollar bill into the tip jar, only to expertly fish it out as soon as the cashier turned her back.

Amanda shook her head with wonderment. 'He's like this all the time,' she said. 'Just when you think he might do something that isn't horrible, he surprises you with something even worse.' While Steve waited impatiently for his drink, he angled for a peek down the blouse of an old woman.

Perry was still puzzled. 'This is one of your shows?'

Amanda nodded. 'Up until a few years ago, it was the top show on Channel Blue. When it started going down in the ratings, I was assigned the job of reviving it. But it hasn't been easy.'

'I don't understand,' Perry said. '*This* is really a show.'

'Steve is a Jacuzzi salesman in Encino,' Amanda said. 'He's unfaithful to his girlfriend, he steals from his job, he lies to his friends, he cheats at golf, he rents his condo out for pornographic film shoots during the day, and on his holidays he goes to Mexico, buys prescription drugs and sells them at a profit to poor cancer patients. Every Sunday after the service at his church, he goes to fellowship and steals coffee filters. He has the most amazing amalgamation of bad qualities of any living being in the galaxy, and he's the reason I brought you here. All we have to do is figure out a great new story idea for Steve, and we can save Earth. What are your thoughts?'

'My thoughts?'

'Work with me, Mr Bunt. We don't have much time here.'

'This is crazy,' Perry said. 'Are you telling me that your biggest show is some asshole from Encino?'

'Not just some asshole,' Amanda said. 'The biggest asshole *ever.*'

'I don't get it. I thought you were some kind of advanced civilisation with superior intelligence.'

'No matter how smart you are, Earthles being cruel and selfish is entertaining. You're just going to have to take my word on that.'

'You're sadists.'

'Look at the stuff you all watch for fun – football, boxing, wrestling, humiliating reality TV, demeaning game shows, ultra-violent movies. Because we're more advanced, we've eradicated the lame justifications for witnessing debasement. We take our entertainment straight.'

Perry was about to argue this point when the door flew open and the two security guards walked into the room, one short and squat, the other tall and thin.

'You're both going to have to come with us,' the short one said.

CHANNEL 9

THE IDEA THAT WILL SAVE THE EARTH

The two security guards stood in the doorway. 'You are in violation of company rules,' the tall one said to Amanda.

Perry stood frozen in fear. As was his wont, when confronted by an authority figure, be they the lowliest substitute study-hall teacher or the most menacing alien security guard, he had begun perspiring profusely. Amanda, meanwhile, seemed bizarrely unconcerned. As if trying to get more of a reaction, the tall guard stepped to within a few inches of her face and glared at her. 'We have a situation here. You have brought an Earthle into the station.'

'Who cares?' Amanda said. 'He's harmless. Look at him. He's certainly not a threat.' Though Perry understood the strategy behind this, he found Amanda's casual discounting of his dangerousness annoying. 'I know, I know, I shouldn't have brought him in. Just zap his brain with your collar and let's forget about it.'

'No.' The tall guard cocked his head and eyed Perry, who involuntarily recoiled from the menacing gaze. 'He's been here before. We need to erase more than his brain.' Perry did his best to steady his shaking legs – he needed them to get out of here.

'Let's not get ahead of ourselves,' the short guard said. 'We should all talk to Mr Pythagorus. If you could both come with us?'

The two guards strode into the room and Perry saw his chance. With all the speed he could summon, he darted to his right, scurried around the guards, slipped through the open doorway and sprinted down the hallway. He glanced over one shoulder and was pleased to see that no one was following him, only to look ahead and nearly run into the tall security guard. He staggered to a stop, barely avoiding a collision.

'Hey, how did you—' he said, before the guard grabbed him.

Perry struggled, his arms flailing. Something came off in his hand, and when he glanced down to see what it was, he saw, to his horror, the guard's face dangling between his fingers. With a groan of annoyance, the guard snatched his face from Perry and smoothed it back over the steel tube that protruded between his shoulders. Amanda and the short guard walked by and the tall guard, his face still a little crumpled around the edges, pushed Perry down the hallway after them.

Perry, still breathing hard, caught up with Amanda. 'What the hell are they?'

'Copbots. Or, more specifically, good copbot/bad copbot.'

'Where are they taking us?'

'To see my boss.'

Perry could feel a wave of sweat breaking onto the small of his back, drenching the seat of his pants. 'What are you going to tell him? How are you going to explain what we were doing?'

'I don't know. Just remember, you don't know anything. I never told you what we're doing here.'

'Hey, guys. What's going on?' Dennis the receptionist sauntered down the hallway towards them, idly munching popcorn from a paper bag. He noted the security-guard escorts. 'Is there some kind of problem?' he asked with forced nonchalance.

Amanda glared at him. 'What happened to you?' she whispered. 'You were supposed be a look-out.'

'I was,' Dennis replied under his breath. 'I looked and I got out.'

'You were supposed to *warn us*.'

'There wasn't enough time,' Dennis whispered. Amanda smirked. 'Come on, Manda. You know I wasn't bred for bravery.' Then in a conversational voice he said, 'Hey, you should check out the feed in screening room seven: bunch of rich guys seeking enlightenment dying in a sweat lodge – totally *hilarious*,' and bustled off. A large hand smacked down onto Perry's shoulder. It felt like a turkey vulture had landed.

'No talking,' the tall security guard growled. 'Keep moving.'

After walking for what seemed like blocks, Perry and Amanda were herded through the doorway of a large office. At one end, behind an improbably large desk, a nine-year-old boy in a suit, his hair stylishly spiked with gel, sat watching an array of screens floating in the air and talking to no one Perry could see.

'Look, just tell him I loved what he did with the tsunami,' the boy said. 'Everyone here loved it. And we loved the Russian earthquake, too. But just not as much. It just wasn't as *disastrous* as we were expecting.'

Perry glanced at Amanda. '*That's* your boss?'

She shrugged. 'It's a youth-oriented industry.'

The boy executive, still staring intently at his screens, gestured for Amanda and Perry to sit down. Perry read the shiny silver nameplate on the front of his desk:

NICHOLAS PYTHAGORUS
PRODUCTION EXECUTIVE IN CHARGE OF EXECUTIVE
PRODUCTION

Nick, as he was known to both friends and enemies, was indeed a prodigy – most children employed by Galaxy Entertainment were thirteen or fourteen before they attained executive positions. But Nick had everything: youth, style and a keen business sense. Today, he also had a terrible headache. He had won the job of producing Earth's finale by presenting an ambitious plan to accomplish this well under the budgets of his rivals. But cutting corners had taken its toll. After only two months of escalating cataclysmic disasters, he was two weeks behind schedule and way over budget, with the bulk of Armageddon to come.

'Look, I don't care how many megatons or how deep, all I'm saying is, it wasn't enough. It was more like an earth-quiver than an earthquake.' Nick paused. 'I'm not trying to be hurtful here, but I thought we all agreed that this was going to be an event foretelling *the end of the planet*, not merely an opportunity for another benefit concert.'

Perry noticed a peculiar statue on the shelf behind Nick Pythagorus: a gold naked woman held a planet in her hands. The naked woman, though only ten inches tall, appeared to be alive, and the planet she held was a swirling mass of red and purple gasses. He leaned over to Amanda. 'What's that?'

Amanda followed his gaze and chuckled. 'It figures he'd have that out for everyone to see,' she replied. 'It's his Orby.'

'His what?'

'The award the Academy of Television Arts and Sciences gives every year for extra-planetary production. It's supposed to be about quality but everyone knows it's just politics.' Amanda glanced at Nick, then continued to speak softly to Perry. 'Nick won his for the Iraq War, but he lucked into it. The guy who should have won was the producer who got President Bush elected in the first place.'

'A producer got Bush elected?'

Amanda nodded. 'Yeah, and Karl's still pissed about being overlooked. He won't even *talk* to Nick.'

Perry was distracted by the sound of Nick exhaling impatiently.

'Look, I don't have time for this,' the boy said. 'Just tell him I loved it, but I have some notes. And we definitely need to talk before Flight 240. I just received the script and have some concerns – *especially* after Russia. I don't want the plane to bounce off the damn reactor. Bye.' Nick waved his hand and several of the floating screens flew in tight formation into his desk. He turned to Amanda and Perry. 'Writers,' he muttered. 'I ask for an earthquake and I get a shiver; I ask for a simple terrorist act and they turn it into this whole song and dance.'

The boy executive turned his attention to one of the remaining floating screens, which played a video of the two security guards walking in on Perry and Amanda. Nick smiled and sat back in his chair.

Maybe this isn't going to be such a bad day after all, he thought.

He had always perceived Amanda as a rival, albeit one at a decided disadvantage; on his side were youth and ruthless ambition, on hers were merely creativity and intelligence. And while her advantages were just as often disadvantages in the entertainment business, she had unsettled him on occasion with her innovative ideas. Now, with this huge violation of company policy, she was as good as unemployed.

Contemplating this fine turn of events, Nick leaned back in his chair. 'What gives, Mandy? Seriously. I know you've always been soft on Earthles, but *bringing one in here?*' He laughed in a short burst. 'Have you completely lost your mind?'

Amanda stared into space as if lost in thought. Perry, by now a sopping wet knot of fear, couldn't take it anymore. 'I don't know anything!' he yelped.

Amanda glanced at Perry with a bemused expression, then turned to Nick. 'He's lying,' she said. 'He knows *everything*. I even told him about the finale.'

Perry stared at her, his jaw agape.

'It really doesn't matter,' Nick Pythagorus said. 'Just by being here, he's off the channel. And you, Mandy, will have difficulty finding employ as a barker on an amusement asteroid.' He swivelled to the security guards. 'Escort him to the Green Room.' The tall security guard moved in quickly and grabbed Perry by the collar.

'Don't you want to hear his pitch?' Amanda said.

Nick frowned. 'What?'

'He has a great idea for a show. I think it could keep us on the air.' For a moment, Perry was certain that he couldn't possibly be the 'he' she was referring to. But then she smiled at him like a proud mother entreating her six-year-old to share a story with a family friend. Perry, who hadn't had a great idea since VHS was a format, suddenly felt like he was sitting on a trap door over a bottomless pit.

Amanda continued obliviously. 'Mr Bunt may be an Earthle, but he also happens to be a fantastic writer. That's why I contacted him. We've tried everything we could think of. I thought maybe he could come up with an idea that would save our jobs and you know what? I was right.'

Nick chuckled derisively. 'Come on. An Earthle writer? Entertainment on this planet is *bullshit*. Please. They still enjoy watching people *pretending to be other people*. For Adam's sake – they watch grown men giving each other brain damage while chasing a ball. And if you were going to go crazy and hire an Earthle, *Perry Bunt*, for crying out loud? Why not Lucas or Spielberg?'

Amanda frowned. 'Do you think I'm an idiot? Do you think I'd risk everything for less than the best idea I've ever heard? How much is your finale running?'

Nick shifted in his seat. 'I don't know. Twenty trillion or something.'

'Last thing I heard was it was over thirty. You know it's going to be at least fifty by the time you roll credits.'

Nick flung one hand out over his desk. 'What the fuck does that have to do with anything? You bring some Earthle into my office and start riding me about *my* budget? Get to the damn point.'

Amanda leaned into him. 'I know you have a lot riding on this, but even you have to admit that we would be heroes if we found a way to boost ratings, save the channel *and* avoid spending that last twenty trillion.'

Nick pursed his lips. After a moment, he sighed. 'What the hell.' He nodded to the security guard, who released Perry and stepped back. 'I've got a couple minutes. Give me the pitch.'

Nick and Amanda stared at Perry, who felt the trap door open up beneath him.

CHANNEL 10

THE SECOND FLOOR

Take every anxiety dream you've had – every classroom in which you've heard for the first time about a final, every crowded street you've walked down naked, every stage on which you've forgotten your lines – multiply them times ten, add the fear of imminent death and the destruction of the world, and you have a sense of what Perry felt while boy executive Nick Pythagorus waited for his literally world-saving idea.

'Well—' Perry began. 'Um, it's kind of complicated. I don't know if, uh, I can sum it up in a couple minutes.' He shot a panicked look at Amanda, who still appeared ridiculously calm.

'Also,' she said, as if Perry had actually said something, 'I don't think we should pitch it here.'

Nick flinched. 'What?'

'We need the boss in the room.'

Nick laughed hollowly. 'You can't go over me.'

'Why not? You're all ready to toss my writer into the Green Room. I don't feel like this is a friendly environment.'

Nick didn't take long to do the math. If, by some fluke, the Earthle's idea was promising, it wouldn't help him if he appeared to have obstructed it. On the other hand, if the idea was terrible, as he suspected it was, Amanda would be digging her own grave deeper by pitching it to the President of Channel

Blue. Plus, she'd no longer be his problem to deal with. 'OK,' he said. 'But the Earthle still goes in the Green Room when it's over.'

'Fine,' Amanda said, standing. Within seconds, she and Perry were walking back down the long hallway. Perry glanced over his shoulder at the security guards, who now followed at a discreet distance.

'I thought I wasn't supposed to know anything.'

'Change of plan.'

Perry waited for Amanda to say more, but she didn't.

'What's the Green Room?'

'It's a place for Earthles who've been compromised.'

Perry swallowed. 'What does that mean?'

'Sometimes on-air talent discovers too much about aspects of the production and for some reason can't be erased. We put them in the Green Room.' She said this with a trace of impatience, as if she was being forced to tell Perry what a tree was.

'What happens to them there?'

'They serve as extras. Sometimes they even get speaking parts.'

'When you first told me about Channel Blue, you said that you'd rescued me from the Green Room.'

'So?'

'So . . . you made it sound like I would've been killed if I'd gone there.'

Amanda shook her head impatiently. 'We don't kill. We haven't killed any living beings for *millennia*.'

Perry regarded her sceptically. 'You just put them in situations in which they happen to die.'

'We can't stop people from dying – everyone dies.'

'Especially in the Green Room?'

'Look, if we nail this pitch, the Green Room won't even be an issue.'

Perry glanced around furtively before speaking. 'Amanda, I hate to break this to you, but there is no pitch.'

'I know.'

'But you told him—'

'I had to get him interested. He wouldn't have let us go unless he thought you had something.'

'But I don't! I have nothing!'

'Something will come to you, Mr Bunt.'

Perry didn't have the heart to tell her that her faith in him was misplaced. They arrived at a bank of elevators. 'Now that we're working together,' he said, 'do you think you can call me Perry?'

Amanda laughed. 'I'm sorry, force of habit. We're trained to keep a respectful distance from the talent.'

Amanda pressed her fly tattoo against a set of elevator doors. They shot open and she entered the car. Perry followed her in. On the control panel were two round illuminated buttons, 1 and 2. Amanda pressed 2 and the doors closed. As the elevator shot up with a gentle whirr, it occurred to Perry that the building they were in had only one floor. Light flooded into the car. They were suddenly high above the building, standing in a translucent box surrounded by nothing but sky. Perry's stomach dropped as Ventura Boulevard and the flat roofs of drab buildings disappeared quickly below them. He grabbed onto the railing to steady himself. 'What's going on?' he gasped.

Amanda gazed out on the shrinking coast of California as if she'd seen it a million times. 'The channel's corporate offices are on the dark side of the moon.'

Perry watched breathlessly as clouds raced past. 'No one can see us?'

'All anyone sees from the outside are images of sky projected onto each surface. For all practical purposes, we're invisible.'

The sky became a darker blue, then indigo. Stars blinked out of a purple haze and below them the vast blue-white plain of the Earth became a crescent, then an immense oval, then a blue pearl surrounded by darkness. Perry was so struck by the beauty of this sight that he momentarily forgot about the doom that awaited both him and the world below.

He turned back to Amanda, who examined her nails. He was more mystified than ever by this woman, the product of a race of people who could create something as sublime as an elevator to the moon but also enslave and destroy an entire planet in the name of entertainment. 'If your civilisation can do this,' Perry said, 'why do they want to watch *us*?'

'They don't anymore,' Amanda said. 'That's the problem.'

'You know what I mean. Why go to all the trouble to come across the galaxy and spy on Earth when you've got everything figured out?'

Amanda stared into space. 'It's a complicated question, and one I can't answer in the short time we have. Besides—' She looked at Perry. 'You need to be thinking about the new show.'

Perry's mind was full of things – unfortunately, none of them resembled an idea. 'I don't understand why you think I can do this. I don't know anything about your audience.'

'I showed you some of our programming. Think along those lines. Focus on Steve Santiago.'

'But Steve Santiago doesn't make any sense. I mean, no one I know would enjoy watching him for even a minute. He's just a douche bag.'

Amanda considered this. 'To us, Steve's incredibly—' She searched for the exact word. 'Exotic.'

'Why?'

'In many ways. For example, no one in Eden has believed in any sort of deity for thousands of years. We think it's hilarious that someone like Steve can do all these horrible things to other people, then go and pray to a god and think that he's been forgiven. That is truly extraordinary.'

Perry nodded. 'OK, what else?'

'Well, just *everything*. Everything that Steve is – selfish, petty, arrogant, aggressive, vindictive – is remarkable. You have to understand: these aren't traits our viewers come into contact with.'

'Why not?'

'They've been weeded out.'

'*Weeded out?*'

'They were all vestiges of our origins as animals, when we had to compete every day for survival. And though we no longer evince these traits, we still find them entertaining. The same way you might enjoy seeing, I don't know . . . monkeys playing at the zoo.'

'But what do you mean by *weeded out*?'

'You know. Nobody wants those traits, and they certainly don't want them for their children.'

Perry stared at Amanda. 'You're all . . . what? Genetically altered?'

Amanda nodded.

'Even you?'

Amanda rolled her eyes. 'You think my parents would have left me to *chance*?'

Perry now gazed at Amanda's features in a different light, the hazel eyes that crinkled magnificently when she laughed, the cascade of luminescent blonde hair, the perfectly placed freckles. He had often thought of her beauty as being too good to be true and now he'd found out that it was. Or was it? He recalled an argument about fake breasts he'd once had with a studio executive. In the middle of a party in the Hollywood Hills, the executive had argued that it didn't matter whether a woman had real or fake breasts, while Perry had clung to the notion that knowing they were fake did in fact diminish the experience of fondling them. (Later that night, as fate would have it, Perry found himself drunkenly kissing an actress and eagerly fondling breasts the size and texture of water balloons. Telling himself that this experience was not in fact all it could be in no way diminished his disappointment when the actress, in a moment of sobriety, disengaged herself from Perry, buttoned up her blouse and disappeared from his life forever.) Did Amanda actually appear any less attractive to him now? Did he crave holding her in his arms any less than a moment before? Of course he didn't.

'Dennis said he wasn't bred for bravery,' Perry said.

'The human genome contains only 28,422 genes, which isn't much when you consider that a flatworm has over 10,000. So even if your parents hire the best genetic programmer in the galaxy, you can't have everything.'

'So what were you bred for?'

'I'm a Grade 4 genotype,' Amanda said without a hint of boastfulness. 'It's a long list, and we really should be focusing on the pitch.'

'Just give me a taste.'

Amanda sighed. 'Deductive reasoning, memory, risk-taking, tenacity, ambition, language skills, imagination, empathy, artistic ability, physical coordination—'

'Christ, is that all?' Perry interrupted. 'No bowling ability? What about feet that don't smell?'

Amanda frowned. She was usually not opposed to a joke – after all, 'sense of humour' was one of the pronounced traits that Perry had prevented her from listing. But now wasn't the time. 'We should be coming up with ideas.'

'What about Dennis. What was he bred for?'

Amanda had to think about this for a moment. 'I'm not sure. He has really nice hair.'

Perry snorted. 'Now those are priorities.'

'Don't scoff. Good genes are why we don't have any war or hunger or murder. That was all left on the laboratory floor a long time ago. Without the need for senseless aggression, we have time to enjoy our lives.'

Perry considered this. 'So you're bored.'

'No,' Amanda said, a glint of defensiveness on her armour of calm. 'We have a great deal of leisure time.'

Perry felt his pulse race. 'Which is why you need to watch us, right? Without us murdering each other, you people have nothing to do with your lives.'

Amanda frowned. 'No matter what you think about us, you and your planet are going to be in reruns soon if we don't come up with a pitch. Now, what do you have?'

Perry furrowed his brow and tried to appear deeply thoughtful, as if on the verge of a breakthrough. Unfortunately, his mind was filled with only one endlessly repeating thought: *I have no idea.*

The blinding white surface of the moon raced towards the elevator until it seemed to surround them. Perry remembered something Amanda had said during one of their classroom chats.

'When you told me your boyfriend lived far away, is this what you meant?'

Amanda laughed. 'Oh no,' she said. 'The moon would be

easy. Jared works in administration back on the home planet. We hologram three times a week if we're lucky.' Amanda stared at the expanding moon with what seemed to Perry like wistfulness and he averted his eyes, angry with himself for bringing up the topic. The elevator lurched slightly to one side and fell into an easy lunar orbit, skimming from light into dark. As night enveloped the elevator, the dark side of the moon slid into view. Giant illuminated letters appeared on the surface, and Perry stared at them transfixed until he could read the entire message. It read:

THIS IS WHERE THE INSANITY BEGINS

Next to the huge, bright letters was a giant arrow pointing directly at Earth. As they descended over the 'T' in 'THIS', blinding light filled the elevator. Perry squinted his eyes while Amanda slipped on a pair of sleek dark glasses. 'We've actually received complaints about it from passing spacecraft,' she said. 'It's good publicity, though. And we've needed every bit of it.'

Perry couldn't reply because the elevator was suddenly plummeting towards the surface of the moon. As the chalky ground rapidly rose up to meet them, he braced himself against the railing for impact. Then the elevator slowed, twisted down into a small crater, and slipped soundlessly below the surface. Before Perry had a chance to react, a soft chime sounded – *bing* – and the doors slid open, revealing a large, brightly lit hallway. Amanda's heels clicked as she strode out onto the shiny floor. 'Welcome to Base Station Blue,' she said. 'I'll see you after decontamination.'

'What?' Perry said as two figures, one tall, the other short, both in white coveralls, approached him.

'Right this way, sir,' the short one said. Perry stared at

them. As impossible as it seemed, they were the two security guards from Galaxy Entertainment.

'Amanda!' he shouted.

Amanda paused. 'Don't worry. They're different models – copbots retrofitted as decontaminators. They're perfectly harmless.' She continued on her way.

Perry reluctantly let the two all-too-familiar-looking figures lead him through a sliding door into a shiny, glassed-in chamber. The tall one sealed the door and both decontaminators picked up long metal wands.

'Disrobe, please,' the short one said. Perry slowly removed all his clothes down to his white briefs (which, to his dismay, were stained).

'*All* of your clothes,' the tall one barked. Perry hesitated, then pulled off his underwear. The decontaminators exchanged a glance and the tall one raised up his rod, which emitted a blue pulsing charge that travelled in a straight line towards Perry's crotch. Perry felt a strange sudden warmth and glanced down to see that his pubic hair had vanished. He looked like some grotesque pre-pubescent version of himself.

'That's it,' the short one said, gesturing to a door that Perry hadn't noticed. 'There are some new clothes for you outside.' Perry stepped through the door into a room that was empty, except for a bench on which a blue velour tracksuit was neatly folded.

Moments later, Perry, dressed in the blue tracksuit, emerged into a hallway, where Amanda waited in an identical blue outfit.

'Why didn't you tell me they were going to burn off my body hair?' he said.

'Oh, I forgot about that,' Amanda said, studying a small screen she held in one hand. 'We haven't had any pubic hair for a thousand years – they must've thought it was a potential source of contamination. We're in luck. The President of Channel Blue will see us right away.' She glanced up at Perry. 'Any ideas yet?'

'How am I supposed to have ideas when two robots are shooting fireballs at my crotch?'

Amanda slid the screen into one of her pockets. 'There's still time.'

'Amanda, I hate to say this, but I don't even have a *notion* of an idea.'

'You will.'

Perry shook his head. 'What have I done to give you the impression that I work well under pressure? Because I'm going to tell you right now: I don't.'

Amanda appeared completely unfazed. 'Something might come to you.'

'How can you possibly be so calm?'

'Would it help if I panicked?'

'I don't think anything would help. I'm the wrong man for this job.'

Amanda shrugged. 'It's too late to get anyone else.'

Perry wanted to scream. 'Listen to me: I don't have an idea now and I won't have one fifteen minutes from now.'

'You seem really tense.' Amanda regarded him thoughtfully, tapping her lips with one finger. 'I know what might help. An orgasm.'

Perry felt a sudden surge of adrenaline. He looked furtively up and down the empty hallway. 'You think?'

'Absolutely,' Amanda said. 'Why don't you masturbate before the meeting?'

Perry couldn't disguise his disappointment. 'What?'

'I know you're under a lot of pressure – an orgasm might

relax you. Actually, I wouldn't mind one myself.' Amanda pulled a small box from her pocket, shook a purple pill into the palm of her hand and swallowed it. She shook out another pill and offered it to Perry.

Perry eyed the pill suspiciously. 'What is it?'

'MORE.'

'More? More of what?'

'Masturbatory Orgasm Response Enhancer. Watch.' Amanda tapped her hand just below her stomach and immediately began breathing hard. As Perry watched with both embarrassment and avid interest, she threw back her head and moaned ecstatically, then smiled at Perry without a shred of self-consciousness. 'Whew,' she said. 'Sure you don't want one?'

Perry was suddenly aware of a hairless bulge in his pants, the longer-lasting result of Amanda's quick climax. 'If there's one thing I don't need a pill to help me with, it's masturbation.'

'But this makes it so much quicker, easier and more intense,' Amanda said. 'Before MORE, we wasted huge chunks of our lives in the absurd quest to have sexual intercourse with each other.' She shivered with revulsion. 'Like animals in heat, dying for a chance to rub membranes and put our mouths all over each other. You know, like . . . you. Now we're free.'

Perry couldn't conceal his disappointment. 'You don't have sex?'

'I knew someone who tried it once in college.' Amanda cringed. 'Yuck. It's amazing that such a violent, ugly act ever became confused with love, just because of its association with reproduction.'

'So you've never—'

'No!'

'Then—' Perry tried to pick out the right words. 'What do you *do* with each other?'

'Physical intimacy,' Amanda said. 'You know, snuggling, cuddling, spooning. Acts that are truly worthy of the concept of love.'

'Kissing?'

Amanda wrinkled her nose and shook her head. 'Kissing originates from apes chewing food for their young and spitting it into their mouths. No thank you.'

'Never?'

'No!' Amanda studied Perry's face. 'Are you OK, Mr Bunt? You look pale.'

'I'm fine.'

'Are you absolutely sure you don't need to masturbate?'

'I'm fine!'

'Maybe later then.' Amanda dropped the purple pill into Perry's jacket pocket. 'If you get tense during the meeting, go ahead. Everyone will understand.'

Perry still couldn't wrap his brain around the idea of a world devoid of almost everything he cared about. 'If you don't kiss or have sex, how do you show someone you really care about them?' he asked.

'What?'

'How do you show love towards each other?'

'I wasn't aware that love was something that had to be shown,' Amanda said. 'You either feel it or you don't, right?'

Perry shook his head. 'You must be fun at parties.'

'I am,' Amanda said.

'I was being sarcastic.'

'I know, but we're on the moon now. The Earthle irony doesn't fly here.' She smiled at Perry patronisingly. 'We find that it's more efficient to say what we mean. So while we're here, give it a try. At least until we get through this meeting.'

'I'd be happy to,' Perry said, as sarcastically as possible.

A small two-seater vehicle appeared out of a slot in the wall and hovered in mid-air. 'Here's our ride,' Amanda said. She sat down in one seat and gestured for Perry to join her. He stepped warily into the floating car, which immediately sped off down the empty hallway. Advanced civilisations sure have long hallways, Perry thought. The car turned a corner and was suddenly surrounded by other men and women of all races, walking and floating in various directions and speaking different languages, all wearing blue tracksuits. The men had the compact bodies, full heads of hair and chiselled features of movie stars, while every woman evinced an ethereal, stunning beauty that made Perry feel awestruck and inadequate at the same time. It was as if Hollywood had cast a futuristic version of the United Nations.

Perry now understood why Amanda didn't seem to realise how attractive she was. Among these people, she was *typical*.

'Why the blue suits?' Perry asked.

'Why not?' Amanda said. 'They're very comfortable.'

'No one wants to wear anything different?'

'Oh, you mean *fashion*?' Amanda laughed. 'Another vestige of our animal origins – plumage and whatnot – a *huge* waste of time and money. Very entertaining, though. One of our most popular shows features live feeds from changing rooms all over Earth.'

The car passed through an immense domed atrium lined with hallways and doors. 'My apartment's right up there,' Amanda said, pointing halfway up into the maze. 'I'd show it to you if we had more time.'

Perry felt a tingle of excitement about the possibility of being with Amanda in her apartment before he realised that without kissing or sex, there would be no point. 'So you live on the moon?' he said.

'Of course,' Amanda said. 'You didn't think I'd live down there, did you?'

Perry sighed. 'You know, you keep insulting the Earth as if I'm not from there. How am I supposed to take that?'

'I'm sorry,' Amanda said. 'Sometimes I forget. Here we are.'

The car floated to a stop. Amanda jumped out and started trotting briskly down the hallway. Perry stepped out of the car, pausing to watch it disappear into a slot in the wall.

'Mr Bunt!' Amanda called. Perry caught up with her and together they walked through a massive sliding door into an office unlike any he had ever seen. For starters, one entire wall was glass and overlooked the surface of the moon and the black emptiness of space. The other walls were filled with small screens showing live feeds from Channel Blue – children vomiting at birthday parties, construction workers hitting their fingers with hammers, motorists slamming their cars into garage walls – but in this office, Earth seemed very far away. Against the backdrop of distant stars was a massive desk flanked by shelves of trophies, among which Perry recognized several golden Orbys. A large man with a shock of bright white hair wearing a blue velour jumpsuit sat in an armchair behind the desk, staring out into space. Amanda and Perry sat down and the man spun around to face them.

'So . . . what've you got?' he said with a distinctive low drawl.

Perry had heard this voice before. It was the voice of The King.

The man in the armchair was Elvis Presley.

PITCHING TO THE KING

He was older, an incredibly well-preserved man in his eighties, but clearly Elvis. Perry stared at him with a frozen smile on his face, unable to speak. The man behind the desk, for his part, stared back at Perry expectantly. Amanda jumped in to end the stand-off.

'As you've heard,' she said, 'Mr Bunt has come up with a new show that will save Channel Blue.'

'You've taken a lot of risks, young lady,' the man with the white pompadour drawled. 'For yourself and for the company.'

'It was worth it, as you'll see.'

The man glanced quickly at Perry then back at Amanda. 'I confess I'm doubtful,' the man said. 'No one wants to keep Channel Blue on the air more than I do. I've always had special feelings for the Earthles and their amusing hijinks. But there's no way to sugarcoat space trash – the ratings have been down a wormhole lately.'

'Then we have nothing to lose,' Amanda said. 'We're about to blow the whole thing up and write it off anyway, right? Any programming we get out of it at this point is pure profit.'

The man nodded slowly. 'I'm no expert on Earthle writers, but if we're going down this road, why not Lucas or Spielberg?'

Even in his stunned state, Perry felt annoyed. 'You haven't heard of him, but Mr Bunt is the best,' Amanda said. 'I have total confidence in him. I wouldn't be wasting your time if I didn't.'

The President of Channel Blue fidgeted his hands on the top of his desk, then turned to Perry. 'All right,' he said. 'I'll hear your idea.'

Perry stared at the older man. 'I'm sorry,' he blurted, 'but I have to ask. Are you Elvis Presley?'

The man nodded. 'I started as a field producer on Earth,' he said with a note of finality that indicated he wasn't interested in elaborating. Perry heard the note but still couldn't help himself.

'What are you doing here?'

Amanda glared at him. 'Mr Presley would like to hear your idea. He's a very busy man.'

'Right,' Perry said. 'Of course.' The butterflies that Perry had felt in his stomach for the last day suddenly became eagles. *Why had this happened to me?* he wondered. Why did he, of all people, have a chance of saving the Earth? It was bad enough to be killed by aliens, but to be responsible for the Earth's destruction as well? He shook his head, trying in vain to clear it.

'He does have an idea, doesn't he?' Elvis said.

'He sure does,' Amanda replied. She turned and gazed directly at Perry, her eyes shining. 'And it's a winner.'

Perry returned her gaze and, despite his nervousness, found himself smiling broadly. She believed in him! How crazy was that? And if she believed he could pull this off, why shouldn't he? After all, wasn't he the seven-year-old who believed so intently that he was destined for greatness that he risked his life on a clothesline? And wasn't it only a few years ago that, riding a powerful gust of cash, he had glided to the upper stratosphere of Hollywood screenwriters? Hell, he'd faked his way through a hundred meetings just like this one and come out of them with million-dollar deals. OK, not *exactly* like this one – he'd never pitched an idea to a deceased rock star on the moon in order to save humanity – but wasn't it really just the same thing? Convincing someone you had the answer they were searching for, even if you didn't?

Perry continued smiling, trying with every ounce of his being to summon the confidence he'd left in the Hollywood Hills. 'My idea,' he said aloud, almost as if trying out the phrase. 'My idea is very simple, very straightforward.' So far, so good – Elvis leaned forward as if to give him his full attention. Now what? Perry thought. Then he remembered a valuable artefact from his glory days of taking meetings: *When in doubt, restate the obvious.*

'Channel Blue was successful for years. Now, it isn't.' Keep going, Perry thought. Just keep going. 'In the beginning, your viewers watched because they found the people of Earth to be ridiculous, ludicrous and generally horrific.' Elvis nodded slightly. Yes, Perry, thought. It's working! He had him! 'What about that changed? Did the people of Earth become less ridiculous, ludicrous and generally horrific? I don't think so. What changed,' continued Perry, gaining steam, 'is that your viewers got sick of them. So what do we do about it? How do we give people a new look at Channel Blue and bring them back?'

Elvis regarded him intently. Amanda listened raptly. Perry opened his mouth . . . and nothing came out. Just like that, he'd hit a wall. He was a dry, barren husk, bereft of ideas. Once again, he was a fraud, an out-of-work screenwriter living in a crappy apartment who was in way over his head. He could feel the flop sweat surge out of his brow as he desperately surveyed the office, searching for anything to smash the lock on his brain.

'Are you going to tell me?' Elvis said. 'Because I don't feel like guessing.'

Then, Perry saw it. On one of the small screens showing Earth people humiliating themselves, Perry recognized Steve Santiago, the galaxy's most reprehensible creature, lying in bed asleep, his hair tucked in a hairnet. Above the bed was a graphic portrait of Jesus Christ, the kind of painting that had always made Perry feel slightly woozy – Jesus gazed heavenward while a bloody, thorn-encircled heart emerged from his chest.

And suddenly, Perry had the answer.

'Steve Santiago has a vision,' Perry said. 'Jesus appears before him. And Jesus tells him that he's going to destroy the Earth and all of humanity unless Steve becomes a good man. To save his life and the life of everyone on the planet, Steve tries to go from being the galaxy's most-selfish to least-selfish individual.'

Without missing a beat, Amanda smiled. 'I told you it was great,' she said. Perry felt the euphoric rush of a condemned man suddenly set free.

Elvis nodded slowly. 'Smart,' he said. 'But having Jesus appear . . . Well, we don't like to introduce visions that much. Our audience doesn't care for it when they sense we're manipulating folks down there, ever since the damn Sixties. A lot of folks think that's when Channel Blue lost its way.'

'Look, no one's suggesting we introduce LSD to an unsuspecting population,' Amanda said jumping in. 'Or mullets or Humvees or women's shorts with writing on the buttocks, for that matter. And we're certainly not suggesting rock and roll.' Amanda said this provocatively to Elvis, who gave a hint of a smirk. 'What we're talking about here is one heavenly vision with a potentially limitless up-side.' Amanda's eyes sparked to life – Perry could see that she was good in meetings. 'Steve's quest will prove to our audience that the Earth's inhabitants aren't all selfish, apathetic slugs. We increase sympathy while delivering our bread-and-butter: failure and humiliation. Steve Santiago trying to be good? It's going to drive him crazy. I personally can't wait to see it.'

Elvis shrugged. 'Two days,' he said and swivelled his chair so that it once more faced the distant reaches of space.

CHANNEL 12

THE BIGGEST STAR ON EARTH

'What just happened?' Perry asked, when he and Amanda were once more walking down a large lit hallway beneath the moon's surface. Amanda didn't answer; she pushed a screen into Perry's face. On it were a variety of Renaissance portraits depicting Jesus Christ.

'Which do you like?' she asked. When Perry hesitated, she said, 'Come on, Mr Bunt, you heard him, we only have two days to make this work. We have to start casting immediately.'

'Are you serious?' Perry asked. 'That wasn't a real idea. I was just stalling, trying to buy us a little time.'

'Well, it worked,' Amanda said. 'Now we have to produce.' They came to a bank of elevators. Amanda pressed the down button and with a soft chime, one of the elevator doors opened. They stepped into the car and she pressed 1. The doors slid closed and the elevator lurched up out of the moon and into space.

'If we're going to have a chance, we need to present Steve with his heavenly vision when he wakes up, which is one hour from now.' Amanda pointed at a sombre Jesus on her screen. 'What do you think? Vengeful enough? Or should we go for something a little more, you know, apocalyptic?'

Perry was so overwhelmed by questions he couldn't focus. 'Elvis was a producer for Channel Blue?'

Amanda, restraining her impatience, explained that when

Channel Blue's ratings sank in the fifties ('Even the wars were boring,' Amanda noted), Elvis Presley, then a mere segment producer for Galaxy Entertainment, came up with the idea of encoding the message '*Have Sex and Go Crazy*' into sounds that could be broadcast to Earthles. This message became so popular that Elvis was sent to the planet to broadcast it personally and eventually became the star of his own show.

'A lot of our field producers end up celebrities in your culture,' Amanda said. 'It's one of the hazards of stirring things up, I guess.'

'Like who?'

'Jimi Hendrix, Kurt Cobain, Fatty Arbuckle. When their contract with the channel's up, they get "killed off" and go onto their next gig. Not Elvis, though. He stayed on and worked his way up to President of the channel. He's like me – a true Earth fan. This whole finale's tearing him up.'

Perry was unimpressed. 'Not enough for him to stop it.'

'He's giving your show a shot, isn't he? Here we go.' Amanda held up a portrait of an angry Jesus wielding a large sword. '*This* is our saviour.'

Perry couldn't help having terrible misgivings about his half-baked idea. 'Look, even if by some miracle Steve Santiago became a saint, and everyone else on Earth became caring and considerate, wouldn't your viewers get sick of that, too? Isn't Channel Blue built on how selfish we are?'

Amanda considered this. 'The sheer novelty of Earthles behaving decently would definitely attract viewers. Then, yes, you're right – eventually people would get bored and stop watching. But at least they'd take no pleasure in seeing you destroyed. There'd be no ratings bump to that at all.'

As the elevator entered the upper reaches of Earth's

atmosphere, Amanda relayed instructions on the appearance of their Jesus to the special effects department. Perry heard a familiar ringing from his pocket. He dug out his cell phone and noticed that he had three messages, all from GALL. The phone rang again and Perry answered it. 'I have Dana Fulcher calling for you,' spoke an imperious voice, and before Perry could make his excuses and hang up, his agent was purring in his ear.

'*Perrrrryyyyyy*, where have you been?' Dana Fulcher of Global Artistic Leadership Limited was using her overly friendly voice, the voice she used when she was heated in pursuit of someone or something that she wanted. Perry had never heard it directed at him before. 'We've been literally tying ourselves in knots trying to get a hold of you.'

In the interests of brevity, Perry chose to let Dana have her egregiously figurative 'literally'.

'I've been busy,' he said. 'What's up?'

Dana laughed as if Perry had tickled her while telling her the funniest joke in history. 'Oh Perry, you are too much. "The Last Day of School" is what's up. I've set up pitches for this afternoon.' Perry guessed that Dana had run his movie idea by someone in a greater position of power, and that someone had liked it. His failure to return her calls had then created a false sense of urgency, which, in Hollywood, was really the only kind.

'Sorry,' Perry said. 'I'm busy.'

There was a confused pause. 'Busy?' Dana said, barely able to conceal the incredulity in her voice. 'With your *teaching*?' The word 'teaching' was said with such a perfect combination of condescension and disgust that Perry had to take a moment to marvel at it.

'No,' he said. 'Something else.'

'What is it?' Dana said. 'What's more important than selling a script?'

'I can't talk about it.'

'Is it another project?' Dana's voice sounded both annoyed and hurt.

'Yes,' Perry said as he watched Los Angeles spread out beneath him. The elevator was plummeting towards Ventura Boulevard.

'Oh Perry,' Dana said. 'Tell me you aren't doing TV again. Please tell me that.'

The elevator slowed as it slid back into the roof of the Galaxy Entertainment building. 'I've got to go,' Perry said and hung up. The doors slid open and Amanda charged out. Perry followed her and came face to face with . . . Jesus. The famous Nazarene glowered and held a magnificent sword over his head. Perry gasped, taking a step backward. An attractive red-headed woman stepped out from behind Jesus.

'What do you think?' the woman asked.

'Let me hear a line,' Amanda said.

'Steve Santiago!' Jesus bellowed with a deep, metallic voice that sounded like it had been recorded at the wrong speed. 'Thou art a terrible sinner!'

Amanda seemed unimpressed. 'Isn't Jeff available?'

'He is and he isn't,' the redhead said. 'You know Jeff.'

'I can work on the line,' Jesus said. 'I just got the script thirty seconds ago.'

'I'll let you know,' Amanda said and took off down the hall at a trot.

'You'd better hurry,' the redhead called after her. 'We go to air in twenty.'

Perry scurried to keep up with Amanda. 'Where did Jesus come from?'

'He's a facsimilon,' she said. 'They're a species of shape-shifter – kind of like your jellyfish but a lot more sophisticated. We often use them for visions, dreams and hallucinations. Most of them are expert visual mimics, but their imitations of the human voice are always a little dodgy. And they need scripts – they can't improvise at all. Jeff is the best we have, but he's temperamental. Fortunately, he owes me a favour.'

Amanda stopped at a door with a star on it and rapped sharply. There was no response. She opened the door and stepped in. Perry followed her into a small room, illuminated solely by the small round lights surrounding a make-up mirror against one wall. In front of the mirror, draped across a small platform, was what appeared to be a white terrycloth towel. It quivered when they entered the room.

'Jeff, I need your help on this,' Amanda said, addressing the towel. The towel, in turn, emitted a cacophony of low noises that sounded like the rumble of a train through mud. Amanda shook her head. 'You know I can't understand you like that.'

The towel groaned with impatience. It rose into the air, expanding and contouring, colours racing across its surface in patterns until, to Perry's complete shock, Amanda's twin stood in front of him, identical down to the smallest freckle on her nose.

'I've told you several times,' the twin said in a tinny voice deeper than Amanda's, 'no more Jesuses, no more Yahwehs, no more Angels of Death, no more ghosts. You know how limiting they are. You know how easy it is to get pigeonholed.'

'I do,' Amanda said. 'And you have so much more to offer, Jeff.'

'Thank you,' said the second Amanda. 'Would you tell the idiot executives that? All they want are icons and archetypes. There's no depth there, there's nothing to play.'

'I tell them all the time,' Amanda said. She took both of her twin's hands and gazed directly into her eyes. 'You know how much admiration I have for your integrity and the quality of your work.' Perry watched in disbelief as Amanda reached out and smoothed the blonde hair of her twin. She seemed to be flirting with herself. 'And I'm not asking you to do this lightly. But we need you on this pilot and it's a rush job.'

Amanda's twin sighed. 'Why must I always save these thrown-together productions? Why?'

'Because you're the best,' Amanda said. 'And it's not all gloom-and-doom. Remember who I cast to play Freddie Mercury in the Prime Minister's sex dream?'

The twin chuckled. 'Oh Amanda, I just can't say no to you.'

Amanda smiled. 'You'd better get going. You have your lines and the address?' Amanda Two nodded. 'Then break a leg.' Amanda and her twin cheek-kissed, which Perry found titillating, despite its unfathomable strangeness. A panel in the ceiling opened and sunlight pierced the dark room. Amanda's twin melted, falling away until all that was left was a small dark mound on the floor. This mound trembled briefly until the shape of a large crow emerged from it. The crow squawked loudly, hopped once, took flight and soared up through the opening in the ceiling.

Perry was still staring up at the open ceiling when he realised that Amanda was already out in the hallway, the sounds of her shoes clicking away from him. He tore after her and caught up. 'That was incredible. Does he always turn into you like that?'

'They have an easier time communicating if they assume the appearance of whomever they're talking to,' Amanda said.

'Where do they come from?'

'There's no time for questions, Mr Bunt. We're about to go live to air.' Amanda arrived at a door marked Control Room D and pushed it open. Perry followed her into a dark room dominated by screens that lined the walls. Technicians silently worked at a console in front of the largest screen, which showed Steve Santiago sleeping peacefully in his hairnet and sleep mask. Amanda guided Perry by the elbow through the darkness to the second console, where a large green slug creature covered with eyeballs sat in a swivel chair.

'Guy,' Amanda said, 'this is Mr Bunt. He's the writer.'

The slug creature nodded the top portion on its slithery head and around half of its eyes focused on Perry. 'I never forget a face,' said the creature. The wide slit at its base flattened itself out into what appeared to be a smile. 'Welcome to the team.'

'We're lucky to have Guy directing our pilot,' Amanda told Perry.

'Oh stop,' said Guy, oozing a viscous yellow liquid that poured down one side of its gelatinous green body. While Perry fought the urge to gag, Amanda steered him to the console at the very rear of the room, where Nick Pythagorus was already seated. In front of him was a bottle wrapped in a festive ribbon.

'Amanda,' he said. Amanda nodded curtly. 'We've got our A team on this one. We'll make it work.' Nick smiled at Perry, who noticed that the boy executive still had some of his baby teeth. 'Congratulations on the pick-up,' he said, sliding the bottle down the console towards Perry. 'I obviously underestimated you.'

Perry examined the bottle.

'Cassiopeian Burgundy,' Nick said. 'The best wine in the galaxy. You might as well know that a lot of people around the station have been very sceptical. "A show by an Earthle? Are you crazy? That'll never work! What a stupid idea!" But I believe in you, Mr Bunt. I think we may have a hit on our hands.'

Perry smiled, unsure. 'Thank you.'

'Quiet, please,' one of the technicians said. 'Three, two, one . . . cue heavenly vision—'

On the screen, a shimmering pool of light appeared at the base of Steve Santiago's bed, accompanied by ethereal sounds. Steve stirred and opened his eyes. The pool of light congealed into the form of Jesus Christ, complete with white robe, sword and a deeply furrowed brow. Perry noted that this Jesus seemed even angrier than the one he and Amanda had met in front of the elevators.

Amanda leaned forward to Guy. 'Nice effect,' she told him.

The director chuckled. 'Just wait till he starts waving that sword.'

'Is that Jeff?' Perry asked.

Amanda nodded. 'He's the best.'

'Steve Santiago!' On the screen, Jesus bellowed in a *basso profundo* that shook the control-room speakers. The Jacuzzi salesman sat up in bed, pure terror on his face. 'I have come for thee!'

Steve fell onto the floor and, quivering all over, pulled himself up on his knees. 'Lord?'

'Thou art a terrible sinner!' Jesus shouted.

Tears sprang from Steve's eyes while an unmistakeable wet patch spread in the crotch of his boxer shorts. 'Yes, Lord,' he whimpered. 'Yes. I am.'

Amanda turned to Perry, her eyes filled with excitement. 'This is good stuff,' she whispered. 'Steve never soils himself. The mere thought of it horrifies him.'

Jesus glared down at the trembling sinner. 'While I gave my life to redeem you, thou hast shown me nothing but wickedness,' he intoned. Steve nodded his head, sobbing plaintively.

Amanda leaned forward to Guy. '*I care nothing for your womanly tears*,' she said.

'I care nothing for your womanly tears,' Jesus on the screen said, eliciting another crying jag from Steve.

'Take it on home,' Amanda said to Guy. The director's towering head nodded.

Jesus waved his sword and a fierce roar shook the walls of Steve Santiago's townhouse. 'I will blot out you and all of Man from the Earth!'

Steve moaned, beyond terrified. 'Please no! Please just . . . give me another chance!'

'There is only one way in which my hand will be stayed,' Jesus said. 'That is if you, Steve Santiago, undertake to change yourself from evil to good. Will you do this?'

Steve nodded his head fervently. 'Yes, Lord. Yes!'

'You make this vow right now before me, to lead a life of righteousness?'

'Yes, Lord! I swear it!'

'Then I will give you this one chance,' Jesus spoke, and with a whirl of his sword, vanished from Steve Santiago's bedroom.

Steve stared at the spot where Jesus stood, blinking incomprehensibly. He rose slowly to his feet on shaking legs and walked into the bathroom.

A whoop of celebration went up in the control room. 'Did you see him?' one of the technicians said.

'We've got a hit!' Guy said, many of his eyes widening in excitement.

'Fantastic!' Amanda said. She hugged Perry and he nearly passed out from sudden, ecstatic joy. 'We couldn't have asked for a better start.' Perry couldn't believe it – yesterday he'd been a poor screenwriter without a single production to his name. Today, not only had one of his scripts been produced, it was being shown throughout the galaxy, reaching an audience of which the greatest writers in Hollywood could only dream.

'Hold on,' Nick said. The boy executive was watching one of the smaller monitors. 'Put the bathroom on the main screen.' The large centre screen filled with the image of Steve Santiago bent over the bathtub, using his fingernails to pull a tile off the wall. The control room fell silent.

'What's he doing?' Perry said.

'He's got a peephole that looks into the shower of his neighbour,' Nick said, unable to conceal his glee. 'The amazing thing is, she's fifty and weighs 200 pounds.' Nick pulled the bottle of wine from Perry's hands. 'You won't be needing this. I knew it wouldn't work.' Perry gaped at him, confused by his sudden change in tone. 'You don't get it, do you? Your show's done. Finished. Understand? You're cancelled.'

Perry turned to Amanda, who, for the first time in Perry's memory, appeared shaken.

'It didn't work,' she said. 'Steve couldn't change for five minutes, much less a series.'

The two copbots entered. The tall guard's face was still crumpled around the chin where Perry had yanked it off the previous day.

'Take him to the Green Room,' Nick said.

The tall guard smiled and grabbed Perry by the collar. 'With pleasure,' he said. 'Say goodbye, Earthle.' Before Perry had a chance to, however, he was yanked from the room. The last thing he saw was Amanda's face watching him go, suddenly pale in the light of Steve Santiago's bathroom.

CHANNEL 13

CANCELLATION

Once more, Perry found himself in a Galaxy Entertainment elevator. But this time, the car was plummeting into darkness. Flanked by the two robots staring straight ahead, Perry contemplated the sudden cancellation of his first and seemingly last show, as well as the dire consequences thereof. He was being taken somewhere awful to die, that much was certain, and the fact that the entire planet was also doomed didn't make it any easier. His thoughts flew far afield. He thought of his best friend from the second grade, the first person he'd ever known well who'd died. On his eighteenth birthday, the friend had drunk too much beer and fallen off the back of a tractor into a threshing machine. At the time that Perry heard the news of the tragedy, death seemed completely abstract, like Mongolia or any other foreign country you'd never visited and never planned on going to. But then, in the last couple years, he'd been provided with ample opportunities to contemplate his mortality, since professional failure in Hollywood expertly simulated death: you lost everything, including your friends, and were forced to move to a less desirable place.

He thought of his parents. He wished now that he had called them more often. He'd always put off calling until he had some good news to tell them. But for the last two years he hadn't had any. And now this. At least they wouldn't have long to contemplate their son's short, unfortunate life before the world ended. And it gave him no small comfort that they would never know of his final failure, when the Earth had come falling towards his outstretched glove and he had dropped it.

He suddenly thought of Debbie Drimler, a development executive he'd dated back when he'd been successful. Debbie was pretty, smart, had a great sense of humour and, most importantly, liked him. Then, on their third date, while they were sitting in a Beverly Hills restaurant discussing spirituality, Debbie had absent-mindedly opened and shut her denim pocketbook over and over again. Perry hadn't thought much of it at the time, but when he went to call her back later that day he couldn't get the image out of his head. Suddenly, they were man and wife sitting at the Oscars. He was about to collect his award and she was opening and closing that damn denim purse. The world watched them wondering: How could that incredibly successful screenwriter be with that compulsive woman? And who brings a denim purse to the Oscars? And Perry hadn't called her – that day or ever again.

Now Debbie had her revenge: He was about to die and all he could think of was her.

How would death happen? he wondered. The Green Room was apparently Galaxy Entertainment's version of Gitmo, a dungeon for prisoners it couldn't prosecute but couldn't release. Perry swallowed hard and wiped his sweaty palms on his jeans. What terrible tortures awaited him before he became the latest victim of the Earth's finale? The elevator slowed and Perry felt his heart accelerate as it came to a stop. The doors parted and he squeezed his eyes shut, awaiting the blows of his jailers. Instead he heard . . . music. Soft, calming music. He opened his eyes to see: A pristine carpeted lobby with light green walls. The copbots escorted him from the elevator, then stepped back into it. The doors closed and they were gone.

Perry recognised the music. It was an instrumental version of 'Suspicious Minds'.

A pretty young woman holding a plain white envelope suddenly appeared next to him. 'Welcome, Mr Bunt. We've been expecting you. Today you'll be playing the role of Distressed Passenger No. 72.' She handed him the envelope. 'This envelope contains your script. The rest of the cast is waiting for you.' She pointed to a door at the end of the lobby. 'Make yourself comfortable. The director will be joining you shortly to talk about your scene.'

Perry stood frozen, unsure. The young woman smiled at him again. 'Go right on in,' she said. 'And please let any of the assistant casting directors know if there is anything we can do for you.' Perry walked slowly with his envelope through the door, stepping into a large room with green walls and green couches. While there seemed to be over a hundred people scattered amongst the furniture, there was little noise or conversation.

Another pretty young woman, who Perry recognised as identical to the first except for being blonde instead of brunette, approached him. 'Hello, Mr Bunt,' she said. 'Can I get you water, coffee or any other beverage?' Perry shook his head. 'Feel free to help yourself to the buffet.' She gestured over to a sumptuous table of food set up along the far wall. Succulent fruit platters and trays of glazed doughnuts glinted reassuringly in the muted light. 'If you're not hungry, just have a seat wherever you'd like.'

Perry walked slowly to the first group of couches and studied the faces of the men and women sitting there. Most were reading books or magazines, a few dozed, and a few sat staring straight ahead with expressions of tranquil anticipation on their faces. Amongst them, Perry noticed Ralph, the homeless man who frequently made him uncomfortable on his morning coffee runs. Identifying him wasn't easy: Ralph had been given some kind of makeover. He was cleaned, shaved and wore a polo shirt and khakis. Perry took a seat on the couch next to him.

'Ralph?' he said.

Ralph looked at Perry and seemed to recognise him immediately. 'Hello, Buddy,' he said. 'Isn't this exciting?'

Perry wasn't sure how to respond. 'Do you know what we're doing here?'

'Of course, Ralph knows,' he said. 'Ralph's known it for years. The aliens have been watching us. Ralph kept telling people, and every now and then these weird men in blue would take Ralph into their van and shoot something at Ralph's brain that made it feel all fuzzy, and they'd do it again and again but Ralph would tell them, you can't shoot nothing at Ralph's brain on account that he's a veteran. Ralph's an American hero. You can't shoot the brain of an American hero.'

Perry stared at Ralph, trying to make sense of his blather. Ralph pointed to both sides of his head. 'Firefight in Tikrit. Two steel plates.' He beamed with pride. '*Nobody* can shoot Ralph's brain.'

Perry suddenly understood why he, along with Ralph, had been privileged with the terrible knowledge of Channel Blue. 'After a while they just said, "OK, Ralph wins. Ralph can be in the show."' Ralph clapped his hands with delight. 'Ralph can't believe it. Ralph is First Class Passenger No. 12!' He pulled a folded-up piece of paper from his pocket and read from it deliberately.

'*God help us!*' Ralph paused for a moment, savouring the line. 'Ralph can't decide. Do you think it should be, *God* help us! or God help *us*!? Ralph wants to get it right. You can only say it once when the plane starts crashing.'

Perry blinked. 'A crashing plane?'

'Oh yes,' Ralph said. 'That's what the whole show's about: our flight. It's called *Flight 240*. Cool, huh? Gives me chills, just hearing the title.'

Perry swallowed. '*Flight 240*?' He remembered that in his visit to Nick Pythagorus' office, he had heard the boy executive discuss a flight in connection with the finale. He vaguely remembered something about an airplane crashing into a nuclear power plant.

'Uh huh.'

'Do you know anything else about . . . the show? Anything else about what happens?'

'We crash into a nuclear reactor and all kinds of people die. What's your line?'

Perry stared at him. Ralph motioned to the white envelope in Perry's hand. Perry tore it open and removed a single sheet of paper. It was blank except for the following:

DISTRESSED PASSENGER NO.72
We're all going to die! Yaaaaaah!

Ralph peered over Perry's shoulder at the paper. 'What does it say?'

Perry heart was pounding. 'We're all going to die. Yaaaaaah.'

Ralph chuckled. 'You're going to have to do better than that,' he said. 'Come on, Buddy. This is your big opportunity. Half the galaxy's going to be watching.'

Perry looked around, trying to contain his panic. He slowly

pulled his cell phone from his pocket. No service. He slipped it back in. He leaned closer to Ralph and spoke in a hushed voice. 'Ralph, listen to me. Everyone who gets on that plane is really going to die.'

'Yeah,' Ralph said, smiling. 'That's what's going to make the show so exciting to watch.'

Perry shook his head. 'You don't understand. Everyone is going to die *for real*. And the plane is really going to crash into a nuclear power plant. It's all part of their series finale. They're destroying the Earth.'

'That's *cool*,' Ralph said. 'You must have read the script. Can you get Ralph a copy?'

Perry had to restrain himself from yelling. '*I'm not talking about a script*. They are really crashing that plane. And if we get on it, we are really going to die, along with a lot of other people.'

By now, several other cast members were watching the exchange between Perry and Ralph. A large grey-haired man seated on the other side of Ralph pulled on his sleeve. 'What's he saying?' he said.

'He's read the script,' Ralph said excitedly.

The man broke out in a smile. 'How about that? How does it end?'

'Everyone on the entire planet dies,' Perry said.

'Wow,' said the grey-haired man. 'Boffo.'

'I know,' Ralph said. 'My mother's going to love this. She likes all those shows where the world ends. Like the one with Fresh Prince and his dog.'

Perry rubbed his head, trying to contain his impatience. 'No one's going to be able to watch it, because no one will still be alive.'

'Right,' Ralph said, smiling. 'That's a good one.'

'I can't believe my luck,' the grey-haired man said. 'Twenty years I've been a janitor at this cable TV company. Yesterday, I walk through the wrong door and there's a giant slug sitting there. Next thing I know, they're offering me a part. Just goes to show, it can happen any time. Never give up. Nearly sixty years old and I've got my first acting job!'

Perry sat back on the couch, defeated.

'Can I have your attention please?' the blonde casting assistant said from the front of the room. Her voice was amplified to a perfect volume, though Perry couldn't see any microphone. 'We're very fortunate to have the show's director here to say a few words to all of you. Please welcome Richard DeLong.'

The room applauded as a lanky man in tinted glasses stepped through the door. He wore freshly pressed jeans and a bomber jacket with the Channel Blue logo stitched over the breast pocket.

'Hello, everyone,' he said. 'I just want to thank you all for being part of this. This is a great project and all of us at Galaxy Entertainment are very excited about it. As many of you know, Earth has been the setting of some of our most popular shows over the years, and we think what we're doing here today will become an instant classic. Now, you've all been specifically chosen because of your interest in what we're doing, and we appreciate that. So give yourselves a round of applause.' Everyone in the room applauded, except for Perry, who watched with disbelief as the director continued.

'Now, in a few moments, you'll all be taken up to our set, the Los Angeles International Airport. Pretending to be passengers, you will board Flight 240.' A smattering of excited applause greeted the announcement of the titular flight. 'Once the plane takes off, remember: just relax and be yourselves until you hear the right engine explode. That will be your cue to say the lines you've all been given. Let's have a quick rehearsal, OK? When I say *boom*, that will be the engine exploding.'

The room filled with the sound of excited actors unfolding sheets of paper. 'Ready? OK, here we go. BOOM!' The room exploded in a cacophony of hysterical screaming.

Next to Perry, Ralph shouted, 'God help us!' over and over again, changing the emphasis from word to word each time, while the grey-haired man next to him simply yelled, '*Noooooooooo*!' at the top of his lungs.

After what seemed to Perry an incredibly long time, the director said, 'That was awesome! Give yourselves another hand!'

After the applause died down, Richard DeLong continued: 'Just one more thing: The plane might take longer than you think to hit the ground, so keep up that great energy even if it seems like you're doing it for a really long time—'

Perry couldn't take it anymore. He jumped to his feet. 'We're really going to die! Don't get on that plane! It's really going to crash and we're really going to die!'

The director chuckled. 'That's great, I love it, but let's save it for the scene, OK?'

Ralph frowned at Perry. 'That's not even your line.'

The brunette assistant casting director appeared next to Perry and took him by the arm. 'Come with me, Perry,' Amanda said. Perry turned. The woman wasn't Amanda, but she sounded exactly like her. 'I'm speaking through the casting bot. Follow her. I'm in the next room.'

Richard DeLong continued addressing the room as the assistant casting director led Perry through a door and into a corridor, where Amanda waited. Perry wasn't sure he'd ever been so happy to see anyone.

'Thank God,' he said. 'Can you get me out of here?'

She nodded. 'I told them you weren't right for the part and you've been recast. Let's go before Nick finds out.'

Perry started to follow her, then paused. He looked back through the open door at Ralph, who was studying his lines while silently moving his lips.

'Hold on,' he said. 'I need to bring someone.'

After Perry slipped back into the green room and escorted Ralph out, the three of them hurried into an elevator. The doors slid shut and their car ascended. 'When the doors open, go straight through the lobby to the street,' Amanda said. 'It would've been much easier with one of you. But if you act like you know where you're going, maybe no one will notice.'

'Ralph still doesn't understand why he couldn't do his part,' Ralph said.

'You weren't right for it,' Perry said. He turned to Amanda. 'Are you coming with us?' She shook her head. 'What are we going to do?'

'About what?'

'About the finale? Remember? The destruction of Earth?'

Amanda took a deep breath. 'I'm sorry,' she said. 'We tried. There's nothing more I can do.'

Perry felt his pulse throbbing in his temples.

'Ralph had a good line,' Ralph said. 'He was really looking forward to that plane crash.'

'You're not doing it, Ralph!' Perry barked, then turned back to Amanda. 'That's not good enough.'

Amanda frowned. 'I rescued you from the Green Room. I saved your life.'

'Only so I can die with the rest of the planet.'

'If there were anything else I could do, I'd do it.'

'Can't you throw some switches in the control room? Anything to slow it down a little?'

Amanda shook her head. 'I've already broken the Producers' Code. And even if they weren't watching me, this is too big a production – they've been planning it for too long and there's a lot of money on the line. We have hundreds of stations like this all over the world—' Her voice trailed off. 'No one could stop it at this point.'

'Ralph would have been great,' Ralph said.

'Shut up!' Perry yelled. Then, to Amanda, 'What if I came up with another idea?'

'I'm sorry,' Amanda said. 'We had our shot. Nick is running the show now.' The elevator slowed. 'Head to your right, through the double doors, and don't stop until you get to the street.' The doors slid open and they stepped out. The hall was empty. 'Go,' Amanda said.

Perry hesitated. 'What's going to happen to you?'

'They're shipping us all back to corporate headquarters in two weeks,' she said.

Perry gazed at Amanda. She stared back at him, unwavering. He walked towards her until they were inches apart. Her eyes widened.

'Run,' she said. Perry looked over his shoulder to see several tall security guards running towards them. 'The lobby,' she said. 'I'll slow them down.'

Amanda spun towards the charging copbots and yelled, 'I have an ache in my right leg, my mouth is dry, and my breathing is irregular!' The security-guard stampede stopped suddenly and the guards all stared into space, confusion on their faces. She turned back to Perry and Ralph. 'Why are you still standing there? You've got maybe twenty seconds. Go!'

'Why did they stop?' Perry asked.

'The first generation of bots were medical computers. You can still stump them with the right symptoms. Now *move!*'

Perry grabbed Ralph by one arm and steered him towards the double doors. He stopped at the doors and turned back to Amanda, who, improbably beautiful in the harsh light of the hallway, stood like a sentinel before the silent mob of robot security guards.

'Goodbye,' Perry said. She gestured impatiently for him to go. Instead, he ran back to her, took her in his arms and kissed her. While the kiss lasted – and Perry had no clue as to how long this was, whether it was three seconds or a minute – every nerve ending in his body seemed to end in his lips, which felt fused with Amanda's. For a few dizzying moments, he had no idea where he ended and Amanda began, or even if it was necessary to make such distinctions. They separated and stared at each other, stunned. Amanda, in fact, appeared as if she'd just seen a ghost. 'What was *that*?'

'I kissed you,' Perry said.

'I know. But . . . What made you . . . What did—' For the first time in her life since a teaching bot had taught her to speak at the age of fourteen months, Amanda Mundo was at a loss for words.

'Symptoms psychosomatic,' one of the guards said.

'Go! Now!' Amanda said. Her urgency was warranted: Perry saw that the guards, all repeating the words 'symptoms psychosomatic', had come back to life and were trotting towards them at a brisk clip. Perry grabbed Ralph and bolted through the double doors into the lobby. They raced across the shiny floor to the glass doors. The guards, now sprinting, were quickly closing in on them.

'Faster!' Perry urged Ralph.

'Ralph doesn't even want to go,' Ralph gasped. 'Why is Ralph even running?'

They burst through the glass doors and hurled themselves

down the granite steps to the sidewalk of Ventura Boulevard. But the blue-shirted guards were suddenly all around them, and there was nowhere to go.

CHANNEL 14

THE SEASON FINALE

With the strength of a true coward, Perry flailed his body against the security guards. But the copbots were locked onto him, their talon-like grips digging into the muscles of his arms and legs.

Like soldier ants expertly transporting two unwieldy crumbs of bread, the guards picked up Perry and Ralph and carried them back towards the entrance of Galaxy Entertainment. Perry, though exhausted, had a sudden inspiration. 'I have a headache . . . and seizures . . . and rashes—' He searched his brain for symptoms. 'And a stiff neck. I have a stiff neck!'

With no hesitation at all, the guards barked 'Meningitis!' and continued on.

'What's going on here?' a voice demanded. The guards paused in their rush to the double doors. An agitated meter maid appeared on the edge of the fray. She was brown, plump and exceedingly short, resembling a Bosc pear in a tight beige uniform. On top of her head sat a brimmed cap that appeared to have been knocked to one side. A shiny nameplate on her jacket read:

SERGEANT DORIS SANCHEZ
LOS ANGELES PARKING AUTHORITY

Glaring at the guards, the meter maid straightened her cap with exaggerated effort to emphasise the enormity of its unseating.

'You got a problem? I would say that you do. Because right now, you all are infringing on the abilities of the Los Angeles Parking Authority to proceed in the timely accordance of its duties, being the swift determination of unlawful spatial inappropriateness in a vehicular manner and the speedy legal punishment thereunto.'

The security guards seemed nearly as stumped by this tirade as by Amanda's list of symptoms. The sergeant turned her steely gaze to Perry and Ralph. 'Are you being molested by these rent-a-cops?' she asked. 'Because their jurisdictional integrity ceases to exist at the juncture of this sidewalkular vicinity.' She turned back to the security guards, who seemed to melt away under her inspection. 'And what's with you carbon-copy motherfuckers anyway? You all clones or some shit?'

The guards released Perry and Ralph and backed up the stairs together with such perfect synchronisation that they appeared choreographed.

'We were only removing trespassers from the premises,' said one.

'No need for any trouble,' said another.

'There will be no trouble at all,' said Sergeant Doris Sanchez, 'as long as you respect the authority of the Los Angeles Parking Authority, of which I *am* the authority.'

A retreating guard brushed past Perry. 'You're going to be dead in three weeks anyway,' the voice of Nick Pythagorus whispered in his ear. Perry spun around but saw only the back of the last guard disappearing through the double glass doors of Galaxy Entertainment.

Sergeant Doris Sanchez shook her head. 'Carbon-copy

motherfuckers,' she muttered to herself as she turned to inspect a meter. The meter had a minute remaining on it, so she took her time writing the ticket.

'Come on,' Perry said to Ralph, and nudged him down the sidewalk.

* * *

Even by the standards of Los Angeles, Perry and Ralph made an odd sight walking down Ventura Boulevard: Perry, still in a blue velour suit with his cell phone pressed to his ear, and Ralph who, despite his fresh khakis and polo shirt, paused at every garbage receptacle to pick out empty cans and bottles.

By the time they made it to the end of the block, Perry had called the Los Angeles field office of the FBI and, without revealing his name, told a receptionist about the fate awaiting Flight 240 from Los Angeles International Airport. Ralph, meanwhile, continued to complain bitterly about losing his chance at stardom. 'Ralph could've been an American hero *and* a galactic superstar,' he said.

Perry grabbed Ralph and spun him around. 'Listen to me. Just for one moment, try turning down the crazy and listening.'

Ralph glanced down at Perry's hands, which appeared comically small on the homeless man's shoulders. Perry couldn't believe he was manhandling a large lunatic, but for the moment he seemed to have gained his attention. 'Right now, you and I are the only two people on Earth who know about Galaxy Entertainment and aren't their prisoners.'

Ralph nodded. 'Yeah?'

'We know that they're going to destroy the Earth within days.'

Ralph nodded again. 'Right.'

'It's not a show, Ralph.'

Ralph shrugged. 'OK.'

'So, since no one else will believe us, you and I have to figure out a way to stop Galaxy Entertainment from destroying the Earth. It's up to *us*.'

For a moment, Perry thought he was making headway. Then Ralph furrowed his brow. 'Uh . . . why is that?'

Perry sighed. 'Do you *want* them to destroy everything?'

Ralph considered this. 'You have to admit: it'll look great on TV.' He seemed to lose interest in the conversation and reached into a trash can for a beer bottle. Perry shook his head and walked on.

'Relax, Buddy!' Ralph called after him. 'It's not like it's the end of the world!'

* * *

Amanda sat her in her office at Galaxy Entertainment, packing the contents of her desk into a blue plastic container. Normally, this kind of mundane organisational work helped clear her mind, but not this afternoon. It was hard for her to know how she felt. She expected to feel trepidation about her job ending, or anxiety about the repercussions of rescuing the Earthles from the Green Room, or anger at the way the finale had been mishandled. Instead, she felt completely exhilarated. And it all seemed to be a result of the absurd – no, the absolutely preposterous – kiss.

Before the kiss, she had never considered Perry Bunt or any Earthle in anything remotely resembling a romantic context. She wasn't sure she did now, either. To do so would be ludicrous, as ridiculous as befriending a fish. She was practically a different species than Perry and his planetmates, and while she was willing to admit that he was pleasant enough and pretty smart for a random product of fornication, the idea of sharing any sort of intimacy with him was mind-boggling. And yet they had, and now Amanda couldn't seem to order her thoughts with any clarity. Beneath them seemed to be a pulsing lava field of giddiness. What was wrong with her?

After the copbots had escorted her back to her office 'pending further investigation of a security breach' and left her alone, she'd taken a MORE pill, thinking it might help calm her down. She'd quickly achieved orgasm so many times that she'd had to avoid physical contact with the furniture to keep from passing out. She stood completely still in one corner of her office, feeling more agitated than ever.

At one point, she found her thoughts veering into completely bizarre territory. She actually began to work out scenarios that would save Perry Bunt from his planet's destruction. This seemed so insane to her on so many different levels she couldn't begin to quantify them. Besides the fact that any rescue of on-air extra-terrestrial talent was against the Producers' Code as well as various laws, numerous ethical considerations and everything else, what would she do with him, assuming she could save him? He couldn't possibly fit in with Edenites, given his terrible genetics and minuscule IQ. All the things he didn't know! And if he knew them all, would he even want to be alive, much less exist in a world that considered him inferior?

Amanda picked up the silver nameplate on her desk. It read:

AMANDA MUNDO
EXECUTIVE EXECUTIVE PRODUCER

She stared at it, lost in thought. What was even more bizarre than the thought of saving Mr Bunt was the thought now occurring to her: that letting Earth destroy itself was wrong. Not just wrong from a programming point of view – she had always thought that to be the case. But *ethically* wrong. As if the Earth was somehow different from the planetainments that routinely self-immolated during sweeps weeks every year. As if the pathetic residents of these backward worlds wouldn't in fact be better off in a state of non-existence, spared their ridiculous and completely futile strivings. What an idea! And what about the ethics of keeping Earth alive? Beyond prolonging the suffering of its miserable inhabitants, what if the civilisation somehow evolved to a point that it was able to export its selfishness and aggression to other worlds? No. Not even the most soft-hearted scholar of ethics would support saving Earth from itself.

But still . . .

Amanda rubbed her fingers at her temples, trying desperately to bring some kind of logic to her thought process. She knew what would help.

'Jared,' she said, and the top of her desk was instantly covered with a three-dimensional hologram of the head of her boyfriend, Jared Corley. Like every Edenite man, Jared was stunningly handsome. He had chiselled features and deep, soulful eyes that peered out from under a full head of lustrous golden hair. Yet it was the quirks that no genetic programmer could have predicted that attracted Amanda, most notably the way his mouth became slightly crooked when he smiled, like now.

'Hey, hotshot,' he said. Amanda already felt better. She and Jared had met at the Academy during the second week of classes, becoming inseparable for two years. While she remained fixed on her goal of producing Earth, his interests lay in administration. When Amanda was given her first planet, he had taken a job at Galaxy Entertainment's headquarters on Eden, working his way up to Vice President in Charge of Planetary Acquisitions. She'd promised him she'd be back after her stint on Earth. He didn't like the idea of her taking a job so far away, but long-distance relationships were often the best choice for ambitious young Edenites. Without any personal distractions, they'd both been able to throw themselves into their jobs.

'Hey, Jer.'

'What trouble are you in now?' His tone was light but Amanda found herself wondering if there was any disapproval beneath it.

'What have you heard?'

'The usual galactic gossip. That you smacked down Pythagorus in front of the King.' Jared chortled. Like every male over ten, he hated the idea of a nine-year-old executive. 'That you found some Earthle with an idea to save the channel and ruined the little boy's big plans. Wish I'd been on that feed.'

'Well, you need some refreshing. The new show didn't work. Nick is getting his finale after all.'

Jared appeared unfazed. 'Hey, what did you expect? It was written by an *Earthle*, right?'

Amanda felt defensive even though she knew it was completely inappropriate. Jared was right; no one could have expected an Earthle to save Channel Blue.

'It was a good idea,' she said. 'I think it would've worked with anyone other than Santiago.'

Jared shrugged. 'Live by the jerk, die by the jerk.'

'I guess. But I really thought it would work.'

'You gave it a shot, right? It was worth it. Now when Earth finales, you won't have any regrets.'

Amanda couldn't tell if he was underselling this setback for her benefit or whether he really believed it. She took a deep breath. 'I'm not sure what's going on, Jer. I've really been doubting myself lately.'

Jared frowned. 'Really?'

'I can't help feeling that there's something more I can do here.'

'Amanda, we've had this conversation before, and I know that you know that there's absolutely nothing you or anyone can do with Earth. They've tried everything with that planet, the best minds in the business – and I'm including you in there, hotshot – and it always turns to crap.' Jared was in full-on big brother mode, the way Amanda liked him least. Sometimes she just wanted him to listen and instead he came at her like an advice-show host with only a few seconds before the commercial break. 'And no one – *no one* – is going to hold it against you when that marble melts. Trust me, you'll feel a whole lot better when you're here back home and Earth's in reruns. A big part of this business is knowing when to cut and run, take your losses and get out. You're going to land on your feet just fine.'

Amanda found herself wishing they'd isolated a gene for cliché usage before Jared had been conceived. She waved one hand through the air. 'I know all that. But haven't you ever—' She tried to find words that wouldn't make her sound completely crazy. 'Haven't you ever come across a planet that you knew was worth saving? And felt . . . bad because you know it shouldn't be finale-ed?'

Jared furrowed his brow, considering this. 'I suppose so. But that's the vocation we've chosen, right? If it were easy, anyone could do it.'

After a beat, Amanda nodded. 'Right.'

'You OK, hotshot? You seem a little distracted or something.'

'Have you ever kissed anyone?' It came out of her mouth before she knew she was saying it.

Jared's eyes widened and he laughed in short nervous bursts. 'Are you kidding me?' He scrunched up his face. 'Adam's ghost! What's gotten into you today?'

'I don't know.'

'Are you going Earthle on me?' He arched his eyebrows so she'd know he was joking.

'No, my mind's just been wandering, I guess.'

'Well, get it back in its pen. I recommend a couple of stress pills and the rest of the day off.'

'Maybe you're right. I'll talk to you later.'

Jared's magnificent face lingered on her desk. 'Seriously, hotshot. You OK?'

'Yeah.'

'Remember, it's just another show.'

'I know, I know.'

'This is our calling. This is what you wanted to do.'

Amanda nodded quickly. 'I know. Bye.'

Jared vanished. Amanda stood and paced around her desk. Talking to him hadn't helped at all. In fact, she felt more disconcerted than ever. What was going on? Her reverie was interrupted by the appearance in the middle of her office of a scruffy pig wearing children's pyjamas. The pig squealed with annoyance and tugged at the pyjama bottoms with its teeth.

Amanda watched the pig with a deep reverence. This was the closest she'd ever been to an animal, even though this wasn't really an animal *per se*. The pig was a hologram that appeared in every production office throughout the galaxy every day at precisely noon Eden Standard Time, as mandated by government order. Its purpose was to remind employees of the crucial role that entertainment played in the maintenance of the Edenite civilisation. To Amanda, it was as if the hologram's creators had been thinking of her, because on this particular day, the pig brought her quickly back to Earth – in a manner of speaking.

If she was busy putting together a production or up against a deadline, Amanda would often ignore the pig. But today she watched it intently while reciting to herself the story she, and every other Edenite, had been taught before they could remember:

Many centuries ago, the people of Eden had conquered space, colonised planets, eradicated war, poverty, disease and, most importantly, their basest animal instincts. They could work as much or as little as they wanted, could travel the length of the galaxy in a week, and lived, on average, 200 years.

They were also bored stiff. Just bored, bored, bored.

Their entire evolution had been predicated on overcoming challenges to their well-being; now that wellbeing was all they had, they lost their bearings. Violence, a relic of the distant past, returned with a vengeance. Edenites fought each other out of sheer tedium. Riots broke out. Two planets blew themselves up out of sheer desperation for something to do.

In short, the people of Eden were boring themselves to death.

The plague of senseless destruction spread through the empire to its seat, the planet Eden itself, where thousands of weapon-wielding citizens marched on the capitol, shouting, 'There's nothing to do!' and 'Life is far too easy!' On the giant video screens set up around the capitol building, Eden's democratically elected president begged for calm. The crowd jeered and booed, drowning him out: 'We're sick of calm!', 'Stick your calm you know where!' and 'We're going to calmly burn this world to the ground!'

Then, in a twist of fate that saved humanity, the image on the screen changed from that of the President to that of a pig dressed in a child's pyjamas. The rioting crowd fell quiet as they watched the pig struggling to wriggle free from its human vestments, a spectacle broadcast by all the major news networks. Would it escape the pyjamas? No one could say. An entire empire watched, transfixed. When the pig finally did succeed in pulling his head through the top and, with a frantic shake of its hindquarters, casting off the bottoms, billions of viewers laughed and cheered. The crowds surrounding the capitol quickly disbanded to return home and replay it again and again.

The pig, it turned out, had escaped from a farm just outside the capital, where the owner's son had dressed it in his pyjamas. When the boar ran onto the capitol grounds, it was automatically picked up by a surveillance camera. A security guard was so distracted by watching it on one of his monitors that he'd accidentally switched the feed onto the big screens surrounding the capitol.

Thanks to this pig, our leaders recognised the importance of entertainment to our empire's security and well-being. Thanks to this pig, the events that nearly destroyed Eden, the Great Stultification, have never repeated themselves. Thanks to this pig, the human race was saved from self-destruction.

The pig's name . . . was Adam.

By the time Amanda came to the end of her recitation, the hologram had vanished. She stared wistfully at the spot it had just occupied. This is our calling, she thought. This is why we do what we do. Without entertainment, there would be nothing but chaos and death.

'Contemplating your sudden downfall?' Nick Pythagorus, an unpleasant grin on his face, had managed to slip into the office without her noticing, which was not that surprising given his height of four feet. 'Actually, I'm surprised to find you here. I thought you might still be gallivanting with your Earthle boyfriend.'

Amanda blushed. At first she wasn't sure what was happening – she thought it might be a delayed head rush from the MORE pill.

Nick chortled. 'Oh my heavens, you're *blushing*,' he said. 'Look.' He picked up the silver nameplate from Amanda's desk and held it so she could see her reflection. 'What's next? Will you be sprouting body hair?'

Irritated, Amanda grabbed the nameplate and slammed it back on her desk.

'And aggression,' Nick said in wonderment. 'You are really doing your genetic programmers proud today, Mandy.'

'What do you want, shrimp?' Amanda said, angrily biting off each word. She knew she was playing right into the boy executive's hands, but it still felt good.

Nick's expression became grave. 'You know what you did, right? By letting the Earthle go, you ruined a great sequence in my finale.'

'*Flight 240* was derivative, gratuitous and random,' Amanda snapped back. 'I also believe it broke laws prohibiting the direct endangerment of on-air talent.'

'They were all volunteers,' Nick said. 'But I'm not here

to parse issues of extra-planetary entertainment law. The good news is that the rest of the finale is on track. And to make sure it stays that way, you're confined to station. You can finish packing up your things and that's it.'

Amanda inhaled deeply to avoid screaming. 'You have no right to do that. I'm not your prisoner.'

'No,' Nick said, 'but you'll soon be one nonetheless. For all your violations of the Producers' Code, I would expect a minimum of two years on a suitably miserable asteroid. But that's for a board of enquiry to decide. In the meantime, my job is to keep you from wrecking what's left of the production.' Nick waved his hand and a pair of copbots entered.

The short one touched the bill of his cap. 'Afternoon, Ms Mundo.' The tall one merely glared.

Amanda stood. 'I will not be guarded like an animal.'

'I'm sorry, Amanda. The President agrees with me.' Nick was using his quiet voice now, the one that sounded like he really cared. 'We think you may be suffering from a case of Satanism.'

Amanda stared at him, incredulous. This was one of the most serious accusations that could be levelled against a producer. Satanism was a mental disorder named after Leslie Satan, a former Galaxy Entertainment executive. Over a century earlier, Leslie Satan was the producer of a small plan-etainment in the Crab Nebula when the executive in charge of the production, attempting to increase the planet's low ratings, gave him the note to introduce nuclear weapons to the planet's residents. Leslie Satan refused to do so, arguing that nuclear weapons in the hands of the planet's short-sighted rulers would quickly bring about its end. Satan was over-ruled and sure enough, the planet quickly destroyed itself (while, it should be noted, winning its time slot for the very first time).

Leslie Satan subsequently quit Galaxy Entertainment and founded CREEP, the Committee to Re-Evaluate Entertainment Policies, which for years sought to increase government regulation of what Satan labelled 'the exploitation of lesser life forms for the benefit of the entertainment-industrial complex'. Failing to do this, Satan took his committee underground, where it became known as The Movement, a scourge to productions all around the galaxy. Not only had The Movement blown up satellite cameras and bombed relay stations, but Movement agents, who were often disgruntled former employees of the entertainment industry, had insinuated themselves into planet populations to subvert the intentions of Edenite producers. It was widely know that such agents had been active on Earth, introducing, among other things, antibiotics, civil rights, solar power and meditation. Satan himself, adopting heavy disguise, had made memorable cameos as advisers to Gandhi and Martin Luther King Jr, preaching non-violence to the Earthles before Galaxy could detect his presence and chase him back into space.

Now 195 years old, Leslie Satan continued to elude capture by the Edenite government and to fight what he called 'entertainment colonialism' from the deck of a ramshackle spaceship that cruised the galaxy, usually scant light years ahead of his pursuers. His latest polemics were even crazier than his earlier rants – in speeches passed around the galaxy via pirate channels and sub-space frequencies, he'd stunned even his followers by suggested that products of fornication should not be considered lesser life forms. He'd announced a 'POF revolution' and predicted that one day, a POF would appear who would unite his genetically random brethren into an army that would end POF subjugation and conquer the galaxy.

As a result, to be accused of Satanism was akin to being

accused of insanity. Amanda saw Nick's game for the power play it was.

'I am perfectly well,' she said. 'You know I am. I've always thought ending Channel Blue was a bad idea, and it still is. Just because I disagree with you doesn't mean I'm sick.'

'Just admit you lost this one.'

'Are you going to have the bots make me do that, too?'

'Stubborn,' Nick said. 'I'm learning a lot about you today.'

'Get out.' Amanda picked up the nameplate and threw it. The tall bot's arm shot out and intercepted it inches from Nick's head. Nick calmly took it from the guard and set it back on Amanda's desk.

'You'd better hang onto this,' he said. 'In a couple of months, you're going to need it to remind yourself of who you were.'

THE MIGHTY PEN

Perry stepped out of a taxi in front of his apartment, carrying two large shopping bags. One contained two tubs of ice cream, a box of chocolate, a package of chocolate-chip cookies, two takeaway bacon cheeseburgers and an order of fries packed into white bags with the grease already seeping through them, a carton of Camels and a large bottle of a very smooth, very expensive single malt Scotch. If the world was ending, Perry reasoned, he was going do everything possible to enjoy it.

The other bag contained a new Mossburg 500 pump-action shotgun and two boxes of shells.

After climbing the steps to his front door, he realised that he'd lost his keys, probably while stripping naked for the robots on the moon. He unceremoniously lifted a potted plant, smashed his kitchen window and climbed in.

Perry turned on the TV, opened the single malt and lit a Camel. He was sweaty, dirty and exhausted – he hadn't slept in nearly two days – but right now sleep seemed out of the question. What if the world ended while he was in bed?

Going through the pockets of his blue tracksuit, he found the little purple MORE pill Amanda had given him on the moon. *What the hell?* he thought and knocked it back with a gulp of whisky. He crossed his legs and groaned as the most amazing orgasm he'd ever experienced rippled through his entire body. He sat gasping in the aftermath, wondering how this could be. There was no trace of moisture in his pants, and he hadn't even had time to become erect. He uncrossed his legs and it happened again, even stronger, a sliding, rippling earthquake of ecstasy rolling outward from his crotch to his scalp and toes. He gasped for breath like a fish on a dock. This was too much.

He sat back in the chair and came; he hunched forward and came again. He sucked in air, hyperventilating.

Dear God, he thought, *this pill's going to kill me.*

Moving very, very slowly, as if his body were composed of nitroglycerine, he stood. This seemed to keep the orgasms at bay. It was also helpful that the local afternoon news had started. If there were such a thing as an anti-orgasm, it would be brought on by watching the local news.

Today's leading stories were the usual litany of murders, natural disasters and pandemics that you might not associate with the end of the world had you not spent the last twelve hours trying to postpone it. Sandwiched amidst these dire reports was news that Flight 240 out of the Los Angeles International Airport had been cancelled due to 'unspecified concerns'. The correspondent standing by live at the airport wasn't able to talk to any of the passengers, who were being taken to 'an undisclosed location to be reunited with their families'.

Perry watched the TV as familiar faces from the Green Room were herded onto a bus. He was about to turn it off when the anchorman said, 'And finally, the general assembly of the United Nations was disrupted today when the Iranian delegate complained about a pen. Yes, you heard me correctly: A pen.' The anchorman smirked. 'We haven't seen the offending implement yet, but apparently it was enough to vanquish world peace for at least a day. Tomorrow? My bet's on buttons.'

The two anchormen then kidded each other while holding up their pens: 'Come on, Joe, you're really cheesing me off with that thing.' Perry watched this, his face ashen. *They've sent out the pens*, he thought. *How long did the receptionist say it would take the world to end from here? Three weeks?*

The Earth was on the brink of extinction and no one could even see it. Perry pulled out the new shotgun and the box of shells. He crouched down too quickly and experienced another incapacitating orgasm. Steadying himself against the couch, he stood deliberately, lifted the shotgun and opened the chamber. While thanking God for the permissive gun laws that he had thought for years to be a national tragedy, he slid the shells into the empty chamber, the way the clerk at the K-Mart had shown him. He knew it would be a doomed mission, but he figured he could maybe cause enough damage to the control room of Galaxy Entertainment to slow down production. A shell slipped out of his grasp and clattered to the floor. Bending down – slowly – to scoop it up, he paused. He had the feeling of being watched. He now realised that he'd had it ever since he entered his apartment. Then he heard a sound, a buzzing. He followed it to his left, just in time to see an insect land on top of the TV.

A fly.

Perry tiptoed until he was standing directly over it. The insect pivoted towards him. He was now close enough to see a glint of metallic blue on its abdomen. With a rapid motion, he cupped his hand and slammed it down. Did he get it? Yes – he felt it crawling up onto his palm. He quickly folded his fingers into a loose fist.

'Enjoying the show?' he asked the trapped fly. 'How about this?' He raised his hand, intending to smash it against the wall. Then he had a better idea. He walked into the kitchen and found an empty peanut-butter jar in the recycling bin. He released the fly inside the jar, screwed on the lid, and set it on top of the TV. He squatted down until he was eye-level with the fly.

'Amanda,' he whispered. 'Amanda, are you watching?' The fly sat on the bottom of the jar, motionless. 'If you're watching, do something. Fly in a circle.' The fly continued to stare at him, inscrutable.

Perry inhaled. 'OK. I have something to say to you, whoever's watching,' he said. What now? Perry's mouth was dry. He needed another idea to save the Earth, but following through on a project had never been his strong suit. Unfortunately, there was no other project to go on to. This was it. He forced his mouth to talk. 'You think we're all selfish, aggressive idiots on this planet. You think we don't deserve to live. But you're wrong.'

Perry felt acutely aware of how lame this sounded. This was why he was a writer and not an improviser. He wished he had a few minutes to write something down. But if anyone was watching, who knew how long they would continue watching?

'The people of Earth are basically decent people. If you don't know this, it's because you're only being shown the Steve Santiagos of this world. You haven't had a chance to see anyone be a decent human being. Well, now you are.' Perry hesitated. He surveyed his apartment and spied his wallet, which he'd set on top of a bookcase. He picked it up and removed his ATM card, brandishing it at the fly. 'Right now, I am going to remove all my money from my bank account and give it to the poor.'

The fly seemed to take this in. But, in fact, the fly was only thinking about how to get out of the jar. This was because the fly was just a fly, and not a camera for Channel Blue. However, one of Channel Blue's satellite cameras did happen to be passing over Perry's house at that moment, and the image of an Earthle conversing with a common housefly was deemed bizarre enough to set off an alert from an automated screener at a relay station. This machine's job was to sort through the millions of video feeds radiating from Earth and narrow them down to the half per cent that might qualify for entertaining viewing on Channel Blue. After noting the Earthle–fly interaction, the machine communicated with the satellite, which fixed all its lenses on Perry's house and summoned camera flies in the vicinity of Perry's apartment complex. They entered through the broken kitchen window and flew to the best vantage points for viewing Perry. The machine then alerted a technician at the Ventura Boulevard control room. While Perry left his house and walked to his car, this technician pulled in the various feeds and watched as Perry took the jar with the fly in it, buckled it into the passenger seat of his car, drove to the closest branch of his bank, withdrew $478 from the ATM (the entire contents of his checking account after his end-of-the-world spending spree) and made his way to a poor neighbourhood on the other side of Ventura Boulevard, where small crumbling stucco houses nestled like embarrassed hobos behind overgrown front yards.

Perry parked his car and walked down the street, holding the jar containing the fly in one hand and a wad of twenty-dollar bills in the other. He passed boarded-up homes and stripped-down cars. Normally, he would have ventured through a neighbourhood like this with great trepidation. Today, he felt fearless. After all, he was here to help.

He walked for an entire block and still couldn't find anyone to give his money to. Then he came upon a small girl pushing a rusty tricycle through a front garden covered with weeds. She wore a dirty white dress clearly too small for her, but as far as Perry was concerned, she was perfect. She was poor.

'Hello, little girl,' Perry said. 'This is for you.' He peeled off two twenties and offered them to the girl, who hesitated. She eyed Perry and the bills suspiciously.

'Go ahead,' Perry said. After a moment, she reached out and took the bills. She held them in her hands, gazing at them, her awe tinged with disbelief. A breathtaking smile broke out on her small face. Perry smiled back. 'What are you going to do with that money?'

She blinked at the two bills. 'Take Grandma and Grandpa to dinner,' she said softly.

Perry held the fly jar out towards the girl. This was good stuff.

'What the fuck?'

Perry turned to see four teenagers walking down the sidewalk towards him. They were large, but their clothes were even larger. In fact, it wasn't immediately clear whether the boys were wearing the clothes or the clothes were wearing the boys. One teen stepped into Perry's face.

'Whaddaya doing, freak?' He turned to the little girl, 'What's he doing to you?'

'He gave me money,' she said.

'He did *what*?' the teen said.

Perry suddenly realised how ridiculous and possibly sinister he appeared: a dishevelled white man in a blue velour tracksuit giving cash to a child.

'Do you need some money?' he asked the teens. 'You see, I'm just trying to help out a little. We could all use some help, right?' He extended a shaking hand filled with cash.

The four teens laughed in short, barking breaths, then set upon Perry. The glass jar slipped from his hand and crashed to the sidewalk.

Since Perry was busy being beaten, he didn't see what happened to the fly inside the jar and assumed it was gone. But the fly hadn't flown far. It had found a perch on the top of a nearby parking sign, next to a row of other flies – the perfect vantage point, it turned out, from which to watch Perry Bunt demonstrate the basic goodness of the Earth's people.

CHANNEL 16

MAN ON A MISSION

'Per? Per? You OK?' The words seemed to come from a hundred miles away. Perry opened his eyes and saw his neighbour Noah Overton standing over him. Noah appeared relieved. 'Jesus. What happened to you?'

Perry was lying on the sidewalk next to the overgrown garden, surrounded by shards of broken glass. All of his money was gone. He had a crushing headache and what felt like bruises all over his body. He slowly sat up and felt his face to see if it was all still there. It was.

He told Noah about the confrontation with the teenagers. 'I must have blacked out when I hit the pavement,' he said.

Noah's large brown eyes welled with concern. 'What were you doing over here in the first place?'

How could Perry begin to explain his last-ditch attempt to show aliens that the Earth's residents were worth saving? As Noah helped him to his feet, he heard a buzzing sound. He assumed this was a side-effect of the concussion until he saw a swarm of flies above him. 'Weird, huh?' Noah said. 'Never seen that many flies. As if they don't have enough problems around here.'

Perry smiled slowly. *They were watching. Goddammit – they were really watching!* And the longer he could keep them watching, the better the chances of postponing the finale. He turned to Noah Overton. All the features that

Perry had come to disdain in Noah's face – the innocent doe-like eyes, the pert superior nose, the down-turned smug mouth, the pubic half-beard, the shaggy, artfully messed-up hair – now seemed brilliant to Perry. Better than brilliant.

'I know I haven't been the best neighbour,' Perry said. 'But I want to change.'

Noah furrowed his brow. 'What do you mean?'

'I've decided that you're right. We have to save the planet.'

'That's great,' Noah said, a little uncertainly.

'And *you* are the perfect person to help me do it,' Perry said, angling his face up towards a nearby hovering fly. 'You are a good person. You're unselfish – compassionate – you're always looking for ways to help other people. Isn't that true?'

Noah regarded Perry warily. 'I'd better take you to the hospital. You should get checked out.'

'I've never given you any credit, but you *really care*. And you're trying, really trying to make a difference.'

'Seriously, Per – you might have some brain damage or something.'

'You just saved my life.'

'I just drove around the corner and saw you lying here. Anyone would've stopped.'

Perry turned to the white van parked at the curb with its safety flashers on. On its side was written: DAILY BLESSING MEAL DELIVERY. Perry smiled triumphantly. 'You were delivering meals to the hungry!'

'Shut-ins and seniors, mostly,' Noah said. 'I was just on my way back to the church to pick up more.'

'Let's go then!' said Perry. 'Let's go help people! Because that's what we do here on Earth all the time, right? We help people.'

Noah hesitated. 'Are you mocking me?'

'No, no,' Perry said. 'God, no. Why would I do that? You're such a good person.' Noah gave Perry a long look, then led him to the van.

The two men drove through sun-baked rows of decrepit bungalows to the Church of St Jude, which towered over the clapboard hovels with its gothic spires and, at the tip of its centre tower, a large cross bordered with neon tubing. This cross provided a beacon, though probably not the one its builders had in mind: Disoriented drivers trying to find their way back to nicer neighbourhoods learned that they only needed to drive away from the cross.

Perry, sitting in the passenger seat, interviewed Noah exhaustively on all the organisations he worked for and the just causes he believed in until Noah interrupted. 'Man, what's with all these flies?' He picked up a street atlas and swatted at a fly on the dashboard.

Perry gasped and yanked the atlas out of Noah's hand. 'Don't do that. The flies are good. You have to trust me on this.'

Noah shook his head. 'Per, I feel like you're going through something really heavy right now. You want to talk about it?'

'I want to talk about *you* and all the work you've done for this planet.'

Noah sighed. 'Look, it's OK. I've done counselling at rehab centres.' He glanced meaningfully over at Perry. 'I'm serious. You can tell me what you're on.'

They pulled into the nearly empty parking lot of the church. While Perry was interested in helping Noah load more dinner trays into the van, Noah thought Perry's enthusiasm might be put to better use as a volunteer at the shelter and directed him across the parking lot.

The shelter for displaced persons at St Jude's occupied the

basement of a block-like annexe that was built onto the side of the hundred-year-old sanctuary in the 1970s in an ecclesiastical splurge of cement and stucco. Perry followed a ramp down the side of the building and pulled open a heavy metal door. The first thing that hit him was the smell, an odd combination of cleaning solvents, body odour and human filth. Then, as his eyes adjusted, he saw a large, drab, windowless room filled with benches and mostly inert bodies, some sitting up at tables over metal trays of shapeless food, others lying down on the floor next to shopping trolleys full of what appeared to be garbage. One side of the room opened onto a kitchen, where volunteers stood at a steam table serving food to a long line that shuffled slowly by. At a nearby table, a group of leathery men, dressed as if they had walked by an exploding thrift shop, gazed at Perry standing in the doorway, a blank stare from dull eyes. The room was a violent, mocking contrast to the sunny afternoon outside.

Perry couldn't help but smile. This is the perfect place, he thought. They'll see Earthles helping other Earthles. If this doesn't make them realise what good people we are, nothing will.

'Shut the damn door!' a large man wearing a ski cap yelled from a bench.

Perry hesitated, unsure if the man was yelling at him.

'The flies, man! You're letting in flies!' The man was right: to Perry's great joy, flies were zipping around him through the doorway. He shut the door, but slowly.

After asking the servers at the steam table, Perry located the volunteer coordinator, Father Michael, a handsome young priest wearing a short-sleeve tunic and carrying a clipboard. It was Father Michael who had expanded the meals-on-wheels programme into a fully-fledged soup kitchen. While the other priests at St Jude's were initially dubious about Father Michael's enthusiasm for helping the poor, it had paid great dividends for the parish. While membership at other churches had dwindled in recent years, overall attendance at St Jude's had actually risen as the homeless filled masses after breakfast and before dinner.

'Excuse me, Father.' Perry navigated across the busy dining area and approached the young priest. 'Noah Overton said I should talk to you. I'd like to help.'

'I'm sorry,' the priest said. 'We don't start volunteers on Thursdays. Come back on a Monday or a Wednesday.'

Father Michael clearly considered their discussion over, but Perry continued standing in his path. 'I really want to help and I'm here today.'

The priest shook his head. 'Unfortunately, I'm extremely busy right now – I'm literally going out of my mind.' While Perry fought the urge to offer the priest an exorcism, Father Michael said, 'You'll have to come back' and slipped through a door marked 'Staff Only'. Above the door was a TV mounted on brackets. The sound was off but Perry saw a sombre news anchorman and the words:

SPECIAL REPORT – CRISIS IN THE MIDDLE EAST

Perry fought the urge to panic and desperately surveyed the room around him. He noticed a muscle-bound man with a buzz cut mopping the floor.

'Excuse me,' Perry said. 'If there's some other work in the shelter you need to do, I can take over here.'

The man eyed Perry suspiciously, then continued mopping. Perry noticed several flies landing on a nearby table. 'You must really care about people,' Perry said to the man.

'What?' the man said.

'You're a volunteer, right?'

The man chuckled derisively. 'I busted some guy in the face,' he said. 'I was either down for assault or community service.'

'Oh,' Perry said. 'But you are still here helping, aren't you?'

The man glared at Perry. 'You queer or something?'

'Uh, no,' Perry stammered. Sweat sprang out of his forehead. 'I just wanted to point out that it doesn't matter why you're here . . . you're still doing a good thing . . . making that floor so . . . shiny and . . . bright.'

The man brandished the mop like a club, waving it in Perry's face. 'Get the fuck away from me!' he snarled. Perry jumped back and quickly made a wide arc around the man towards the main entrance. Here he fixed on an old woman, gnarled and leathery, attempting to push a shopping cart loaded with bags through the metal door. One of the cart's cracked wheels had become caught on the threshold. Perry rushed to her assistance.

'Let me help you with that,' he said. He took hold of one end of the rusty cart in order to pull it through the door.

'Don't touch my cart,' the old woman said.

'I'm just going to help you get it through the doorway.' Perry gently tugged at the cart.

'*Nooooo!*' The old woman yanked the cart away from Perry with all her strength, slamming it backwards into the doorjamb and causing it to topple over onto one side, sending myriad shopping bags onto the floor of St Jude's Shelter for the Displaced.

* * *

Amanda carried the container holding all her Earthly possessions down the hallway towards the elevators, closely followed by two security guards. While passing a screening room, she heard hysterical gales of laughter and poked her head in the doorway. Dennis the receptionist and an associate producer rocked convulsively in their seats. On the screen, Perry Bunt ran around a dark room chased by an angry old woman. The old woman, amazingly fast for her size and age, was occasionally able to lunge at Perry and deftly pummel him with her fists. Encircling this chase were rowdy homeless men and women, cheering on the spry senior.

'What's going on?' Amanda asked.

'Hey, Amanda.' Dennis gasped for air and wiped tears from his eyes. 'They were going through the selects this morning and came upon that Earthle we brought in here. Remember? The one who had a show for five minutes?' Amanda nodded her head, watching as Perry slipped on a food tray and fell to the floor of the shelter. Dennis paused to chortle ecstatically, then continued. 'He's totally hilarious. He thinks he can stop the finale by showing us that Earthles are basically good, but—' Dennis fought back another fit of laughter. 'But the more he tries to do it, the more abused he gets!'

Months later, when Amanda would think back to the last days of Channel Blue, she would often ask herself when she first felt what might be called love for Perry Bunt. This is the moment she often came to: seeing Perry on his lost humiliating crusade, running at full speed from a crazy old lady. It made no sense to her in the moment or even later, but there it was. She wasn't coming down with a case of Satanism. She wasn't going crazy. She simply cared deeply about the fate of an Earthle risking everything to save his planet. And like every great producer of entertainment, she had the audacity to think that other people would, too.

'How long have we been tracking this feed?' she asked the associate producer.

'Half an hour,' he said. 'A technician sent it to me a few minutes ago.'

'Are you going live to air?'

The associate producer glanced away, clearly uncomfortable. 'Not sure Mr Pythagorus will go for that.'

'Do it,' Amanda said.

The associate producer nervously smoothed his hair with one hand. 'I'd like to. I mean, this is good stuff. It's just that you and this Earthle are kind of on the outs right now.'

Amanda glanced over at her shoulder at the two guards, who kept a respectable distance in the hallway. 'I'm still your boss,' she said.

The associate producer shook his head. 'I'm sorry, Amanda. I'd love to help you out, but I can't.'

* * *

After several volunteers, Father Michael, and two other priests pulled the old homeless woman off Perry, it fell to Noah Overton to escort him off the premises. When they walked out of the basement door, Perry paused, surveying the sky and the dingy walkway. *Where are the flies?* Panic gripped his stomach. Where had all the damn flies gone? Had they stopped watching?

'I'm sorry, Per,' Noah said. 'I know you really want to help, but you were making everyone really uncomfortable in there. You have to go.'

Perry fought down his agitation. If he was going to show the sympathetic side of Earth, he needed Noah's help. Jesus

– his neighbour was practically the poster boy for hopeless causes. Now more than ever he needed to appear sane and rational. 'Noah, you have to listen to me,' he said. 'If I can't show that human beings are capable of being good, the Earth is going to be destroyed.'

Noah's great brown eyes were tinged with sadness. 'It's hard to see you like this.'

'If I gave you a jar full of flies, would you carry it around with you?'

Noah shook his head. 'Why would I do that, Per?'

'Why have all the flies been following me around?' Perry took a deep breath. It was now or never – he had to tell him everything. 'Because they're *cameras*.' He fixed Noah's doubtful expression in the steadiest gaze he could muster. 'An alien race has been watching Earth for entertainment, but they've decided to blow us up because they're sick of watching. The thing is, they've only been watching the worst of the worst. We have to show them what we're capable of!'

Noah sighed. 'Promise me you'll get some help.'

Perry finally saw what he'd been searching for: a blue fly perched on the wall nearby. He smacked the wall and nailed it. 'You see?' Perry said, holding his hand up to Noah's face. 'It's a *camera*!'

'No, Per,' Noah said softly. 'That's a fly. A very dead fly.'

Perry examined his palm and saw what appeared to be an unappetising smudge of wings and fly guts. 'You have to look at it closely. I swear to God, there's a camera in there somewhere.'

Noah turned away. There was nothing more he could do. 'Goodbye, friend.' With a final mournful glance, he entered the shelter and left Perry outside, wiping his hand on his blue velour pants and staring at the sky.

CHANNEL 17

THE PROPHET

Perry crossed the church parking lot, scanning the air for flies. A passing nun glanced at him furtively and bustled by. He could only guess at what he looked like in his dirty blue tracksuit, bruised, beaten and haggard after two days without sleep. But he didn't care anymore. The naked burka girl pens had been sent out; a crisis was escalating in the Middle East and the Earth had only days before Nick Pythagorus' machinations reduced it to rubble.

Perry didn't see any flies but he had to assume that someone up there was still watching. He had to because it was Earth's only hope. And if they were watching, he had to do everything in his power to be perceived as the kind of person that you wouldn't want to kill. In other words, he had to do some good – as quickly as possible. Now that the homeless shelter was off-limits, that meant helping someone out here.

He looked around the half-empty parking lot. Birds sang in the trees and a passing car radio played salsa music. It wasn't exactly a war zone. Still, there had to be something he could do.

He heard shouting and turned towards it. A run-down park bordered the parking lot. At one end, a small cluster of homeless people sat on decrepit swings and playground equipment, eating boxed meals from the shelter. They watched as two men shoved each other, scuffling and shouting among the wood chips. One held a cupcake that the other struggled to reach.

Perry trotted across the asphalt and entered the park, accelerating into a run as he approached the fight. Without hesitating, he grabbed the scraggly man holding the cupcake.

'Stop this!' he shouted. He took the cupcake out of the man's hand and threw it as hard as he could. It sailed like a frosting-covered comet over the playground equipment. 'No one gets the cupcake!'

Perry's actions were so decisive that both men dropped any pretence of aggression and stared at him, confused. Perry, in turn, felt an obligation to explain his sudden act of pastry vandalism.

'There's no more time for fighting. We have to start being good to each other or the world is over.'

'Because of the aliens?'

Perry turned to the man who'd been attempting to grab the cupcake and realised, to his shock, that it was Ralph.

In the hours since Perry had seen him, Ralph had somehow deteriorated back to his dirty, shambling homeless configuration – and then beyond, to an even more dilapidated state. It was if he had left Perry on Ventura Boulevard and rolled up and down a hill of garbage for the next five hours.

Perry had decided that he wasn't going to waste any more time talking about aliens to people who thought he was crazy to begin with, but since Ralph had brought it up, Perry nodded. Ralph's eyes grew wide. It was as if two puzzle pieces in his broken brain had slid together.

'It's not a show,' he muttered.

'No,' Perry said.

'*That's* what you were trying to tell me. Right, Buddy? The aliens are crashing our planes because we're not good to each other!'

'Basically, yes.'

The other homeless regarded Perry and Ralph sceptically. This seemed to spark some fire in Ralph, who turned to the scraggly man he'd been fighting for the cupcake and strode directly towards him with his arms outstretched, like an old-fashioned movie monster closing in on a victim.

Perry cringed. But to his surprise, Ralph threw both arms around the scraggly man.

'I love you,' he said. After what seemed like minutes to Perry and probably hours to the scraggly man, Ralph released him, turned to the rest of the group and pointed emphatically at Perry: 'Listen to this man! He knows what's going on!' The homeless stared at Perry, who was still trying to catch up with this odd chain of events. 'Tell them, Buddy,' Ralph urged. 'Tell them how we're all going to die and how it's not a show. How the aliens are going to destroy the Earth.'

The motley group waited for Perry to speak. Perry had never enjoyed public speaking – it was one of the reasons he'd become a writer. It was always so much easier to seem witty when you spent hours writing it beforehand. When he'd been a successful screenwriter, his awkwardness in meetings had been considered charming; the way he sometimes paused for an uncomfortably long time before speaking was thought to be an endearing eccentricity that only confirmed his status as a savant. After his fall, however, these same qualities were viewed as terrible liabilities and proof that the failure of his screenplays was no accident.

'Well,' Perry said after a long pause. 'It's true.'

'Ralph told you!' Ralph bellowed to no one in particular,

then turned his intense blue eyes back on Perry with disconcerting focus. 'What can we do, Buddy? Tell us! What can
we do to save ourselves?'

'Help each other,' Perry said. 'Just . . . try to be decent
and . . . unselfish.'

'No one gets the cupcake!' Ralph yelled ecstatically.

'No one gets the cupcake,' one of the other men repeated,
as if to see how it sounded coming out of his mouth. The
other homeless continued to focus their attention on Perry,
their scepticism now tinged with interest.

'It may even be too late,' Perry said, warming up to his
speaking role, 'but we have to hope that it's not. We have to
hope that the aliens are still watching us, and that everything
we do or say will have a bearing on whether they decide to
destroy the Earth.'

As he spoke, he noticed that more homeless from the
shelter were approaching, attracted by the commotion.

'Tell us more, Buddy,' said one leathery woman to Perry.
'How did you find out about these aliens?'

'Yeah,' said a toothless man. 'Do they have those disgusting
big white heads?'

'No,' Perry said, and proceeded to tell the growing group
how he had found out about Galaxy Entertainment and their
plans for Earth. Sometime during his story, the bells above
them tolled for seven o'clock mass. No one in his audience
made a move towards the church.

By the time Perry had recounted his journey to the shelter,
the crowd listening to him had tripled. The men and women
leaned forward, straining to hear him, occasionally yelling,
'Louder!' to Perry or 'Shut up!' and 'Quiet!' to someone else.
Ralph worked the periphery of the crowd, bringing listeners
in closer to Perry and fielding questions. Perry noticed Father

Michael standing towards the rear of the crowd, his arms folded across his chest.

During one pause in Perry's story, the priest cupped his hands around his mouth and shouted, 'It's not too late to attend mass! If you're interested, please join us in the main sanctuary!'

'No thanks,' a homeless man replied. 'We're listening to Buddy.'

Father Michael, unfazed, shouted again, 'Please come and join me in a prayer for peace! The Middle East needs our prayers tonight!'

'We're not playing with that God stuff anymore!' Ralph shouted back. 'There are aliens trying to destroy the planet! We have to stay out here and help each other.'

Father Michael smiled, maintaining his calm. 'I'm happy you want to help each other,' he said. 'But there are no aliens. There is only God. Your friend Buddy here—' Father Michael extended his arm to Perry, 'does not speak for God.'

A chorus of jeers rose from the crowd. Perry, mortified, waved his hands and shouted for them to be quiet.

Father Michael stepped closer to Perry and fixed him with a steely gaze. 'What's your game here?' he said with disconcerting calm.

'My game?' Perry said.

'Leading these lost souls astray,' the priest said, advancing on Perry. 'If you really want to help them do good, why not encourage them to come into church?'

Emboldened by the support of the crowd, Perry held his ground against the priest. 'It's not enough to sit in church. They've already watched us sitting in church.'

Father Michael arched his eyebrows. 'By "they", I suppose you mean . . . the aliens?'

Perry nodded. 'They're not impressed that people think

they can go into church and be absolved for anything bad they've done. They actually thought it was hilarious for a while, but now they think it's another example of why we should be destroyed.'

As Perry spoke, he saw Father Michael quietly give up on having a reasonable conversation. 'I see,' the priest said. He turned back to the massing crowd and spoke with his commanding baritone. 'When any of you become tired of this crazy talk about aliens, the church will be open to you!'

'Crazier than a virgin birth?' shouted back the toothless man.

'How about raising the dead?' came other voices.

'What about God talking from a bush?'

'Crazier than a talking snake?'

The crowd continued heckling Father Michael until he marched back into the church wearing an expression of righteous indignation. Then it turned its attention back to Perry and demanded that he repeat different parts of his story again, answer questions, and give advice. Perry had used up all his adrenaline. As the sun sank below the horizon and the fluorescent lights that bordered the park flickered on, he felt overwhelmed by fatigue. He sat down but still had trouble keeping his eyes open. On his fourth or fifth time reciting the disasters that would end the world, he slumped over onto the grass and slipped into a deep dreamless sleep.

* * *

Perry woke to the ringing of church bells. He opened his eyes and saw the words: THIS END UP. It took him a few moments to realise that he was lying inside a refrigerator box that had been propped over him like a tent.

'He's up!' a familiar voice said. Perry raised his head from a balled-up down vest and saw that Ralph was gazing down at him, flanked by two homeless men Perry vaguely remembered from the night before. Perry stretched his limbs beneath a makeshift quilt of dirty coats. He felt stiff and sore.

'We've got some food for you, Buddy,' Ralph said, holding a boxed breakfast from the shelter. Perry wiped the sleep from his eyes with one dirty blue sleeve and crawled out from under the box. He emerged into the morning light and was immediately set upon by Ralph and the other ripe-smelling men, who grabbed him and lifted him onto Ralph's shoulders.

'Let me down!' Perry shouted.

'No, Buddy,' Ralph said. 'They all want to see you.'

Perry surveyed his surroundings, disoriented and blinking in the bright sun. When his eyes adjusted, he saw that the park was now filled with hundreds of people standing shoulder-to-shoulder, all facing Perry. They weren't just homeless, either. There were men wearing ties, well-dressed women, schoolkids with backpacks, men and women wearing blue velour tracksuits. Many held crudely made signs that read: 'We Love You Buddy', 'Save Us' and 'No one Gets the Cupcake'.

They saw Perry and a huge cheer went up amongst them.

'What's going on?' Perry asked when Ralph had set him back down.

'They've all heard about the aliens and what they're doing,' Ralph said. 'They want to hear from you what they should do to save the planet.'

'Speak to us, Buddy!' one of the crowd shouted.

'No one gets the cupcake!' another yelled, and the chant was eagerly taken up and repeated over and over.

Perry waved his hands for them to stop. A sudden silence descended as if he had pressed a mute button. He studied their smiling expectant faces and cleared his throat. 'Be nice to each other,' he said. 'That's all. Stop thinking about yourselves for a day. Go help someone.'

The crowd seemed to nod as one, then broke into a burst of enthusiastic applause. 'More!' they shouted in a cacophony.

'Talk to us, Buddy!'

'Talk about the aliens!'

'That's it!' Perry yelled. 'Go somewhere else and be good people! That's all!' The crowd cheered and made no move to go anywhere. If anything, they seemed to huddle closer to Perry.

'We love the Buddy!' an excited Latino man shouted, and this chant was also taken up by the crowd. 'We love the Buddy!' they shouted. 'The Buddy is love!'

'Get out of here!' Perry shouted, as if haranguing a pack of wild dogs. 'Go! Shoo!'

Ralph rested one large hand on Perry's shoulder. 'You've got to give them more about the aliens,' he advised. 'Maybe you could tell them another story about Elvis. Like maybe you two had a jam session on the moon.'

Perry shook his head. 'The point is to get people out there doing good things. It's not to have them listening to me talk.'

Ralph appeared confused. 'But you're the one person here who can save us,' he said. 'You're the one true Buddy.'

'My name isn't even Buddy!' Perry shouted. 'It's—'

At this moment, Perry noticed two officers of the Los Angeles Police Department picking a path through the crowd, making their way towards him. One of the officers caught his eye.

'Excuse me, sir,' he said. 'This crowd is considered a non-permitted assembly and, as a result, is a disturbance of the peace. Until you file for the proper permits, you must disband immediately.'

'I've been trying to,' Perry said. 'Watch.' He turned to the crowd. 'Go away!' he shouted. 'This is illegal! You all have to leave the park!'

'No!' the onlookers shouted back.

'Never!'

'Not without you!'

'Don't worry, Buddy,' Ralph said, scowling at the officers. 'We'll never leave you.'

'But I want you to!' Perry yelled. 'I'm serious! Get out of here!'

'He's testing us!' Ralph shouted to the crowd. 'He's testing our faith in him! Are we going to let down Buddy?'

'*No!*' the crowd roared back.

The two officers turned to each other to discuss the situation. In the parking lot, Perry could see Father Michael and other members of St Jude's clergy watching intently. Next to them was a group of shelter volunteers that included Noah. It was hard to read their expressions, except for Noah's. Noah shook his head sadly.

'I'm sorry, sir,' one of the officers said to Perry. 'At this time, we need you to come with us. No charges will be filed, we just need the crowd to disperse.'

'Fine,' Perry said. He turned and followed the officers, but Ralph lunged and grabbed his arm in a vice-like grip.

'We won't let you arrest him!'

'They're not arresting me, Ralph,' Perry said, but his words were drowned out by an angry roar from the surrounding crowd, which quickly transformed itself into a mob. Cans, rocks and bottles showered down on the two officers, who were jerked and pulled like puppets by the onlookers before tearing themselves free and escaping to the perimeter of the park.

Ralph beamed ecstatically. 'We showed them!'

'Are you crazy?' Perry yelled.

Ralph lowered his great head like a scolded child. 'You seem angry, my Buddy. Have I done something to upset you?'

Perry staved off the urge to throttle the large homeless man. 'Haven't you listened to anything I've said? We have to be good to each other!'

'Right,' Ralph said. 'And we saved you. That's good, right?'

'Listen to me,' Perry said. 'I'm leaving the park now. Don't try to stop me.'

Ralph's eyebrows dipped in consternation. 'Why would you leave us? We believe you. We love you.'

'That's nice, Ralph, but it's not going to help the Earth if the aliens see us fighting over how we're going to be good.' Perry stepped around Ralph and began making his way through the crowd to the sidewalk. Incredulous faces watched him go.

'Stop him!' Ralph roared. 'He's giving himself up to save us!'

The crowd closed in on Perry like a fist, surrounding him on all sides.

'That's not true,' Perry told his captors as calmly as possible. 'Nothing will happen to me. I'm just taking a walk. I need to go to the bathroom.'

'Don't believe anything he says!' Ralph yelled. 'He'll do anything to help us!'

Despite Perry's protestations, his followers pushed him back towards Ralph while several police department trucks pulled up to the edge of the park. Riot police in helmets, flak jackets and shields took up positions around the crowd's perimeter. Seeing this, Perry begged and pleaded to be released, but unfortunately the followers who surrounded him were those who had managed to get the closest to him during his twelve hours in the park, and were thus his most loyal acolytes. Their love for him and his fight to save Earth from the aliens was so great and pure that they would entertain no notion of letting him go.

The police fired tear gas canisters into the crowd and waded in, waving riot batons like beaters flushing game birds from the brush.

* * *

Perry sat in a holding cell. He had a black eye, a fat lip, a sprained arm, and was still vomiting every fifteen minutes from the after-effects of tear gas. His cellmates comprised of several large men who viewed him with a mixture of contempt and derision. Every time Perry went to the seatless toilet in the corner to throw up, he saw them shake their heads in disgust.

Though the police had originally not intended to charge him with any crime, the fierce nature of the ensuing confrontation and the number of policemen injured required some reprisal towards the responsible party. Perry had been charged with disorderly conduct and intent to riot and was told that, due to a large influx of arrests, he wouldn't even be arraigned for several hours. Allowed one call, he had phoned Noah and had left a rambling message that would no doubt reinforce the belief that he had gone completely insane. And, in truth, he had. He had gone momentarily insane with the hope that he could stop the inevitable. But he couldn't. As he was being booked, he had overheard two policemen talking about an escalating war in the Middle East.

War. Perry couldn't believe what he was hearing. You had to give them credit: Nick Pythagorus and his colleagues knew exactly what they were doing.

Perry heard a distant buzzing and stood. He quickly surveyed the cell. 'Has anyone seen any flies?' he asked his cellmates. They glared at him. Perry sighed and sat down. *It doesn't really matter*, he thought. *It's all over.* Even if the aliens were still watching, every attempt he'd made to prove the people of Earth worth saving had been a complete disaster. If anything, Galaxy Entertainment would have even more justification for blowing up the planet. This depressing reverie was interrupted by another surge of nausea. He staggered over to the toilet.

'Give it a rest, freak,' a bald man in a vest growled as Perry discovered, deep within, new frontiers of his stomach that needed emptying.

'I can't,' Perry choked out. 'It's the tear gas.'

'You stop puking,' the bald man said, 'or I will shove my fist down your throat.'

Perry wiped the corner of his mouth with a tattered blue sleeve. 'I'm no expert on these things, but if what you really want to do is to stop me from puking, I don't think putting your fist down my throat will help.'

The bald man leaped up with puma-like speed and grabbed Perry by the hair. 'You making fun of me?' he said. 'You want me to kill you?'

'Honestly,' Perry said, 'it doesn't matter.' The bald man grabbed the seat of Perry's pants to ram him headfirst into the cement-brick wall when a guard appeared on the other side of the bars.

'Let him go,' he said. The bald man reluctantly dropped Perry to the floor. The guard opened the cell door. 'Bunt.'

'Yes?' Perry said.

'Your uncle's here.'

Perry blinked. He had only one uncle, a senile octogenarian

living in a Midwestern convalescent hospital who hadn't known his name in years.

'He wants to see you. Let's go.'

Perry followed the policeman to what looked like an interrogation room, with mirrored glass along one wall. 'Wait here,' he said and exited. After a moment, a distinguished-looking middle-aged man with a trimmed grey moustache entered. He wore an expensive suit and a pair of designer eyeglasses. He seemed to be deeply upset.

'Perry, Perry, Perry,' he said. 'What kind of mess have you got yourself into now? Thank God your parents don't know.'

Perry was quite sure that he had never seen this man before.

'Do you know the strings I had to pull to get you out?' the man said. Perry could only gape at him. 'Well, come on, don't stand there like some garden gnome waiting for pigeon poop. Let's go.'

The man opened the breast pocket of his suit and Perry watched incredulously as three flies flew into it. The man patted the pocket closed, then held out his left arm and pulled up the cuff of his shirt. A tattoo of a blue fly adorned his tanned wrist.

'I'm a producer,' he whispered. 'Let's go.'

Perry followed the man out of the interrogation room into a hallway. They walked until they came to an elevator. Inside the elevator, below the button for the lowest floor of the parking garage, was a key slot. The man pressed the inside of his left wrist against it, the doors closed and the elevator descended sharply, whirring as it gained speed. Perry's stomach dropped. The man stared ahead impassively while Perry felt tension pulling his shoulders up around his ears – the last time he'd gone down this fast was to join the passengers of a doomed airliner. His nervousness wasn't alleviated when the elevator doors opened to reveal a long corridor with green walls and an instrumental version of 'Teddy Bear' playing softly in the background.

'This way,' the man said officiously, having dropped all pretence of knowing Perry. He opened one of several doors along the corridor and held it for him. Perry swallowed and stepped into what appeared to be a large dressing room. At one end, Amanda Mundo stood before a floor-length mirror in a sleeveless white evening dress that clung to every curve of her body. She fastened the stud of a diamond earring in one ear and noticed Perry.

'Come on,' she said. 'We're going to a party.'

CHANNEL 18

THE STAR

For the first time in his life, Perry Bunt was a writer on a hit show. Not only that, he was also the star.

True, Amanda had experienced some difficulty working around Nick Pythagorus to get the show on the air in the first place, but once she did, viewers tuned in immediately. According to the detailed ratings recorded every millisecond, Perry's audience grew across all demographics with lightning speed. By the time he was kicked out of the homeless shelter, nearly every satellite camera over North America was focused on his plight. And when he became the prophet of St Jude's Park, Channel Blue received its highest rating in ten years. Viewers across the galaxy could not get enough of the guy being abused while trying to save Earth.

Amanda's hunch had been right – in the vernacular of her profession, Perry Bunt was a POF with relateability, a product of fornication for one and all. In short, Perry was POFFO.

'So the execs didn't have a choice,' Amanda said. 'They had to postpone it.' She brushed an eyelash with mascara. 'I have to admit – I enjoy dressing up like an Earthle.'

Perry stood by the doorway mesmerised, afraid to move because it might wake him from this dream. 'Postpone it?' he repeated in a daze.

'The finale.' Amanda popped open a tube of dark red lipstick. 'They're postponing it.'

Perry couldn't believe what he was hearing. 'Really?'

'Yeah. When Nick found out, he went into a full-on tantrum. People always forget he's just nine years old. He kept pounding his fists and accusing me of sabotaging him, but I could honestly say it was all you.' Amanda glanced at Perry and gave him a half-lipsticked smile that compounded his state of stupefaction. She was so beautiful his teeth ached.

'You did it, Mr Bunt. You saved Earth.'

The words met Perry's ears but didn't immediately enter them – they rolled around in circles like a ball on a roulette wheel until they clicked into place. Then he jumped into the air, whooped, and without thinking, lunged forward, wrapped Amanda in his arms and kissed her full on the lips.

Amanda wriggled free and stared at him in amazement. 'You did it again.'

'Yeah,' Perry said. He stepped backwards and clumsily ran one arm across his mouth, painting the dirty blue sleeve with a streak of red lipstick. 'I'm sorry. I guess I got caught up in the moment.'

The sound of a throat being cleared made Perry turn to the middle-aged man who had helped him escape from prison. In all the excitement, Perry had forgotten he was still in the room. The man had removed his jacket, tie and glasses, and appeared considerably less distinguished. With his deep tan and serene expression, he looked like someone who'd spent every day of his life lying on the deck of a yacht sipping Bloody Marys.

'This is great stuff,' the man said. He grinned widely, revealing luminescent teeth of a colour not found in nature, and peeled off his grey moustache. 'Seriously. Really, really great stuff. But I'm afraid that, as great as it is, it's not the show that captured the imaginations of our audience.'

'This is Marty Firth,' Amanda said. Without showing a hint of embarrassment, she smoothed down her dress, picked up her lipstick and turned back to the mirror. 'He's Channel Blue's *Executive* Executive Executive Producer.'

'I also host a show on the channel,' he said, eyes twinkling. Perry could tell that Marty never had a problem talking about himself. '*Earth Mirth with Marty Firth and Vermy*. It's been the launching pad for many careers, both on the channel and throughout the galaxy.'

Amanda capped her lipstick. 'Once your show took off, Galaxy brought Marty in to run it.'

Marty Firth grabbed Perry's right hand with both of his, shaking it as if doing so with enough intensity would eventually cause Perry to dispense the secret of the universe. '*Very* pleased to meet you,' he said. 'I *love* the work you've been doing. Absolutely *love it*. Amanda can tell you all the stars of Channel Blue I've discovered. I've produced Steve Santiago, I've produced Pol Pot, I've produced Charlie Manson, and you are without a doubt the most promising star I've ever worked with.'

Perry wasn't sure about how he felt about being in this group, but such was the power of Marty Firth's aggressive charm and blinding smile that he felt at great pains not to appear ungrateful. 'Thank you,' he said.

'No, thank *you*!' Marty pronounced. 'I'm 120 years old. I don't have one organ in my body that I was born with – except for my eyes, and my eyes have never seen anything like you. *Thank you!* Thank you for saving our channel. All the wonderful hours of programming we've produced out of this little planet—' Marty shook his head as his only original organs misted over.

'I'm going to be honest with you, Mr Bunt. I've been in

this business for many years and worked on a lot of different worlds – so very many. But nothing comes close to the sheer volume of comedy and drama we've managed to wring out of this little blue nugget and you wonderful, crazy Earthles.' Marty gazed into the distance blissfully, transported by sheer wonderment. Then his smile disappeared, as if a storm cloud had passed in front of the sun. 'But despite all that, they were going to *shut us down*. Before you started running around like a lunatic giving all your money away, we were *done*. I mean, you saw it, right? They sent out the damn pens!'

In all the excitement, Perry had forgotten about the finale already in progress. 'That's right,' he said. 'They've declared war in the Middle East!'

Marty chuckled and pawed the air with one hand. 'Relax,' he said. 'Half an hour ago, a mysterious computer virus disabled the Iranian and Israeli missile systems. Neither knows about the other's virus, so both sides are suddenly urging further peace talks.'

'So predictable,' Amanda said into the mirror, a blush brush in one hand. 'Only weakness can save them from wiping each other out. It's a wonder the fools didn't do it years ago.'

Perry glared at her. 'You're acting like I'm not here again.'

'I'm sorry,' Amanda said. 'But you have to agree that the absolute worst thing you can do to an Earthle is to give him power.'

Marty nodded philosophically. 'Yes, but of course it's those refreshingly brutal and selfish qualities that attracted so many viewers to Channel Blue in the first place. They just got a little too much of a good thing until this man—' His arm shot out towards Perry, gripping him firmly on the shoulder. 'Until this *legend* changed everything. Our research shows that you appeal to every single demographic, right across the board. I haven't seen anything like that since Jeffrey Dahmer. Can I get you anything, Mr Bunt? Some food, perhaps? Something to drink?'

Perry shifted uneasily. 'I still feel sick from the tear gas.'

'Of course, of course,' Marty said, chuckling. 'Brilliant performance, by the way. Just brilliant. The way you begged the police to release all your dirty followers as you were being beaten and dragged? Priceless.'

'It wasn't a performance,' Perry said, unable to keep the annoyance out of his voice. 'I was trying to keep people from getting hurt.' The darker side of his success on Channel Blue, which up until now had been kept in abeyance by the postponement of the Earth's destruction, bobbed to the surface of his consciousness. *What kind of creatures are these Edenites?* he wondered. *What kind of monsters would consider people getting hurt 'entertainment'?*

'That worked out well, right?' Marty said, his eyes filled with mirth. 'How many ended up in the hospital?'

Perry stood. 'I'm glad it all worked out for you and your channel, but I'd like to go home now.' Perry never thought he'd feel this way, but after two days of little sleep or food combined with multiple beatings and humiliations, his crappy little apartment and its lumpy fold-out bed struck him as the closest thing to paradise.

'I'm sure you would,' Marty said, though he didn't show any sign of moving away from the door. Perry couldn't help notice that the producer had what appeared to be a white worm emerging from one ear. What made this even more unusual was that the worm had two eyes that blinked open and stared intently at him.

'Um . . . You have a, uh, worm in your ear.'

'Oh, that's just my parasite,' Marty said, completely unfazed.

He looked sideways towards the worm. 'Vermy, did you come out to say hello?'

Perry stared slack-jawed at Marty and the worm. 'You have a parasite.'

'*Everyone* has parasites,' he said. 'Even parasites have parasites. But this happens to be a very special one: *Vermis solium.* I purchased him on a planet in the Sirius sector just sixty years ago.'

Perry watched with disbelief as Marty reached up to his ear and stroked the worm affectionately on the top of its little head.

'Why?'

'Why?'

'Yes. Why would anyone purchase a parasite?'

'Parasites have an incredible talent for remaking other life forms to suit their needs. The *Vermis solium* crave travel, rich food and excitement, and will change their hosts to get those things. And that's exactly what Vermy's done for me.' As if on cue, Vermy disappeared back inside Marty's ear.

Repulsed, Perry turned to Amanda. 'Do you have one of those things inside you?' She shook her head matter-of-factly.

Marty Firth laughed. 'We don't all have the benefit of superior genetic programming like Ms Mundo's. My parents weren't rich and had to cut costs on my conception, particularly when it came to the more expensive traits, such as ambition and tenacity. As a result, I was a wayward and listless young man. Vermy changed all that. Within days of insertion, it had altered my brain so that I would get it all the things it wanted. Since it came aboard, I've produced planets all over the galaxy, winning sixteen Orbys for my work and becoming quite famous and wealthy. I've become what you might call the perfect host.' He chuckled and looked at Perry with a glint in his eye. 'You know, if you were ever able to afford one, a brain parasite might be the best thing that ever happened to you.'

'No thanks,' Perry said, unable to conceal his disgust. 'I'd actually like to go now.' He took a step towards the door, but Marty continued to block his path. The producer and Amanda exchanged a quick glance.

'The thing is,' Marty said. 'You can't.'

'What do you mean?' Perry searched out Amanda's eyes, but she returned to the mirror with a powder compact.

'You're the star of your own show,' Marty said. '*Bunt to the Rescue.*'

Perry grimaced. '*Bunt to the Rescue?*'

'Number nineteen in its time slot for 27-year-old males. They love it; you're a hit.'

'It's a terrible title.'

Marty shrugged. 'Titles are hard. We didn't have a lot of time. It's not like you gave us any warning, you crazy planet saver.' Marty playfully chucked Perry under the chin.

Perry instinctively wiped his face with his sleeve. 'Well, you can call it whatever you want. Right now, I need to take a shower, get something to eat and go to bed.'

'Food and hygiene can be arranged, my filthy little hero. In fact,' Marty said, patting Perry's head, 'I'd say a haircut is an absolute must. No offence, but there's nothing more unap-pealing than a balding man with long hair. Sleep, however, will have to wait. You see—' Marty turned both of his palms upwards. 'Everyone wants to see more. Of you. Of your incredibly heroic self-sacrificing exploits. You're in the public eye now; you can't just disappear on us. You're too famous.'

In all the time that he'd fantasised about becoming famous – a lot more than he'd like to admit – Perry had never fantasised about wanting the fame to end. Then again, he'd never imagined that his fans would live light years away and want to see the Earth destroyed. 'Then the show's over,' he said. 'I quit.'

'Again, you can't.'

'How are you going to stop me? Try to kill me again? Is that something your viewers would enjoy seeing?'

'No,' Marty said. 'At least not right at this moment. What they want to see is you doing your thing. That thing you do so well.' Marty twiddled two fingers and made his hand 'run' across the air. 'You know, scurrying around, trying to save a planet.'

'But there's no reason to save it anymore. You just told me the finale isn't going to happen.'

Marty, who hadn't felt sheepish about anything since acquiring his brain parasite sixty years ago, did his very best to appear that way. He widened his eyes, licked his lips and grimaced. 'Not at the moment.'

Amanda snapped a compact shut and dropped it on the table. 'It's just a postponement, Mr Bunt,' she said. 'We have to prove that we can sustain a hit series. In the meantime, they're keeping their options open – they can put the finale back into production at any moment. Right now, *Bunt to the Rescue* is the only thing stopping them. If it ends or the ratings dip, we're back where we started.'

Perry's stomach sank. He collapsed into a chair and rubbed his head. He stared at Amanda with disbelief. 'So you would kill an entire planet and all the life on it because I won't . . . perform for you?'

'It's not up to us,' Marty said. He extended both hands over his head. 'The audience is our master.'

'Your audience is *insane*!' Perry shouted with a vehemence that surprised him. 'They're spoiled sadistic psychopaths with nothing better to do than to watch the suffering and death of innocent people.' Marty and Amanda both gazed at Perry impassively. 'For God's sake, we're living, flesh-and-blood beings, just like you. We're *alive*!'

Marty glanced over at Amanda. 'Is he going to go there? Because if he is, I'm telling you right now, there is no way I'm going to be able to keep a straight face.'

'Go where?' Perry demanded.

'The "sanctity of life".' No sooner had Marty said it than he burst out in paroxysms of laughter.

Perry scowled at the producer. 'What about it?'

Marty struggled to catch his breath, wiping a tear from one eye. 'Do you know how many planets there are in this galaxy, how many living beings there are on all those planets? No one's even been able to count them yet, and that's just *this* galaxy – one tiny pinprick in the known universe! The universe is *lousy* with life. Please. It's about as scarce as hydrogen.'

Perry remained defiant. 'That doesn't justify what you're doing to us.'

Marty smiled pleasantly and turned to Amanda. 'Is he always this way? I thought Cheney was difficult.'

Amanda shrugged. 'I guess the whole thing is still a bit of a shock. You know Earthles – they always take a little longer than you think they should.'

'Again, I'm *right here*,' Perry said.

Amanda turned to him and smiled. It was the sort of patient, long-suffering smile that Perry had seen on the face of his schoolteachers throughout his education, but coming from Amanda it made his heart accelerate. Again he felt the anger boiling in his stomach dissolved by the beating of his heart. *Damn her*, he thought. *Why does it have to be her?* He was once counselled by an elderly screenwriter never to fall in love with anyone in the entertainment business – advice he'd managed to follow, mostly by default. What would that screenwriter make of his present dilemma?

'Mr Bunt, you've achieved your goal,' Amanda said. 'You've saved Earth.'

'Though as far as our viewers are concerned,' Marty said, jumping in quickly, 'you still think the world is ending. And if I had it my way, those viewers would be right – we wouldn't have taken you off the set.'

'You'd have left me in jail?'

The producer chortled. 'Oh, you wouldn't have *stayed* there,' he said. 'We had numerous scenarios to gain your release. My favourite involved two corrupt cops, a ladder to the roof and a four-story drop onto a flatbed truck carrying mattresses. It would've been *spectacular*.' Marty seemed momentarily lost in a happy dream, then continued. 'But Amanda here convinced me you'd benefit from a little hiatus between episodes.'

Amanda frowned. 'He'd given up,' she said. 'He wasn't going to be of any use to us.'

'Hey, we're here, right?' Marty said. 'I just want Perry to know how important it is that he maintains that desperate, naïve attitude that made him a star in the first place.' He reached over and massaged one of Perry's shoulders.

Perry pushed the hand away. 'I'm not your puppet,' he said.

'Definitely not,' Marty said agreeably. 'If you were, I wouldn't even need to be having this conversation with you. I'd just stick my hand up your ass and we'd start rolling. Now, where was I—' Marty rubbed his hands together. 'Ah yes, the importance of your ignorance. Our audience loves authenticity above everything else. They want *real* drama, *real* comedy, *real* excitement. It's not anything approaching what you call 'entertainment' down here. Edenite audiences are not like children; they don't like to pretend. If someone dies onscreen, they really have to die; if someone saves a planet, they really have to save that planet. They're very sophisticated – they know the difference. In short, if anyone out there watching catches on that we're working with you behind the scenes, they'll switch to a robot fight on Alpha Centauri faster than you can say "ratings disaster". Then—' Marty dramatically slashed one finger across his throat. 'We're *all* dead. Not literally, of course. You and Earth would be dead. Amanda and I would have to find new jobs. And Channel Blue would exist only in reruns—' His eyes teared up again. 'Something that, twenty years from now, people might catch a glimpse of late at night and think, *Wow, that was a great channel, I wonder why they shut it down?*' He studied Perry closely. 'Do you really want to be the answer to that question?'

'I don't give a shit about your channel,' Perry said.

'Then how about your seven billion fellow cast members?' Marty said. 'Are they worth your time?' He shrugged, opening his hands to the sky. 'I don't know. You have to tell me.'

Perry glared at Marty. He thought he could see the white tip of a parasite peeking out of the producer's ear. He shook his head and sighed. 'What do I have to do?'

CHANNEL 19

SAVIOURS OF THE PLANET

Two hours later, Perry reluctantly resumed his starring role in his hit series, *Bunt to the Rescue*. The current episode required him to put on a new Armani suit while riding in the back of a stretch limousine that was speeding through Beverly Hills. Since he'd had limited experience with nice clothes, accomplishing this was taking a ridiculously long time and no doubt supplying laughs to viewers throughout the galaxy – especially when, wearing nothing more than underwear and an unbuttoned dress shirt, Perry leaned forward to pick up a dropped cufflink and the limo braked suddenly, sending him sprawling to the floor. He lay there wondering how hilarious his butt crack looked peeking out the top of his boxers.

As Marty Firth might have said: if someone falls on their face onscreen, someone really has to fall on their face.

Perry was en route to a charity function at the estate of Del Waddle, the richest person in Hollywood and the tenth richest man in the world. Even in his glory days as a successful screenwriter, Perry had never actually met the man. The only time he'd come close was when one of his screenplays – a thriller called *Dead Tweet*, about a man who is able to exchange e-mails with the deceased – came tantalisingly close to being produced by Waddlevision Studios, only to be shelved when, according to his agent, Del Waddle baulked at the action star cast as the leading man, saying that the star, for all his on-screen exploits, was a 'pussy' in real life. Other than this, Perry knew little more about the billionaire than what the public knew: that with an unparalleled combination of business savvy and a knack for knowing what fantasies people wanted to see on their large and small screens, the young mogul, after inheriting a few radio stations from his father, had constructed a conglomerate so massive that it could only exist in an era in which the word 'monopoly' was used mainly to describe a board game. 'Vertically integrated' was the phrase now used to describe such awesome entities, and Waddlevision was the Everest of them all.

Waddlevision could take a simple children's fable, produce it as a movie, distribute it, merchandise it, spin it off into a theme-park attraction, a TV show, a Broadway musical and, finally, a movie based on the Broadway musical, all released with their own hit soundtrack albums and effusive critical praise as 'perfect family entertainment' by the newspapers, magazines and websites also owned by . . . Waddlevision.

But Waddlevision was only the beginning. Del had leveraged his outsized control over media into control over almost every aspect of American business. He owned airlines and Bolivian shirt factories, armament brokers and chains of preschools. As a result, he had a net worth of over forty billion dollars, which was more than the gross national product of most of the Earth's nations. But despite his mansions, fleet of private jets and liner-sized yacht with its own basketball court, Del went out of his way to portray himself in the media as 'just a regular guy who caught some breaks'. He had married his high-school sweetheart, given millions to charities and regularly held large benefit dinners at his various mansions. Newspapers (not just the ones he owned) were full of accounts of his philanthropy.

Today, Perry was on his way to a $10,000-a-plate dinner for one of Del's pet causes, the Little Greenies Foundation, an organisation devoted to educating children about the perils of global warming. Perry was using this function as a pretence to get close enough to the billionaire to ask for his help in saving the Earth. In so doing, he was about to give the famous media mogul his biggest audience of all time.

An hour earlier, while Perry shaved in a bathroom next to the underground dressing room, Marty Firth had explained to him that Edenites were fascinated by super-wealthy Earthles. They couldn't get enough of men who spent their lives acquiring vast, unspendable sums of money at the expense of other earthly pleasures and relationships, only to die and have that money mean nothing to them. Marty told Perry that he planned to use this fascination with pointless wealth to increase the audience of *Bunt to the Rescue*.

'You know that money is the only thing that makes a difference to most Earthles,' Marty had told him. 'And, after the debacle at St Jude's, you realise that inspiring the masses to become better people isn't enough without a real organisation behind you. Del Waddle can give you that organisation.'

Perry frowned. 'But he's already giving his money away. And I'm just going to sound crazy. Why should he give away more of it because a crazy man shows up at one of his benefits and tells him to?'

'Remember: you're on a mission,' Marty said. 'You're desperate. You'll do whatever it takes.' When Perry continued to stare at him blankly, Marty waved his hand. 'You're the star – you'll figure it out.'

Perry shook his head. 'I've known rich people. They really like hanging onto their money. That's why they're rich.'

Marty smiled the crinkly, eye-twinkling smile that Perry

had quickly come to loathe. 'No one ever said saving Earth was going to be easy.' He then excused himself to consult with other producers about 'setting up shots'. Perry took the opportunity to slip back into Amanda's dressing room. He needed to talk to someone about his misgivings. 'The upcoming episode', as Marty referred to it, seemed like a Sisyphean task at best. If Earth's survival depended on Perry making an effort to redeem the planet in the eyes of its viewers, there were certainly better ways to do it.

He found Amanda attempting to fasten a string of pearls around her neck and offered his help, which she gratefully accepted. Her initial enthusiasm for dressing up like an Earthle had subsided. 'I don't know why anyone would do this,' she said. 'Such a waste of time.' With the necklace in place, she turned and looked at Perry. 'So, what do you think?'

Perry had fallen in love with Amanda when she'd worn her blue Galaxy Entertainment jacket and no make-up. Now, seeing her in the evening gown, radiating the same effortless beauty on a much larger scale, he thought he'd pass out from blood rushing to places it didn't normally go, and certainly not in such volume.

'Not bad,' he managed to say, and was about to discuss his problems with the new mission when Marty entered.

'Your limo's ready,' he chirped. 'Come on, superstar. Let's go save the planet.'

* * *

Perry finally had his second cufflink in place when the limousine, which seemed nearly a block long, turned into a mansion-lined street and pulled up to an imposing wrought-iron gate. In the distance, he heard his driver talk into an intercom. After a few moments, the great gate opened soundlessly and the limo drove through.

Perry reached into the breast pocket of his jacket and removed an engraved invitation on thick creamy card stock that probably cost more to print than Perry spent annually on clothes. When Marty gave him the invitation, Perry had wondered how viewers were going to believe that a poor screenwriting teacher would be able to afford ten thousand dollars for a dinner when he'd just given all his money away.

'You had a retirement account with the Writers' Guild,' Marty said. 'We took it out of there.'

When Perry had protested, Marty cheerfully reminded him that retirement funds were now wishful thinking at best to the lead character in *Bunt to the Rescue*.

The limo continued driving through a landscape of trees and lush meadows with no house in sight. Just when Perry was convinced that they had somehow become lost in a wilderness area in the middle of Beverly Hills, a white mansion fronted with ionic columns and topped with gleaming solar panels came into view. The limo nosed its way into a bevy of other stretch limos that fanned out like shiny sticks of liquorice before the mansion's entrance. Perry thought that it was a good thing the partygoers were financing a foundation to educate children on global warming, since they clearly weren't up to it.

The driver opened Perry's door and he cautiously emerged, half expecting his flung-together outfit to fall apart when confronted by gravity. Miraculously, it stayed intact. Attempting to exude the air of someone who actually belonged at such an exclusive address, Perry nodded to his driver and walked from the limo.

'Tuck your shirt in.' Amanda's voice rang in his ear. He

noticed her standing with a group of other beautiful people by the mansion's entrance. She appeared strangely at home in the plush surroundings. He watched as she turned away from the group and opened her Louis Vuitton purse, releasing a small swarm of flies into the air. 'Don't look at me,' she said in his ear. 'Remember, you don't know me until we're back underground.'

Amanda and Marty had repeated this so many times that Perry thought he would scream: Amanda is your field producer, but you don't know Amanda. She's there to guide you through the episode but can't help you in any other way.

Perry tucked in his shirt while walking towards the front door. 'I'd be looking at you even if I didn't know you,' he muttered softly.

'And don't talk to me,' the voice in his ear said. 'What are the viewers supposed to think?'

'That I talk to myself,' Perry said. From the other side of the driveway, Amanda scowled at him. Perry smiled back at her and she turned away.

'Stop messing around and get in there,' she said. Perry showed his invitation to a woman with a clipboard standing at the door and walked between two huge bronze doors depicting scenes from the Old Testament. Perry recognised them as reproductions of 'The Gates of Paradise', the famous baptistery doors in Florence, and he wondered what Del Waddle did when he had a fight with his wife – there was definitely no way to slam these without heavy machinery.

Perry crossed the marble floor of a gaping entryway, pausing to navigate a busy ant trail of white-suited caterers dashing back and forth with shiny silver trays. He finally came to another set of double doors that opened onto a lawn so rich and lushly green in the dying afternoon light that Perry wanted to drop to the ground and hump it. A tastefully designed sign informed him that 'The grounds of the Waddle Estate are maintained with reclaimed water'. All around the green expanse were clusters of beautiful and immaculately dressed partygoers.

Perry perused the perfectly tanned and tucked faces of the saviours of Earth. Everywhere he turned his head he saw movie stars, studio heads, and A-list directors. If a bomb went off, Perry thought, Americans would have no choice but to start reading again. No writers, however. Even the most sought-after screenwriters weren't sought after for an event like this. At such a happy, carefree occasion, no one want to be reminded that they were all dependent on some greasy little computer jockey's imagination.

Seeing all these outstanding individuals in one place, Perry felt even more fraudulent than usual. To seemingly underscore this feeling, a few of the partygoers glanced over at Perry and quickly looked away. No one was faster than the Hollywood elite at telling who did and didn't belong.

Between the conversing partygoers frolicked laughing children of all ethnicities garbed in the official uniform of the Little Greenies: green cap, green neckerchief, and a T-shirt reading 'Save the Planet'. At one end of the perfect lawn, a group of pale and serious young men played acoustic music on a stage. Perry recognised them as a popular rock band that had just released its sixth consecutive platinum album. He couldn't fathom what it would cost to have them play at a party, let alone play softly.

He took a sparkling flute of champagne off a passing tray and sipped it. The vaporous elixir playfully tickled the back of his tongue and made him instantly happy. He realised that he'd probably never tasted real champagne before. As the soaring strains of another international hit emerged from the original artists and the Southern California light became even more golden, he surveyed the glowing glade before him, the bubbling fountains, the amazingly attractive, charming people, none of whom – women or men – Perry would throw out of bed, especially after his second sip of champagne.

And he realised that he was in deep, deep shit.

Who, standing in this beautiful preserve of the rich, would believe that the Earth was in real and immediate danger?

Perry snapped out of his reverie when a large bald caterer yanked the champagne flute out of his hand, scowled at him and strode off. He was about to protest when Amanda's voice purred in his ear. 'I told him to do that.' Perry turned and saw her in the distance walking towards the stage, her back to him. 'I told him you're a recovering alcoholic.' Perry started to speak. 'Again, no response is necessary. You're desperate and you're here on a mission, don't forget that. The group just to your right: there's your man.'

Perry turned to a nearby conversation cluster and saw, among several men in expensive suits and women in designer gowns, Del Waddle. Unlike the rest of his guests, Del wore jeans – the ultimate power statement at a gathering like this – a baseball cap from one of the teams he owned and a 'Save the Planet' T-shirt. He was tastefully unshaven and, in one arm, held an adorable young girl wearing a Greenies cap and neckerchief. Perry steeled himself and walked towards the group.

'Watch it, mister!' Perry looked down to see that he'd nearly stepped on one of the Greenie children, a boy playing in the grass with a ball painted to resemble the Earth.

'Sorry,' Perry said.

'Go fuck yourself,' the child said.

Perry realised that, peering up from under the green hat brim, was none other than Nick Pythagorus.

CHANNEL 20

THE PHILANTHROPIST

Inside a control room within the Galaxy Entertainment building on Ventura Boulevard, all hell was breaking loose. The Nakeeth director, his many eyes swivelling wildly, faced thirty-six monitors, many of which showed Nick Pythagorus confronting Perry Bunt. He yelled at the assistant director and oozed several pints of dark green liquid onto the control board. The assistant director, in turn, yelled at his technicians, who then yelled at each other.

In the middle of this chaos, the calm in the middle of the storm, sat Executive Executive Executive Producer Marty Firth, munching on a sliver of goat's-cheese quiche, which both he and Vermy were enjoying immensely. This was what live television was all about, Marty mused. These were the moments that made him feel truly worthwhile.

'Didn't we know this guy was loose?' the director shouted in a guttural voice, fixing Marty in the gaze of a dozen eyes. 'How is it that we didn't pick him up earlier? We only have 500 cameras pointed at this crapstand!'

Marty shrugged. Everyone in the company knew Nick had been fired, had shed his fly tattoo and jumped the grid. But this sort of thing happened all the time – you didn't shut down productions because some nine-year-old former executive was out there somewhere, nursing a vendetta.

'Don't worry about it,' Marty said. 'He'll be gone by the

time we come back from the commercial break. Amanda, can you take him out?'

At the Beverly Hills estate, Amanda was already trotting across the lawn towards Perry and Nick. She nodded discreetly. 'Good girl,' Marty said and returned with gusto to his quiche.

The latest episode of *Bunt to the Rescue* had been moving along fine until moments earlier, when a production scanner had picked up a 'casting irregularity' on the set. It took several seconds to identify the irregularity as a DFE – Disgruntled Former Employee.

With surprising frequency, DFEs 'went native', often divulging information to Earthles that caused shows to be cancelled or rescheduled. Sometimes their bitterness would lead them to establish communication with Leslie Satan and join The Movement, working to destroy the productions they once nurtured. Nick Pythagorus was now one of these.

Nick's fall had been precipitous, even by the standards of the intergalactic entertainment business. Before satellite cameras trained their lenses on Perry Bunt in St Jude's Shelter for the Displaced, Nick had been the wunderkind who would shepherd Earth to its ratings-grabbing ruination. But on hearing that his finale was being postponed for a second time, young Nick had lost it. While youth definitely had its advantages, self-control was not one of them. He had pitched a full-out tantrum on Marty Firth's desk, giving Marty no recourse but to fire him and send him back to the moon with a security escort. Nick, however, had quickly slipped the guards, removed all his tracking devices and used his knowledge of Channel Blue to elude detection.

Now standing at the party next to a surprised Perry Bunt, the fired executive knew he didn't have much time to do what he'd come for, but he loathed Perry so much that it was hard to resist a little abuse. 'You stupid Earthle sap. You have no idea what you're part of, do you? No idea.'

Perry stared down at the boy, unsure of how to react. *Was this part of the show?*

'This is not part of the show,' Amanda said into his ear. Perry could see her trotting quickly towards Nick's back, out of the boy's view. 'He's not supposed to be here. Walk around him and get to Del.' Perry tried to do as he was told, but Nick blocked his path.

'Your girlfriend's not being honest with you,' he said. 'We can wreck you if we want to because we made you.'

Perry frowned. 'What?'

Nick exhaled, exasperated. 'You writers are so damn stupid. I'm going to lay it out for you, OK? You and this whole planet are nothing more than—'

Amanda's left hand clamped down on his shoulder. 'Nicholas, you're being a very bad boy. You know it's nap time.' She pulled him away from Perry, but Nick dropped down, slipping from her grasp, and ran towards the house. Amanda followed him at a brisk trot. Perry watched her go, unsure of what to do.

'Go to Del,' her voice rang in his ear.

Perry remained where he was, watching Nick and Amanda disappear behind well-dressed guests. What was Nick trying to warn him about? What had he said? That Amanda was lying to him, that 'we made you'. What did it mean? Again, Amanda seemed to anticipate his thoughts. 'He's still upset because we ruined his plans for the finale. Now he's trying to ruin our show. Don't let him. Go to Del now.'

Perry took a deep breath, turned and walked towards the circle of partygoers that included Del Waddle. He found a gap between the casually dressed billionaire and a bearded man in a dinner jacket and gingerly wedged himself into it.

'It's really too much,' the bearded man was saying. 'I mean, he apparently really believes that aliens are going to destroy the Earth.' Perry froze. What the hell was going on? Did they already know who he was and why he was here? No one was looking at him, but maybe that was part of the show – to see how he'd react.

'What do they call it again?' asked a mean-faced older man.

'Buddyism,' said the bearded man. 'Apparently, their prophet is a homeless guy named Buddy who was taken away by the police and hasn't been seen since.'

The older man raised his champagne glass. 'God bless the LAPD for making more prophets than we know what to do with.'

The group laughed except for Perry. He warily took a slow step backwards when Amanda's voice came into his ear. 'Stay there,' she said. 'They're just talking about the religion you started. It's been in the local news. They have no idea you're Buddy.'

'I'm not Buddy,' Perry muttered under his breath. 'There is no Buddy.'

'Quiet. They're starting to look at you.'

Sure enough, the partygoers were casting sidelong glances in his direction. Perry smiled. 'Buddy, huh?' he said awkwardly. 'That's a good one. People sure are crazy.' The group stared at him, nonplussed.

Del shrugged. 'Well, if it gets people to do good, who cares what motivates them, right?'

'Oh come on, Del,' said an older woman with dozens of gold bracelets on one forearm that shimmered and clanged as she spoke. 'They're deluded! It's just another case of religion turning people into total idiots.'

'Opiate of the masses,' snorted the bearded man.

'More like the children's cough syrup of the masses,' the older woman said, and everyone laughed, including Perry, who probably laughed a little too hard in his effort to seem like one of the gang.

Del peered over at Perry and extended a hand. 'Del Waddle,' he said. 'I don't believe we've met.'

'We haven't,' Perry said, shaking his hand. 'Perry Bunt.'

'Welcome, Perry,' Del said.

Perry smiled nervously, his mind whirling through different approaches to becoming 'the crazy guest' at the party.

'This is your opening,' Amanda said in his ear. If there had been an earpiece or anything tangible in there, Perry would've torn it out and flung it to the ground. Unfortunately, he'd taken a pill back in the dressing room and had been stuck with Amanda's voice in his head ever since.

'Thanks for supporting Little Greenies.' Del gestured to the small girl in his arms. 'This is my daughter, Wynd.' 'Wynd' was pronounced 'Wind', and although Perry couldn't hear the 'y' in the girl's name, he knew enough about Hollywood to assume it was there.

'Hello, Wynd,' Perry said. 'Mr Waddle—'

'Del,' Del said. 'Please.'

'Del. I was wondering if I could have a quick word with you.'

'OK.'

'In private.'

'That would be great,' Del said, looking past Perry to someone more important at the party – namely, everyone. 'But I have a lot of guests to say hello to. Maybe later on.'

'I think you'll be interested,' Perry said. 'It's about saving the Earth.' The other guests exchanged glances – Perry's 'crazy guest' credentials had officially been presented. Del, however, seemed as composed as ever. He put his daughter down on the grass. She ran off, joining other children in chasing an actor dressed as an angry smokestack with a moustache. The smokestack, Captain Carbon, was an important teaching tool in the Little Greenies program.

Del watched the laughing children scamper away. 'Well, I guess I have to hear the rest now, right?'

Perry took a breath. 'This is going to sound crazy, but it's absolutely true.' He struggled to find the right words. 'The Earth is going to be destroyed in a matter of days unless we become better people – unless we help each other more than we've ever helped each other before.'

Several guests rolled their eyes. 'Hello security,' the woman with the bracelets said in a low voice. But Del didn't blink. 'I'm into that,' he said affably.

'Would you consider giving more of your money to charity?' Perry asked.

Del gave a folksy laugh. 'Well, Perry, do you know how much we're raising at this benefit? Three million dollars. And that's going to keep the Little Greenies in greenbacks for years to come.'

'I mean serious money,' Perry said. 'You have forty billion dollars. I know you give a lot to charity by normal standards, but come on. Three million? Thirty million? It's nothing to you. You've got houses, planes, boats, and none of them are going to do you any good if the Earth ends.'

The guests now openly glared at Perry. The bearded man stepped between Del and Perry, lowering his large head into Perry's face. 'What gives you the right to be so rude to our host?' he seethed with resplendent brie breath.

'Now, now,' Del said, pulling him away from Perry. 'Maybe

Perry's right. Maybe I don't give enough to charity. We should all give more, right?' The group nodded noncommittally. 'I'll definitely give it some thought, Perry. Thank you.' He patted Perry on the back and began to walk away. But Perry's hand darted out and grabbed the billionaire's arm. Del whirled around, stunned – no one had touched him like that since he'd acquired his first TV station.

No one was more surprised than Perry. He'd never been this aggressive with his most obnoxious student, much less the tenth richest man in the world. 'It has to be now,' Perry said. He dug the benefit invite out of his pocket. 'Look. I spent ten thousand dollars on your benefit today. That's 35 per cent of my annual income. Will you agree right now to give away 35 per cent of your income?' For the first time in their interaction, Del seemed speechless. He shook his head for a moment, then laughed.

'You know what?' he said. 'Let's do it.'

'Right now?' Perry said.

'Right now,' Del said. 'Follow me.' Del started off towards his mansion. The bearded man put a hand on Perry but Del waved him off saying, 'It's fine, it's fine.'

Perry followed the billionaire across the lawn through smiling faces that turned towards Del like flowers following the sun. Del opened a side door of the great house and gestured for Perry to enter.

Perry stepped into a vast room that defied easy classification. It appeared to be part study, part den and part games room, containing a billiard table, a widescreen TV, pinball machines and a kitchenette – in other words, it was a room that belonged to someone who had way too much money. As Del closed the door behind them, Perry studied the wall of vintage movie posters and noticed one for his favourite movie,

Casablanca. He turned back to Del, saying, 'Nice pos—' and this was all he could get out before a foot slammed into his stomach. He gasped for air and crumpled to the floor.

Del kicked off his sandals and pulled his shirt off, revealing a hairless, perfectly muscled torso, the product of a full-time staff that included nutritionists, dietitians, personal trainers, martial-arts instructors and cosmetic laser technicians. He met Perry's stunned look and said, still smiling, 'Get ready to die, bitch.'

CHANNEL 21

A VERY SPECIAL EPISODE

Perry was naïve about multi-billionaires. When Del Waddle seemed to respond to Perry's arguments for giving away his money and saving the world, Perry thought, with some vanity, that the rich man was in fact responding to his arguments. Amanda, however, was not so naïve. Having worked at Channel Blue for several years, during which she'd had ample time to study Earthle behaviour with some objectivity, she knew that Del was lying and became instantly concerned when he escorted Perry towards his house. She also noted that Del Waddle's security detail, a dozen hulking former Special Forces commandos squeezed into dinner jackets for the occasion, were now shadowing Del.

She gave up her pursuit of Nick Pythagorus and turned back to Perry, who she could see walking with Del across the great lawn, a hundred yards in front of her.

'Don't go into the house,' she said. 'Stay outside with the guests.' When Perry didn't stop walking, she chalked it up to his usual stubbornness. 'Stop!' she commanded with enough urgency for the man standing at the buffet to return a second piece of red velvet cake he'd slipped onto his plate. When Perry vanished inside the mansion with Del, Amanda trotted with urgency towards the entrance. 'Marty, what's going on? I've lost contact.'

Marty sat in the control room, stirring sugar into a vanilla latte. Vermy dangled from his ear, attracted to the sweet steam that in many ways reminded it of its human host. 'No reason for concern,' he said. 'I took you out of his head.'

Amanda stopped in mid-stride. 'What?'

'Yeah. We want him in the house.'

Amanda snapped on a pair of sunglasses. On the right lens she accessed the feed from inside the mansion, which showed Del kicking Perry in the stomach. In the left lens, Marty, with Vermy, stirred his coffee.

'This was not in the script,' Amanda said. 'We did not agree to violent content.'

Marty smiled. 'You're too close to the material. This is what our viewers want to see.' Amanda, on a hunch, manipulated the images in her right lens, quickly scanning through background material on Del Waddle. Because so many channels were broadcasting so much material on any given day, and no producer could possibly keep up with developments on all the different shows, Channel Blue maintained an extensive database on every Earthle. Amanda had been given the impression by Marty that this was Del Waddle's Channel Blue debut, but she quickly saw that this wasn't true. By examining the archives, she saw that he'd been featured in several shows, and what she saw made her accelerate her pace towards the house.

Marty watched her on one of the monitors. 'Calm down, Amanda. Check out the ratings right now. We just passed *Nebula Sluts*.' Amanda continued walking. 'Did you hear me? At this moment, we've got the number fifteen show in the entire galaxy.'

'You set him up,' Amanda muttered, pushing her way past well-heeled guests who stared at the glamorous woman in the sunglasses talking to herself.

Marty and Vermy shrugged in her right lens. 'We knew that it might be explosive, I'm not going to lie to you.'

'You already have,' Amanda said. 'He could die in there. What happens to the show then?'

'Anything could happen. But that's the way it is with Blue. Anyway, it's all been approved.'

This brought Amanda to a sudden halt. 'Since when?' she asked.

Marty licked his coffee stirrer. '*Bunt to the Rescue* is a mini-series, not a franchise.'

'You have no right to make that call.'

'I get paid to make that call, and right now, you're the only producer in the galaxy who thinks it has legs.'

Amanda stood still, fuming. Laughing party guests strolled by her.

Marty adopted a conciliatory tone. 'I'm sorry. I would've told you, but I didn't have time to deal with artistic differences.'

Amanda resumed walking towards the house. She pulled off her sunglasses, dropped them to the lawn and crushed them under one high heel. She pulled off one of her earrings and prepared to deal it the same fate.

'Don't do this, Manda,' the earring squawked in her hand. Marty's voice had an urgency she'd never heard, and she stopped inches from the entrance into which Del had led Perry. 'Seriously. You're a great kid with a lot of potential. If you go in there right now, it *will* be over. Not just the show, Channel Blue, and Earth – I'm talking about your entire career. Don't do it, honey. Don't throw everything away like this.'

* * *

Perry had been beaten up a few times since becoming a star on Channel Blue, but he now realised that those rough drubbings at the hands of street toughs, prisoners and the LAPD were completely amateurish compared to what was happening to him right now in Del's den. Perry did his best to run and dodge the blows Del rained down on him, but Del tracked him down mercilessly, cutting him off before he could get to the door or crawl under a table and beating him backwards. It seemed that everywhere he turned fists and feet rained down on him.

'Amanda!' he shouted. 'Amanda, I need some help here!'

This amused Del. 'Amanda, whoever she is, can't help you, Perry,' he said, landing another right hook that sent Perry sprawling over a water purifier. 'Nor can anyone else.'

Del had always pushed himself to excel in every field of endeavour. Since acquiring his first billion, he had devoted himself to a monk-like study of kicking ass. He'd flown to Thailand and lived in a hut in the jungle to train with masters of Muay Thai. He'd spent seven months in Brazil sleeping on the floor of a one-room concrete bungalow with a dozen swarthy men to learn the discipline of *ju-jitsu,* which inspired Ultimate Fighting. He regularly sparred with the greatest fighters in the world, flying them in and paying them thousands of dollars an hour to beat him – though, truth be told, not very hard. All these hours of training were now culminating in this magnificent moment, when such brutality, in Del's mind, was not only fully justified, but the only solution to the insult posed by Perry.

Between punches and kicks, Del embarked upon a running monologue to explain, in case there were any doubts, why Perry deserved this treatment. 'You come to my home and question my generosity? In front of my guests? In front of my *daughter*? And *grab my arm*?'

Perry tried to say 'I'm sorry,' but even these two short words did not seem to fit between blows.

'I am now showing you what having forty billion dollars means,' Del said. 'Do you know what it means?' Reeling from the last few punches to his head, it took Perry a moment to realise that his tormentor was awaiting a response. Del snapped a quick punch to Perry's jaw that sent sparks of pain down to his toes. 'I'm asking you: do you know what it means?' Perry shook his head. 'It means that later tonight, when you're found dead in a car at the bottom of a ravine off Mulholland Drive, no one will ask any questions.'

Perry moaned and clutched his jaw. Was this really part of the show? They couldn't have known. Why would they have set him up for this? Wasn't he the star of the show that was saving Earth? On the other hand, didn't they know everything? And hadn't Nick Pythagorus tried to warn him about something like this? What had he said? Perry's addled brain couldn't focus. 'Amanda!' he yelled.

The door opened and Perry turned hopefully. But the huge man in the dinner jacket who appeared in the doorway seemed to have no immediate interest in interrupting the proceedings. He stood impassively by the door until Del, catching his breath after another few punches, glanced over at him. 'Well?'

The man consulted a piece of paper that looked like a note card in his massive hand. 'Single,' he said. 'No connections with anyone important. Works part-time teaching at Encino Community College. Otherwise, he's an unemployed screenwriter.'

Del turned back to Perry and smiled. 'Even better,' he said. 'I might get a medal for killing you.' He pulled back a fist and advanced on Perry, who staggered backwards into a wall and sank against it, raising his arms over his face in what he recognised as a futile gesture. He closed his eyes, waiting for the blow to fall. Typical – here he was on his first hit show and it was already time for a Very Special Episode.

But no punch came.

Or . . . the punch had been so lethal, Perry hadn't felt it and was already dead. He opened his eyes and peeked around his upraised arms. Del still stood in front of him, but now his face was frozen in a terrible grimace. Standing behind the billionaire – and appearing strangely serene – was Amanda Mundo. She was pulling his arm straight back while planting one of her high-heeled shoes against the small of his back. Del suddenly howled with pain and collapsed onto the floor, where he lay motionless.

The dinner-jacketed man grabbed Amanda around the neck with an arm the size of a log – for a moment, she looked like a doll being toyed with by a giant. Her calm expression, however, didn't change. With blinding speed, she swung her right fist back and punched him square in the Adam's apple. He made a choking, gurgling sound and grabbed at his neck. She slipped from his grasp, bent her arm and lunged towards him in a precise, seemingly effortless movement, jamming her elbow into the centre of his ribs. His knees buckled and he sprawled onto the floor, moaning.

Perry still sat with his back against the wall. 'Remind me not to piss you off,' he said, slowly lowering his arms. Amanda saw his face and gasped. She pulled a handkerchief from the jacket pocket of the guard, who continued to writhe on the floor, like a fish flopping on a dock, and stepped over him to Perry. Dabbing some of the blood from his face, she leaned into him and whispered in his ear: 'Follow my lead.'

Unlike Marty Firth, Amanda believed that saving Perry's

life wasn't inconsistent with keeping *Bunt to the Rescue* on the air. She had a plan that would accomplish both. She wiped Perry's nose and said, in her regular voice, 'I recognised you at the party. You're Buddy, aren't you?'

Perry stared at her, mystified. Unfortunately for Amanda and her plan, she had whispered into the ear Del Waddle had boxed moments before with a deafening blow. All Perry could hear in that ear was a loud ringing sound.

'What?' he asked. 'What are you talking about?'

'I knew I had to save you,' Amanda continued, doing her best to prompt Perry with her eyes. 'I was at the park. I heard your teachings.'

Perry felt like his head might explode. 'Amanda, will you please tell me what's going on?'

Amanda gave him a low, swift kick in the shin. 'How do you know my name? We've never met before. You're Buddy and I'm one of your followers.'

Perry rubbed his shin as tears welled up in his eyes. 'Is this what's happening now? You're going to beat me up, too? Have you stopped producing the show? For the love of God, please tell me what's going on!' He whimpered pathetically.

Amanda sighed. 'I was pretending to be your follower,' she told him, dropping the ruse.

Perry was both relieved and confused. 'Why?'

'So the viewers wouldn't know who I was.'

Perry nodded, understanding at last. 'Are they still watching?'

'I hope so. But now, thanks to you, they know I'm a producer.'

'And that's bad?'

'Well, it's not good. The whole thing looks like a set-up. And our audiences hate set-ups.' Amanda smoothed back her hair, considering their options. From the floor, Del Waddle moaned in pain.

'Well, if we still have a show,' Perry said, 'I'd like you to teach me to fight.'

Amanda distractedly shook her head. 'No. Your inability to defend yourself is a huge part of your appeal.'

'How did you learn to do that?'

'We don't have any violence in our culture, which gives us an advantage in any sort of physical combat with Earthles. We can contain our emotions in order to apply the right technique at the right time. It's basically physics.' Perry's nose had begun bleeding again. Amanda handed him the guard's handkerchief. 'Are you OK, Mr Bunt?'

'I was much better five minutes ago. What took you so long?'

Amanda helped Perry to his feet. 'I had to make a very tough call. You know the parameters we're working with—'

'Screw your parameters! He was going to fucking kill me!'

'Maybe. But I just broke every rule in the Producers' Code by walking in here. We may not even have a show anymore.'

'I don't give a shit!' Perry flipped off the ceiling with both hands. 'Fuck you, you sick alien motherfuckers!' He gave Amanda the same benediction. 'And you too, for that matter.' He took a step towards her and nearly teetered over.

Amanda steadied him against the wall. 'I had no idea that Del was going to try to kill you.'

Perry regarded her sceptically. 'No idea,' he said. 'That runt Nick Pythagorous tried to warn me, but you had no idea. What kind of producer are you?'

A brief flush of irritation passed across Amanda's face. She took a bottle of water off a nearby table and noticed that the guard, groaning softly, had nearly succeeded in using the table to pull himself up off the floor. Amanda deftly plonked him over the head with the bottle, sending him back down. This time he lay in an inert state next to Del, who also showed no sign of consciousness. Amanda cracked open the water and handed it to Perry. 'Nick didn't know anything about this.'

'Really? Well, he also told me you weren't being completely honest with me, and based on the last few minutes, I'm inclined to agree.'

'Drink,' Amanda said. Once Perry had placed the water bottle to his bloodied lips, she continued. 'This may be hard for you to understand, but there are forces working against us, forces that will do anything to keep us from producing content. Nick has aligned himself with a renegade producer by the name of Leslie Satan. Satan heads up a group that exists to destabilise productions all over the galaxy called The Movement.'

Perry couldn't help laughing, even though it hurt in four different places. 'The Movement? Somebody named themselves The Movement? Satan's movement? Is that what we're talking about here? Let me guess: is it hot and evil?'

Amanda rolled her eyes. 'We don't have the concept of Satan that you have here on Earth. Or movements, for that matter.'

Perry stared at her. 'I almost died just now and instead of explaining to me what the fuck is going on, you're babbling gobbledygook about Satan and movements and—' The motion of Perry's lips suddenly ceased when Amanda strode forward and placed hers firmly on top of his. Because she was an inexperienced kisser, having experienced only two kisses previous to this one, this was much more awkward than she'd intended, and for a moment she found herself sucking on one of Perry's bloody nostrils before getting the correct lip-to-lip alignment.

Amanda would have preferred not to kiss Perry, but at this moment she felt like she had no choice. She knew that Marty Firth was right: as soon as she walked into Del's den, she was introducing a significant new element to *Bunt to the Rescue,* one that could destroy it. Even though Earthles were regularly manipulated by the producers of Channel Blue, the viewers didn't want to know about it. Like meat-eaters horrified by the spectre of the slaughterhouse, they wanted the illusion that their entertainment was pure and pristine, free of any real consequence or calculation.

Amanda knew that when she came to Perry's rescue, Marty would probably cut away to a car chase or dwarf-tossing or some other staple of the channel's programming. She also knew that Perry would ask a lot of questions that she couldn't adequately answer. Her only hope was to shock Marty and the channel's viewers into watching more and Perry into talking less. Thus, the kiss.

It was as unpleasant as she remembered: the bizarre mouth-on-mouth sensation, the unavoidable exchange of saliva, the breathing issue, the primordial ooze of darting tongues like single-celled sea creatures bumping in the dark. She did notice, however, that it was decidedly different being the kisser than the kissee. Just as grotesque, definitely, maybe even more so, but also more raw and – there was no other word to describe it – *fascinating.*

When she pulled back from him, Perry was stunned, his anger completely dissipated as if she'd sucked it right out of him.

'That's the third kiss,' he said.

'So?'

Perry smiled, but it hurt his cracked lips so he stopped. 'Earthle custom. You don't kiss someone three times that

197

you're not serious about. The third kiss means you're going to do something more.'

'Earthle customs,' Amanda mused. 'I also enjoy how you shake hands to show each other you're not carrying swords. And call the thirteenth floor the fourteenth floor. And say "Bless you" because an evil spirit might have crawled into your head when you sneezed.'

'Now you're just making us sound crazier than we are.'

'That would be impossible.'

The crackle of walkie-talkies came down the hallway. Amanda drew back the curtains from a picture window, picked up a footstool and shattered the large pane in an explosion of glass. She stepped casually over the jagged splinters into the backyard, turning back to Perry.

'Coming?' she asked.

Perry, his body aching with every motion, followed her out into the evening.

While most of the guests were gathered at the opposite end of the spacious lawn, a group of Little Greenies watched curiously as Perry and Amanda emerged through the broken window. The strains of another earnest international hit could be heard over the clinking of glasses and party chatter.

'Can you run?' Amanda asked Perry. He reluctantly nodded. He actually wasn't sure what would happen when he started moving quickly – whether his body would stay in one piece or collapse into parts. 'I think the closest wall is this way,' Amanda said, pointing to a large stand of oaks and pines next to the winding driveway.

'What about a car?' Perry asked, unconsciously leaning towards the driveway.

Amanda shook her head. 'Del has a small army, they'll be watching the limos. Our best bet is getting to the street.'

The hiss of walkie-talkies and urgent voices emerged from the house behind them. 'Now,' Amanda said. She kicked off her high heels and sprinted towards the trees. Perry did his best to follow, grimacing and holding one badly bruised arm close to his body as he ran.

Once they reached the trees, Perry staggered to a stop, bent over and put his hands on his knees, gasping for air. 'Jesus, I feel like shit.' His eyes adjusted to the darkness. Standing alert in her bare feet among the pine needles, her skin glowing in the moonlight, Amanda resembled some mythological goddess of the forest – all she needed was a garland in her hair and some fairy sidekicks. She watched a group of thugs in dinner jackets assemble in front of the broken window, pointing towards the woods and talking into their walkies.

'We have to keep going,' she said, tugging at Perry's arm. He reluctantly pulled himself up to standing and ran after her as she bounded like a gazelle through the trees. By contrast, he felt like a rusty old tank flattening a path through the scrub brush. They'd run another fifty yards before she stopped suddenly and cocked her head at an angle. 'What's that?'

Perry paused and heard the distant sound of excited barking.

'Dogs,' he said. 'Can you believe that? What a cliché. Del Waddle has storm troopers *and* guard dogs.'

Amanda wasn't amused. In fact, Perry saw a look he'd never seen on her face before. It was so unique to her self-assured features that it took him a moment to identify it. It was fear. Pure abject fear.

'Dogs?' she said in a faint, faraway voice. 'I didn't know he had dogs.'

'What's the big deal? Just work 'em over with some of your alien kung fu, and they'll be yipping all the way back to the kennel.'

Amanda shuddered and shook her head emphatically. 'I don't know anything about dogs. We don't have the genes for it.'

'The genes?'

'You all have pets, it's part of your over-identification with animals. We don't. No one's had any pets for hundreds of years. They're a huge waste of time and resources—' The fierce barking grew louder. Amanda swallowed. 'If I'd known he had dogs, I would've gone to the limos.'

'I thought you said we wouldn't make it.'

'Of course, we would have made it. I just thought a chase scene would be more interesting than getting into a car and driving away.' Perry blinked at her, dumbstruck. 'We have to do *something* to keep people watching! This talking *blah, blah, blah*—' Amanda moved one hand back and forth between them. '—is not interesting to *anyone*.'

'Well,' Perry said, 'getting torn apart by guard dogs might change that.' Even in the moonlight, he could see Amanda turn pale. They could now hear the panting of large carnivores racing towards them through the underbrush.

CHANNEL 22

WHAT EARTH STANDS FOR

Amanda was visibly shaking. She clung to Perry in a way that, despite the direness of the situation, he thought he could get used to.

'What are we going to do?' she said in a high voice that was nearly unrecognisable.

Perry had no idea, but for the first time since he walked into the control room of Galaxy Entertainment, he felt unafraid. Maybe it was Amanda's fear that had pushed him in the opposite direction. Maybe surviving so much head trauma in the last couple days had made him stupider. Whatever the reason, he found himself unusually calm as he listened to Del Waddle's approaching guard dogs.

'We can't outrun them,' he said. 'Look for a tree to climb.'

They looked around, but none of the trees had branches they could reach. Perry could now see dark forms approaching under the trees. 'German Shepherds,' he said. He'd researched attack dogs when he was hired to rewrite a B-movie entitled *Kickin' It Doggy Style*, which concerned an inner-city hip-hop artist who used a pack of dogs to get revenge on a drug gang.

'What are we going to do?' Amanda repeated hysterically, tugging at his jacket.

Four large German Shepherds broke into the clearing, growling ferociously and bounding towards them, the moonlight glinting off their jagged teeth. Amanda whimpered.

'Stand behind me,' Perry said. She scrambled around him, cowering. He planted his feet and held his right hand straight out, palm outstretched.

'*Sitz!*' he commanded in a gruff German accent. '*Bleib!*' The dogs froze in their tracks as if someone had yanked them on invisible leashes. After a moment of brief uncertainty, they sat. They studied Perry, panted and cocked their heads.

Amanda stood up from behind him. 'What just happened?'

Perry slowly lowered his hand. 'They sometimes train them in German. I just told them to sit and stay.'

Amanda smoothed her dress with one hand. 'Well,' she said, suddenly very matter-of-fact. 'We'd better keep going.'

Perry wasn't sure, but he thought this might be the closest Amanda Mundo had ever come to being embarrassed.

'After you,' he said. They continued running through the woods, leaving the dogs in a perfect stay behind them.

Minutes later, they came to the wrought-iron fence that encircled Del Waddle's estate. Perry had forgotten how tall it was, and he certainly hadn't remembered the sharp iron spearheads that lined the top. Even if he'd been perfectly healthy, he would have had trouble scaling it. In his present condition, with a torso that felt like a giant bruise and an arm that hung from his shoulder like an overcooked noodle, climbing it would be impossible.

He was about to tell Amanda this when he saw her leap halfway up, shimmy effortlessly to the top and, with a perfectly timed forward handspring, vault over the spearheads, landing perfectly on the other side. In the words of so many annoying gymnastics announcers, she'd stuck it.

'I can't climb,' Perry said. Amanda frowned at him through the bars. 'I'm too beat up.'

She looked both ways along the fence. 'There has to be

another way through,' she said, then took off, trotting along the fence towards the gate they'd driven through. Perry turned in the same direction, shadowing her.

They'd walked twenty feet when he heard what sounded like lawnmowers. 'They're here,' he whispered to Amanda. They turned and followed the fence in the opposite direction, scrambling urgently through the brush. When Perry slipped around a tree next to the fence, he came face to face with the muzzle of a gun.

Del Waddle stood unsteadily, like a man in pain. He pressed the barrel of a large handgun firmly into Perry's forehead.

'Amanda, run!' Perry yelled. Before Amanda could react, Del aimed the gun through the steel posts at her, freezing her in her tracks.

'Don't move, you witch . . . or whatever you are,' the billionaire barked. Two security men drove up on an all-terrain vehicle. In the moonlight, Perry could make out a bumper-sticker: THIS VEHICLE POWERED 100% BY THE SUN. One security guard shined a bright light into Perry's face. Squinting past it, Perry could barely make out Del Waddle cocking the gun aimed at Amanda.

'Well, Perry. Looks like you just got some company in that car crash off Mulholland,' Del said. The handgun went off with a loud pop and Perry yelped. He charged Del but there was suddenly nothing to charge – Del had collapsed to the ground.

'He's shot!' one of the guards yelled.

Perry looked over at Amanda, who remained standing on the other side of the fence, completely unfazed. 'Are you OK?' he asked. She nodded.

The two guards ran to Del, who lay moaning up against a tree. Perry climbed onto the idling solar-powered ATV and, pulling on one of the handles, drove away.

In moments, he had blazed a trail through the brush to the driveway. He turned onto the pavement and soon found himself at the front gate, which opened automatically. He accelerated through it. Amanda waited on the other side, standing nonchalantly as if she were waiting for the bus. She climbed on behind him and they took off, speeding past dark Beverly Hills mansions to the lights of Sunset Boulevard.

'What happened?' Perry shouted back to Amanda. 'He shot you!'

'When the bullet hit my shield, it must have ricocheted back into him.'

'Your shield?'

'Yeah,' Amanda said. 'Before my Earth assignment I produced this small planet near Rigel. It had a really weak atmosphere and there were constant meteorite showers. Every-one working there had shield chips implanted in their necks.'

'I don't understand.'

'A shield is a force field designed to repel any object that comes at you faster than a hundred miles an hour.' Amanda said this as if she were a little put out having to explain it. 'I meant to have the chip removed when I moved here, but I keep forgetting. Take a left on Sunset.'

'Where are we going?'

'Back to the station.'

Perry backed off the ATV's throttle. 'Is that such a good idea, considering they just tried to kill me?'

'We have to find out if we still have a show. And the truth is, they could kill you any time, if they wanted to.' Though Perry found this far from comforting, he turned left on Sunset Boulevard and sped past the bright lights of the Strip. Passers-by stopped and stared at the ATV driven by a bloody-faced man in an expensive suit.

They took Coldwater Canyon over the Hollywood Hills and pulled into a gas station across Ventura Boulevard from Galaxy Entertainment. The concrete building appeared suitably dark and foreboding. Amanda dismounted the ATV.

'I'll find out what I can,' she said. 'Lock yourself in the restroom and don't open the door until I call you.'

'I thought you said they could kill me at any time.'

'They can, but why make it easier for them?'

Perry smiled tightly. 'Good luck.'

Amanda nodded and stepped into the street. She turned back and said, 'You might want to wash your face while you're in there', before jaywalking barefoot across the boulevard, her flowing white dress flickering in the headlights. Cars honked their horns, but were unable to disrupt her sure and steady pace.

Perry watched until she was safely across and headed to the restrooms. He found the men's room locked and was about to go to the office for the key when the door opened and what appeared to be a dwarf in a black fedora exited the lavatory, pausing to hold the door open for him.

'Thank you,' Perry said.

'No problem,' the dwarf said. 'I hope you die in there.' Perry froze in his tracks. The dwarf peered up at him. Nick Pythagorus glared from beneath the hat's brim.

'Gotten a clue lately?' Nick asked. Perry could only gape at the boy executive. 'Jesus, you fucking POFs are so dense. Do I have to spell it out to you?' Nick sighed with great annoyance. 'OK, listen to me, you idiot writer. We made you. Your precious planet that you love so much, that you're dying to protect, is nothing more than a lousy amusement park. And everyone on it is nothing more than—' A helicopter suddenly hovered overhead, drowning out Nick's words.

'What?' Perry said.

'All of you!' Nick yelled. 'You're literally just a bunch of—' The roar grew louder. The wind from the helicopter's main rotor knocked Nick into Perry, and the boy grabbed onto one of Perry's pockets for balance. Perry looked up. The helicopter now seemed to be just a few feet overhead – he felt like his eardrums might explode. When he looked back down, Nick was gone. He spun round, but there was no trace of him. The helicopter rose back up into the air and flew away.

After a moment of feeling completely creeped out, Perry entered the restroom. He turned on the light and yelped in terror: a bloody, disfigured face stared back at him. It took him a moment to realise that it was his reflection. No wonder Amanda had suggested he wash. He turned the handle of the rusty hot water faucet and waited until the trickle of water was warm before gently splashing it onto his face.

He was drying his hands with a paper towel when he heard a car pull up outside the door.

'Open up!' It was Amanda's voice. Perry threw away the towel and stepped out of the restroom.

Amanda sat in the driver's seat of a Galaxy Entertainment service van. 'Get in,' she said. Perry couldn't help noticing that her manner was oddly gruff.

'What did you find out?' he asked.

'Nothing,' she said, annoyance lacing her voice. 'They wouldn't even let me past the lobby. I knew where the keys to the van pool were, so I picked this up.'

'What do we do?'

'I don't know, Mr Bunt. What do *you* want to do?'

'Go home and get some sleep.'

Amanda shrugged. 'Then get in.' Perry climbed into the

passenger side. While fastening his seat belt, he noticed that Amanda's feet were still shoeless.

'Nick Pythagorus paid me another visit,' he said.

Amanda didn't seem surprised by this. 'Yeah?'

'He told me that the Earth was just an amusement park.'

Amanda shook her head. 'He's lost his mind. It happens a lot to young executives. They have no experience with failure so the first time they lose, they completely self-destruct.'

'Then an odd thing happened.'

Amanda glanced over at him. 'Are you really waiting for me to ask?'

'He disappeared.'

'What do you mean?'

'He disappeared. A helicopter flew over, he grabbed me, and then he wasn't there anymore.'

Amanda shrugged. 'Well, maybe you should stop talking to him.'

'I really didn't have a chance to talk—'

'*Whatever*,' Amanda said. She started up the van and accelerated out of the gas station, taking a hard right onto Ventura Boulevard.

They drove in silence for a moment. *What the hell is wrong with her?* Perry thought, but said, 'What are you going to do now?'

Amanda's eyes remained on the road. 'I don't know, Mr Bunt. I don't seem to have a job anymore. Maybe I'll look for one while you get your beauty sleep.'

'Are you mad at me for some reason?'

'You say you want to save the world, then you change your mind and just want to sleep.'

'I haven't had a decent night's sleep in three days!'

'*Ooh, widdle baby needs his nappy-nap*,' Amanda spoke in

a disturbing singsong voice. 'Guess I chose wrong, huh? You don't have what it takes to save Earth. Maybe you never did.'

Perry's face flushed. 'What the hell's wrong with you?' he said. 'Why're you talking to me like this?'

Amanda didn't respond. Perry stared at the cold set of her features as she steered the van beneath a freeway overpass, pulled over to the curb, shifted into park and turned off the ignition. He looked around. He recognised this place. This was where Amanda parked his Ford Festiva before she revealed to him the workings of Channel Blue.

'Do you see any flies?' she asked. They searched the van. He shook his head. Amanda did one more inspection, then fixed her eyes on him and broke into a huge smile. 'We did it.'

Perry considered the possibility that the alien producer had gone completely insane. 'What?' he said guardedly.

'We're still on!' she shouted. Perry continued to stare at her. Amanda proceeded to talk unbelievably fast while tucking her hair behind her ears. 'I couldn't tell you, because they're still watching. It's bigger than ever. *Bunt to the Rescue* has won the last three time periods hands-down!' She giggled and took both of his hands in hers.

Perry wasn't sure what to think, but her joy was infectious. He found himself grinning back at her. 'Really?'

'Yes. When I walked into the station, they practically gave me a medal! They all said they'd been completely wrong about you and the show.' Amanda took a deep ebullient breath. 'Marty Firth came up to me and admitted – *to my face* – that killing you off for ratings was the biggest mistake of his career!'

'That was big of him,' Perry said, unimpressed.

'The viewers love you. And they love me. Isn't that incredible? I never dreamed of being on camera. And they love it, love it, *love it* when I'm mean to you. That's why I was just acting that way. They love that unresolved tension between us. Oh, Mr Bunt. It's so incredible. We've got a hit!' Amanda fell into Perry's arms and kissed him on the lips as if it were the most natural thing in the world. And, for that moment, it was – until she pulled herself away. 'We can't do that anymore,' she said. 'We need the unresolved tension.'

'Right,' Perry said, disappointed. They stared out of the windshield for a moment, then slammed together like the last two cars in a demolition derby, tumbling between the seats onto the metal floor of the van, their hands feverishly groping each other as if bare skin held the secret to eternal life.

If there was one thing that Perry hated writing, it was a sex scene. Like car chases, sex scenes were obligatory in Hollywood blockbusters. The audience expected that at some point the hero and heroine, naked but not too naked, would flail their perfectly toned and hairless torsos against each other. Which posed a question: in an age when limitless pornography of all dispositions is within a click away, how do you make a simulated sex act between two movie stars interesting? The answer was: you didn't. Everyone knew what was going to happen. The only thing you could do was make it quick – something Perry never had a problem with, in theory or in practice. In one script he'd written:

INT. BEDROOM – NIGHT
Tim and Veronica make passionate love.

Done! Let the movie stars hash out how much they will or will not show. Let the director figure out how to make their unoriginal mimicry of original sin interesting.

In Perry's reality, however, sex scenes were *never* obligatory.

If anything, they were the opposite: optional to the point of not existing at all. The frantic kissing and groping amongst discarded evening wear on the floor of the cable service van was no exception. He couldn't believe it was happening but also couldn't afford to doubt the reality of it: It was way too close to his fantasies for comfort.

Amanda broke off a long kiss with her hands still in his pants. 'And we definitely can't do this,' she said between hot breaths.

'Right,' Perry said, quivering in ecstasy.

They resumed their plunder of each other's bodies. Within moments, Amanda lay naked on the floor of the van with her legs wrapped around Perry, his pants bunched around his ankles.

Perry and Amanda made passionate love.

'*Especially* not this,' Amanda moaned.

'No, never,' Perry groaned.

'Because *nobody* does this,' Amanda yowled.

'Nobody!' Perry agreed, shouting at the top of his lungs. 'Nobody! No!'

'No! No!' Perry yelled as they feverishly gyrated against each other. 'No! No! *Nooooo*!' And with that last 'no', Perry Bunt offered the biggest 'yes' possible in the known universe. He launched his own DNA deep into the galaxy of cells known as Amanda Mundo, searching for life where no man had gone before.

Moments later, they sat panting on the floor of the van, sticky and naked, staring into space. The van's windows were fogged and the air inside more humid and foetid than a city park portable toilet in mid-summer. But Perry and Amanda were oblivious, lost in a post-orgasmic stupor.

For his part, Perry was mostly relieved. He'd spent the

frantic minutes of coitus pouring all his energy into a single thought: please don't come to your senses. To be with someone so beautiful, someone whom he'd thought about for so long seemed impossible; at any moment, he was certain she'd realise what she was doing and push him away. But miraculously, she hadn't.

Now what? Perry thought. He'd saved the Earth, become famous and made torrid love to the most beautiful woman in the universe. He'd never been so happy in his entire life. Still, he couldn't help thinking: *there has to be a catch.* Nothing this good ever happened to the characters in his screenplays. And if it did, it would be followed immediately by a sudden reversal. But nothing was reversing – or versing, for that matter. He was simply sitting naked in a van parked beneath a freeway overpass on Ventura Boulevard.

'So,' Perry said, breaking the silence. 'Do you think fornicating might make a comeback?' Amanda laughed. 'Come on. Better than the pills, right?'

'Different, that's for sure.' She peered down at her sweaty body as if it belonged to somebody else. 'I feel like I just rode a rusty bicycle through a swamp.'

Perry frowned. 'I have to say, that's pretty far down on the list of things I was hoping to hear.'

'I'm sorry, Mr Bunt, but you have to understand that this was absolutely the craziest thing I've ever done – and will ever do – in my entire life.'

'Again,' Perry said. 'Not anywhere near the top.'

'The sheer primitiveness of it!' Amanda shook her head. 'We were absolutely like two animals.'

'You're moving up the list,' Perry said.

He now had a chance to consider Amanda's body as something more than a blur of flesh. Unlike 90 per cent of humanity and 100 per cent of visitors to nude beaches, Amanda looked better with her clothes off than on. His eyes wandered around her phenomenal breasts, a gravity-bending combination of natural fullness and pertness that would cause any self-respecting Beverly Hills plastic surgeon to slit his own throat with a scalpel. And the ass! When she turned to gather her clothes, it was as if he was suddenly in the presence of a heavenly orb, an incredible clefted sphere of life-affirming roundness. Then he considered (very briefly) his own body, which from years of sitting at a computer had grown thick in the middle and spindly everywhere else. And really, was there anything quite as laughable in nature as the penis? In its current, nearly hairless state – courtesy of the decontaminating robots on the moon – it appeared even more ridiculous than usual, an odd worm with far too much skin. Or a tiny, faceless Shar-Pei puppy, without any of the cuteness. In any case, it wasn't pretty. He self-consciously grabbed his underwear, held it over his crotch, and gazed back on Amanda's smooth, flaw-less form. Maybe there was something to genetic engineering.

Amanda turned around and slipped her underwear up over her long legs, and he noticed something else. Two inches below her navel there was an indentation, a kind of second navel, except that it was an almost perfect perforation.

'Is that a scar?' he asked, then immediately regretted blurting out such a personal question. But Amanda didn't seem to mind.

'No. It's my shunt.'

'Your what?'

Amanda blinked. 'For elimination.'

Perry felt repulsed but tried to show concern. 'I'm sorry. Did you have some kind of surgery?'

She laughed. 'We all do. Everyone has one.'

Perry blinked. 'It comes out of there?'

'It's much cleaner and more efficient than the way you do it. Plus, we don't have to squat over our own excrement like filthy animals.'

Perry stared at Amanda as she slipped her dress over her head.

'You Edenites are too much. You look like humans, you act like humans. . .'

'Why would you say something like that?' Amanda snapped back, offended.

'You're like humans in every way except the way that matters. You're like humans who are so afraid of being animals that they've forgotten how to be human.'

'I have no idea what you're talking about.' Amanda smoothed her dress, glimpsing her reflection in the rear-view mirror. 'But if being human means fouling yourself every time you go to the bathroom, then who would want to be that? Put your clothes on, I should get you home.'

Perry unfurled the underwear he held over his crotch and slipped them on. 'I'm afraid to ask,' he said, 'but what's the next episode?'

'I don't know. They were still working on the script.'

'Great,' Perry said. 'I'll probably be asking Mike Tyson to help me save the world.'

Amanda laughed and slipped into the driver's seat. 'I doubt it,' she said. 'You're now very valuable to the channel. They won't make the mistake of risking your life again.'

Perry stood up and, crouching to avoid the roof of the van, stepped over to where his pants lay in a tangled heap. 'Isn't it going to be weird when your viewers see the van drive out from under the freeway a half hour after it went under in the first place?' He picked up the pants and there was a sharp clink of metal as something fell out of one of the pockets onto the floor.

'They'll make an edit back at the station,' Amanda said. 'We've got a delay because of transmission time. No one will know the difference.'

Perry spotted a small, inscribed gold plaque glinting up from the van's floor. He remembered Nick Pythagorus at the gas station, grabbing his pocket as the helicopter descended. Perry picked up the plaque and read it.

532ND ORBY AWARDS
BEST SENSELESS VIOLENCE
NICK PYTHAGORUS
PRODUCTION EXECUTIVE IN CHARGE OF
EXECUTIVE PRODUCTION ENTERTAINMENT AND
RECREATIONAL TERRESTRIAL HABITAT

He read the last line twice before it hit him. 'Earth,' he muttered to himself.

The insane ravings of Nick Pythagorus suddenly made complete sense.

They'd made us.

CHANNEL 23

BREAKING CONTINUITY

Perry gaped at the small plaque in his hand, unable to move.

'Come on, let's go,' Amanda called from the driver's seat. She turned over the ignition and started the van. In a daze, Perry shuffled to the passenger seat. She glanced over. 'You forgot to pull up your pants,' she said.

He stared at her. 'When were you going to tell me?'

'I just noticed it now.'

'Not my pants. Earth. When were you going to tell me what it was?' He reached out and dropped the plaque on the dashboard in front of her.

Amanda turned off the ignition.

'Were you ever going to tell me?' Perry asked.

She gazed out the windshield. 'I don't know. Probably not. I thought about it. I really did. But you already have so much on your mind, I thought it was better if you didn't know everything.'

'Start talking.'

Amanda furrowed her brow. 'There's no point,' she said. 'It won't change anything and you won't like it.'

'I don't care!' Perry barked, surprised at his own ferocity. 'I want you to tell me everything. Right now.' He picked up the plaque. '"Entertainment and Recreational Terrestrial Habitat." How long have you people been here?' Amanda looked away. 'Did Galaxy Entertainment create the Earth?' She shook her head. 'Then who did?'

'Please, Mr Bunt,' Amanda said. 'Don't make me.' Perry opened the door of the van and stepped onto the sidewalk. 'Gerald O. Davidoff,' she blurted.

Perry pulled his legs back in and closed the door. 'And who the hell is Gerald O. Davidoff?'

'He was a travel agent.'

Perry sighed. 'This is not getting any clearer.'

'He was leading a tour of the western galaxy and discovered it.'

'What?'

'What do you think? Earth. There was basically nothing here. A few animals, some primitives. The dinosaur bones and ruins of some ancient civilisations were what brought in the tourists originally – along with the beaches, of course. Then the re-enactors found out about it.'

'The who?'

'Re-enactors. Civil War buffs. They liked it because it had geographical features very similar to Eden at the time of the Civil War.'

'You had a Civil War, too?'

Amanda shook her head. 'No. We had *the* Civil War. Yours was a re-enactment.'

Perry blinked. 'Our Civil War never happened?'

'It did, in a way. Over and over again. The re-enactments became so elaborate, in fact, that Davidoff brought in thousands of actors to fill out the world, as well as plants and animals to make it look more like Eden. He also re-created other eras from Eden's barbaric past: Renaissance Land in Europe, Pharaoh Park in the Middle East, Samurai City in Japan. Tourists loved them all. Everything was incredibly popular and he kept expanding. Before long, the northern hemisphere was filled with theme parks. The rest became hunting preserves and beach resorts.'

'Wait a second,' Perry said. 'How long ago was this?'

Amanda frowned. 'When the Civil War happened. You know when that was, right?'

Perry rubbed his face. 'This doesn't make any sense. What about the thousands of years before that? What about *history*?'

Amanda shrugged. 'Your history is our history. I mean, there were a few Stone Age tribes scattered around when the first ships arrived, but nothing really to speak of.'

'What happened to them?'

'They were given jobs working at the theme parks. Believe me, they were happy to get out of the dirt.'

Perry clamped both hands on his head to keep it from exploding. 'So everyone on Earth is . . . *descended from theme-park workers?*'

'You're getting ahead of yourself. I told you this wasn't worth getting into.'

'Keep talking.'

Amanda sighed and fiddled with a lock of her hair. 'Galaxy Entertainment came in and started broadcasting the Civil War battles and the ratings were good. Good enough that Galaxy hired Gerald O. Davidoff as a programming executive and turned the planet into a studio. They surrounded it with cameras, filled it with flies and towed in the moon from the asteroid belt as a reflector.'

'What?'

'They needed more light for night shoots. That was the beginning of Channel Blue. But it wasn't anything like it is today. It was still, for all intents and purposes, a historical re-enactment channel. Decent ratings, but very limited in its way.' Amanda took a breath. She seemed to be warming to her story. 'What changed everything was when the actors went on strike. They were still being paid as theme-park employees and demanded to be upgraded to a television rate. Plus, they all had to live down here and you know what that's like. Less than ideal. But Davidoff and Galaxy decided they couldn't pay actors scale and still make a profit, so they replaced them all with POFs.'

Perry regarded Amanda. 'You're going to tell me what that is, right?'

'Products of fornication. Genetic programming has been around for a thousand years, but there have always been Edenites who fall through the cracks – as it were. Mostly criminals and lunatics. So Davidoff rounded up POFs from all over the galaxy, shipped them here, and reprogrammed their memories so that they would believe they'd lived on this planet all their lives. At first it was a complete disaster: these were psychos and sociopaths, after all. They wouldn't take direction or follow a script. The Civil War re-enactments were disastrous – the POFs refused to do anything the same way twice. Ratings plummeted, tourists stopped coming, and Earth started losing money. Davidoff figured he had nothing to lose, so he fired his directors and cut the POFs loose from the script to see what would happen.' Amanda's eyes sparkled. 'It turned out to be the greatest decision in broadcasting history. The Civil War became bloodier than anyone thought possible and the ratings went through the roof. But that was just the beginning: The planet was suddenly filled with crazy violence, assassinations and fornication – *lots* of fornication. And wars! The Austro-Prussian War, the Franco-Prussian War, the Russian-Turk War, the Anglo-Zulu War, the Sino-French War, the Russian-Circassian War—'

'I get it,' Perry said. 'A lot of wars.'

'And that was just in our *first three seasons* on the air!'

'Let me get this straight,' Perry said. He was trying his best to stay calm. 'Everyone on Earth—' He took a breath and started again. 'You're saying that we're all murderers and lunatics?'

'Don't be silly,' Amanda said. 'You're all the *descendants* of murderers and lunatics.'

'*All* of us?'

Amanda nodded. 'Is that so weird? You read the news. You didn't think people normally behaved like they do here, did you? The World Wars, the genocide, the massacres, the random killings – more mayhem and violence every day than 3000 channels can show.' She shook her head in awe. 'It's been a history totally different from ours. Our Civil War was a lesson to us, the beginning of a new era in which we learned to channel our aggression into the pursuit of a balanced civilisation. Your history—' Amanda gazed at Ventura Boulevard, her eyes filled with awe. 'It's a history no one could have imagined. Terrible and shocking, beautiful in moments, but mostly tragic and *always* compelling.'

Perry stared numbly out of the window, his face frozen in a shell-shocked grimace. His mind whirled, struggling to process the onslaught of disturbing information. The Earth was only 150 years old, a theme park that had been turned over to maniacs – thirty-two of which were his great-great-great grandparents. *No*, he thought, *it can't be true.* And yet, why would she make something like this up? What was her motivation? Why lie to him now? He'd forced her to tell him. Unless . . . it had all been arranged this way. Unless this was just another part of the show. No. It couldn't be. He knew them well enough to know they wouldn't like this.

Yes, he was being tortured and they loved that, but they liked their torture on the outside where their flies and satellites could see it. To the galaxy, this was just dead air.

They made us.

It explained a lot, actually. Now he understood why Galaxy Entertainment was so cavalier in its decision to destroy Earth. They considered it *theirs*, after all. Perry had seen enough of his screenplays decimated by the whimsical notions of studio executives to know that there was nothing pretty about being owned. They owned your script and could do whatever they wanted to it. Why should owning your planet be any different?

It also explained the contempt that Amanda and the other executives had evinced for Earth's inhabitants, the 'Earthles'. To them, he and his fellow criminal lunatics would always be something less than human. And if Earth's own tortured (and short) history had shown anything, it was that this superior attitude was a slippery slope towards mass murder.

Finally, it explained the bizarre hoops he'd been forced to jump through. With a sinking feeling in his stomach, Perry realised that *Bunt to the Rescue* was at best a Sisyphean exercise. A show, even a hit show, would never be more than a postponement of the inevitable. As long as Earth was the property of Galaxy Entertainment, its end was only a few lost ratings points away. It is possible to hold a loaded gun to someone's head and not kill them; but if you keep it there, eventually you will.

Amanda studied the hardening expression on Perry's face. 'I know this can't be easy to hear—'

Perry spat out a derisive laugh. 'Oh no. It's fine. I mean, if the planet has to be owned by someone, at least we're in good hands. It's not like we're being threatened with annihilation by a bunch of aliens who have destroyed hundreds of other planets just like ours.'

Amanda shook her head. 'It's not like that. All of us who care about Earth know that a planet like this happens once in millennia. You could put POFs on every habitable world in the galaxy and never reproduce what happened here. It's magic, pure magic – that's the only way to describe it. You can't wreck it all for short-term gain.'

'Yeah,' Perry said. 'Why blow it up before we can do it to ourselves, right? Wouldn't that defeat the purpose of the whole exercise? Because we will do it. You know we will, don't you?'

Amanda squinted at Perry, trying to read his attitude. 'You're being ironic.'

'Am I?'

'I think I may have more faith in your planet than you do.'

'Oh really? That's rich. Honestly. That is beautiful.' Perry's mouth twisted into a sneer. 'You talk about how sick we are. But this is all you, isn't it? This is all part of *your* "balanced civilisation". Nice balance. You get perfect genes, thousands of channels and orgasm pills. We get suffering, murder and death.'

'I can't go into our entire history right now,' Amanda said, 'but you have to understand that planets like Earth are the reason we survive.'

'Then you shouldn't,' Perry snapped back. 'Jesus – don't you see? *You're* the ones who are sick.'

Concern flickered across Amanda's face. 'Mr Bunt, you have to believe me when I say I have always been the biggest fan of Earth and its people, ever since I was a small child. I mean, I had posters of it on my wall.' She took Perry's hand in her own and smiled. 'How else can you explain what just happened here?'

Perry gazed at the woman sitting across from him. Only

moments before he had held her in his arms and had felt that he knew her. Now he realised he never would. He pulled his hand away.

'That's easy. I thought I was in love with you. Though you probably don't understand that. I'm sure that "love" is one of those terrible animal traits that got left on the laboratory floor.'

Tears filled Amanda's eyes. 'It isn't,' she said, 'though right now I wish it was.'

Perry opened the door and stepped out of the van. His feet touched the cracked sidewalk and he started walking, his steps echoing off the overpass. It felt good to be out in the air. That's something he never thought he'd feel in Los Angeles. He heard her clamber out the door, her feet following him down the sidewalk.

'Don't do this,' she called after him. 'Mr Bunt, I'm on your side.'

Perry kept walking.

'Perry!'

The shock of hearing his first name from her lips caused him to stop.

'If they see you walk out from under the freeway, they can't edit it. One shot will be us together in the van, the next will be you walking alone. You're breaking continuity.'

Perry smiled ruefully. 'Exactly.'

Amanda stepped backwards, as if the wind had been momentarily knocked out of her. She steadied herself. 'You're killing the show?'

'What a shame,' Perry said. 'Your big hit. Your on-air debut.'

Amanda's pale face flushed with hurt and anger. 'It's not about that.'

'I'm sure you'll be able to find yourself another monkey to torture.'

'You're the only one who can stop the finale!'

Perry kicked a loose chunk of concrete from the sidewalk into the gutter. 'If what you've told me is true,' he said, 'the world needs to be taken out of its misery.' He walked away, and this time she didn't try to stop him.

CHANNEL 24

DEAD AIR

It took Perry more than an hour to make it back to his apartment building on foot. As he walked, yahoos in passing cars yelled unintelligible things at him. He'd found this to be a peril of being a pedestrian in Los Angeles – so few people walked, especially at night, that they became deserving of taunts. Granted, he was wearing a bloody, rumpled Armani suit, which probably didn't do much to reduce the freak factor.

He arrived at his street and hiked up the steep grade from Ventura Boulevard to the Wellington Arms. He paused halfway to gaze out at the giant round light reflector in the sky – tonight at its full intensity – and the shimmering lights of all the fornicators below, spread out in an endless sprawl towards the horizon. All of them were doing whatever they needed to do to get ready for sleep and another day of entertaining their alien overlords, all of them no less pitiable than advanced Alzheimer's patients, completely ignorant of who they really were and the imminence of death.

Those alien bastards, Perry thought. *Those monstrous shit-fearing fuckphobic freaks.* He took some small satisfaction in knowing that by walking off when he did, he had created a terrible story problem for the producers of Channel Blue. One moment, he and Amanda were driving along Ventura Boulevard; the next, Perry was walking alone along the sidewalk. Because the decisive moment of *Bunt to the Rescue* had occurred beneath a freeway overpass in a flyless van, no viewer would ever understand what had happened. And in television, even the television of the future, incomprehension was death.

Perry found his apartment much the same as he had left it. It appeared as if a rodent, probably a squirrel, had slipped in through the broken window and taken a few bites of the cheeseburger he'd left on the table. But that was it. His possessions, his worthless possessions, were all present and intact. He picked up the shotgun and opened the chamber. There was still a shell in it. He laughed, remembering his lame plan to stop the world's destruction by shooting up an office building.

Why had he ever cared about the world anyway? What was it to him? It had served only as a stage for his humiliation. Not only his, but that of everyone around him. That's how it had been set up. The dice were loaded, which is why Earth's residents kept rolling snake eyes. A planet of suckers.

He opened a bag of chips and noticed a few flies buzzing around. *No way*, he thought. He found another empty jar in the kitchen and methodically trapped all of them. Sure enough, metallic blue glinted from their thoraxes. Of course they weren't giving up. Hit shows came along once in a blue moon; they were going to do everything they could to keep *Bunt to the Rescue* on the air, even if it no longer made sense.

What the hell? Perry thought. *The audience is out there, waiting. Give 'em what they want.*

Perry raised the jar up to his face. The flies immediately ceased their fidgeting and pivoted so that Perry stared straight into their compound eyes. He cleared his throat and smiled.

'Hello, alien masters, and welcome back to *Bunt to the*

Rescue,' he intoned, adopting a deep announcer's voice. 'Here's what you missed while Perry Bunt was fornicating with Amanda Mundo under the freeway. Yes, that's right. A dirty, lowly, stupid Earthle sexing up his producer. Sorry you missed it? I'm sure you are. Because you love the fornication, don't you? Almost as much as you love the killing. Because your pathetic sterile civilisation has wiped out anything that was vaguely pleasurable about being alive.'

Perry knocked a cigarette out of the pack of Camel Lights, lit it on a gas burner and took a deep drag. Damn, it felt good. Why had he ever stopped smoking?

'Anyway, Amanda and I fornicated. Did I mention that already? And it was fantastic. And after we fornicated fantastically, there occurred something that we call in the screenwriting business a "major reversal". I learned that this whole planet is nothing more than a glass bowl stocked with insane goldfish for your amusement. You might have trouble understanding this, seeing how you've always thought of me as something less than human, but I found this news very disturbing. For many reasons. Not the least of which was the fact I thought I was in love with a woman who believes this depraved experiment is justified.'

He took another drag on the cigarette. 'But I digress. Where was I? Right. After the fornication and the discovery of this disturbing news, Amanda and I had an argument – no physical violence, so I don't think you would've been interested – and I quit the show. That's right. I will no longer be rescuing your—' Perry took another drag, recalling the exact words. 'Entertainment And Recreational Terrestrial Habitat. So go ahead and blow it up. In fact, if I could, I'd do it for you, as long as I could take every one of you with me.'

Perry hunched in close to the jar, cigarette smoke fogging

the glass. It might have been his imagination, but he thought
he saw the flies take tiny steps backward. 'Because if there
were any justice to this universe, you would each die a
horrible, painful, lingering death. Nick Pythagorus, if you're
watching, thank you for the plaque, but you should be playing
with toys, not planets. Nine years old or not, I'd love to kick
you in your smirky little face right now. Marty Firth, you
no-talent brown-nosing hack, I'll kill myself on the air if you
let me take your Orbys and shove them one at a time up
your ass. You're the real parasite – that white thing in your
ear should have *you* removed. Elvis, I was happier when you
were dead, you fat freak. You don't cancel me, OK? I'm
cancelling you! And I never got a chance to tell you: I hate
your music. You sound like a drunk hillbilly with the hiccups.
As for your entire so-called "advanced civilisation"—' Perry
glanced down at the flies.

They lay on their backs, legs in the air.

He'd been officially pre-empted.

Perry unscrewed the lid and poked at the motionless flies
with a chopstick, but they were unquestionably victims of
dead air. He poured them down the garbage disposal and
made his way to the bathroom, where he peeled off his filthy
suit and took a shower, moaning as the water came into
contact with his battered body. He dried off, put on whatever
clean clothes he could find, ate another bag of chips and
collapsed onto the fold-out bed.

He woke the next morning to the sound of his ringing
phone. It took him a while to realise that he was back home.
His first sensation was relief. This lasted for about two
seconds before he remembered what Earth stood for. The
ringing continued. He groaned and put a pillow over his
head until it stopped. Unable to fall back asleep, he slowly

sat up, feeling every bruise. The phone began ringing again. Exasperated, he picked it up.

'What?' he demanded.

'Perry,' a female voice said. 'Perry, do you have any idea how long I've been trying to get a hold of you?'

'Who is this?'

There was a stunned silence on the other end of the line, the silence of someone completely unused to their voice being unrecognised. 'It's Dana. Fulcher.'

'Oh.' Perry hadn't recognised his agent's voice simply because she never called him directly. The irony that it took the end of the world for his agent to call him was not lost on Perry. 'What do you want?'

'Where've you been?'

'Busy.'

'We didn't know what happened to you. We thought you might have run off and joined Buddy.'

Perry was sure he'd misheard. 'Who?'

'Buddy. The leader of the new cult all the crazies are joining? It's all over the internet.'

'I haven't been on-line lately.'

'Perry, you've got to tell me what's going on. Are you with another agency?'

'No.'

'Then why haven't you taken my calls?'

'Because I don't have the time.'

'I've got an offer for your pitch.'

'My pitch?'

'*The Last Day of School.*'

Perry couldn't help laughing. He couldn't believe he'd ever made a living thinking up such dumb ideas. 'Thank you, but I'm not interested.'

For a rare moment, Dana Fulcher was stunned into silence. 'Not interested?'

'No. You were right. It was desperate.'

Perry could almost hear the gears turning as his agent tried to comprehend words she'd never heard from a writer's lips. 'Well, I have some other news: *Dead Tweet* is back.'

Perry frowned. '*Dead Tweet* is dead. Del Waddle killed it.'

'Del Waddle's the one who's dead. Car crash. They found him off Mulholland Drive.' Perry's mind whirled. The bullet that bounced off of Amanda's force field must have killed him. And since no one would've wanted to explain how the billionaire shot himself while trying to kill two of his party guests, they faked up a crash.

'Huh,' Perry said.

'Very tragic, of course. But with every ending is a new beginning, circle of life, you know, *hakuna matata* and all that.' Dana paused for maximum dramatic effect. 'I'm putting *Tweet* back in play.' When Perry didn't respond, she continued confidently, 'Del was the only one standing in its way – everyone else over there *loved* the project. I'm getting you in the room with the VP of Development tomorrow.'

'Don't bother,' Perry said.

Dana emitted a guffaw of disbelief. 'Perry, I've been literally killing myself to make this happen.'

Normally, Perry would've let his agent have her 'literally'. But today was different. 'No, you haven't.'

'What?'

'If you were literally killing yourself, you'd be dead.'

Dana Fulcher clucked her tongue. 'Perry, I know what "literally" means.'

'No. You literally don't. But I'll give you an example: I am literally hanging up.' He hung up the phone and, with one

smooth jerk, yanked the cord out of the wall. It felt so good
he couldn't believe he hadn't done it years ago. His cell phone
began ringing, vibrating itself across the kitchen counter. Perry
picked it up, walked out to his balcony, and threw it as hard
as he could. He thought maybe he heard it shatter on the roof
of the house below, but he couldn't be sure.

Since his kitchen was nearly empty and he was famished,
he drove the Festiva to his local diner and gorged himself on
eggs, bacon, pancakes and black coffee. A few dozen other
descendants of criminals and lunatics were packed into the
booths and tables around him. A television in the corner had
the sound turned off, and showed the grim visage of the
anchor of the evening news. You knew something was
seriously fucked up when the evening guy was on in the
morning. Sure enough, the chyron below him read: 'Middle
East Peace Talks Cancelled'. Perry sipped his coffee. Channel
Blue's producers had called off the computer virus, thus
putting the conflict that would thankfully never be known
as 'The Stripper Pen War' back on track. It would never be
known as that, of course, because no one on Earth would be
left alive to write about it.

How did he want to spend his last couple of weeks alive?
Perry considered this question. By different paths, he kept
arriving back at the same answer: with Amanda. Despite
everything, he couldn't escape the memory of holding her
on the floor of the cable service van. And the tears in her
eyes when he'd left. *Dear God*, he thought. *I'm like a Jew
in love with Eva Braun*. He shook his head. It could be
worse. If the world wasn't ending, he'd torture himself like
this for years.

He was signalling the waiter for his bill when a beautiful,
blue-eyed brunette approached his table. Though stylishly

dressed, her eyes were swollen as if she'd been crying and there was a red welt on the right side of her jaw. 'Perry Bunt?'

'Yeah?'

'Hi. You probably don't remember me.'

Perry stared at her. 'I'm sure that I would.'

'We met at a premiere party for a film I produced a couple years ago. I'm Cheyenne Ross.' She extended her hand. Perry stood and shook it. 'Just wanted to say hello. I mean, you seemed like a nice guy then and—' She smiled, embarrassed. 'Wow. This is awkward.'

Perry, having no memory of this woman, was at a loss as to what to say. 'No, it's fine,' he finally said, feeling incredibly lame.

Cheyenne stared at him and her considerable lips began trembling. Tears welled up in her eyes and she smeared them across her chiselled cheekbones with one hand. 'I'm so sorry,' she said.

Perry stood frozen. How had he become the guy that made beautiful women cry? He picked up a napkin from the table and handed it to her. 'Are you OK?' he said.

She shook her head. 'I just had a huge fight in the parking lot with my boyfriend,' she sobbed. 'He hit me.'

'Jesus,' Perry said.

'I don't know where to go,' she said. 'I came in here and saw you. I just know I don't want to be out there.' She wept openly. Diners at the other tables glanced over.

Perry put a hand on her back. 'Please, sit down,' he said. He guided her into his booth. 'Do you want me to call the police?'

Cheyenne shook her head. 'No,' she said. 'Is your car parked on the street?'

Perry nodded.

'Could you give me a ride home?'

'Of course.'

Cheyenne broke into a breathtaking smile and took one of Perry's hands in both of hers. 'Thank you so much,' she said. 'My hero.'

Perry's smile faded away. He suddenly turned Cheyenne's left hand to one side and pushed up the sleeve of her suit jacket. A blue fly tattoo peeked out from behind her cuff. He released her hand. 'You're a producer, all right,' he said.

Classic move, Perry thought. Entertainment executives look upon creative enterprise as nothing more than machinery – a collection of interchangeable parts that, when assembled properly, generated money. So it followed that the overseers of Channel Blue had assumed that all they needed to do was replace one pretty producer sidekick with a new one and *Bunt to the Rescue* could pick up where it had left off.

Cheyenne stared steadily back at Perry, her tears gone. 'What gave me away?'

'You had me until the hero line. That was terrible. Amanda didn't feed you that, did she?'

Cheyenne shook her head. 'Amanda's not on the show anymore.'

Perry did his best to appear uninterested. Cheyenne moved closer to him – which Perry, despite himself, found titillating – and whispered with sweet warm breath into his ear. 'Come on. Why not play along for a bit?'

Perry shook his head. 'Forget it.'

Cheyenne smiled. 'You can't blame us for trying, can you? *Bunt to the Rescue* is huge.'

'I'll say this one more time,' Perry said in a low, even voice. 'I'm not rescuing you, or the Earth, or anyone else for the entertainment of a bunch of monsters out in space.' He suddenly became aware that the other diners were glaring at him. He picked up the bill and started towards the till. Cheyenne put one hand on his arm.

'They want you. They want to watch you help people and save the planet. Why turn your back on that?'

Perry considered this. It wasn't a bad question. 'I guess maybe because none of it's real.'

'Real?' Cheyenne laughed. 'Are you serious? You're a writer. Since when did you care about reality?'

'Since I realised how hard it is to come by.'

'Please.' Cheyenne brushed back hair from her forehead and froze Perry with her piercing blue eyes. 'I want to work with you, Mr Bunt. Give it another chance. Let's save the world and have some fun.' She gave a sly smile that fluttered his heart. 'Hey, we could even fornicate a little, if that's what you want. Kissing, I don't know, we can talk about it. But I guarantee we'll have a great time.'

'Yeah,' Perry said. 'Until we don't and your bosses send out some more stripper pens. Leave me alone.'

But Cheyenne wasn't done. Before Perry could reach the door, she turned to the other patrons and called out, 'He's Buddy!' At first, there was little or no reaction. A few diners gawked at Perry, muttering among themselves. Then, before he knew what was happening, several had jumped to their feet and were striding towards him. Perry dashed into the parking lot, started up the Festiva and gunned it into the street as they poured out of the diner.

When he returned to his apartment, he found Noah Overton waiting at the front door, pale and trembling. Noah apologised adamantly for thinking that Perry was insane and told him that he'd had a vision the night before in which the three men he admired the most – Gandhi, Martin Luther King Jr and

Dr Albert Schweitzer – had appeared at the foot of his bed and told him that the Earth was indeed in grave danger and if it was going to be saved, Noah needed to join forces with Perry Bunt.

'I know it sounds weird,' Noah said. 'But it was so real.'

Perry explained to Noah that it hadn't been a vision and that visions didn't really exist; they were all special effects produced by alien producers to elicit specific types of behaviour from people living on Earth. Gandhi, King and Schweitzer were actually facsimilons, shape-shifting extra-terrestrials that can adapt to any shape or form.

Noah stared at Perry for several moments. 'I didn't think this was possible,' he said, 'but that's much weirder than what I just told you.'

Perry opened his front door. 'I hate to break this to you, but Earth can't be saved. Not by you or me or anyone else. It's out of our hands.'

Noah's jaw jutted out. 'I don't believe you. We have to keep trying. If I've learned anything from my work at the food bank—' Perry slipped into his apartment, slammed the door and locked it. Noah pounded on the door. 'I won't let you give up, Perry!' he yelled through the broken window. 'I'm staying out here until you talk to me!'

Great, Perry thought. *If I'm going to spend my last few days alive being annoyed, I might as well be with my parents.* He threw a few things into a backpack and walked back out the door, opening it in mid-pound. Noah fixed him in a determined gaze. 'You have to hear me out,' he said.

'I'm driving to the airport,' Perry replied.

'Then I'm coming with you.'

Perry shrugged and Noah followed him down to the street. While Perry drove the Festiva down the 405, Noah sat in the passenger seat and spoke to him about various issues affecting the planet – from plastic bottles to disappearing honeybees to childhood obesity – and how each could be solved. Perry didn't bother telling Noah again about the upcoming series finale that would render all his solutions moot, mainly because it was easier to drive and let Noah's words wash over him like talk radio. He felt freer than he could ever remember feeling. The sense that his life had been a disappointment and that he had failed to live up to his potential, a nearly suffocating gloom that had enveloped him for years, was completely gone. He wasn't alone anymore. As it turned out, everyone on Earth would fail to live up to their potential.

The freeway was unusually open and Perry celebrated his new freedom by seeing how fast the Festiva could drop down the south side of the Sepulveda Pass. When the speedometer needle quivered above 100, Noah was startled out of his rant. 'Should we really be going this fast?'

'No,' Perry said, squeezing it up to a 105. 'Definitely not in this car. It's not a good idea at all.' They rapidly approached the airport exit. When Perry turned sharply from the off-ramp onto Century Boulevard, a lit-up police motorcycle pulled up behind them and sounded its siren. Normally this sight would have sent Perry's gut into panicky spasms, but he was still celebrating. 'Should we run for it?' he asked Noah.

The young man gaped in horror. 'God, no!'

Perry wondered briefly whether Noah had ever had a sense of humour. Are people actually born without it? Is it stripped away from them? Or does it just stop working from disuse, like a muscle? Perry pulled over and the police officer, a large black man, strode up to his window.

'Licence,' he said.

Perry pulled his wallet out and gave the officer his driver's licence. 'I may have been going a little fast back there,' he said.

The officer didn't respond. He glanced at Perry's licence and handed it back to him. 'Did you write the movie *Kickin' It Doggy Style?*'

Perry, now quite confused, nodded slowly. 'I rewrote the script. They never made the movie.'

'There's an APB out on you,' the officer said. 'I need to escort you directly to City Hall.'

Perry frowned. 'Excuse me?'

'The mayor needs your help.'

'*My* help?' Perry smiled. 'I'm a screenwriting teacher.'

'I understand that,' the officer said. 'A drug gang in South-Central has been using dogs to kill people. The mayor needs your expertise.'

Perry stared at the very serious policeman at his window. 'Nice try,' he said. He reached out for the left cuff of the officer's uniform and slid it up his bulky forearm.

The inside of his wrist was unmarked.

The officer glared at Perry. 'What the hell do you think you're doing?' he said.

'Yeah, Perry,' Noah said from the passenger seat with great concern. 'What the hell are you doing?'

'You're not a producer,' Perry told the policeman. 'But you're being manipulated by one. Maybe your chief, maybe the mayor. Who knows?'

'What?' The cop practically spat the word into Perry's face.

'Am I under arrest?' Perry said.

'No. As I told you, I have orders to escort you.'

'Then tell the mayor I decline your . . . escortion.' The word sounded dirty, which made Perry giggle. 'I have a plane to catch.'

He started up the Festiva and roared back onto Century Boulevard. In the rear-view mirror, the cop, stunned, watched him go. Noah glanced over his shoulder, worried.

'Shouldn't you go with him?' Noah said. 'Why don't you want to help?'

Perry lit a cigarette and took a deep drag. 'You know the alien producers I told you about earlier?' Noah nodded warily.

'They're trying to trick me into being a hero. But I won't let them do it because it's what they want, and ever since they created the Earth and populated it with the dregs of their society, they've been able to do whatever they wanted with us. Not this time.' Noah stared at him, his eyes wide enough that Perry could see white all the way around the irises. 'Sorry you asked?'

'I'll get out here,' Noah said.

Perry pulled over. Noah opened the door and stepped out onto the pavement. Perry leaned out his window and yelled, 'Do yourself a favour – get laid!' before speeding off.

He pulled the Festiva up to the departures area of the Los Angeles International Airport and stepped out. As he sauntered towards the automatic glass doors, an airport security guard sprinted up to him. 'Do not leave your car there!' he shouted. 'It will be towed and impounded!'

'Promise?' Perry said and entered the airport. He strode by the snaking line for Economy and bought a first-class ticket with a credit card he'd found in a stack of junk mail that morning. He nearly pranced through the security checkpoint, leaving behind his blocky running shoes on the conveyor belt. He'd never liked them. Padding down the linoleum in his stockinged feet towards the departure gate, he bought a new iPod, a surfing magazine and a bizarrely large box of chocolate.

He boarded the plane and planted himself in his first-class seat. Luxuriating in its comfort, he was forced to contemplate a life misspent in the economy cabin. How had it happened? This was so much better. Even when he could easily have afforded first class, he would often choose coach, just to save a few hundred dollars. And where had it got him?

'Another, please.' He motioned to a smiling saintly woman in a perfect red uniform with a swirl of the ice in his glass. She quickly took his glass and refilled it for the third time with twelve-year-old whisky, despite the fact that passengers were still filing on – their eyes dead in preparation for the hours of confinement in a steel tube, breathing the farts of their neighbours. The coiffed middle-aged woman in the seat next to him had not risked eye contact with Perry since he'd boarded and created something of a stir trying to jam the immense box of chocolate under his seat. But now, as he sipped another whisky, she glanced over and asked him something.

'What?' Perry said loudly.

'Your music!' she said. 'It's coming through your headphones!'

'Right.' Perry made no move to turn down his new iPod. *Poor woman*, Perry thought. He wouldn't want to sit next to him, either.

The chipper, cartoon-like voices of ABBA soared into 'Waterloo'. He'd ordered the album through the internet by clicking the first artist on an alphabetical list. He'd always disliked ABBA. Now he wondered why he'd bothered. He realised now that there was absolutely nothing to dislike about them. It was like loathing the sky or detesting water. Why waste the energy? For the sake of his 'artistic integrity'? Ha! As if that had ever got him anywhere. So much of life would've been easier if he'd just *given in*.

The plane took off and Perry, now quite drunk, revelled in the miracle of flight, though now he had to wonder if it was a miracle or just some artful special effect concocted by Channel Blue. Either seemed equally probable at this point. Were there really ever any Wright Brothers? Or were they just day players in a period drama?

The plane bounced in turbulence over the Sierra Nevada but Perry was now deep into 'Dancing Queen' and his surfing magazine. He'd never learned to surf and now obviously never would, but he'd always loved to watch the exultation and triumph of the wave riders; for a moment they were masters of their fate, conquerors of nature's infinite force and the chaos of the universe. It must be nice to feel that way, Perry thought, even if for a moment, even if it's only an illusion.

More turbulence. The plane was now chattering through the stratosphere, diving and climbing precipitously. While the passengers around him clung grimly to their armrests, staring straight ahead with sublimated terror on their faces, Perry read about the Lizzy Surf Slam and sang tonelessly to 'Fernando'.

The flight attendant interrupted him. She was no longer smiling.

'Excuse me, Mr Bunt?' Perry removed his headphones. 'The pilot has requested your help in the cockpit.'

Perry stared at her for a moment before breaking into a smile. 'Oh my God,' he said. 'You almost had me.' This set-up had the greasy fingerprints of Marty Firth all over it. Perry shook his head in admiration. He had to hand it to the producers of Channel Blue: They didn't give up easily.

The flight attendant, jostled by another severe swoon, clutched the back of Perry's seat. 'I don't understand.'

'The pilot and co-pilot have food poisoning.'

The flight attendant made an almost perfect 'O' of surprise with her mouth. 'How did you know?'

'You need someone to land the plane.'

'Yes.'

'And even though I'm not a pilot, I will follow you to the cockpit and sit in the pilot's chair. As soon as I put my hands on the controls, the plane will level off and I'll be credited with saving everyone's lives.'

The plane bucked fiercely and the flight attendant, flung down the aisle, caught herself on the back of the next seat. 'All I know is that I've been asked to bring you to the cockpit! Will you come or not?'

'I'm sorry,' Perry said, 'but I'd like to finish my article.' He slid his headphones back over his ears.

The flight attendant glared at Perry and walked backwards up the aisle. The middle-aged woman next to him, who'd watched this exchange with increasing aggravation, could no longer contain herself. 'What the hell is wrong with you?' she shouted at Perry. 'Get up there and help them!'

Perry turned and regarded her calmly. 'The plane's not going to crash,' he said. 'If they'd wanted it to, it would've already happened.' He returned to his surfing magazine just as the plane shook once more and plummeted towards Earth. The cabin filled with the screams of terrified passengers, along with one off-key voice exultantly singing:

When you're near me, darling
Can't you hear me?
SOS
The love you gave me
Nothing else can save me
SOS . . .

CHANNEL 25

BACK TO EARTH

Perry disembarked the plane under the judgemental eyes of the crew and his fellow passengers. By all accounts, the pilot had miraculously recovered from his bad prawn dinner just in time to land the plane in the severe storm, saving lives that Perry had cast to the wind with his refusal to help. Perry meanwhile had managed to fall asleep in the midst of the drama, his open, drooling mouth a gaping taunt to the other passengers.

Well-rested and content, Perry padded in his socks to the airport's taxi queue and took a cab to the small town he'd called home for the first eighteen years of his life. Since leaving he could count on one hand the times he'd returned; escaping its boundaries had been like taking off a straitjacket he'd been forced to wear all his life – this was the place he'd had to flee to lose his virginity – and coming back usually felt like being forced to put it back on.

But today was different. Today Perry actually took pleasure in seeing the landmarks on his way into town, their contours enhanced by the Technicolor glow of autumnal colours. There was the cornfield where he'd received his first French kiss, the park where he'd drunk his first beer, the vacant lot next to the park where he'd been sick on beer for the first time, the high school where he'd tried desperately to fit in before he'd realised that he didn't. He wasn't smart enough to be a geek, he was too paranoid to be a stoner (a single inhalation of marijuana gave him the power to read everyone's mind and interestingly enough, everyone was thinking the same thing: 'Perry Bunt is a loser'), while his inability to complete a single pull-up made joining the jocks out of the question.

Instead, Perry had started a literary magazine. *From the Brow of Zeus* served mainly as a vanity press for his own stories, which ranged from the embarrassingly autobiographical to the dementedly self-aggrandising. Perry's hope that becoming a published author would make him instantly popular and girlfriend-worthy lasted only until the school's budding recycling programme received a substantial boost from the first issue. When it became apparent that no one was interested in reading *From the Brow of Zeus* except his parents – who seemed deeply troubled by it and discreetly sent a copy to his psychiatrist uncle (Perry came upon an article on his mother's dresser titled 'Is Your Child a Serial Killer?') – he heaved a soaring 'Hail Mary' pass for popularity towards the end zone. Perry volunteered to become the school mascot.

Upon donning the costume of a big-headed Titan for a football game, Perry immediately realised why the job had been up for grabs. While encased in the twenty-pound head and trying to see and breathe through saucer-sized nostril holes, he was expected to prance up and down the sidelines, waving a large plastic sword. The combination of heat and oxygen deprivation caused him to throw up just seven minutes into the first quarter. He staggered to the locker room, a journey made all the more difficult by the unavoidable pool of his own vomit swishing around inside the Titan's jaw.

Since that day, he'd rarely worn a hat, let alone a mask.

Normally, memories such as these made it impossible for him to enjoy his homecoming. Today, however, they amused him. After all, they were all part of a long-running comedy. And when your show is coming to the end of its run, what else can you do but replay the unforgettable moments?

His parents were shocked to see him, beyond the fact that he was shoeless and drunk and hadn't bothered to let them know he was coming. They naturally suspected that some terrible predicament had motivated his arrival, which of course was true. But Perry presented the visit as a lark, a spur-of-the-moment chance to catch up with his family. 'Life is too short to be out of touch,' he was shocked to hear himself say.

There were no surprises: His mother wept and smothered him in a wet embrace, his father smiled and disappeared into the garage where a fence post on the lathe needed attention. But again, none of this bothered Perry. He felt strangely non-judgemental of his parents. For the first time in his life, he saw them for who they were without taking their eccentricities personally. In fact, he found himself rather enjoying his mother's operatic emotionality and his father's autistic-like remoteness, as if his parents were characters in a familiar play. Because he no longer nursed any expectations of satisfactory interactions with them, he actually engaged in enjoyable small talk with his mother and profound conversations with his father.

He accepted everything completely because nothing was going to get any better – this was the way it was going to be.

The Earth's final days wound down in a happy haze. While the 'situation in the Middle East' continued to spiral out of control – the Russian army had invaded Pakistan, God knows why – Perry slept ten hours a day and let his mother stuff him with comfort food. No flies, blue or otherwise, buzzed around him, and no suspicious strangers asked for his help. He walked alone through brilliant orange leaves and read a dusty volume of Herodotus he found on a bookshelf in the living room. He stood in his parents' kitchen with a long sharp knife and sliced a Pink Lady apple, purchased from a nearby farm stand. *It might be the last thing I'll ever eat*, he thought, sliding cool tart wedges into his mouth. It was like nothing he'd ever tasted before, this ultimate apple. Every bite might be his last, so every bite became the best bite ever.

Maybe this was what it took to be happy, he thought one morning, sitting in the backyard watching a crow soar above the brown razed cornfields. If only he'd spent more of his life with the world about to end.

One evening, Perry wandered into town and stopped at a bar for a beer. Darlene Brickton took his order. Tall and blonde, Darlene had been the hottest girl in his high school class and, to Perry's eyes, hadn't change that much. It was as if the high school cheerleader had been freeze-dried into a barmaid – she had lost the succulence of her quintessence but was still ravishing.

They struck up a pleasant conversation, which would have been impossible if Perry hadn't known the world was ending. Even after all these years, he would've been too intimidated. No longer. Darlene didn't remember him, of course, but like most popular people, took it on faith that Perry had known her. She told him that she'd been married twice – no kids 'thank God' – and was back in town, working at the bar until she figured out the next step. 'That's something no one has to worry about,' Perry wanted to say, but couldn't work out how to say it without sounding like a hippy, a nut or a creep.

Darlene talked about watching all her friends from school become their parents 'without so much as a fight'. She didn't want that happening to her.

'You know what?' Perry said. 'I know this for a fact: it's not going to happen.' Darlene smiled at him, touched by his confidence. Of course, he didn't go on to tell her that no one was going to have a chance to turn into anything other than space dust.

After Darlene had brought him a couple beers, the second one on the house 'for old times' sake', Mitch Thalmer entered the bar. Back in high school, Mitch had been the quarterback of the Titans and the scourge of students like Perry, whom Mitch made a point of torturing when he wasn't busy enjoying the fruits of his immense popularity.

Perry winced involuntarily, thinking of the slaps across the face dealt during the daily re-enactment of *Lord of the Flies* that was called 'gym', now known to Perry as Channel Blue's worst show ever. He and Mitch had definitely done their parts to entertain the galaxy.

Perry was inordinately pleased to see that Mitch was now fat and bald, not to mention drunk. The former football star coerced a beer from the bartender and swigged it while turning his broad sweaty face up to the TV. He demanded that the channel be switched to sports, and Darlene had to explain, several times, that even the sports networks were tuned into the escalating crisis in the Middle East.

'Who cares about that?' Mitch said loudly enough for everyone in the bar to hear. 'I hope they all kill each other. It doesn't affect me any.'

'That's true,' Perry said, amazed to find himself speaking his thoughts aloud. 'You're a piece of shit now. In a few days, you'll just be a dead piece of shit.'

Mitch's head pivoted to Perry's table and the drunk man's legs, as if on automatic pilot, staggered towards it while the large hands at his sides curled into squab-sized fists. He shuffled to a stop in front of Perry's chair, breathing audibly through his nose. 'What the fuck did you just say?'

Perry was more than happy to repeat himself. Exhibiting quick reflexes for so drunk and fat a man, Mitch pulled one hulking fist back and hit Perry squarely in the mouth. For a moment, Perry did nothing. In fact, other than the blood oozing from his upper lip, his expression barely changed. Then, very deliberately, he stood and stared at Mitch, who towered over him.

And he smiled.

It turns out that knowledge of the world's imminent demise gives you a decided advantage in a bar fight. So much of fighting turns on the fear, or lack thereof, that results from that first punch. When Perry, his lip bleeding, smiled at Mitch, the large man had lost the fight, even though Perry hadn't thrown a punch. In fact, it was Mitch who threw the second punch as well, but was so discombobulated by Perry's reaction to his first that he swung wildly and missed. Before he could regain his balance, Perry gave him a shove and Mitch fell, banging his head on the foot of a barstool.

It really wasn't clear how much of the former quarterback there was until he lay knocked out on the floor, sprawled like a vast continent on a dark-green sea of linoleum. Patrons were forced to circumnavigate Mitch to buy a drink or use the toilet. Eventually, the bartender revived him with a splash of cold water. Perry helped lift the large dazed man and get him into a cab.

'Thank you,' Darlene said. 'He's been coming in here and driving me crazy for weeks. Maybe this'll give him pause.' Whenever someone used the phrase 'give him pause', Perry thought about someone being given paws. In this case, he imagined Mitch Thalmer in the back of the cab with large cat paws, which made him smile. Darlene interpreted this smile as more proof that Perry was the coolest guy in the world and invited him to walk her to her car.

Later that night, Perry found himself on Darlene Brickton's couch, passionately making out with the former cheerleader. He vacillated between intense desire and great awe that the subject of so many fantasies was now literally (yes, *literally*) in his grasp. But when he gingerly swept a hand up under her blouse, she pulled back. 'So . . . it must be nice, living in LA,' she said.

'It's not that great,' Perry said. He leaned forward to resume their explorations, but she continued to speak, confounding him.

'When you were out there, did you hear about this guy they're calling "The Buddy"?'

Perry wasn't sure he'd heard her correctly. 'The what?'

'"The Buddy". I guess he was a homeless man who preached in some park in Los Angeles and started this whole religion. He told people that the Earth is being watched by aliens who've become sick of us, because we're so selfish and violent. We have to become better people or they'll destroy the planet. That's supposedly what all this stuff in the Middle East is about.' Perry stared at her with complete disbelief, which Darlene took as a judgement of her credibility. 'I know, it sounds completely crazy. But after I heard about it on the radio, I couldn't stop thinking about it.'

'Huh,' Perry said. 'That is weird.' He kissed her on the lips, but she now seemed distracted. *Great*, he thought. Somehow he'd managed to cock-block himself.

'This is his picture.' Darlene pulled a folded piece of paper from her jeans pocket and handed it to Perry. Perry unfolded it and saw a printout of a photo taken from a distance in St Jude's Park. Perry's face had been blown up into a jumble of pixels, which someone had then gone about Photo-shopping into something resembling a human. In the process, they'd turned Perry's thinning hair into a flowing mane and his five-o'clock shadow into a beard. The photo didn't resemble Perry so much as a young, demented Santa Claus.

Perry refolded the paper. 'What happened to Buddy?'

'They call him *The Buddy*,' Darlene said. 'It's a sign of respect, I guess.'

Perry was yet again annoyed by the religious movement he'd inadvertently created. 'OK,' he said. 'What happened to the Buddy?'

'After he preached for two days, the police came and took him away. When his followers went to get him out of jail, he'd completely disappeared. They say the aliens didn't like him telling the people on Earth what they were doing so they took him away.'

'Do you actually believe all this?'

Darlene shrugged. 'I don't know. I've been reading about Buddyism on the internet and in some ways it makes complete sense. I mean, I don't know if I believe in aliens and all that, but when I think about watching all the things that we do from outer space, it makes you want to become a better person.'

'You know what I think?' Perry said, setting aside his picture.

'What?'

'I think that if the Buddy were here, he'd want us to love each other and take care of each other right here, right now.'

Darlene smiled with recognition. 'I think you're right.'

'It's about living in the moment,' Perry said, kissing her.

'Yes,' Darlene replied, kissing him back, once more completely engaged. 'Why not spend more time loving each other—'

'It totally makes sense,' Perry said between gasps of air. Darlene's right hand reached down towards his crotch. 'I love the Buddy!' he blurted.

The next morning, when Perry woke up in a strange bed next to the hottest girl in the school, he thought for a moment that the world had ended and he was in heaven. Then he remembered the events of the previous night and was so filled with happiness that he couldn't sleep anymore. He was even thrilled to have created a new religion, especially the fact that it was a religion that seemingly encouraged beautiful women to have sex with less attractive men. That was definitely something he could believe in. Careful not to wake Darlene, he dressed and slipped out of her parents' house.

The morning was warm and he took a leisurely walk home, reflecting on his great turn of luck since Earth had begun its death throes. If Thomas Wolfe had gone home again with the knowledge that aliens would soon be ending the world, he would've found it not only possible but deeply gratifying. Perry had finally been able to become the cool, contented guy he knew himself to be deep inside simply by not caring anymore. It was that easy.

When he strolled through the front door of his parents' house around noon, his mother hugged him and Perry didn't even mind the intense guilt infliction that immediately resulted from his night away.

'A girl came by to talk to you,' she said, 'and I didn't even know when to tell her you'd be back.'

Perry frowned. 'When did she come by?'

'Just a few minutes ago. She said it was important so I told her she could wait. She's out back.'

Perry sighed. Maybe he'd been too cavalier, leaving Darlene

without so much as a note. How could she know that there wasn't any point? He should apologise. He went out the back door and saw her standing at the edge of the property, gazing at the razed cornfields across the road. But as he neared her, he couldn't help noticing that the girl wasn't Darlene.

Amanda Mundo was standing in his parents' garden.

They stood for a moment in silence, surveying the dead corn. 'Looks like the world *will* have to end before I get rid of you,' he said in a not-unfriendly way.

Amanda smiled at him. 'Have fun last night?'

He felt the blood rush to his face. In all his end-of-the-world exultation, he'd forgotten that their cameras could still find him. 'Look,' he said, 'she and I knew each other at school and—'

'Save your breath,' Amanda interrupted. 'That's not why I'm here.'

Perry couldn't help feel disheartened by her seeming lack of jealousy. He also couldn't help but be irritated by how happy he felt to see her. 'I'm sorry about the way I stormed off the other day,' he said. 'I know you're not as bad as the rest of them, but you were there and got all the blame.'

'That's not why I'm here either,' she said. 'I'm here because we have to get the show back on track.'

Just like that, the cool contentment Perry had cultivated since coming home gave way to irritation and anxiety. He took a deep breath, trying to regain his equilibrium. 'We already had this conversation. There's no point.'

'There is now,' Amanda said. 'We're doing the show.'

Perry took two steps away from her. 'No, we aren't. I don't know where your glass elevator is, but go ahead, get back in it and tell Elvis and Marty and whoever else that it ain't gonna happen!'

'I don't work for them anymore,' Amanda said. 'I quit the channel.'

Perry frowned suspiciously. 'That doesn't make any sense. You love your job.'

She took a slip of paper out of her pocket and handed it to Perry. 'I had to fly here on an *airplane*. Full of Earthles. Economy. Would I put myself through that if I still worked for the channel?'

Perry glanced at the boarding pass. 'What happened?' he asked.

Amanda didn't answer. She gazed out at the fallow fields stretching in a flat brown plain to the horizon. 'By the way, where are we? This place is depressing.'

'It's called the Midwest. You might know it from pie-eating contests and threshing-machine accidents. And you really shouldn't be here. Those pens are doing their jobs. It's already a World War in the Middle East, even though nobody's calling it that. You should be far, far away, well on your way back to Planet Wonderful.'

Amanda fixed her eyes on Perry. 'I can't live there anymore,' she said. 'And since I can't live in the world I come from, we have to fix this one.'

CHANNEL 26

IMPLANTED ON EARTH

It turned out that while Perry was busy becoming the golden boy of the apocalypse, Amanda's luck was heading in quite the opposite direction. When she returned to Galaxy Entertainment, all everyone wanted to know was what she'd done to piss off Perry under the freeway. No one gave a damn about what had happened to her, it was all about getting the Earthle back on the show. *What were you doing under there?* they'd asked her repeatedly.

Of course, telling them that she and Perry had been having coitus on the floor of a service van was out of the question for many different reasons, the main being that she wasn't sure herself why she'd done it. What was she thinking? Had she completely lost her mind? She had, obviously, but now she was sane again, and if not for the irritating stickiness she felt all over her body, she might have been able to convince herself that it had never happened.

Almost convince herself.

In any case, her animal regression had served to confirm the degenerate sordidness of such an act and to ensure that nothing like it would ever happen again. She thought: *I now know why we're a product of something more than fornication.* But no sooner had she thought this than she caught herself reliving the entire unseemly act in her memory, as if she had *enjoyed* it. But she hadn't. Had she?

All of this was going through her mind while Marty Firth and the other producers were questioning her like a common criminal. *Why did you park? You know we're on a tight production schedule. What did you tell him?*

Without any reference to what came before, Amanda told them that before his forced removal from the gas station, Nick Pythagorus had managed to slip his Orby plaque into Perry's pocket, and that Perry had discovered it, figured out what it meant, and walked off the production.

'Then what are you doing here?' Marty said. He and Vermy stared at her as if she were a ghost. 'You should've gone after him.'

'He hates us!' Amanda yelled, catching Marty off guard. He definitely wasn't used to being yelled at. Edenites typically didn't raise their voices unless there was a fire in the next room or an avalanche bearing down on them. They knew that there were very few cases in which communication wasn't hindered by shouting. Everyone in the conference room stared at Amanda in shock. 'He hates us and doesn't want to have anything to do with us and I don't blame him.'

Amanda felt her face flushing. It was the second time this week. *What the hell is going on?* She was acting like the worst kind of Earthle girl, the kind who rode her emotions like a destructive tsunami through life.

'Well, Amanda,' Marty Firth said slowly, as if speaking to a lunatic, 'you need to talk to him, convince him to stop behaving like an infant. It doesn't matter whether the Earth is an amusement park, a zoo or a rabbit farm, it's not going to be *anything* unless he cooperates. I mean, he's jeopardising *this entire production.*'

'You talk to him. I'm done.' She stood and walked to the door.

'Get back out there or you're off the channel,' Marty said.

'Fine,' Amanda called back. 'Just blow it up so we can all go home.' She ran into her office, deactivated all the sensors, and was trying to clear her head when Dennis burst in.

'You've got to see this,' he said.

'Not interested.'

'Oh, you will be.' He activated the main screen on her wall and Perry Bunt's face loomed before them. 'Amanda and I fornicated,' Perry said. 'Did I mention that already?'

Amanda buried her face in her hands. She knew that no one in the galaxy would believe Perry, that they would ascribe his hysterical ranting to the bitterness of an Earthle facing the imminent destruction of his planet. But this was small consolation.

Dennis attempted unsuccessfully to contain his jubilation. 'You should see Marty going crazy out there. He wants to put it on the channel *so bad*.' But he couldn't, Amanda knew. This footage would effectively kill *Bunt to the Rescue* and Marty still hoped – futilely, she was certain – to bring it back on the air for another few profitable episodes before Earth was finale-ed.

Of course, the footage would still find its way out there; beyond the established broadcast networks, there were thousands of pirate channels devoted solely to outtakes from around the galaxy. Within moments, Perry's rant would appear on one of them with a chyron reading something like: 'Bitter POF Claims To Have Had Sex with Producer' and everyone she knew would see it. Given the recent popularity of *Bunt to the Rescue*, she wouldn't be surprised if it became the Most Viewed Outtake for seconds, maybe even minutes.

After Perry insulted Marty and Elvis and his feed was cut

off, Dennis turned to her. 'Everyone's saying it couldn't possibly have happened,' he said.

'What?'

'You having sex with the Earthle.'

Amanda sank back in her chair and rubbed her forehead. 'What do you want, Dennis?'

'As crazy as it sounds, I just want to ask the question. I thought I saw a little something between you two the other night. And for all his Earthleness, Perry Bunt doesn't seem like the kind of guy who would make up something like that.' Dennis leaned forward. 'Did you have sex with an Earthle?'

Amanda closed her eyes and wished she could disappear. 'Just leave me alone.'

'I've heard it smells awful. Did it smell awful?'

'Out!' Amanda stood and pushed Dennis into the hallway. 'Go eat your popcorn while you can.'

This time, she locked the door. She sat down at her desk and felt something she hadn't remembered feeling before, and she didn't like the feeling at all. It was shame. She only knew what to call it because she'd used the word frequently in Channel Blue programme guides to describe episodes of her shows. Now, like so many of the Earthles' repellent attributes, she was taking on this one as well. And there was more, coming so quickly it was hard to sort out. She also felt hatred for Earth and especially for Perry Bunt, a dark, smouldering contempt that boiled in her stomach like bad food.

She rested her forehead on her desk. The surface came to life with the magnificent chiselled features of her boyfriend, Jared. She'd forgotten to turn off her phone.

'Hey,' Jared said, his voice laden with concern. 'Are you OK?'

Amanda would've preferred that he yelled at her and hung

256

up, but of course he would never do that. The year that Jared was born, empathy was one of the most popular traits for boys. She nodded back at him. 'Yeah,' she said. She dreaded asking the next question, but felt like she had to. 'Most Viewed?'

Jared nodded. 'For almost thirty seconds now.' He shuddered. 'I can't believe that Earthle. You expect them to be unevolved, but what a thing to say. Ick.'

Amanda tried to hide her irritation and think of things to say that were true. 'If I don't see another one, I'll be happy,' she said.

'Well, you won't have to. You can head straight to the moon and ditch that dirt clod.'

There was a pause and Amanda felt buffeted with wave after wave of unpleasant emotions: loathing for Perry Bunt, disgust with herself, and intense dislike of Jared for being so reasonable.

'I did it,' she finally said.

'What?'

'I had sex with him.'

After a beat, Jared burst out laughing. 'Oh my God,' he said.

Amanda found herself forcing a smile, going along with the joke that wasn't. *Why am I pretending?* she thought. He didn't need her to. She could insist that she had indeed experienced coitus with an Earthle and he would've found some way to understand it. That was it, she decided. She didn't want him understanding anything else about her.

'You totally had me,' Jared said, wiping away tears of laughter. 'Working on Earth has done nothing to tame that wicked sense of humour.'

'No.'

'Well, here's some good news.' Jared perused a screen.

'You've already cycled out. It's down to third Most Viewed. Hold on. Still dropping. Forty-second!' Jared smiled with relief. 'It's all those mutants being hunted on *Crazy World 26*.'

Amanda smiled wanly. 'Thank goodness for mutant hunting.'

'They can shorten a cycle, that's for sure.' Jared's eyes remained fixed on his screen. 'Still dropping. Down to eighty-ninth! You watch. In another thirty seconds, some mom giving birth to seventeen children will make it disappear completely.' Jared focused back on her, his bright blue eyes each the size of serving plates on her desk. 'Now do me a favour. I'm serious now, Manda. Get out of there. Go to the moon, do your exit work, and get back here. I want to be with you.' He smiled. 'And hey, if you decide you actually want to experiment with sex, I guess I'd be up for trying it. Earthle-style. No kissing, though – I have to draw the line somewhere.'

Amanda laughed falsely and hated herself for it. She told Jared she was on her way home and hung up.

She felt a tremendous sense of relief as soon as she arrived on the moon. Nobody stared at her in the hallways as she made her way to her apartment. Maybe Jared was right. She'd cycled out and the entire humiliating incident was safely behind her.

She spent the rest of the week packing up her belongings and wrapping up her shows. She produced final episodes for several series, including an elaborate finale for Steve Santiago, in which the Jacuzzi salesman, on one of his jaunts to Mexico to buy cheap prescription drugs for resale to cancer patients, was kidnapped by a drug gang and brutally sodomised in the basement of a Tijuana bar before dying in a knife fight. The moment before life ebbed from his body, Jesus Christ (Jeff) appeared before him and said, 'Told you.'

The ratings were better than they'd been, but still not great. The way in which Amanda's other shows ended wasn't much cheerier. Earth was now all about bad endings. Amanda didn't protest or ask questions. She just produced. There's nothing anyone can do now, she told herself. For the first time, she felt resigned to Channel Blue's cancellation, and she had to admit it was a relief.

On the day she was scheduled to catch a ship home, she woke early to take care of the last formalities. At the exit centre, the receptionist processed her transfer application and waved her into the examination room. There she sat in a rotating armchair while two Class 3 medibots wheeled out of the walls and scanned her. Once they had completely retracted, she stood and stepped to the exit. But the door didn't open. Instead, a pleasant voice said, 'Dr Roberts needs to follow up on your exam.'

A different door opened and Amanda walked through it into an office where a fully sentient Class 5 docbot sat behind the desk. Like all docbots, it was named Dr Roberts, after the author of the first software, and it was configured to appear as an older fatherly male with a white jacket and white hair. The desk in front of Dr Roberts was covered with homely objects like souvenir paperweights and fishing lures, props intended to reassure the patient. Docbots had always had the most human-like aspect of any of the helper bots. This, according to history, was because Edenites had at first refused to go to them with their health concerns. While it was one thing to depend on a robot to guard your house, fix your car or take out your garbage, it was quite another to engage one in a discussion about anal itching.

'Hello, Amanda,' Dr Roberts said, smiling. 'Or should I say: Congratulations!'

Amanda paused. 'Why?'

Dr Roberts chuckled warmly, which is what docbots were

programmed to do when they didn't understand a patient's question. 'We need to update our medical records,' it said. 'Who was your genetic programmer?'

Amanda frowned, confused. 'I don't remember the name, but my records have been in the medibase since my conception.'

'Not for you, Amanda,' Dr Roberts said lightly. 'I meant for your child.'

Amanda stared at the docbot blankly, which prompted the machine to give her more information. 'It seems that you had a fertilised ovum implanted in your uterus, but we have no record of it.'

Amanda shook her head. 'That's not possible.'

A screen lit up behind Dr Roberts, showing what appeared to be a lumpy pink golf ball floating underwater. 'That's your blastocyst,' the docbot said cheerfully. 'Now, as you know, while women still have the option of choosing this method of pregnation, *in utero* fertilisation can be relatively risky. In order to safely track the baby's development, we need to know where you had the implantation performed.'

In the back of a van, Amanda thought. How had this happened? Nobody got pregnant. Nobody had sex either, of course, but *definitely* nobody got pregnant.

The panic in her throat kept her from thinking clearly; her thoughts were coming in shabby clumps instead of the ordered rows she was accustomed to. She stared at the lumpy pink golf ball on the screen and felt a strange flutter in her heart that made no sense to her at all. It certainly looked like the product of fornication. Could the medibots already detect the genetic randomness of the cells rapidly subdividing in her uterus? *No*, she decided, *they're probably not even programmed to consider it*. That would be like programming them to recognise a disease that was eradicated a thousand years ago.

The docbot was programmed to prompt a patient who was silent for more than twenty seconds. 'It may be of some help to know that, according to our measurements, you had it done a week ago.'

'Of course,' Amanda said. 'How could I have forgotten? I took a weekend in Antares, had it done. It's something my boyfriend and I have been talking about, and I figured with Channel Blue getting cancelled I'd have some time to, you know, pregnate.'

Dr Roberts was all smiles. 'Well, I'm sure he'll be a perfectly programmed baby boy.'

'Boy?' Amanda said, unable to conceal her shock. Up to this moment, she hadn't really thought of the blastocyst as a person at all.

'Yes.' The docbot frowned. 'That is what you ordered, isn't it?'

'Definitely,' Amanda said, recovering. 'I've always wanted a . . . boy.'

'Then congratulations,' Dr Roberts said. 'Who did your genetic programming?'

Amanda stood. 'I'm sorry – I have to run. I'll send all the records to the medibase. Thanks for reminding me.'

She charged out of the exit centre and practically ran back to her apartment. She deactivated all screens and sensors and did some breathing exercises to slow her heartbeat. She considered her circumstances, then packed a bag and took an elevator back to Los Angeles.

'It was such an odd sensation,' she told Perry. They still stood in his parents' backyard. He stared at her dumbfounded, a pose he'd assumed minutes earlier and was having trouble breaking out of. 'In a matter of minutes, my key beliefs had been pulled out from under me.'

She couldn't imagine that the being growing inside her was somehow less than any Edenite. As a result, she could no longer justify feeling superior to products of fornication. This, in turn, led her to the realisation that the vaunted rationality of her people was a sham, and that the trauma of the Great Stultification had broken her culture's moral compass: the idea that almost anything was justified in the name of entertainment was despicable. It had led the greatest minds and technologies in the known universe into a dark business that resulted in the torture and killing of other human beings. And yes, she, Amanda, had been a part of that. As she neared Earth in the elevator, she felt her sense of deep shame grow with the approaching planet.

The doors opened. She walked briskly down the hallway, hoping she wouldn't run into anyone she knew, mainly because she didn't want to have to look anyone in the eyes. She felt that if she did, they would sense her terrible judgement. When she came to the first unused screening room, she ducked in. She knew that they'd given up on *Bunt to the Rescue*, but she also knew they'd keep cameras on Perry, just in case he decided to resume his heroics or do something entertaining. He hadn't, as it turned out, but that didn't matter to Amanda. After she'd obtained a fix on his location, she grabbed her bag and slipped into the lobby, moving as fast as she could without appearing to rush.

She'd nearly made it to the glass double doors when Dennis called after her. 'Amanda. What are you doing here?' She paused and composed herself as best she could. Dennis approached, munching from a bag of popcorn. 'I thought you were heading home.'

'I am,' Amanda lied. 'Jared asked me to bring him some popcorn.'

Dennis smiled and sidled up to her confidentially. 'I've already shipped three containers of it home,' he said. 'I'd send more, but I hardly have any room for my personal belongings as it is.' He chatted idly about his packing struggles and how great it was that, even though the Earth was being finale-ed, they would soon be on their way home again – until Amanda excused herself, saying she only had a few minutes before she was expected back on the moon, and headed out of the door. She walked down Ventura Boulevard until she found a taxi that would take her to the airport.

'I didn't have any other options,' Amanda explained to Perry. 'I can't have this baby on Eden.' She took a deep breath. 'Which is why you have to meet with the President of the United States and tell him how to save the world.'

CHANNEL 27

THE SERIES COMEBACK

Amanda's plan was brilliant, a testament to her tremendous abilities as a producer, a veritable treatise on effective planning, a perfect example of her grasp of the macro and micro and everything in between.

It was also preposterous and couldn't possibly succeed.

It involved a large donation of cash (courtesy of Channel Blue's prop room, which she'd raided before her departure), the fancy clothes from the Del Waddle gig (dry-cleaned, thank God), a photo opportunity with the President of the United States, and a plan, so far unwritten, to save the world.

But the entire time she was talking, Perry wasn't really listening. He could only think two thoughts: *I'm going to be a father!* and *I can't possibly be a father!* Back and forth these thoughts pulsed in his brain, like the two filaments in a strobe light, or the two notes in a Philip Glass symphony. Then another thought intruded, this one a darker chord: *Why is she doing this to me?* Here he was enjoying his last carefree days before Armageddon – he'd finally stopped wanting to be with her and had actually found some kind of happiness, or at least maybe the closest that he, Perry Bunt, could come to experiencing that Brigadoon-like emotion – and then she suddenly showed up, roaring back into his life with, of all things, an embryo in her uterus!

Normally, Perry was very cautious about birth control,

not that he'd had a lot of recent opportunities to practise it. In a distant, more sexually active time, he'd prided himself on maintaining deposits of condoms in his bedroom, his car and inside the filter casing of his Jacuzzi. Fancying himself an evolved man, he was never one to fob off the responsibility of unfertile sex onto his partner. But he hadn't brought it up for discussion on the floor of the service van – other matters seemed more pressing – and of course now he was paying the price.

He could hear the narrator of a school sex-ed film in his head: 'Even when your partner is from outer space, discussion of birth control is *mandatory*.'

'I don't understand,' Perry said. Amanda had just come to the part of her plan in which they arrived at the White House for a photo opportunity with the President. She was showing him the engraved invitation, which he was far too distracted to consider. 'You don't fight, you don't shit, you don't have sex, but you still get knocked up? How can that be?'

'*In utero* conception is technically impossible,' Amanda answered. 'It's not supposed to be part of our genetic make-up. So there must be a recessive gene that no one knows about. It's not an issue, of course, because it's almost never put to the test.'

'I would say that it's an issue,' Perry said. 'It is most definitely an issue.'

'I obviously had no idea this was going to happen.'

'Great. Fantastic. Like I don't have enough to think about right now.'

Amanda arched her eyebrows. 'It doesn't seem like you're doing much thinking. You've been living with your parents, drinking beer and having sex with a barmaid.'

She was right, of course, but it only made Perry more

irritated. 'That's my business, OK?' he said, his voice rising. 'I'm not the one blowing up the planet.'

Amanda stared at him. 'I know you hate me and Eden and everything we've done here, and I can't say that I blame you. But don't hold it against the baby.'

'Baby?' Perry choked out a burst of incredulous laughter. 'I can't believe you! Is this what happens? You people have sex once and your brains go out the window? You come from a civilisation that doesn't even reproduce outside of a laboratory and suddenly you've got a *baby*? It's a bunch of cells the size of a pinhead! You'd rather be on a planet dying with a bunch of losers because of a pinhead?'

'I suppose,' Amanda replied. 'Though I guess I would describe the situation somewhat differently.'

Perry shook his head. 'Baby or no baby, you need to get out of here.'

Amanda took a deep breath. 'You of all people should understand. Products of fornication have no opportunities in my world. I can't be responsible for bringing a baby into that situation.'

'*No one's forcing you to have a baby.* You have other options.' As soon as the words left his mouth, Perry regretted them. But Amanda remained matter-of-fact.

'I don't,' she said. 'I'm not sure you'll understand, because I'm not sure I do.' She averted her eyes, formulating her words. 'As a rule, Edenites don't believe in fate. The concept of destiny is something a child might believe, but not an adult. Adults know better. But this—' She brushed her hand across her stomach. 'This is beyond my understanding. I mean, I supposedly don't even have *the gene to reproduce*. And beyond that, the probability becomes even more miniscule. We're talking about a series of events, each less probable than the one before it: leaving my coat in your class; your walking through the security door at Galaxy Entertainment; the steel plates in your head shielding your brain from the collar; your attempts to save the world and getting beaten up, which made you a star on Channel Blue, which threw us together in a van under the freeway where we lost our minds for several seconds.'

'I think it was more like a few minutes,' Perry said.

'Whatever. This is a series of events that is so impossibly ludicrous—'

'I wouldn't really call it *ludicrous*.'

'It was!' Amanda practically shouted. 'In my wildest dreams, I couldn't have come up with something like this. In all the years I've watched Earthles do the craziest, most ridiculous things, I could never have imagined something like this happening. Could you?'

The truth was that Perry could have, and actually, several times, had, but he would never admit to it. 'Maybe not, but you make it sound like some kind of freakish event.'

'That's a perfect way of describing it – *a freakish event*. And you were the one who always told us in class how we shouldn't use freakish events in our scripts. How, if there was a coincidence after the first act, the audience wouldn't buy it and feel cheated. Why? Because in real life *it never happens*.'

Perry nodded. 'Yeah, OK, so no self-respecting writer would have anything to do with this. What does that prove?'

'That there's something going on here! And while I'm not prepared to call it God or fate or destiny, I'm not prepared to undo what's already been done. And part of me does think—' Amanda's voice trailed off for a moment. 'Part of me thinks that I was meant to have this boy with you.'

Despite himself, tears filled Perry's eyes. He quickly blinked them away, but it was too late – they'd already derailed his rage. *Damn it, she was doing it again.* He felt his anger melt into a pool of warm mush that collected in his chest, making every heartbeat reverberate throughout his entire body. Amanda stared at him. 'Are you helping me or not?'

After a moment, Perry took the invitation from her. Engraved script invited 'Mister Perry Bunt' in 'appreciation for his generous support' to a meeting with President Brendan Grebner in the Oval Office at eleven the following morning. Perry shook his head. 'The President's posing for photos with campaign donors while there's a war in the Middle East?'

'He doesn't know it's the last one,' Amanda said. 'He thinks there's going to be another election, which tend to be very expensive. He shakes a few hands, poses for some pictures. It's part of his job.'

Perry continued to gaze sceptically at the invitation. 'I could go to the President with the most convincing argument in the world, but he'd never buy it. I'll be the crazy guy in the White House. It'll be like Del Waddle's all over again, only worse.'

'I've thought of that,' Amanda said. 'You know that the President is a deeply religious man, right?' Perry nodded. He hadn't followed the last presidential campaign very closely – like half of his fellow citizens, he preferred complaining to voting – but he did know that Brendan Grebner had talked frequently about his faith in God and how it would help him govern the nation. In a paradox that only Edenites would find entertaining, citizens of the United States preferred leaders who received advice from an invisible being whose existence was, by its very nature, impossible to prove.

'The night before I quit Channel Blue,' Amanda continued, 'I asked Jeff to stop by the Lincoln Bedroom and visit President Grebner.'

It took Perry a moment to realise what she was saying. 'You gave the President a vision?'

Amanda nodded. 'Jesus Christ told President Grebner that the world was about to end, but that Perry Bunt would be coming to see him soon with a plan to save it. When the President shakes your hand, all you have to do is tell him your name. He'll know why you're there.'

Perry couldn't help smiling. 'That's good.'

'You wrote the original scene – I'm just doing what producers do best.'

'What's that?'

'Steal from writers.'

Perry smiled. He knew there was a reason he'd conceived a child with this woman. 'And what will I say to the President when he asks me how to save the world?'

'The usual: stop being selfish, stop killing people, stop poisoning the planet—'

Perry shook his head emphatically. 'I'm going to need more than that. He's the President of the United States, for God's sake. Even if he thinks Jesus sent me, he's going to want specifics.'

Amanda waved one hand impatiently. 'I'm not worried about that. There's a million things he could do to make Earthles seem less repugnant. If you can get him to cancel a single bombing mission, or melt down one nuclear weapon, that might be enough to keep us on the air.'

'Maybe,' Perry said. 'But if we're going to do this, we need to do it right. We need a concrete plan to save the world.'

'Fine,' Amanda said. 'We'll come up with something on the plane.'

Perry remained unconvinced. 'What makes you think anyone will be watching? You quit your job. And I quit

269

whatever I was doing. How do we know anyone's even out there anymore?'

'They're still tracking us. Marty's not stupid.' Amanda glanced up at the sky. 'All right, he's more than that, he's really smart, the most talented producer I've ever worked with.' She winked at Perry. 'He knows we're going to try something. He'd be foolish not to watch. Whether they'll put us on the air is a gamble. It depends on how successful we are. But I don't think they'll be able to resist. Series star Perry Bunt and the most powerful Earthle joining forces to redeem the planet? Our viewers will eat it up.'

'They only like it when I fail,' Perry said.

'They do enjoy your failures,' Amanda admitted. 'But I think I know our audience. They're ready to see us succeed.'

By the way she said 'us', Perry could tell that she wasn't just talking about the two of them.

He stared at the invitation as if trying to find, between its engraved words, another flaw with Amanda's plan. 'If we're doing this, we have to move,' she said. 'The last flight for Washington leaves in an hour.'

Perry handed the invitation back to her. 'There's only one way I'll go. You have to promise me that if it doesn't work, you'll get out of here.'

After a moment, Amanda nodded.

'I mean it. If we can't slow down the end of the world within twenty-four hours, you will find yourself an elevator and go straight to the moon.'

Amanda sighed. 'I already agreed. Now let's go.'

'Wait,' Perry said. 'I need you to ask Jeff one more favour.'

* * *

Noah Overton was eating brown rice and mung beans alone in his studio apartment, fretting about a feud between two volunteer teachers in the reading programme he was organising, while also feeling guilty about obsessing over his petty problems when so much else was wrong with the world. The Middle East was going up in flames and here he was, worrying about his reading programme. In such states of guilty agitation Noah spent most of his waking hours.

'Noah,' a lilting voice said. Noah bolted out of his chair and turned. Gandhi was standing in his living room – *freaking Mahatma Gandhi* – right there next to his futon, wrapped in a white robe, beaming beatifically.

'Not again,' Noah said, his eyes widening in terror.

'Yes, and this time, you must pay attention to your vision!' Gandhi said, gently chiding Noah in his sing-song elocution.

Noah staggered backwards until he bumped into the couch. 'What is it? What do you want?'

'You are a very lucky young man,' Gandhi said. 'You have one more chance to save the world.'

CHANNEL 28

MEETING WITH THE PRESIDENT

Perry saw the pillars of the White House through the limousine's tinted window and felt a shiver run down his spine. He had never paid much attention to politics. Like most Americans, he took it as a given that most politicians were venal, power-hungry con artists, while paradoxically respecting the offices they filled. Ever since he was a young boy, he had held a special awe for the presidency. Maybe it was the special phone they carried that could start a nuclear war, or their pictures on the money, or the fact that they had their own theme song, 'Hail to the Chief'. The thought of meeting the President still gave him goose bumps.

'There it is,' Perry said, his voice tinged with wonder.

Amanda, who felt no such awe, nodded noncommittally. In her white evening dress, she was reading the document that Perry had, at five in the morning in a sleepless delirium, titled 'How to Save the World'. During his flight from Los Angeles to Washington, Noah Overton had come up with 315 immediate steps the President of the United States could take to improve life on Earth, and they filled over fifty pages. While Amanda slept through the night in the bedroom of their suite at the Willard-Intercontinental Hotel, Noah and Perry stayed up in the next room, whittling and honing the document until, at ten pages, it seemed almost reasonable.

The limousine turned right onto Pennsylvania Avenue.

Numerous groups demonstrated in front of the wrought-iron fence that separated them from the White House lawn. Perry pushed the button that lowered the glass partition between the back seat and the driver. 'What's going on?' he asked.

The driver glanced in the rear-view mirror. 'There's always folks out here. Everyone's got something to say, I guess.'

The limousine, caught in heavy morning traffic, crept by the protestors. Perry could now read their signs, and he saw that their complaints did indeed cover a wide spectrum. There were protestors for peace, against abortion, for Jesus, against government, for Israel, against Israel, and a strange group of demonstrators who wore blue tracksuits and waved signs reading: 'Hurry Before the Aliens Come' and 'No One Gets the Cupcake'. The limousine slowed to a stop behind a stalled car, and one blue-clad young man pushed a placard against Perry's window that depicted a handsome prophet with a flowing beard and the words 'The Buddy Is Love'. It took several moments for Perry to recognise himself – or rather, an artist's version of a Photoshopped cell phone picture of himself. The limousine pulled away. Perry shook his head in disbelief. 'Did you see that?'

Amanda was still reading 'How to Save the World'. 'What?'

Perry turned and looked out the rear window. The blue tracksuits were now just little dots among the other protestors. 'Never mind.'

The limousine passed through a security gate, then joined a parade of other limousines sliding up under the west portico of the White House in perfect choreography, each pausing to disgorge its well-dressed passengers before moving on.

As Perry and Amanda emerged from their limo and walked to the entrance, Amanda tucked 'How to Save the World' back into its manila envelope and handed it to Perry. 'Nicely done,' she said.

'Not too crazy?'

'I don't think so,' Amanda said. 'But then, I'm not from around here.'

Perry gazed up at the formidable mansion. His grandparents had brought him here when he was eleven. At that time, he'd felt butterflies in his stomach walking through the east portico with the other tourists. Today he felt those same butterflies, only more of them. Today he wasn't just sightseeing on the ground floor, he was going upstairs to meet the man of the house. And more than that, he was going to ask for his help in saving the country, the world and his unborn son.

No pressure, he thought.

Yet as he made his way through the security checkpoint and showed a poker-faced Secret Service agent his invitation and drivers licence, he felt a strange elation. In one hand he held 'How to Save the World'; in the other, he held Amanda's. Just having her next to him instilled in him an irrational confidence. Then, as if to prove him right, a fly buzzed by his head and down the long hallway filled with grandiose oil paintings of bewigged presidents. He didn't have a chance to see if the fly was blue, but it had to be a good omen. 'Watch this, you alien couch potatoes!' he wanted to yell after it. 'You want to see a desperate plan to save Earth? I've got it right here!'

Perry, Amanda and the rest of the well-dressed visitors gathered at the bottom of a staircase, where they were met by an officious man in a dark suit.

'I want to welcome you all to the White House,' he said. 'We will first proceed upstairs to the Oval Office. There you will all have an opportunity to meet the President. Photography is permitted, but since the President's time is limited, he cannot pose with each of you. If you would like a photo with the President, we ask that you have someone else take it while the President is shaking your hand—' He went on in this manner and Perry found himself impatiently grinding his teeth. Finally, the protocol was dispensed with and the officious man led the visitors up the stairs.

When Perry followed the group into a homely room and was told that it was the Oval Office, he was sure there'd been some mistake. But on closer inspection he saw that it was in fact the room he'd seen for years in photographs and movies, only smaller and older-looking. The officious man set about arranging Perry, Amanda and the rest of the visitors into a single-file line. They stood like birds on a wire for what seemed like several minutes until a door Perry hadn't noticed opened and two Secret Service agents strode in. They circulated around the room, scrutinised the visitors, then drifted back to the walls and became as still as statues. More minutes passed. Then, through yet another door, a tall, handsome white-haired man charged in, while talking to two younger men who trailed him. The tall man was unmistakably President Brendan Grebner.

'First make the call,' he said, looking at a paper on his desk. 'We need more information.' One of the younger men nodded and headed out the way he'd come in. The President glanced at papers on his desk, seemingly oblivious to the dozen strangers standing in a straight line in front of him. Finally, he looked up and smiled.

'Welcome, folks,' he said. 'I need to apologise. The situation in the Middle East has made things a little chaotic this morning. But I'm glad you all could come by—' He proceeded to shake hands with each visitor, starting at one end of the line and working his way down at a brisk pace, exchanging pleasantries along the way. 'Hi there, where're you from?' 'Welcome to the White House, what's your name?'

Perry and Amanda stood towards the end of this line, but at his present pace, the President would soon be upon them. Perry nervously fondled the manila envelope and tried to generate more saliva; his throat suddenly felt like a desert cave. Amanda squeezed his hand and smiled.

'Remember,' she whispered, 'it's just another show.' Perry couldn't help smiling back.

President Grebner was now shaking hands with the man standing next to him. Perry started to extend his hand but the man was blathering on about some biofuels plant. Finally, President Grebner pulled himself away and stepped over to Perry, who took a deep breath and offered his hand.

'Good morning, Mr President. I'm Perry Bunt.'

For a fleeting second, Perry thought he saw a trace of recognition in the President's eyes. But then, to his surprise, the President released his hand and moved on, quickly saying hello to Amanda and one other visitor before vanishing through yet another door.

Perry watched the door close behind the President, panic building in his gut. He leaned in close to Amanda. 'What just happened?'

Amanda shook her head. 'I don't know.'

'Are you sure he was awake when you gave him the vision?'

'Yes, I'm sure. He wept. He wet his pyjamas. Oh no. Perry.' Amanda was looking down. It was then that Perry realised he was still holding 'How to Save the World'. 'You didn't give it to him.'

'He didn't give me an opening!'

'Well, we have to get it to him. Something has to happen here or no one's going to watch the show. You know as well as I do that it's not even considered a scene if nothing happens to move the story along.'

'I know the rules of scene structure,' Perry replied tersely.

The visitors, led by the officious man, were filing out of the Oval Office. Perry and Amanda looked around desperately.

'Put it on his desk,' Amanda hissed. Perry, sweat beads forming on his forehead, took two steps towards the President's desk when the officious man arrived at his side.

'Right this way, sir,' he said, gently placing his arm on Perry's elbow and guiding him to the door. 'We have White House cufflinks for the gentlemen and White House compacts for the ladies—'

Just before walking through the door, Perry noticed one of the Secret Service agents standing against the bookcase. He thrust the manila envelope towards him. 'Please give this to the President,' Perry said. After an interminable second, the agent deliberately reached out and took the envelope, just as the officious man pushed Perry through the door.

Perry caught up with Amanda at the bottom of the stairs and told her what he'd done. 'It's something,' Amanda said. 'Let's hope it gets to him.'

At the end of the hallway, a woman handed out official White House cufflinks and compacts. Once they were given theirs, Perry and Amanda were directed back out through the Secret Service checkpoint to the driveway. As they were passing through, one of the agents approached Perry. 'Mr Bunt?'

'Yes?'

'Can I ask you to step back into the White House? The President would like to ask you some questions about the document you left for him.'

Perry and Amanda looked at each other with great relief. 'Of course,' Perry said.

Amanda gave him a hug. 'Now go talk his ear off,' she whispered. 'I'll see you back at the hotel.' They kissed quickly and Perry followed the agent back into the White House.

The agent led Perry down the same hallway, but when they came to the staircase that had taken him up to the Oval Office, the agent opened a door and directed Perry into a hidden stairwell. They walked down into the basement of the White House, which evinced none of the historic charm found above ground; the hallways could have been part of any office building. They took several turns and entered a small room where two other Secret Service agents waited, one of whom Perry recognised from the Oval Office. This agent held the manila envelope that contained 'How to Save the World'.

'Did you write this?' he asked.

'Yes,' Perry said. The agent nodded and a hood was slipped down over Perry's eyes, blocking out all light. Perry instinctively ran but almost immediately collided with a wall. One of his arms was yanked back and the sleeve of his jacket pulled up over his forearm.

'I have to talk to the President!' Perry shouted into heavy black cloth. 'Listen to me. The world is going to end if I don't talk to him.' He felt the prick of a needle and felt like he was falling. He wondered where the floor was, but never got there.

* * *

Although he couldn't hear Perry yelling, President Brendan Grebner was actually only ten yards away, strolling briskly down the hallway to a meeting that appeared on no schedules and was accorded the secrecy of a covert military operation. The President turned a corner and entered an elevator that only he was permitted to use, which whisked him down to a sub-basement. Once he'd stepped out of the car, an infra-red scanner shining into his right eye confirmed his identity before unlocking a door into a small office. Inside this office, a middle-aged man with a beard and glasses sat in an armchair facing a larger chair. President Grebner entered, closed the door and sat down in this chair.

'So,' the bearded man said. 'How are you feeling today?'

President Grebner shook his head. 'I'm afraid it's getting worse.'

'Please explain.'

'You remember last week's hallucination?'

'Jesus?'

The President nodded. 'A visitor came to the Oval Office this morning named *Perry Bunt*.' He waited for something to register on the face of the bearded man. Nothing did. 'Did you hear me? Perry Bunt.'

'I'm sorry, I don't know the name.'

'Yes, you do.' The President waved one hand impatiently. 'That's the name the hallucination told me. He said Perry Bunt would have the plan to save the world.' He pointed at the notebook in the bearded man's lap. 'Look back to last week, you must have written it down.'

The bearded man made no move towards the notebook. 'What do you think this means?'

'You're the expert. What the hell does it sound like?'

'I want to know what you think.'

'I just met a visitor to the White House using a name given to me by a hallucination. Which means that the visitor was also a hallucination. Which means I'm still hallucinating. Which means the new goddamned drugs aren't working!'

The bearded man nodded slowly, seemingly oblivious to the President's state of agitation.

'I know the situation in the Middle East has taken a toll on you, and when we're in a fragile state under intense pressure, our minds can play all kinds of tricks on us.' He stroked his beard thoughtfully. 'Maybe the name of the visitor was Barry Bunt. Or Perry Hunt.'

'It wasn't! It was goddamned *Perry Bunt*!'

'Did you ask him to repeat it?'

'You expect me to stand there in the Oval Office, talking to a hallucination?'

'Did his appearance remind you of anyone?'

'No! He didn't look like anyone, he didn't look like anything at all.'

'And this name has no personal significance to you?'

'*Perry Bunt*? Are you joking? What significance could that possibly have?'

The bearded man took off his glasses and cleaned them with a tissue. 'As you know, I'm a man of science. But I also believe there is so much that we don't know that we have to consider everything.'

'English, Doctor,' the President said. 'I've got Jews and jihadis getting ready to incinerate each other; I don't have time for the graduate seminar.'

'I'm saying, maybe you have actually had some kind of religious experience.'

The President stared blankly at the bearded man. 'Are you serious?'

The bearded man shifted in his seat. This was clearly an area he didn't feel fully comfortable discussing. 'I know you've spoken in interviews about getting advice from God—'

'Not *literally*, for crying out loud! Jesus doesn't actually *come to people and tell them what to do*! It would scare the living shit out of them!' The President looked helplessly around the room. His vitriol seemed to suddenly give way to great sadness. 'Doctor, what's happening to my mind?'

'New medication always takes time to become fully effective. You're going to be fine, you'll see. Everything is going to be fine.'

CHANNEL 29

THE TERRORIST

Perry woke to the sound of loud chanting. He sat up, still groggy. He was in a large, windowless cell dressed in an orange jumpsuit. His legs were cuffed to a row of leg shackles bolted to the concrete floor. On both sides and across from him were men in identical orange jumpsuits, shackled just as he was. They had beards and were chanting loudly with their eyes closed, twisting their bodies so that their bowed heads pointed in different directions.

'*Subhaana rabbiyal Alaa. Subhaana rabbiyal Alaa. Subhaana rabbiyal Alaa.*'

The man to his left was splayed out so that he almost touched him with outstretched arms.

'*Allahu Akbar.*'

Without moving their shackled feet, the men stood and continued chanting. Perry lay back down, trying to get his bearings. His head was pounding. He stared up at the dim fluorescent light in the ceiling. He shifted his legs to see how much he could move them. Not much, as it turned out – maybe an inch.

The chanting stopped and the room seemed terribly quiet. The man next to him saw that he was awake, and then turned to the man in the row opposite him and said something in a foreign language.

After a few more minutes, a large steel door opened and

two soldiers in camouflage entered the cell. They walked down the centre aisle and stopped in front of Perry.

'Put your hands out in front,' one of them said. Perry did as he was told. The soldiers put his wrists in handcuffs and locked them, then unlocked his leg shackles from the eyelet in the floor. They lifted him into a standing position and, with a soldier at each elbow, led him shuffling out of the cell.

They passed into a cavernous hallway, also faintly lit by fluorescents. There was more air out there and Perry's mind slowly defogged.

He was clearly a prisoner of some kind, no doubt as a result of the document he'd left for the President. So basically there was good news and bad news. The bad news: he was being imprisoned without even the pretence of a hearing, meaning that his life was in danger. The good news: he was being imprisoned without even the pretence of a hearing, meaning that his life was in danger. Perry now knew from experience that the viewers of Channel Blue took great pleasure in his misery: Perry Bunt in a secret prison in itself might be enough to keep the finale from taking place. But were they watching? He hadn't seen any flies since regaining consciousness, but the satellites had to be picking this up. Hopefully Amanda was safe and could put pressure on Marty to air it. It was a thin hope on which to hang the fate of the world, but it was hope. The scene in the White House had in fact moved the plot along. Once again, a story was happening to Perry. *Bunt to the Rescue* was back in production, if not on the air.

The guards took Perry to a smaller cell. At a table in the centre of the room sat two men: one young with a full head of perfectly coiffed hair in an immaculate grey suit, the other old and bald in a red plaid hunting jacket. They watched silently as the guards sat Perry down in a metal chair and locked his leg shackles to the crossbar.

The young man cleared his throat. 'Dear Mr President,' he said. 'The Earth is in imminent danger. Many of these dangers you know about. But there is a danger even more imminent. For the last 150 years, our planet has been watched by a technologically superior alien race as entertainment. They have grown weary of our selfish and war-like ways and have decided to destroy us. This is the root of the current situation in the Middle East. Unless you take immediate action to show these alien viewers that we are capable of acting in a humane way beyond our own self-interest and thus generate their sympathy, we will all be dead within a week. Here are some steps that must be taken immediately—'

The young man paused. From his lap, he held up the document Perry had titled 'How to Save the World'. 'Let me start with a compliment. The agent who turned your file over to us has been reading crazy letters to the President for thirty years. He said that with this document you have reset the bar. It is arguably *beyond* crazy. Anyone who reads just one paragraph of it starts getting dizzy. So, operating under the bold assumption that you're sane enough to understand what I'm saying, you're probably asking yourself, "Why am I here? All I did was write a crazy letter to the President and walk it into his office. Why aren't I in some psych ward getting an evaluation before being indicted by a federal grand jury on one felony count of threatening the President of the United States, punishable by five years in prison?"'

Perry shook his head. 'I didn't threaten the President.'

The young man returned to the document. '*We will all be dead within a week,*' he read, then smiled at Perry. 'But all of this is academic. The fact is you won't be seeing a grand jury any time soon. The reason, not that we have to give you one, is the text that follows what I just read. This text is what makes you a person of substantial interest to us.'

The young man turned a page and read: '(1) End all military action. (2) Return all military personnel not involved with humanitarian missions to their families. (3) Divert all military funding not concerned with the National Guard to improve education, nutrition and healthcare in the US and around the world.' The young man rifled through the pages. 'And it goes on and on. How did you get into the White House with this?'

'I walked in.'

'Why were you trying to give it to the President?'

Perry stared back at him. 'For the reason I gave in the letter.'

'And that reason is—?'

'To save the world.'

The two men at the table exchanged a knowing look – it seemed that Perry had confirmed their worst fears. The young man drew himself erect. 'Why do you want to destroy this country?'

'I don't.'

'You just said you wanted to save the world.'

'Our country is part of the world.'

'But you didn't mention saving the United States, did you?'

'I want to save it all!'

'But your main concern is with saving the world. Yes or no.'

'Without the world, there'd be no United States.'

'You believe that.'

'It's not a matter of belief,' Perry said, growing frustrated.

The young man stood holding Perry's document. 'The fact is, if the government was to execute even one of your world-saving suggestions, it would destroy our country.'

'That's not true.'

The young man flipped through the pages. '(38) Work with the United Nations to bring peace to all conflicts.' He regarded Perry with a smirk of triumph, then flipped to another page. '(92) Issue an executive order to provide tax incentives for adopting underprivileged foreign-born children.' He flipped again. '(218) Sell off all non-essential assets of the US government – including the 8139 tonnes of gold buried underground – and use it to feed the poor.' He glared at Perry. 'Why not just go over to the Lincoln Memorial and take a big crap in Lincoln's lap?'

'The gold's just sitting there underground,' Perry said. 'It's not doing anybody any good there. We're not even on the gold standard.'

'Don't talk to me about the gold standard!' the young man yelled and threw himself at Perry, pummelling him with his fists. Perry, stunned by this sudden ferocity, fell over onto the floor, where he lay for several moments before the guards, with seeming reluctance, set his chair upright and pulled him back onto the seat. 'You don't know *shit* about the gold standard,' the young man hissed, still seething.

'You're actually right,' Perry said. 'I don't. I just thought it was a valid point, seeing how we have all this gold sitting there under the ground—'

'Shut up!' barked the young man, his face now a livid shade of red. He paced back and forth, rubbing his head as if attempting to calm himself. 'Just . . . stop talking!'

Perry fell silent. The guy obviously had some serious issues with gold.

'Listen and learn.' The young man stopped pacing and turned back to the table. The old man had spoken for the first time. 'This is the new breed. It's the worst kind of terrorism, really, this terrorism of the mind.' The old man gazed intently at Perry with the attention an entomologist might give a rare insect he'd stepped on.

The old man had lived to see many enemies challenge America. But in the fifty-three years he'd spent safeguarding her borders, protecting her from the communists, the revolutionaries, the anarchists and the terrorists, Drummond Nash had run into few operatives as dangerous as he considered Perry Bunt to be. To the elderly spymaster, Perry Bunt was the red flag that warned of a change in the game, the first salvo in a brand new theatre of combat.

This war never failed to surprise the old man. And why shouldn't it? There was no precedent to serve as a guide. It was a war like no other – unconventional, multilateral and, most of all, endless.

Many were the presidents Drummond Nash had seen daunted by the idea of fighting an interminable war. They were weak and needed to convince themselves it could be won in order to fight it. The old man required no such artificial consolations. No one wanted war, of course, much less a war that goes on forever. Yet there was something deeply exciting to him about the concept of Eternal War. He felt like an expert climber who, in the twilight of his career, had come upon a mountain so massive that it had no discernible peak. How could you not be thrilled by that kind of challenge? It was obvious to him that his entire life of service had led up to this ultimate test. And when you thought about it, Eternal War was a more natural state than the old-fashioned ebb-and-flow of human conflict, when great nations would take breaks between wars to manufacture new weapons and breed new soldiers. If you believed that there existed both good and evil in the world, didn't it follow that there should be constant conflict between them? What was the value of good and evil if they weren't eternally bent on mutual annihilation?

Drummond Nash stared at Perry. Here was the eternal enemy's latest escalation, their latest delivery system, their latest weapon. The detainee clearly wasn't what you'd call intimidating, powerful, intelligent, strong of character, or even manly for that matter – but that wasn't the point.

'Make no mistake, Jerome,' the old man told his protégé. 'Evil ideas with a benevolent appearance can turn the minds of a nation's own citizens against it. And what is a nation, even this one, but a mere *idea*? The do-gooders, the so-called humanitarians, don't understand how fragile she is. "Just be more humane." "Just love each other."' Drummond Nash shook his massive head with awe and admiration. 'Few bombs could do more damage. They're like viruses, these ideas. They trick minds into accepting them by disguising themselves as *good* and *kind*, then, once inside, take over and wipe out everything else. We had a taste of it in the Sixties, but this here—' He flapped a large weathered hand in Perry's direction. 'This is a whole new strain. With enough operatives like him, the enemy might never need another bomb. Look at him. He'd like to think us into thin air. He'd like to think us right into the shithole with the rest of the world.' Drummond Nash and the young man glared in silence at Perry, who grew more and more uncomfortable.

'I would love to see him survive one year out in the world he loves so much,' the old man murmured. 'One year.'

'Listen to me,' Perry said with urgency. 'I am not a terrorist.'

The young man, who still seemed agitated about Perry's ideas concerning gold, leaned over and punched him just below the sternum. Perry doubled over, gasping for air.

'Careful,' Drummond Nash said drolly. 'Let's not get too enhanced too quickly.'

The young man snatched up pages from the table, grabbed a fistful of Perry's hair and yanked his head back. 'We want to know who helped you write this and who helped you get it into the Oval Office.'

'I did it myself,' Perry said.

'A lot of this information is classified.'

'You can get it all on the internet.'

'Exactly,' the young man said. 'Who's helping you?'

'I told you, I did it myself.'

The young man stomped on Perry's foot. Perry saw stars and screamed.

'You came to the White House with an Amanda Mundo. What's her real name?'

'That is her real name.'

'It's not. We have no record of her. Where is she now?'

'I don't know.'

'Who helped you?'

'No one.' This time it was a blast to the ribs. 'Where is Amanda Mundo?' The questioning continued in this repetitive vein for a time until, just as Perry was convinced that the young man was going to beat him to death right there, Drummond Nash said, 'Let the Gardener have him,' and Perry was carried back to his cell, bruised and bleeding. There the soldiers laid him out on the concrete floor between the other orange-clad men like a corpse on a slab, locked his leg shackles to the floor, and left him.

'Can I have some water?' Perry muttered before he realised the soldiers had already left. He lay there, a human pulp on the cement, marvelling at the fact that no matter how many times you were beaten, the most recent beating was always the worst. His addled mind recalled his grandfather, who declared every year's Christmas tree the best tree ever. Perry and his parents had called this 'the Christmas tree paradox'. Now he was experiencing an inverse Christmas tree paradox: every beating was the worst ever, and somehow each new one was worst still.

He passed in and out of consciousness until he was forced awake by a sound that made his parched throat and dry mouth seem unbearable: drips of water. He opened his swollen eyes and saw, on the ceiling, beyond the fluorescent light, a crystalline drop of water form slowly, then fall. *PLOP*. Another drop began to accumulate from moisture on the ceiling. Was it dripping like that before? He may have missed it because of the chanting. With great effort, he sat up and traced the drop's fall. The dripping formed a puddle between two prisoners on the opposite side of the room, which in turn became a rivulet that ran across the floor to a crack, where the water disappeared.

No, Perry thought. *It can't be*. He examined the ceiling carefully for the first time, squinting his eyes to peer past the fluorescent light into the shadows above it. There he saw what he was dreading: the dimpling a stonecutter makes when it cuts through solid rock.

'Jesus,' he said aloud. 'We're underground.'

CHANNEL 30

THE TRUE BELIEVER

The bearded men around Perry turned with a clatter of chains and surveyed him curiously. Seeing these helpless prisoners underscored the ridiculous futility of his mission.

'No flies!' Perry shouted to no one in particular. 'And no satellites can reach us! No one can see this! There's no show! We're totally fucked!' The prisoners continued to stare at him curiously. 'Do you understand? No god, not yours or anyone else's, can save us.'

His cellmates muttered to each other and turned away, leaving Perry alone in his despair. Or so he thought.

'You're lucky they don't speak English,' said a clipped English accent. Perry looked over to the bearded olive-skinned man lying on the cement floor, two detainees away from him. He lay motionless, his eyes closed as if he were conserving energy. 'I, however, am not so lucky. What drivel. Flies and satellites, dear God.'

'You speak English very well,' Perry said.

'Because I'm English,' the prisoner replied. 'Unlike you.' He did a dead-on imitation of Perry. '*We're totally fucked!*' He chuckled joylessly. 'If the Queen were here she'd want her language back. Which would be wonderful, because she could take me home with it.'

'Where are we?'

'Well, lying here in my own filth, going over in my mind

everything I know about secret prisons that are no longer supposed to exist, I've narrowed it down to Cuba, Belarus or Israel.'

'Are we underground?'

'I'm no geologist, but if your walls and ceiling are carved out of solid bedrock, you're not in the penthouse of the Savoy.'

Perry pulled himself up to his feet, balancing himself against the chains of his shackles. 'I've got to get out of here.'

'Congratulations. You are the very first person here to have had that thought.' The prisoner laughed. 'The very first.'

'I'm not a terrorist.'

'Of course you aren't. Terrorists never admit to being terrorists.'

'You don't understand. I'm trying to save the world.'

'Now *that* is exactly the sort of thing a terrorist would admit to.'

Perry regarded his cellmate, who continued to lie on the cement with his eyes closed. 'What's your name?'

'Alistair Alexander of London. And yours?'

'Perry Bunt. Of Los Angeles.'

The man's eyes opened. They were a striking shade of olive green. 'And how were you planning to save the world, Perry Bunt of Los Angeles?'

Perry told Alistair everything, from his discovery of the existence of Channel Blue to his most recent efforts to save Earth. Alistair seemed to take the story at face value, only bursting into laughter two or three times. 'Well, it is rather inconvenient that you're underground,' he said when Perry had finished. 'But look on the bright side – if you're right, we might survive a bit longer down here when the rest of the world ends.'

'How about you?' Perry asked. 'Why are you here?'

In his quiet, measured voice, Alistair began telling Perry the story of his life. The child of Yemeni immigrants, fluent in five languages at the age of ten, he had grown up loving language and books. He was now a student of comparative literature at Cambridge University, working on his doctorate. His thesis was tentatively titled 'Voyages Toward Fathers: Sailing Away from Infanticide and Patricide in Literature'. Alistair had chosen this topic as a reaction to the prevailing archetypes of the father–son relationship. His own relationship with his father, a domineering workaholic who had passed away when Alistair was twelve, was troubled at best. When Alistair had sought out his beloved books to understand it, he was chagrined to discover that the iconic stories of fathers and sons in Western civilisation roughly broke down into two categories: either the father offered the son up for sacrifice (Abraham and Isaac in the Old Testament; God and Jesus in the New) or the son killed the father (Kronos poisoned by Zeus, *Oedipus Rex*, *Hamlet*).

The critical deviation from this kill-or-be-killed dynamic was *The Odyssey*, which happened to be Alistair's favourite work. *The Odyssey* tracks both Ulysses' voyage home to Crete from the Trojan Wars and the voyage of Telemachus, Ulysses' son, to find his father.

One day around six months ago (as far as he could tell), Alistair felt inspired by a recent re-reading of *The Odyssey* to fly impulsively to New York City for the weekend. The happiest experience of his father's unhappy life had been a short visit to New York in the early sixties, during which he'd attended a performance at Radio City Music Hall. Alistair's earliest memory of his father was hearing him talk about 'the Rockettes of Radio City'. For his father, the dancing of the Rockettes – their beauty, their seemingly effortless grace – was the quintessence of everything that was magnificent about the world. The Rockettes were the Sirens of his father's Odyssey.

So, in the spirit of Telemachus, Alistair hoped to discover something new about his father by recreating the journey. Everything had gone smoothly until he arrived at passport control in JFK International Airport. When the customs agent asked Alistair to describe the purpose of his visit, he said – with what he realises now was a tad too much whimsicality – 'The Rockettes'. As a matter of course, the agent sent the Yemeni-born tourist interested in America's rockets to another agent for more questioning, who in turn referred him to the FBI.

Alistair quickly discovered a truth about the self-fulfilling nature of criminal suspicion: the longer you stay in custody, the harder it is to get out. The security apparatus is set up to justify itself, and as long as you're inside it, there must be a reason that you are.

Finally, a terrible coincidence doomed Alistair: he was similar in appearance to the only known photograph of a fugitive Yemeni terrorist named Ali al-Zander, a mysterious figure who had introduced rocket technology to the Taliban in Afghanistan. Nothing Alistair Alexander could tell the FBI agents would convince them he wasn't Ali al-Zander, even the obvious argument that no terrorist would be so stupid as to adopt an alias so close to his own name. Since the terrorist al-Zander had never been courteous enough to furnish the FBI with fingerprints or a DNA sample or anything other than the single photo, they were convinced he was Alistair. The British student soon found himself in his present surroundings without a chance to contact his mother or girlfriend, much less a lawyer.

'That's terrible,' Perry said. He had perversely enjoyed Alistair's story in that it had distracted him from his own misery. Now that it was over, though, his thoughts wandered to Amanda. If only he could be sure that she was safe somewhere far away. How terrible to die down here with that uncertainty.

Alistair shrugged. 'It seems somehow fitting that all this happened while I was trying to understand my father. I think one of the reasons he was so cruel to me was that he had a morbid fear of authority. He lived in terror of being picked up and deported back to Yemen. Well, now I've realised his worst fear to the *nth* degree. In some ways, this is all part of the voyage.' He surveyed the cell around him. 'I have my doubts, however, that everyone here will be this philosophical. It no longer matters if they were innocent coming in, they'll all be guilty going out.' He chuckled. 'Who says America no longer makes anything? You make terrorists – with the quality and efficiency with which you once made automobiles. And I'm afraid you'll have many opportunities to sample your fine product in the next decades.' He glanced over at Perry. 'I'm sorry. I forgot that the world is ending soon. Never mind, then.'

'This is exactly *why* the world is ending,' Perry said. 'Galaxy Entertainment set up our planet so that we'd distrust and hurt each other. Terrorism is all about one thing: ratings. It's what they wanted to see, until they got too much of it and decided to kill the monster they'd created.'

'Interesting theory,' Alistair said. 'If I were considering insanity as a lifestyle, I might subscribe to it.'

Perry leaned over and shook the chains around his shackles. 'Has anyone ever escaped from here?'

'I'm afraid you may have read too many boys' adventures: *Count of Monte Cristo* and the like. No one escapes from places like this. We're chained to solid rock, for God's sake.'

One of the prisoners in the far corner of the cell began

chanting loudly. Suddenly, fervent chanting filled the air and the prisoners, except for Perry and Alistair, stood, knelt and bowed in all different directions.

'We never know what time it is, so when one man starts praying, everyone starts!' Alistair shouted over the cacophony. 'And since no one knows where Mecca is, everyone faces in different directions!' He smiled wryly. 'I'm so glad I lived to see the day when I could appreciate being C of E.'

Perry took in the spectacle of the men fervently praying, his heart heavy. *Is this how the world ends? Shouldn't someone at least know which way to pray?* He felt tears running down his face before he realised that he was crying. Alistair noticed this.

'I have to be honest with you, Perry Bunt,' he said. 'I don't believe anything you've told me. But if any of it is true, and if you are indeed a writer trying to rewrite the end of the world, then the story isn't over. It's still your story to write, yes?'

The lock turned in the massive steel door and it swung open. The two soldiers entered and walked down the centre of the cell. The prisoners stopped praying. Perry sensed them tense up around him, waiting to see where the guards were going. When they stopped over Perry and unlocked his shackles, it was almost as if the entire cell sighed with relief.

Alistair, however, sat up. 'What are you taking him again for?' he said. 'He just returned from one of your sessions. Look at him – the blood on his face is still damp!'

The guards didn't seem to hear Alistair as they pulled Perry up to standing. 'He's got nothing for you,' Alistair continued. 'He's a complete lunatic! He should be in a mental institution, not this hellhole!'

As the impervious guards escorted him to the doorway,

Perry remembered the elderly interrogator's last words. He turned back to Alistair. 'Who's the Gardener?' he asked.

Again, he sensed the prisoners tense around him. Alistair appeared distraught. The soldiers pulled Perry into the dank hallway as he heard the English student call after him. 'Write yourself a happy ending, Perry Bunt of Los Angeles! Write yourself a good one!'

Perry was again taken down the cavernous hallway. He tried to keep track of where he was but then realised that he had lost all sense of direction. There was one cave after another, all lined with the same fluorescent lights.

'I'm so thirsty,' he said to his guards. 'Can I please have some water?'

The soldiers laughed. 'Oh yes,' one of them said. They escorted Perry into a bright small room. A doughy woman in glasses and an apron stood next to an examination table. If it wasn't for the setting, she could've been a nursery school teacher. On the floor were a stack of folded towels and two watering cans.

'Perry Bunt?' the woman said cheerfully.

'Yes?' Perry answered, disarmed.

'I'm the Gardener,' the woman said. There was an awkward pause. She reached over and absentmindedly opened a buckle on a strap attached to the table. 'Is there anything you'd like to tell me before we begin?'

'Begin what?' Perry said.

The Gardener gave him a plump-cheeked smile. The soldiers pulled a hood down over his head and strapped him onto the table. He felt a tightening tug on the straps, followed by a falling sensation as the table was tilted at a downward angle. A folded towel was placed over his face, closing off any light that he'd been able to sense through the hood. He had a chance to take two laboured inhalations before he realised that water was running up his nose.

He held his breath. He knew now what was happening to him, knew that it was called 'waterboarding' and had been used on suspected terrorists, had heard the debate between civil-liberties groups who claimed it was torture and national-security advocates who claimed it was an interrogation technique, which he frankly had not really cared that much about because what it really sounded like was a water sport. Now he not so much regretted his lack of interest in the practice as his inability to take a deeper breath before it began happening to him. He was already out of air and the water was still pouring onto his face. His lungs throbbed, pulsing with carbon dioxide desperate to be exhaled.

When he could no longer stand the pressure, when the breath shot out of his mouth and he was forced to take an immediate breath in and the wet cloth sucked up against his mouth, effectively cutting off his air, he realised that the civil-liberties groups and the national-security advocates were both wrong. What waterboarding really turned out to be was drowning. And while Perry had become somewhat inured to thoughts of death since learning of Channel Blue's cancellation, this kind of death was not as abstract as he would have liked. It was terrible and painful and it was happening to him *now*.

Moments before lapsing into a troubled unconsciousness, Perry found himself flipped upright, the layers of soaked cloth on his face, now as heavy as a wet hippo's ass, peeled away. He blinked into the fluorescent light and coughed, sucking in breath only to cough some more.

The Gardener observed this benignly, a small half-smile on her wide face. 'Now do you have anything to tell me?' she said.

Yes! Perry tried to say. *Noah Overton. It was all his fault, he gave me those terrorist ideas, he put me up to it. And Amanda Mundo, it was all her plan, she was the mastermind, she got us into the White House. I don't know if that's her real name – I was just following orders, I'm a nobody, I'm just a teacher at a community college, for God's sake!* But when he tried to speak, he could only cough. 'Noah,' was all he managed to choke out. 'Noah,' he rasped. 'Noah.'

'Oh well,' the Gardener said, shrugging. The wet hood was shoved down over Perry's face.

'*No!*' he managed to scream, realising too late that, in his croaky voice, it sounded a lot like 'Noah'. Tilted back again with the wet towel over his face, he managed one gasping breath before he felt water surging once more up his nose. *This was never meant to be an interrogation*, he thought. *This is an execution.* He started to panic and his chest bucked.

He decided to take Alistair's advice and rewrite this ending. He visualised himself with Amanda, in the house he had owned before his screenplays stopped selling. It was a beautiful house, a modernist three-bedroom, high in the Hollywood Hills, with a swimming pool on a terrace that seemed to defy gravity. He and Amanda were kissing, out there on the terrace, and a child ran up, a little boy. Perry picked him up and hugged him. The child showed him a toy, a wind-up animal, and did something with it that he and Amanda thought was cute and they laughed together. He pretended to push Amanda into the pool and then Amanda really did push him. He did a comical stutter step and fell into the water, laughing, and plunged to the bottom – but then something strange happened. When he paddled, his hands and feet passed through the water with no effect. He couldn't get off the bottom of the pool, couldn't tell anyone up above what was happening – they couldn't even see him down there. He was drowning, dying . . .

And then he wasn't. He was back upright, coughing. The buckles around him were being unclasped. The Gardener gazed down at him, her full flaccid face a picture of distress. 'Are you all right?' she said. 'I am so sorry.'

It was then that Perry realised that there was a newcomer in the room. He wore a full military uniform with ribbons and shiny medals. He had a clipped moustache and a distinct air of authority that belied his youthful appearance.

'The lieutenant here says there's been a mistake,' the Gardener said. 'He's here to take you home immediately.'

The lieutenant gave Perry a warm smile and took him under one elbow. 'Come on, Perry, let's get you out of here,' he said. In a daze, Perry shuffled alongside him into the hallway. The guards followed but the lieutenant waved them off. 'I can handle this,' he said. The guards nodded and walked in the opposite direction. The lieutenant steered Perry around a corner.

'Thank you,' Perry managed to gasp. 'I thought I was—'

The lieutenant pushed him against the rock wall and pressed the cold steel barrel of a pistol against his forehead.

'I've been given the honour of killing you,' he said, 'and I will. But I've also been asked to tell you why. I'm only going to say it once before I kill you, so listen closely.'

Perry was all ears.

'This is why,' the lieutenant said. 'Because your plan has failed.' With that, he took a sharp breath and cocked the gun.

'What?' Perry yelped. 'That's the reason?'

'Quiet!' The lieutenant scanned the hallway.

'I don't even know what that means. What plan?'

'That's all I was told to tell you.'

The gun's muzzle dug into the flesh of Perry's forehead. 'Then I have no idea why you're killing me.'

The lieutenant sighed. While keeping Perry pinned to the wall with one arm, he reached up with the hand holding the gun and pulled down the collar of his shirt to reveal a fresh tattoo: a cupcake with a red slash across it. '*No one gets the cupcake*,' the lieutenant said. 'Got it?'

Perry shook his head. The lieutenant's eyes widened with impatience. 'You wrote that letter telling the President how to save the world,' he hissed. 'Three weeks ago in a park in Los Angeles, before the aliens reached down and took him away from us, the Buddy prophesied that the aliens would destroy Earth. And that's exactly what they're going to do. No false prophet is going to try and stop them. *Now* do you understand?'

Perry had a terrible realisation: like the blue-clad demonstrators he'd seen in front of the White House, the lieutenant was a misguided follower of the religion he'd inadvertently created when he told the homeless about Channel Blue. But it seemed that since his brief stay in St Jude's Park, the religion had metastasised from a benign, slightly bananas belief system into a deadly doomsday cult.

'Listen to me,' Perry said, as calmly as he could manage with a gun to his head. 'There has been a huge misunderstanding. My name is Perry Bunt–'

'I know who you are!' the lieutenant barked impatiently.

'I was the guy at the park in Los Angeles who was trying to get everyone to be nicer to each other so the aliens wouldn't kill us.'

The lieutenant's face scrunched up in disbelief. 'You're not the Buddy!' He fished in the pocket of his jacket and pulled out a laminated card that showed what appeared to be Jesus in a blue tracksuit, his arms outstretched in supplication, levitating over a crowd of adoring followers. 'That's the Buddy!'

Perry shook his head. 'I never said I was the Buddy or even Buddy, for that matter. This homeless guy Ralph called everyone "Buddy" and that's what started it—'

'Brother Ralph? Are you claiming to know Brother Ralph?'

'I don't know about Brother Ralph. I'm talking about Ralph, this homeless guy in Los Angeles who hangs out at this one convenience store—'

The gun smacked across Perry's jaw and he tumbled to the ground.

'Brother Ralph is our prophet on Earth since the Buddy was taken away by the aliens,' the lieutenant said. 'He is only second to the Buddy in divineness.'

That explains a lot, Perry thought. He rubbed his jaw and tried to sit up, no easy trick in shackles and handcuffs. 'Listen to me: no one ever said aliens *have* to destroy the Earth. The whole point is to help each other so the aliens *won't* destroy Earth. And if you help me get out of here right now, there might be enough time. There's still a chance. If I can get above ground or at least somewhere there's a few flies, we could save our lives and everyone else's. Do you understand? We could still save the world!'

'Don't try to seduce me with your lies!' The Lieutenant kicked Perry in the side, sending him back down to the ground. 'Everyone knows that the world has to end!'

Perry tried to sit up again but the pain was too much. 'Why?'

'That's the Word of the Buddy. When the world ends, his prophecy will be revealed to all as the one true Word.'

Perry knew he shouldn't act annoyed at someone with a gun pointed at his head, but he could no longer help himself.

'Are you listening to what you're saying? If the world ends, what's the difference? No one will be here!'

The lieutenant's face turned strangely ecstatic, the eyes opening wide, the mouth smiling broadly. 'Oh yes. I'll be here. And so will thousands of others. The Buddy will come down in his spaceship and save all who believed in his Word.'

'No, he won't! The Buddy doesn't have a spaceship! He doesn't even have a fucking pair of pants right now!'

'Enough of your falsehoods, blasphemer!' The lieutenant knelt down so he could once more place the muzzle of his gun against Perry's forehead. 'Prepare to die.'

'Lieutenant?' A voice came from around the corner. The lieutenant stood and holstered his pistol. A soldier appeared and saw the lieutenant standing over Perry. 'Is something wrong, sir?'

'This detainee was being difficult. What do you want?'

'We have orders for the detainee, sir.'

The lieutenant frowned. 'This one?'

'Yes. Perry Bunt. I checked in Room 6 but was told you'd taken him.'

'Yes,' the lieutenant replied. 'My mistake. Wrong detainee. Please.' The lieutenant motioned to the guard, who helped Perry to his feet. 'Just a moment, private.' The lieutenant took a handkerchief out of his breast pocket and pressed it to Perry's swelling jaw. 'There we go,' he said, then leaned into Perry and whispered. 'If they don't finish you off, I will.'

The guard ushered Perry away. In minutes, Perry, dressed again in the suit he wore to the White House, stood in an office before Drummond Nash. The elderly spymaster now wore a red-plaid hunting cap on his bald head to complement his hunting jacket. A shotgun lay across his desk. Next to him stood a man in a suit who the old man introduced as Dan Whittaker of the State Department.

'Mr Whittaker here will be taking you back to Washington,' he said. 'Today is your lucky day. It seems that the President wants a word with you.' Perry's heart raced. Amanda's plan had worked. It had taken longer than they'd thought, but he was actually going to be able to talk to the President.

'Apparently, he saw your name on a list of detainees,' Drummond Nash continued. 'Why, with all hell breaking loose in the Middle East, he feels the need to interfere with our vital work is not readily apparent.' Dan Whittaker glared at him and the old man realised he'd let his emotions get the better of him. Releasing detainees was something he wasn't comfortable with – understandable because he'd never done it before. He took a deep breath. 'I am bound by the Constitution to obey the President's orders.' He returned his focus to Perry. 'You will be escorted by a security detail throughout the trip, and they will bring you back here as soon as the President is satisfied.'

Drummond picked up his shotgun and began polishing it with a rag. It was obviously his signal that the conversation was over. But Perry wasn't through.

'I want my letter back,' he said.

The old man stared at him, his eyes small and intense. 'We, of course, need the original for your case file, but I'll have a copy brought out to the helicopter,' he said, then turned back to his gun.

Perry nodded. Then he, Dan Whittaker and two guards left the office and entered an elevator. The car rapidly ascended for what seemed like several minutes. Then its doors opened on the enormous wood-panelled lobby. Large heads of dead animals adorned walls under huge rough-hewn wooden beams. A fire roared in a room-sized fireplace. One of the guards slipped a hood over Perry's head. Dan Whittaker pulled it off.

'I'll take responsibility,' he said. The guard nodded uneasily and pocketed the hood. Perry was led out of the hunting lodge where, among Aspen pines, a Marine One helicopter idled.

'Where are we?' Perry asked.

'I can't tell you,' Whittaker said.

They boarded the helicopter. The cabin resembled that of a luxurious private jet. Perry was given a row of large leather seats to himself while his guards took up the two rows in front of him and Whittaker rode in the cockpit with the pilot. The aircraft roared to life and lifted into the air.

Perry peered out the window at spectacular snow-covered mountains. He hoped that Alistair would someday find out how far off the mark he was. The two guards promptly nodded off.

He pushed back his seat and closed his eyes. He wanted to sleep before his meeting with the President so he would seem as cogent as possible, but his nerves wouldn't stop jangling.

'Would you like a coffee or a cold beverage?' a woman's voice spoke.

Perry opened his eyes. Amanda Mundo stood in the aisle.

THE FINAL EPISODE

After leaving Perry at the White House, Amanda had returned to their suite at the Willard-Intercontinental Hotel. There she whiled away an hour watching TV, which had the same fascination to her that watching smoke signals might to a tourist at an Indian reservation. She was about to change out of her evening dress when there was a loud rap on the door. She opened it. Two serious-looking men in suits stood on the threshold. 'Amanda Mundo?' one of them asked.

'Yes?'

'Were you at the White House earlier today?'

'Yes,' Amanda replied, careful not to betray a scintilla of the concern welling up inside her.

'Would you please come with us? We have some questions about your visit.'

Amanda smiled warmly. 'I would love to,' she said. 'That place was so incredible. I had the time of my life. And meeting the President! What an experience it was—' She went on like this for several minutes, making sure that she maintained direct eye contact with both of the men. One minute into her mindless rant, she had both of them smiling despite themselves. Amanda had taught herself flirting while watching Channel Blue as a teenager and rarely had an opportunity to use it.

Finally, one of the men, very apologetically, interrupted

her and said that they really needed to get going. Amanda made a big show out of being upset in an insubstantial, Earthle girl way – 'Oh my goodness! I haven't even changed my dress since I met the President!' – and wouldn't the men please please, *please* let her just go to the bathroom and change super, *super* fast? 'It'll take one second!' One of the men vaguely nodded. She grabbed her purse and was in the bathroom locking the door before they realised what they'd agreed to. She slid the bathroom window open, climbed out and shimmied along a narrow ledge ten storeys above the traffic on Pennsylvania Avenue to the next window over. It was locked. She slipped off one of her heels, smashed it through the glass, slid open the window, pulled herself inside, and walked through the bathroom to a bedroom where Noah Overton lay sleeping off his night-long Earth-saving labours.

Amanda shook Noah awake. 'Perry's in trouble. We have to go.' She spotted his wallet, phone and laptop on the bureau, collected them under her arm and pulled Noah, still blinking groggily, wearing only boxer shorts and a T-shirt, into the hallway.

Another man in a suit stood in the hallway. He saw Amanda, pulled a gun from a holster inside his jacket and shouted loudly for her to stay where she was. Amanda pretended not to hear him and walked towards the elevators, pulling Noah, who was now protesting loudly, with her. The man warned that he would shoot if they didn't stop. Amanda pushed Noah face-first into the ground and pivoted quickly to face the man, who aimed the gun at Amanda's right shoulder and fired. The bullet deflected off Amanda's meteorite shield and ricocheted around the hallway before lodging in the ceiling.

Amanda took seven quick steps towards the stunned man

and kicked the gun from his outstretched hand. She picked it up and held it on him while she backed up to the elevator, pulling Noah with her. 'What the hell are you doing?' Noah whimpered.

Amanda pushed the down button. The man in the suit held his hands out to his sides. 'Don't do this,' he said.

'Yeah,' Noah agreed. 'Listen to him. Don't do this.'

A chime sounded and the elevator doors opened. An elderly couple stood inside with a bellhop and a rolling suit rack. Amanda pushed Noah into the car and stepped in. The doors began to close and the man in the suit charged towards them. When it appeared he might make it into the car before the doors shut completely, Amanda flung the gun through the narrowing gap, smacking him in the forehead. The elevator's occupants saw the man fall backwards onto the carpet before the doors closed completely.

Amanda smiled at the other passengers, who stared straight ahead in shock. She perused the rack of clothes, took a man's suit off a hanger and held it up to Noah. 'I think this is about your size,' she said. When the doors opened, she pulled Noah through the busy lobby of the hotel and out the front entrance, where a line of cabs waited.

They climbed into the back of the first taxi in the queue.

'Jefferson Memorial,' Amanda told the driver. 'And we're going to miss our tour if we don't get there in five minutes.' She took a twenty out of Noah's wallet and set it down on the armrest of the driver, who smiled and punched the gas pedal. The taxi squealed out of the driveway, thrusting Amanda and Noah against the back seat.

'This is insane!' Noah yelled. 'We have to go back! You're a crazy woman!'

Amanda calmly and quietly told Noah that if they had

any hope of saving Perry and the world, they had to stay out of prison. Noah should try to relax and put on the suit she'd stolen for him. 'You have your wallet, your phone and your computer. Did anything else have your name on it?' Noah shook his head. 'Then you'll be fine.'

Noah sobbed softly while pulling on the pants. 'This is really screwed up, man.'

The taxi stopped at a red light on Fourteenth Street and, just before the light turned green, Amanda flung her door open and jumped out, tugging at Noah, half in the stolen suit jacket, to follow her. They trotted down C Street and entered a department store, passed through it and emerged onto D Street. They crossed it, turned a corner and approached a building crowned with large blue letters that read: GALAXY ENTERTAINMENT.

Amanda led Noah into the small café next door to the building. She took his laptop from him and, while he ordered two coffees, sat at a table next to the wall closest to Galaxy Entertainment. By the time Noah arrived at the table, two coffees in his shaking hands, she had hacked into Channel Blue's feeds and was scrolling back through hours of footage. Within minutes she was able to follow unconscious Perry from the White House to Andrews Air Force Base in Washington to a C5 cargo plane flying to Buckley Air Force Base in Colorado. Amanda delved into her memory and reviewed everything she knew about US intelligence operations. 'Drummond Nash,' she said aloud.

'What?' Noah said.

'A former spy chief. He basically runs his own CIA counter-terrorism unit out of some old ICBM caverns in Colorado. That's where they took Perry.' Before Noah could react, Amanda snapped the laptop shut, tossed the coffees into the trash and led him through an emergency exit into an alleyway.

They quickly made their way back to Fourteenth Street and flagged down a cab for Dulles Airport.

At the departures terminal, Amanda bought a ticket to Telluride with a transfer in Denver. She saw Noah to the gate of his flight back to Los Angeles and wished him luck. 'Thanks for all the help,' she said.

'Please don't ever contact me again,' Noah said.

'I'm sorry it got a little hectic.'

'I'm serious. You and Perry are insane. Leave me alone.' Amanda smiled and waved goodbye as Noah boarded his plane.

It was late at night when Amanda arrived in Telluride. She rented a jeep with GPS and drove north for two hours before leaving the freeway. She couldn't remember the exact coordinates of Drummond Nash's hunting lodge, and she ran over dozens of miles of dirt track before arriving at a trailhead guarded by a locked metal gate and a sign that 'prohibited trespassers beyond this point by order of the US Military'. She parked the jeep and caught an hour of sleep before sunlight peaked over the mountaintops.

When there was enough light to see fifty feet in front of her, she jumped the metal gate and hiked quickly up the trail, wishing that she'd stopped in town for some hiking boots and a jacket. When she came to the first barbed-wire fence, she stood motionless until she could discern the infrared lights of the alarm system. Fortunately, it was still dark enough for them to stand out. She crawled under the beams – and the wire – and continued up the mountain.

The patrol caught her about halfway to the top. She figured they must've been watching her with binoculars because they appeared in front of her without warning. The soldiers wore standard-issue camouflage with no identifying patches or emblems, and carried automatic rifles. Amanda made sure to act incredibly surprised, and it certainly helped sell her act that she was wearing a dirty white evening gown and high heels.

'I just had a fight with my boyfriend,' she said. 'I needed to take a walk. I don't know how long I've been walking. Where am I?' She carried on in this vein long enough to slowly close the distance between herself and the two soldiers. When she had moved to within two feet, she kicked one in the knee and punched the other in the solar plexus. They both went down, though one had the presence of mind to pull up his rifle as he fell. She kicked it out of his hands before it went off. Using their handcuffs, she chained them around a tree and gagged them with their socks before moving on.

After another half-hour of steady uphill, she broke through to the summit. A wooden lodge commanded the highest point, surrounded by a vast lawn on which a helicopter idled. As Amanda ran across the open lawn, a group of men exited the lodge. She had nowhere to hide other than the helicopter. She reversed course, keeping the helicopter between herself and the men, ran up the gangway and slipped inside. The cockpit door was open so she dropped to her knees and crawled down the aisle, squeezing under the first row of seats 'so the crew wouldn't see me if they turned around,' Amanda told Perry sitting next to him in the helicopter. 'You could imagine how relieved I was when I heard your voice.'

Perry shook his head in disbelief. 'I can't believe you did all that.'

'I got you into this. I had to get you out.'

'Hey!'

Perry and Amanda looked up. The guard in front of them was awake and pointing his handgun at Amanda. 'Who are you?'

'It's OK,' Perry said. 'She's with me.'

'What is that supposed to mean?' the guard said. 'Where the hell did she come from?'

A sharp, percussive sound like a canoe paddle smacking the side of the helicopter jolted the cabin. The chopper lurched wildly like a bucking bronco having a seizure. The guard, who hadn't been wearing a seat belt, flew across the aisle and smashed his head against the window. Perry and Amanda were flung against the seats in front of them, then spun end over end, violently shaken like rag dolls.

They reached out and managed to hold on to each other before blacking out.

* * *

Drummond Nash sat in his office, polishing his shotgun. He considered getting out for another walk before dinner, but he felt a little low energy, maybe a little 'down in the dumpies', as Mrs Nash called it. *It's this damn work*, he thought.

He could never get over how much waste there was in national security, how much inefficiency. Perfectly good men died all the time unnecessarily. That unfortunately was the nature of the war he was fighting. He had to keep his eye on the big picture, the long view. Lord knows that's what the other side was doing.

Drummond opened up the chamber of the gun and flicked away some grit with his rag. He'd have to do a proper cleaning one of these weeks, but not today. He returned it to its wall-mounted rack and looked at a blue monitor set into the wall, a radar screen he'd had the Air Force install as part of his security perimeter. The Marine One helicopter was no longer even a blip.

You'd never catch me riding in one of those things,
Drummond thought. As he always said, *There was a reason
for fixed wings.* In a helicopter, if one of those metal spinning
things comes loose, you're Spam in a can. So many crashes.
So many that you had to wonder why anyone would risk
riding in one – especially the military variety, which seemed
to drop out of the sky like bricks every day. And there were
rarely any photos of the crash sites or investigations. Once you
heard about a helicopter crash, you just accepted it, just as
you accepted the inevitability of death itself. *Of course there
was a helicopter crash*, you thought. *There are always helicopter
crashes.*

You had to wonder why anyone would take the risk.

His intercom beeped. 'Security One to Orion.'

'Orion here,' Drummond said.

'We're seeing smoke to the southeast. Looks like some
kind of wreck. Should we send out search and rescue?'

'Roger that.'

Drummond sat back in his chair. *You really have to
wonder*, he thought.

CHANNEL 32

HEAVEN IS WHAT YOU WANT IT TO BE

Perry and Amanda opened their eyes. They sat in opposite chairs in an otherwise empty white room. A window looked out onto the night sky. They were both dressed in white.

Perry reached out and touched Amanda's arm. 'Are you OK?' he said.

She nodded. 'You?'

He nodded. 'How can that be?' He tried to remember his last frantic moments of consciousness aboard the upside-down helicopter plummeting towards the ground. Just before blacking out, he recalled wishing that Brent Laskey had been aboard.

'Where are we? How long were we out?' He glanced out the window. 'It's night. We were in the helicopter around noon, right?'

Amanda stood and walked to the window. 'It's not night,' she said. Perry joined her. Outside, the dark dusty surface of the moon stretched out beneath the stars. 'They must have had a fix on us,' she said. 'Froze the helicopter in a field before impact and pulled us off.'

Perry shook his head. He felt a sense of overwhelming relief that put a lump in his throat. 'Jesus.' He clasped Amanda's hand in his. 'I never thought I'd see you again.' Tears rushed to his eyes, and he was surprised to see her eyes glisten as well.

'I know,' she said.

'I never got a chance to tell you. Thank you for coming for me.'

'Any time.'

Perry leaned over and kissed her. She enveloped him in her arms. A strange sound filled the air. At first it sounded to Perry like ice crackling. Then, with a sickening thud in his stomach, he realised what it was.

Applause.

Light streamed through the opposite wall, which then bunched together like a large curtain and lifted up into the ceiling, revealing rows upon rows of seats filled with clapping spectators.

Though they had not moved, Perry and Amanda were now standing on a stage in front of a large audience of incredibly attractive men and women in blue tracksuits. A voice boomed: 'Let's give a big welcome to the stars of *Bunt to the Rescue*, Perry Bunt and Amanda Mundo!' The crowd stood and applauded even louder. A spotlight followed Marty Firth, dressed in a blue dinner jacket, as he trotted across the stage to Perry and Amanda. Vermy, the white worm, jutted from Marty's left ear, gleaming almost as brightly as Marty's smile.

'What an amazing episode, huh, people?' he said in an amplified voice, though Perry saw no microphone. The crowd roared. The jubilant host sidled up to Perry, resting a hand on his shoulder. Perry realised that his arms were still wrapped around Amanda and self-consciously pulled them away.

'Wow,' Marty said. 'We have seen some amazing things on Channel Blue, but you outdid yourself today, Perry Bunt!' He put a fist to his mouth as if to contain his amusement. 'When you told that lieutenant who wanted to kill you that "the Buddy doesn't even have a pair of pants right now", I totally lost it.'

The audience guffawed enthusiastically. Perry stared at Marty, confused. 'Oh yes, we saw all that,' Marty said. 'We always put cameras in the secret prisons. Some of our best programming comes from those facilities, and your antics were no exception. Now let's talk to your co-star—'

Marty swivelled towards Amanda. 'Amanda, where do I begin? Can this lady handle herself or what?' The audience screamed affirmatively. Amanda appeared completely unaffected. Marty laid a hand on her shoulder. 'The smartest thing I did was fire you.'

'You didn't fire me,' Amanda said. 'I quit.'

Marty pretended to cower in anticipation of a punch. 'Whatever you say, Amanda!' The audience laughed. Marty winked at her and continued. 'Welcome everyone to *Earth Mirth with Marty Firth and Vermy Presents a Salute to Bunt to the Rescue*!' An unseen orchestra played a musical fanfare and the audience howled its approval. 'This audience has come from all over the galaxy to be part of our exclusive live Channel Blue tribute to all that you two have accomplished. And we can start with . . . having the *number eight* show in the entire galaxy!'

The audience cheered lustily for what seemed like minutes. Amanda leaned over to Perry. 'This is incredible,' she said. Perry assumed she was commenting on the insanity of the show they'd found themselves a part of, but then she continued: 'We cracked the top ten. Channel Blue's never done that before!'

While Perry tried to take this in, Marty carried on. 'We've got lots of surprises and tributes from some *amazing* special guest stars, but first let's welcome the King himself, Mr Elvis Presley!'

The audience clapped and, to the strains of 'Blue Suede Shoes', Elvis Presley, wearing dark glasses and a powder-blue jumpsuit, sauntered onto the stage holding a gold trophy. 'Hello, Mr Perry Bunt. Now, I know that I'm nothing more than a "hillbilly with the hiccups"—' The audience hooted with laughter. Perry stared at them like a stunned animal, then realised he must appear odd and tried desperately to force a smile, but this came out looking more like a nervous sneer.

'But,' Elvis continued, 'I'm here to present you with this award from the Academy of Television Arts and Sciences. The Orby for this season's Most Promising Newcomer is . . . Mr Perry Bunt!' The audience members applauded and rose to their feet. Elvis slipped the statue between Perry's hands and clapped him on the back. Perry, not sure how to react, examined the statue. A naked gold woman on a pedestal held a swirling red-and-purple planet with one hand and waved at him with the other. Baffled, Perry glanced over to Amanda, who clapped with the audience.

'You know what this means, Mr Bunt?' Marty said. Perry numbly shook his head. 'It means we can't let you die – you're too big a star!' Audience members shrieked with fits of laughter.

Once the hysterics had subsided, Elvis returned to a more conversational tone. 'When this guy first walked into my office . . . Well, if you had told me that he'd be taking home an Orby in a couple of weeks, I would've sent you to a therabot. If you'd told me that he would change the way we think about POFs, I would've signed you up for a brain transplant. I mean, on a planet full of inconsequential individuals, this guy seemed like the biggest loser of them all. Talk about insipid! I've eaten *sandwiches* with more character.' Perry's frozen smile tensed into a grimace while Elvis shook his head in wonderment. 'But that's the thing I love about this business – you never can tell.'

'That's right, Elvis,' Marty said. 'We'll talk more with Perry and Amanda in just a moment, and meet some of the fans here in the audience. But right now we have a very special guest here to sing the theme song of 'Bunt to the Rescue'. Please welcome . . . Baby Jade!' Perry watched as a four-year-old girl in a sparkly blue dress strode confidently onto the stage. If the audience members had cheered loudly for Perry and Amanda, they now seemed on the verge of convulsing, so crazed were their shouts and screams of acclamation. Perry noticed that even Amanda was frantically clapping.

Cacophonous music played and the four-year-old girl danced sprightly around the stage. Amanda watched the prancing child with awe.

'What's going on?' Perry asked her.

'That's Baby Jade,' Amanda said. 'She's been the biggest pop star in the galaxy for *years*.'

'She's just a little kid.'

'They recorded her foetal heartbeat for a dance track and she's been an unstoppable force ever since.'

Perry shook his head in amazement. 'What does all this mean?'

'It's all good news, Perry. The huge production values, Baby Jade, the audience shipped in from Eden – Channel Blue is making a huge investment in the show.'

'I don't care about the show,' Perry said, growing impatient. 'Does this mean they're calling off the finale?'

'You heard Marty – the show's become too big. If they can't let you die, they can't blow up your home, right?'

The news sank into Perry's brain, but he still couldn't believe it. Like a beaten dog, he saw menace in the upraised hand, even if it held an award.

'Really?'

'Look at the statue in your hands. They're not going to finale the Newcomer of the Year.'

'But—'

Amanda brought a finger to her lips. Baby Jade had begun to sing in a smoky soprano.

He had nothing goin' on
Till a lady let him know
That it was time to take a stand
It was time to make a show.

Beaten and battered by his fellow men
But he keeps tryin' again and again
To show that Earthles really care
Even though he doesn't have a prayer—

The music swelled to a loud thumping chorus. The audience members joined in, singing along at the tops of their lungs.

Saving Earth!
Saving Earth!
When it comes to laughter there's no dearth
Since Perry Bunt decided that it's worth
Saving Earth!
Saving Earth!
Just watch that crazy Earthle try saving Earth!

Baby Jade hopped frantically around the stage while repeating the chorus in mind-numbing fashion. Perry didn't know whether he should feel disturbed by the lyrics or comforted that for all the Edenites' supposed advantages over the people of Earth, songwriting wasn't one of them.

Finally, the music slowed and built to a bombastic crescendo. Baby Jade tilted her small head back and wailed.

Saving Earth!
Saving Earth!
Even though it's not even worth
A lousy shovel full of Eden's dirt
He just can't stop saving Eaaarrrrrrrttthhhhh!

Baby Jade held the final note and the audience members jumped to their feet like puppets on the same string, applauding and bellowing their approval. While the four-year-old took numerous bows, Amanda leaned over to Perry.

'Great, huh?'

Perry gaped at her. 'Are you kidding? That was totally insulting.'

'What part?'

'*The whole song!*'

'You're just not used to our music,' Amanda said. Perry was about to argue this point when Marty's booming voice intruded.

'How about Baby Jade?' he shouted to more ecstatic whooping. When the crowd had returned to their seats, Marty carried on. 'Now it's time for a really incredible surprise – please welcome Amanda Mundo's boyfriend, Jared Corley!'

To a huge ovation, Jared Corley strolled onto the stage, all six-and-a-half feet of him, his blond rock-star hair perfectly framing his chiselled features. He gave Amanda a big hug. 'Hey, hotshot,' he said.

Perry couldn't help notice that Amanda seemed happy to see him.

Jared firmly shook Perry's hand. 'Hi, Perry. Big fan of the

show.' The applause wound down and Jared turned to the audience. 'I just wanted to come by and tell these guys how great the show is. And you know what? I still love this woman, even though I fell for a producer – not a *reproducer*.'

The audience guffawed. Amanda smiled, while Perry grimaced. It seemed that joke-writing was another relatively useless field Earthles had the edge in.

'Amanda, as hard as it is to lose you to an Earthle, and as weirded out as I am by the thought of his random genes co-mingling with your perfect DNA, I sincerely wish you both all the success in the galaxy.'

The audience seemed to perceive this as a noble sentiment and greeted it with respectful applause. Perry stared at Jared, unable to believe what he was hearing. To make matters worse, when he glanced over at Amanda, she was glowing.

'Seriously, hotshot, I want to support you in any way that I can. Just as long as I don't have to watch you two have sexual intercourse.' The audience emitted a mixture of titters and disgusted groans. 'Or anyone else. Yuck.'

After more laughter and applause, Jared hugged Amanda again, shook Perry's limp hand, and walked off.

Before Perry could regain his equilibrium, Marty introduced an impossibly attractive celebrity who meant nothing to him but seemingly everything to Amanda, then another and another. The stars sang or danced or played a musical instrument or simply talked about their favourite moments from *Bunt to the Rescue*, usually with a quip that Perry couldn't help but find insulting. 'Can you believe Perry Bunt? Talk about gung-ho! I have seen winged chimps on *Altair 7* that exercised more caution than this guy,' said one famous Edenite, who was introduced as The Galaxy's Funnyman.

When Marty Firth finally announced the end of the show,

Perry couldn't wait to get off the stage. He turned to Amanda, but she was talking animatedly with Jared, so he proceeded to search for an exit on his own. As soon as he had found one and was walking towards it, however, Marty was in his face, telling him that he was needed immediately at a meeting with Channel Blue executives to discuss the future of the series. As if to emphasise the importance of this event, Vermy, dangling from Marty's ear, blinked rapidly.

'There's a crucial press conference tonight – we're flying in all the important entertainment journalists. It won't be like the adoring crowd here who loved everything you had to say.'

'I didn't say anything,' Perry said.

'Tonight will be different,' Marty went on, ignoring him. 'Tonight you'll be facing the sharpest minds Eden has to offer.'

Perry frowned. 'Entertainment reporters?'

'You have to understand that without any war or crime, entertainment is *the* most prestigious beat in our news media. We must prepare you, and not just for the predictable ques-tions—' Marty rambled on, but Perry wasn't listening. On the other side of the stage, Amanda continued her conversa-tion with Jared. He watched as they laughed and hugged. It was what Perry now recognised as an Edenite hug – arms clasped, bodies barely touching, and heads turned away from each other – but it was a hug nonetheless.

After Jared had left, Marty led Perry and Amanda out into another long blue hallway. They walked together for several moments before Perry broke the silence.

'Did you have a nice talk with Jared?' he asked, fighting to conceal his annoyance.

'Yes,' she said. 'He was very supportive.'

Perry stewed on this as they continued walking.

'He wanted to stay but he needed to get back to the home planet. He's got a few planetainments kicking off new seasons.'

Perry smiled wanly. 'Oh wow, that's too bad. It would've been really fun to get to know him.'

Amanda glanced over. 'There's no need for sarcasm.'

'Oh yeah, I forgot. We're on the moon.'

'I meant that Jared is in no way a threat to you.'

'Why would I be threatened by him? Just because he's freakishly tall, looks like a rock star and is weirded out by my lousy genes.'

'His response was completely understandable. You would understand if you knew more about our culture.'

'Well, I definitely don't want to. That entire show made me sick to my stomach.'

Amanda's eyes widened in surprise. 'It was tribute to *us*. What didn't you like?'

'I don't know. How about . . . *everything*? I've never seen so many condescending blowhards. If that was a tribute, I'd prefer torture.'

Amanda stopped. 'I know that cynicism is basically a religion among Earthles, and given your planet I understand why. But can't you give it a rest? Must you *always* see the very worst in people?'

'They compared me to a winged chimp!'

'The winged chimps on *Altair 7* are fabulous creatures. In fact, they always beat us in the ratings. You should be honoured.'

'Elvis said I had less character than a sandwich.'

'When he first met you, that's what he thought. You proved him wrong. You heard him. You changed the way people think about POFs.'

'That song made me sound like a complete loser.'

Amanda sighed. 'Perry, all those people *love* you. That's why they were saying all these things. *That's why we're still alive.*'

'Then I'm not sure we got the best end of that deal.'

Amanda rolled her eyes, further irritating Perry. 'Really? You'd rather be dead?'

'I'd rather be as far away from their love as possible,' Perry responded.

Amanda stared at Perry as if she didn't know him. Though she knew it was irrational, Amanda couldn't help interpreting Perry's disdain for the tribute and Edenites in general as a judgement of her, and who was he, Perry Bunt, to judge *anyone*? Hadn't she given up her career to save his life? He was a *product of fornication*, for Adam's sake. She was a Grade 4 genotype, representing the highest level of genetic craftsmanship in the known universe. She could choose to be with anyone, yet she had given up *everything*, including her dignity, to help save Perry and his planet!

'The Earth is safe. We're together. Why are you acting like this? Is it impossible for you to show gratitude?'

'It's hard to be grateful when they were the ones who were going to kill me in the first place. And if the Earth really is safe, why am I here? Can you tell me that? Why am I still part of their lousy dog-and-pony show? Why don't they let me go home?' The 'me' in the last sentence reverberated uncomfortably between them. 'And if you think Captain Handsome's so damned supportive, why didn't you go home with him?'

'Sorry, sweeties,' Marty said, interrupting. He had doubled back down the hallway to retrieve them. 'We need to keep a move-on, the schedule is exceedingly tight.'

Perry and Amanda continued walking, both dissatisfied by their exchange and the way it had ended. Marty led them to a set of tall steel doors. 'Good luck,' he said, then turned and trotted away.

Perry and Amanda entered a large conference room. At one end was a small stage. On it, four chairs were arranged around a short metal column, and a huge screen displaying the Earth served as a backdrop. Next to the stage, Elvis stood chatting with a striking elderly man. The man wore a long white beard that matched his white hair and seemed somehow familiar to Perry, though he wasn't sure why. Then, with a jolt, he realised where he'd seen him: on the ceiling of the Sistine Chapel.

Elvis looked up and noticed them. 'Hello, Perry and Amanda. There's someone I'd like you to meet.' He swept his arm towards the elderly man. 'This . . . is GOD.'

CHANNEL 33

GOD

Perry and Amanda both stared awestruck at the elderly man. 'GOD is the Founder of Earth and the Executive in Charge of All Production,' Elvis drawled. 'We're very lucky to have him here with us today. How long has it been?'

The elderly man shook his head of white hair. 'Too long, I'm afraid. The whole galaxy needs my attention now and, to be honest, coming back here just made me depressed, so I stopped.'

While Perry stood frozen, gaping at the Founder of Earth, Amanda stepped forward and extended her hand. 'Nice to meet you, sir,' she said.

'The pleasure is all mine.' The elderly man beamed at her while enveloping Amanda's hand in his two large hands. 'Amanda Mundo. Perry's been getting most of the attention, but I want you to know that you are an absolutely vital part of all this. I've been waiting a long time to meet you.' Amanda wasn't sure if it was the beatific expression or the glowing words, but it was all suddenly too much to take. She withdrew her hand. The elderly man continued to transfix her in a benevolent gaze. 'Congratulations on your pregnancy. Such a transformative event.'

Amanda glanced to the side, actually embarrassed. 'Thank you. It was quite . . . surprising.'

'To you and everyone else,' Elvis chimed in. 'When you

told Perry by that dead cornfield, the ratings hit a whole 'nother level. We're talking bigger than robot wrestling, bigger than mutant killing, even bigger than volcano wars!'

'Please Elvis,' the elderly man said softly. 'We know the ratings are doing well. That's why I'm here.' He gazed upon Perry's stunned expression and smiled serenely. 'You can relax, Perry. GOD is just a sobriquet. My name is actually Gerald O. Davidoff. You can call me Gerry if it makes you feel more comfortable.'

In order to speak, Perry had to force the words out of his mouth. 'You're on the ceiling of the Sistine Chapel.'

'Yes,' Gerald O. Davidoff said, his eyes sparkling with mirth. 'Started out as a joke. Back then, they made my hair and beard white to add to my authority. Now they wouldn't have to, would they?'

'So the belief in God—' Perry's voice trailed off.

'He exists!' Gerald O. Davidoff laughed. He shook Perry's hand with an amazingly firm grip for someone close to 200 years old. Perry had never felt such soft, warm hands. 'I am so glad to meet you, son. Earth has always been my baby, but I have to admit I'd given up on her. I was certain that her time had past, that nothing good would ever come out of her again. You proved me wrong. And for that, you have my gratitude.' He patted Perry on the shoulder and chuckled. 'Or should I say, *eternal* gratitude.' Perry found himself smiling back at him. 'Now, we have a lot of ground to cover and not much time.'

Gerald O. Davidoff explained that Edenites all over the galaxy were fascinated with Perry and his sudden rise to fame on a channel that hadn't launched a star in years. The rapid ascent had given way to suspicions that Perry was in fact an Edenite. In the past, various productions had tried to pass off Edenite producers as hapless products of fornication living on planetainments. 'I guess you could say they've been burned a few times before.' He glanced over at Elvis, who looked defensive.

'Hey, we never said I was an Earthle,' Elvis said. 'I mean, we didn't go out of our way to say I *wasn't* one, but we never lied about it.'

'I know,' Gerald O. Davidoff said. 'I'm only saying, they feel like they've been burned. Of course, they know Amanda here is an Edenite. And while the chemistry between the two of you is excellent for the arc of the series, even more questions about Perry's authenticity have been brought about by the relationship.'

'You have to admit, it's an odd one,' Elvis said.

Perry didn't feel he had to admit that, while Amanda readily nodded her head.

'Anyway, it gives us even more motivation to resolve this issue once and for all,' Gerald O. Davidoff continued. 'We have to make it clear to the galaxy's media that Perry is nothing more than a product of fornication. What do you say?' The white-haired executive fixed his penetrating brown eyes on Perry. 'You look doubtful. Are ready for this?'

Perry wasn't. He hated that he and Amanda had quarrelled in the hallway. He glanced over at her, but she wouldn't meet his eyes. Without her as an ally, he felt lonelier than ever. He was exhausted and aching from his escapades saving the world. On top of the abuse he'd endured, the bizarre adulation of the Edenites based almost exclusively on his ability to suffer was infuriating. He couldn't give a crap if the Edenite media thought he was an Earthle, a producer, or a three-toed sloth. He just wanted some kind of assurance that he and the Earth were safe so that he could collapse in a heap somewhere and fall into a deep, deep sleep.

'Do we really need to do this?' Perry asked. The two entertainment executives regarded him inscrutably. 'I mean, isn't it enough that everyone's watching Channel Blue again? Can't we all just go on with what we were doing before?'

Gerald O. Davidoff slowly nodded his mane of white hair. 'Son, I truly understand your desire to get on with your life,' he said. 'I do. After all you've been through? We all understand. But it's not time for that yet. We all want to consolidate the show's success. For that to happen, our friends in the media need to make sure that you're the real thing. You can't blame them, can you? They want to see for themselves that you're really who you say you are.'

'We've already sent them samples of your DNA, of course,' Elvis said. 'That's why we gave you the haircut before the Del Waddle episode. But there'll always be cynics who will accuse us of tinkering with your hair, which leads us to this baby right here.' Elvis smacked the metal column in the middle of the stage with the palm of his hand.

'Why don't you show Perry how it works?' Gerald O. Davidoff said. Elvis gamely hopped onto the stage and sat down on the metal column.

'Normal,' a soothing female voice pronounced.

Elvis smiled and stood. 'It's that easy.'

'Perry, why don't you give it a try?' The elderly executive gestured to the column. After a moment, Perry hauled himself up onto the stage and sat down on it.

'Product of fornication,' the same soothing voice pronounced.

Gerald O. Davidoff smiled. 'You see? It's never wrong. That's why we call it the Stool of Truth.'

Even in his demoralised state, Perry couldn't help giggling. 'Is that really what you call it?'

The founder of Channel Blue stared back at him solemnly. 'Yes.' Perry covered his mouth with his hand like a child caught laughing in church. 'Now, tonight we will begin the press conference with a series of highlights from the series. Then, after Elvis makes a few introductory remarks, you will sit on the Stool of Truth. Having thus settled the issue of your genetic make-up once and for all, we can focus on getting to know the real Perry Bunt—' He swept his hand up towards the immense Earth on the screen. 'Right in front of this beautiful live image of the planet you spent so much effort saving.' He paused and smiled warmly. 'I think it's going to be spectacular.'

'Here are some of the questions you might be asked,' Elvis said, handing Perry a small screen.

Perry read from the screen. *Do you feel like an animal whenever you have a bowel movement? Why do Earthles love dogs and hate people? After defecating, how do you wipe excrement from your anal orifice without being completely repulsed by yourself? What animal do you most feel like when you masturbate?* Perry looked up. 'I'm sorry, but these seem completely insane.'

'To you, yes, I can see that,' said Gerald O. Davidoff in a kindly way. 'But you must indulge them, Perry. Just think of this press conference as your next episode of *Bunt to the Rescue*. Which, of course, it is.'

'I have a question about that,' Perry said, seizing the moment. He tried to phrase the next words as delicately as possible. 'How many more episodes were you planning?' Again God and Elvis stared at him impassively, increasing his discomfort. 'I appreciate everyone's enthusiasm, I really do. I'm very *grateful*,' he said pointedly with a glance at Amanda, 'and I really appreciate being alive. And the Earth not being blown up and everything. But I don't think I can be on your channel anymore.'

'Perry, you're a star,' Elvis said. 'Right now, you are the most famous person on Earth. Isn't that what you've always wanted?'

'What I wanted was someone on Earth to know about it,' Perry thought about saying – but didn't because the last thing he needed was anyone else thinking he was an ingrate. 'Like I said, I appreciate everything. But having experienced fame, I guess I'd rather go back to teaching.'

While Gerald O. Davidoff's expression remained indecipherable, Elvis shook his head and chuckled in amazement. 'You can't be serious.'

'I know you think our lives our worthless down there,' Perry said, 'but right now all I want to do is get back to leading one. I can't keep running around getting beaten and nearly killed so you can keep up your ratings. I can't do it. If that's what you want, you might as well kill me now and get it over with, because I'm not going back to Earth and doing that.'

Elvis and Gerald O. Davidoff exchanged a quick glance. 'Don't worry, Perry,' the elderly executive soothed. 'I promise you that you won't have to. Not ever again.'

Perry stared at the founder of Channel Blue, afraid that he hadn't heard him correctly. 'Really?'

Gerald O. Davidoff grinned. 'My word is good.'

'We're actually very glad you feel this way,' Elvis said. 'The beat-down thing was getting *old.*'

'Your days of being abused by Earthles are *over,*' Gerald O. Davidoff said emphatically.

'*Thank you,*' Perry said, nearly faint with relief. 'In that case—' He turned to Amanda. She stared at him guardedly.

He took a breath and spoke. 'Amanda, I want you to come with me. And I'll work every day for the rest of my life to make you not regret the decision. Would you consider it?'

After a moment, Amanda broke into a smile, and Perry felt the tension between them evaporate into the recycled air. 'Yes,' she said.

Perry smiled back and took her hand.

Gerald O. Davidoff also beamed, evincing an aura of great benevolence. 'How very delightful.'

Elvis pulled off his tinted glasses and wiped his eyes with one hand. 'I swear to God, you have to repeat this for the cameras.' He put his glasses back on. 'Amanda, you are one crazy nutburger. I remember 'bout these pregnant-lady hormones from my days on Earth. You are batshit loony and I love it!'

The founder of Channel Blue stood. 'Spend as much time as you want in here, make yourselves comfortable. Just be sure you both get some rest before the press conference. Unfortunately, I won't be able to stay for it – I'm needed elsewhere. But I have faith in both of you. I'll be watching.' With a twinkling smile, he stepped lightly out of the conference room.

'You're gonna be awesome tonight!' Elvis pronounced, slapping Perry on the back and heading towards the door.

'I didn't really mean that about hating your music,' Perry blurted out. 'I've actually always loved it.'

Elvis paused at the door. 'Truth is, I never really thought of it as music. I was just down there to brainwash teenagers and make them go crazy. And it *worked*.' He curled his lips into a grin and headed out of the door.

When the door shut behind him, Perry ran to Amanda and picked her up in his arms. 'We did it!'

'I told you it would all work out.' Amanda shook her head in amazement. 'Can you believe it? Gerald O. Davidoff himself actually came here to talk to us! About a press conference! That's unheard of. He never gets caught up in details – he's totally a big-picture guy.'

'He said it, right? He said that I don't have to rescue the Earth anymore.'

Amanda nodded emphatically. 'That's what he said. And he never lies. Everyone in the galaxy knows that.'

For the first time in days, Perry allowed himself to feel relief. All the terror he'd been pushing aside welled up inside him and he sobbed in large shuddering spasms. Amanda put her arms around him and kissed his tears. She found his lips and they kissed. Perry broke away and scanned the room.

'There are no cameras,' Amanda said, reading his thoughts.

'Are you sure?'

'Yes. They don't wire the moon. Everyone's here to watch Earth.'

They kissed some more. Perry stroked the side of her face. 'How long until this stupid press conference?'

'About an hour.'

'A whole hour?' He smiled at her. 'That's a lot of time. Especially considering we only need, what was it? *Several seconds?*'

Amanda laughed and punched him. 'I guess I should've said, *the most memorable several seconds of my life.*' They kissed again.

'I hate competing with myself,' Perry said, 'but I think we might be able to better that time.'

'Oh yeah?'

'Yeah. I for one am ready to break a minute.' He backed her up against the stage, unzipped her white jacket and pressed himself against her. 'Let's show up at that press conference sweaty and sticky. Let's really give the galaxy something to talk about.'

Amanda laughed. 'Sounds good,' she said and slid her hands down Perry's pants, catching him completely off guard. He jumped into the air and pulled Amanda with him, causing her to fall backwards. At the last moment, she reached out and steadied herself, placing her hand on the Stool of Truth.

'Product of fornication,' the soothing voice pronounced.

CHANNEL 34

THE POF

Amanda's apartment on the moon was empty except for a couch and a bottle of vintage Cassiopeian champagne that was, according to the tag around its neck, a gift from GOD. It sat in a silver bucket of ice, untouched. Perry sat on the couch and watched with concern as Amanda paced back and forth, pulling on a lock of her hair and muttering to herself. Mostly the muttering was indecipherable to Perry, though now and then it reached an audible volume.

She suddenly stopped in her tracks. 'The Bs in chemistry. No one ever understood those. I had superior deductive powers in my profile, why was I getting Bs? Because I *never had* superior deductive powers.'

'Or maybe it was because the only kids who get As in chemistry are geeks,' Perry said, taking a desperate stab at levity.

'And my hair!' she said, ignoring Perry in favour of the lock in her hands. 'It's supposed to be blonde, but it gets dark sometimes. Sometimes, it's almost *brown*.'

Perry had never seen Amanda like this. She was officially scaring him. 'You must have come across one of these truth stools before.'

'It's not called a truth stool.'

'Stool of Truth, whatever.'

'I have, but I never needed to be screened. My genetic profile has been in the medibase since my conception.'

'Someone must have faked it.'

'That's impossible,' Amanda said. 'No one would try it. And if they did, they'd be caught.'

Perry arched his eyebrows. 'Always?'

'*Always*. Edenite law enforcement isn't the circus you have on Earth. There's almost no crime, and the crime that does happen is punished immediately. That's why nobody ever doubted my profile.' She paused. 'Unless they've known all along that it was false. And that's why they gave me the job on Channel Blue.' She started pacing again, faster than before. 'That makes sense – there must've been hundreds of applicants more qualified than I was.' Her eyes widened. '*That's* why they encouraged me to mingle with the POFs! They wanted me among you because they knew all along I was one of you – that I would do all the awful ignorant things that you like to do—'

'Hey!' Perry said.

'I'm sorry, but it's true. We're disgusting.' Amanda clawed at the flesh of her arms. 'Just the thought of the crappy genes inside every one of my cells makes me want to vomit.'

'Jesus, Amanda, you need to take a breath—'

'I can't help it! I've spent my entire life thinking I was the pinnacle of human genetics when I'm nothing more than . . . someone's random screw baby!'

Perry regarded her incredulously. 'Is that how you think of our kid?'

'No!' Amanda placed a protective hand on her stomach. 'But then I always thought that at least half his genes wouldn't be a total crapshoot.' She stopped herself. 'I'm sorry, that must have sounded insulting.'

'It did,' Perry assured her.

'Someone had it all planned out from the very beginning. Why didn't I see it coming?'

'Amanda, listen to me—' Perry said. But she paced even faster, tugging at her hair.

'*Of course* I couldn't see it coming! I'm a lousy POF, I couldn't see a comet coming if it landed on top of me—'

WHAP! Amanda came to a sudden halt, her hand held up to one reddening cheek. Perry stood in front of her, the palm of his hand stinging from the rapid contact it had just made with Amanda's face. 'I'm sorry, but I had to do that. You're making yourself crazy. You need to take a deep breath—' Before he could finish, she slammed her fist into his chest, knocking him straight back onto the floor. While he wheezed, struggling for air, she took a deep breath and exhaled.

'You're right,' she said. 'That helps.'

Perry slowly pulled himself back onto the couch. 'Glad to hear it,' he gasped.

'There's just no way for you to understand what I'm going through right now. You don't know what it's like to think that your life is your own and then suddenly find out that you're a total tool, some toy for the amusement of a bunch of greedy control freaks—' She paused. 'OK, maybe you do.'

'And you *don't*,' Perry said. 'You know why? You're not a tool. Or a toy.' He rubbed his chest. 'Definitely not a toy.'

'I'm not?'

'No. That's what I've been trying to tell you.'

'How do you know?'

'Because right now, if Galaxy Entertainment knew that you were a product of fornication, they'd be telling *everyone*. They'd put you on that stool tonight and congratulate themselves on finding two POFs for the price of one. But they clearly don't know. So there has to be some other explanation.' Perry thought for a moment. 'Why don't you ask your parents?'

Amanda had been so overwrought that she hadn't considered this. She stepped over to a panel of buttons on the wall next to the couch and pressed one of them. A keypad popped up from the couch's armrest. She hesitated. 'If you don't want to be on the call, stand over there,' she said, gesturing to the wall at the other end of the room. Perry walked over to this wall and Amanda tapped what seemed like a ridiculous number of digits into the keypad.

An excited middle-aged woman with short blonde hair appeared on the wall opposite her.

'Adam's ghost! Amanda! Our big star! Your father will want to hear every word of this – we just watched you on the Marty Firth show! Can you believe that? I was going to call but he said, "She'll be busy, she's a big star now, she has an entire channel depending on her, she doesn't have time to talk to us." What an amazing show! Did you meet Baby Jade? What was she like? Did you ever dream that your job would lead to something so *exciting*?'

'No—' Amanda began, but was quickly overwhelmed by her mother's exuberance.

'That scene in the helicopter with your co-star! So dramatic! Your father and I were on the edges of our seats! How did they make it seem so real?'

'We were in a crashing helicopter,' Amanda said. 'We actually did think we were going to die.'

'Well, it sure looked real to me! So suspenseful! Oh, I have to stop talking, but I'm just so excited! Michael!' she called off. 'It's Amanda! Our famous daughter!'

A distinguished middle-aged man with a full head of

salt-and-pepper hair and chiselled features appeared next to Amanda's mother. 'How's my little rocket?' he said, beaming. 'We are so *proud* of you! What an adventure you've been on. I have to ask you right away: did you really have sexual intercourse with that Earthle?'

Amanda glanced over at Perry, who couldn't lean any closer to the wall. 'Yes,' she said.

'I told them!' Amanda's father chortled. 'The guys at the club have all been asking me, "Did she really do it? Did she really have sexual intercourse?" And I keep telling them, "Of course she did. She's pregnant. The proof is in the pudding, right?" They still don't believe me. I tell them, "That's my daughter – we made a maverick." It's all right there in your genotype. I remember the programmer asking me, "Are you sure you want her to be this much of a risk-taker?" and I said, "Heck yes! Give her the genes that will make her throw herself out into the universe, discover new worlds, make history!" And you know what, rocket? That's exactly what you're doing.'

'I actually have a question about that,' Amanda said quickly, before her parents could interrupt her again. 'I just found out that I'm a product of fornication.'

Amanda's parents became completely still. For a moment, Perry thought there was a technical problem and that the image on the wall had frozen, but then Amanda's father slowly lowered his head. 'How did you find out?' he said.

'They brought a Stool of Truth in for the press conference,' Amanda said. 'I was accidentally screened.'

Her father appeared completely mortified. 'Does anybody else know?'

She shook her head. 'Only Perry. That we know of.'

Her mother cried softly. 'It's true,' she said. 'You came out of my vagina.' She took a deep breath. 'It feels so good to say it, after all these years.' She turned her face up and yelled it out. 'My daughter came out of my vagina!'

'I understand that, Mom,' Amanda said, attempting to remain matter-of-fact, 'but why didn't you tell me?'

'You've been doing so well,' her father said. 'I mean, you might as well be perfect genetically, as far as the galaxy's concerned.'

Her mother began sobbing. 'Please forgive us. We didn't have a choice. We didn't want to lie but we knew that it would be your only chance at having a decent life.'

'Mom, please stop crying,' Amanda said. 'I understand. I just didn't know such a thing was possible. How did you do it?'

Amanda's parents exchanged a glance. The father cleared his throat. 'When your mother started showing, we took some time off at a resort planet in the Vega cluster, out there on the edge of the galaxy. Obviously, we were looking for a world where we wouldn't know anyone. At our hotel, we met a very well-to-do man who was travelling alone. We had dinner with him a couple of nights, and he seemed like someone we could trust. We told him about our situation and, to our surprise, he told us he could help us. He said he knew how to insert a genetic profile for you into the medibase. And it worked. As long as you and everyone else believed you were a Grade 4 genotype, you acted like one.'

'Until the Bs in chemistry, of course,' her mother added.

'Right,' her father said. 'Those were a little worrisome—'

'Who was this man?' Amanda interrupted. 'Why did he offer to help?'

Her father shrugged. 'He never said. He didn't want any money or anything else.'

Amanda shook her head. 'It doesn't make any sense. No

Edenite would break the law no matter how many people it helped.'

'Oh, I don't think he was an Edenite,' her mother said.

'What was he then?'

'We didn't ask any questions,' her father said. 'The less we knew the better.'

A loud high-pitched whine made Perry suddenly jump from the protection of his wall into the middle of the room. 'What was that?' he said.

'The doorbell,' Amanda said.

'It's your co-star Perry Bunt!' her mother said. Amanda's parents turned to take in Perry, who briefly considered returning to his refuge against the wall before realising that it would only make things more awkward. 'Perry, I think you're the most hilarious Earthle ever. Michael and I don't really care for the others – we've never been big fans of Earth. But we like you.'

'Thank you,' Perry said uncertainly.

'You are too much,' Amanda's father said, chuckling. 'Are you going to have sexual intercourse with my daughter again?'

'I-I-I don't know,' Perry stammered.

'I bet you want to, right?'

The loud high-pitched whine sounded again. 'Mom, Dad, I have to call you back,' Amanda said. 'There's someone at the door.'

'OK,' the mother said. 'We love you so much. And I know how much you enjoy your work, but do you think that when you're done with all this Earth business you could come home for a visit? A couple of days at least?'

Amanda agreed to this, pushed a button on the panel, and her parents vanished.

'Thank God,' Perry said. 'Are they always like that?'

'They've always been very supportive,' Amanda said. She pushed another button and a small, bespectacled red-headed boy appeared on the wall. He was standing right outside Amanda's front door.

'Who is it?' Amanda asked.

'Hi, I'm really sorry to bother you, but I'm your biggest fan,' the boy said. 'Could I have an eye scan for my collection? Please?'

Amanda pressed a smaller button on the panel and the image disappeared. 'He must have come here for the show and slipped through security afterwards.'

'Why does he want an eye scan?'

'It's like an autograph. I'll get rid of him quickly.' She walked to the front door and opened it. The red-headed boy scampered past her into the apartment before she could stop him.

'Hey!' Amanda called after him.

'Shut the door quickly,' the boy said, pulling off his glasses and a red wig. 'We don't have much time.'

Perry saw, to his dismay, that Nick Pythagorus now stood before him. 'You again.'

'Yes, me again.'

Amanda strode towards the wall panel. 'I'm calling security.'

Nick blocked her path as best he could. 'Hold on, Mandy. I've got something you're both going to want to see.' He pulled a small screen from the back pocket of his jeans and offered it to her.

Amanda turned to Perry. 'We can't trust him. He's with The Movement.'

Perry laughed. 'I'm sorry. That name kills me every time.'

'What wrong with The Movement?' Nick asked.

Perry laughed again. Amanda rolled her eyes and said, 'I'll be more specific. We can't trust him because he's working

with Leslie Satan. They want to destroy the entire entertainment-industrial complex.'

'Guilty as charged,' Nick said. 'And you will too, after
you read this.' He once more held out the small screen. This
time, Perry took it and read what appeared to be a piece of
business correspondence.

Confidential Memo
From: Gerald O. Davidoff
To: Interplanetary Board Members
Re: Rescuing 'Rescue'

*While ratings remain high, I fear we will face audience
fatigue in the near future without a change of scenery.
Let's not get caught again playing one note for too
long. Yes, the male lead is compelling, but as demonstrated, he will never be able to affect real change on
this habitat and will no doubt deliver just as fine a
performance on another, especially now that the stakes
will soon include a juvenile. New scenery will be a
relief to all concerned. I see no other course than to
proceed with our original plan and find a new venue
for our stars, preferably one of the newer planetainments that show potential for positive story arcs.*

Perry shook his head. 'I don't get it.' He turned to Amanda,
who was reading over his shoulder. 'What does it mean?'

Amanda took the screen and glared at Nick. 'Where did
you get this?'

'They couldn't change *all* the codes after I was fired,' the
boy said. 'They would've had to shut down their entire
network. I hacked in.'

'It's a forgery.' She tossed the screen back at him.

'Will somebody tell me what it means?' Perry asked.

'Then verify it,' Nick said to Amanda. 'It should be easy for you. Do you still have a link with the LA office?'

'Verify what?' Perry asked.

Amanda went to the control panel and pushed another button. A dial popped up from the armrest of the couch. Amanda turned it and a rapid succession of images filled the opposite wall. They flickered by so fast, one after another, that Perry couldn't recognise anything. He thought he saw Drummond Nash setting up cots in his underground office, but he couldn't be sure. Then he saw what appeared to be Ralph speaking to a large rally in front of the White House, but he couldn't be sure about that either. And was that a quick glimpse of Noah Overton filling up jugs of water? Occasionally Amanda would slow the knob and pause on an image, but it would be of a closet or someone's foot – completely meaningless to Perry but greeted with grunts of recognition from Nick and Amanda.

'Could someone please tell me what we're looking for?' Perry said.

'Moving boxes,' Amanda said. 'And they're all over the place.' She pushed the button back down into the armrest and the images vanished. 'Galaxy's pulling out all their employees.'

Perry studied Amanda's expression. 'They're going ahead with the finale, aren't they?'

For a few moments, Amanda didn't seem to know where to look. When she finally met his eyes, he saw that hers were full of tears. 'I'm sorry, Perry. It's really over.'

THE REBEL

'Unfortunately for Earth, the script I put together was perfect,' Nick said, with what Perry thought was way too much pride. 'Earthquakes and shortages in Russia help the nationalists consolidate power, tsunamis and food riots destabilise Asia, and then, to set off the entire tinder box, naked-burkha pens in the Middle East. The only sequence that wasn't properly produced was the terrorist attack in the US. You know, Flight 240.' Nick glowered at Perry. 'Thanks to you. But I even had a contingency for *that*. After your successful press conference, Channel Blue will launch a cyberprobe from one of their satellites into the Kremlin, creating a false nuclear alert. The Russians will launch several nuclear-armed RS-24 intercontinental ballistic missiles at the United States. President Grebner will have no choice but to order an immediate retaliatory strike. As a result, the galaxy's media will have front-row seats to the Earth's immolation – while simultaneously watching you two freak out because you thought you'd saved it. Live television doesn't get much better than that.'

Nick was now smiling rapturously. Perry and Amanda glared at him, and he adopted a more concerned expression. 'I'm sorry it was such a strong script.'

'Contingencies are always incredibly expensive,' Amanda said. 'Especially cyberprobes. And the finale's already trillions over budget—'

'Mandy, *GOD* wants this to happen,' Nick said, holding up his screen as a reminder. 'Expense isn't a consideration at this point. In a weird way, your little show might have sealed the deal. They figure what they're going to lose on the finale they can make up in publicity for future episodes of *Bunt to the Rescue*.'

Perry still couldn't believe it. 'How could GOD lie to me?'

Nick frowned, confused. 'Gerald O. Davidoff was here?'

Amanda nodded and Nick looked crestfallen. 'I missed him?'

'He lied,' Perry said.

'You must be mistaken,' Nick says. 'GOD never lies – even his enemies know that. He's the most successful entertainment executive in the galaxy for a reason: his word is good.'

'It isn't! He just told me I wouldn't have to do the show anymore!'

'On Earth,' Amanda said.

Nick nodded. 'Yeah, that wasn't a lie. They're spinning you off.'

'Spinning me off?' Perry said.

Nick shook his head impatiently. 'You are so slow. That's what this whole show on the moon is about: brand management. They're creating a franchise that they can stick anywhere – the hapless-though-determined Earthle, his genetically superior gal pal, and, coming soon, their little POF. You'll all try to rescue whatever planet they dump you on and the rest of the galaxy will watch.'

Perry glared at the former boy executive, repulsed. 'I won't do it!'

'Then they'll drop you back on Earth and kill you with everyone else. Stick your sweetie here on some crappy asteroid and, when he's old enough, use your son for a sequel.'

Perry turned to Amanda. 'Is this true? GOD would do that?'

Amanda nodded grimly. 'It's a good plan.'

'What?'

'I don't mean that I like it. It's smart, though. Why settle for one series when you can have a franchise?'

'That's why he's GOD,' Nick said.

Perry stood. 'How can either of you talk about the merits of a plan to kill *seven billion people*?'

'You don't know who you're dealing with, Earthle,' Nick said, his voice layered with contempt. 'And you never have.' The boy turned to Amanda. 'Seriously. How do you deal with this imbecile?'

'You little shit!' Perry grabbed Nick, lifted him up and shook him violently.

'Another genius move!' Nick said, his high-pitched voice undulating with every shake. 'Physically abusing the one person who can help you!'

Perry dropped him onto the floor. 'How can you help us?'

Nick sat up, rearranging his clothes. 'Leslie Satan has been tracking this situation closely. He has a solution, and he's asked me to arrange a meeting.'

Amanda laughed. 'The press conference is in less than an hour!'

Nick lowered his voice. 'He's coming *here*.'

'Here?'

'To the moon. The man himself. We can't waste any more time. Come with me.' Nick fetched his red wig and glasses from the couch, put them on and opened the door. 'Come on. It's your only hope.'

Within minutes, Nick, Perry and Amanda had slipped into rented spacesuits and were making their way through an

347

airlock onto the surface of the moon. Strolling the lunar surface was considered a relaxing pastime among the residents of Base Station Blue, so there was nothing unusual about Perry and Amanda moonwalking with one of their young fans. They followed a marked path for ten minutes. When the path came to an end, Nick led them up a steep hill that turned out to be the edge of a crater.

They followed the crater's lip until a boulder the size of a palace blocked their path. Nick scurried around the boulder, followed by Perry and Amanda. On the other side of it, a long flat plain opened up, extending to a range of jagged mountains in the distance. Nick stopped and examined the screen he held in one gloved hand.

'Now what?' Amanda said over their helmet intercoms.

Nick pointed up at a star. It took Perry a moment to realise that this star was rapidly growing and seemed to be approaching quickly. Very quickly. Within seconds, he could see that the star was in fact a motley collection of scuffed-up shipping containers hurtling through space. It slowed as it approached, belching jets of fire from its underside, and dropped down towards the moon's surface, kicking up plumes of dust that showered onto Perry, Amanda and Nick until it hovered just above the lunar plain. The jets cut out and it smacked unceremoniously down onto the ground, where it shuddered like a beached whale, heaving and sputtering, emitting smoke and jets of orange liquid.

Thus far, Perry had only been exposed to Edenite technology through hidden moon bases, streamlined devices, ruthlessly efficient robots and invisible flying elevators. He was transfixed by the sight of this heap burbling before him – it seemed less like a vision of the future than a rogue piece of space junk. After a few moments, one end of the craft dropped onto the ground, revealing an opening. Nick quickly marched towards it. Perry and Amanda exchanged a look, then followed.

After they climbed through the opening into a small dirty chamber, the spaceship closed itself up. Jets of air hissed in around them. Nick took off his helmet and gloves and walked through two creaky sliding doors into a large, dimly lit cabin. Perry and Amanda took off their helmets and joined him.

If a crazy old cat lady ever owned a spaceship, Perry thought, *it might look like this*. Piles of cans, printed material, electronic devices and what looked like spare engine parts filled a large cabin, all covered with nets or strapped to the floor with canvas belts. At one end of the cabin stood a few mismatched chairs on a faded carpet next to a wall of blinking lights and screens. A middle-aged woman in a bathrobe stood up from one of the chairs, a mug in her hand. 'Anyone want something to drink?' she said.

Nick, Perry and Amanda shook their heads. 'Suit yourselves,' she said and approached a set of sliding doors. Only one of the doors opened, forcing her to scoot sideways through a narrow gap. A loud sneeze sounded and Perry's eyes, adjusting to the dim light, now saw that there was someone else in the cabin. Ensconced deep in a worn leather lounger that had bits of yellow foam poking through its cracked brown carcase was an incredibly old man with an eye-patch, smoking a thin cigar. Even in the weak gravity of the moon, he seemed to be exerting a force of will just to maintain any semblance of verticality.

'Please excuse the meagre surroundings.' The old man spoke in a strained, wheezing voice. He laboriously pulled a handkerchief from the pocket of his bathrobe and dabbed his nose. 'We've never put much stock in the material plain. All our resources go directly into The Movement.'

Amanda glared pre-emptively at Perry, who this time was able to stifle a laugh.

'Mr Satan,' Nick said. 'It's an honour to meet you.'

The old man gawked at Nick as if he'd just dropped through the ceiling. 'Who the hell are you?'

Nick appeared flustered. 'Nick Pythagorus. I'm your new agent on Earth.'

'Oh,' Leslie Satan said. 'You're rather small, aren't you?'

'I'm nine years old.'

'I see,' Leslie Satan said. He dropped the thin cigar into a coffee cup and released another great sneeze, covering his mouth with one hand. He grunted and pulled away the hand, which now held a row of teeth. He glanced quickly at the teeth and placed them in the pocket of his bathrobe. 'Damn moon dust. Always irritates my allergies.'

'This is Amanda Mundo and Perry Bunt,' Nick said. 'You gave me the mission of producing them, and here they are.'

'And so they are, so they are,' said Leslie Satan. His one eye stared intently at Perry. 'Perry Bunt.'

Perry wasn't sure what to do, so he nodded.

Leslie Satan returned his nod. 'Surprised to see that I don't have horns and a tail? Earthles usually are. Gerald's little joke, giving Earth's bogeyman my name.' He continued to peer at Perry as if he were searching for something. 'You look different on TV. More impressive.' Before Perry could react, Leslie Satan sneezed again, launching something directly at him. Perry instinctively ducked and the object flew over his head, hit the wall and dropped to the deck of the ship with a small plop. He looked down and saw Leslie Satan's nose.

'Can you get that for me?' the old man asked, his voice even stranger than usual, for he now had two slits in his face where his nose, until very recently, had resided. Perry, concealing his revulsion, reached down, delicately picked up the bulb of flesh and dropped it into the hand of its owner, who pocketed it.

'Have you saved Earth yet? Of course you haven't. Gerald would never let you. Never!' Planting a metal cane carefully in front of him, Leslie Satan proceeded, with much gasping and grunting, to lift himself out of his chair, all the while continuing to speak. 'Do you know why? Because that would demonstrate to the entire galaxy that a lowly product of fornication could somehow effect positive change. We couldn't have that, could we? The whole universe might fall apart!' With a final loud groan, Leslie Satan raised himself into a standing position. Perry realised that he'd been so transfixed by the old man's struggle to get out of the chair that he hadn't heard a single word he'd said.

'Sit down here where I can get a better look at you.' Leslie Satan patted a spotted hand on the distressed lounger. Perry obediently sat. The old man slowly tottered around it until he stood behind him. 'I have none of my original organs. Some of them are third or fourth generation. Like this ship and The Movement itself, I am held together with nothing but hope in the form of a single vision.'

Perry felt warm breath on his bald spot as the old man closely perused the top of his head. 'I received a vision last year when a clogged transceiver steered us into a black hole. I've been trapped in several such singularities and have usually been disappointed. I know many people who have seen the future inside them. But not me – I've always just become constipated. Until this last time, when I actually did receive a vision of what is to come.'

The old man was now poking through Perry's thinning hair as if he was searching for something, a sensation that

Perry found quite disconcerting. 'I learned that one day, on some lowly planetainment – the vision didn't bother to tell me which one – a product of fornication would rise up and lead all the galaxy's POFs in a great war against the Edenites and their terror. The reason I've asked you here, Perry, is that I think you may be the One we've all been waiting for—'

Leslie Satan folded Perry's left ear forward and looked behind it. 'But as it turns out, you are not. You can all go now. Sorry for the confusion.' He pulled a stopper out of the wall and shouted into a small hole. 'Doris! Prepare for lift-off!'

Perry, Amanda and Nick all stared at the old man, confused.

'Go ahead,' said Leslie Satan, motioning with one hand. 'The airlock will automatically close behind you.' Perry stood, unsure of what to do. Leslie Satan now flailed his arm towards the airlock. 'Come now, run along! I don't want to give them too much of a chance to catch me, do I?'

Amanda spoke first. 'We were told you had a solution to our problem.'

'If he had been the One,' Leslie Satan said, pointing at Perry, 'I would've helped him go back to Earth and save it. But he's not, so there's obviously no point.'

'How do you know that he's not?'

'In the vision, I was told that the One would have a star-shaped birthmark on his scalp.' He pointed at Perry. 'He doesn't have anything like that. Just a couple of moles – which you should have someone look at, by the way. Now please, I'm on a tight schedule.'

Nick stepped over to the old man. 'I can help you. I know their codes; I know their infrastructure. I can help you *destroy* Galaxy Entertainment.'

Leslie Satan seemed exhausted by the very thought of this. 'It's hardly worth the time. Galaxy's only the fifth largest entertainment conglomerate in the known universe. If it goes down, the others will assimilate its holdings and nothing will change.'

'Please,' Nick said. 'Let me come with you.'

'Sorry,' Leslie Satan said. 'I really don't have the room.'

His lower lip began to quiver, and Nick suddenly looked very much like the nine-year-old boy he was. 'I don't have anywhere to go! I was counting on you!'

Leslie Satan raised a hand and, after a second, sneezed. He reached into his pocket, pulled out his handkerchief and dabbed the two slits in the middle of his face. Perry couldn't help noticing that one of the old man's ears had come loose and was dangling from the side of his head by a flap of skin. 'You seem like a very nice little boy, but we just don't have the thrust for additional passengers.'

Perry had been trying to contain his irritation with Leslie Satan – after all, the old man seemed on the verge of sneezing himself into bits – but something about the lameness of this excuse pushed him over the edge. 'Why don't you get rid of some of this garbage?' he said, gesturing to the piles around them. 'And if you really love POFs so much, why not help us stop GOD from killing seven billion of them – even if I *don't* have some lousy birthmark? What kind of movement is this, anyway?'

The tiny, ancient, nose-less man seemed like he just wanted to take a nap.

'Look,' he rasped. 'We have to pick our battles carefully. There's no point in getting involved with Earth. Not only are all the inhabitants completely unaware of the forces controlling their lives, but I doubt they would be able to do anything about it if they did. I mean, normally I would fight on behalf of *any* people of random genetics, but the Earthles—' He shook his head. 'They're impossible. I shouldn't have to tell you. We all saw the show, by the way, which was great. I mean, truly hilarious. I am a fan.' The old man's face cracked into a toothless grin. 'The more you tried to help them, the more they hurt you! So you know the situation. I've spent time down there. I've tried my best, but it's no use. If I went down right now and tried to help them, they'd kill me, steal my spaceship and try to use it to kill their enemies. There's just no point.'

'But—'

Amanda quieted Perry with a look and turned to the leader of the Movement. 'Isn't there *anything* you can do to help us?'

The old man wearily considered this, then leaned over, pulled the stopper out of the wall and shouted into the hole. 'Doris! Bring me two dischargers from the bridge closet! Make sure they're full!'

After a few moments, the middle-aged woman in the bathrobe shuffled back into the room carrying two shiny metal tubes with red pistol grips. She gave them to Leslie Satan who, grunting with effort, handed them to Amanda and Perry.

'What are these for?' Perry asked.

'It's the most powerful firearm we have,' Leslie Satan replied. 'With a little luck, you can use them to blow up the moon base before their bots take you out. Eventually, of course, they'll come back here and finish you off, along with your planet, but it'll buy you a little time anyway.'

'What about me?' Nick said. 'Where's my discharger?'

'I don't give guns to children,' Leslie Satan said. 'Now please, all of you, off my ship. There's a massive rebellion on a CrazyPlanet near Corvus 9 and I'm running very late.'

There seemed nothing left to say. Perry, Amanda and Nick turned and walked back to the airlock. When they'd almost reached the door, Nick suddenly darted behind one of the piles of refuse.

'What are you doing?' Amanda said.

'I'm stowing away. When he's stuck with me, he'll realise how useful I am to The Movement.' Nick's eyes darted furtively. 'You'll give me away, keep going!'

Perry glanced at Amanda, who nodded. The two of them stepped into the airlock and, after putting on their helmets and gloves, stepped through another hatch, down a ramp and back onto the lunar surface. The fuselage closed quickly behind them and, almost before they could get out of its way, a column of fire lifted the strange craft away from the moon. They watched as it became a small glint of light among the stars and then disappeared.

'I never thought Satan would be such a let-down,' Perry said.

Amanda brushed white dust off the visor of her helmet. 'At least Nick isn't our problem anymore.'

Perry nodded. 'There is that to be grateful for.' He slipped one gloved hand around the pistol grip of the discharger. Despite his general distrust of guns, it felt good. Yes, he was still a product of fornication on a moon filled with smarter and more powerful enemies, but now he had *firepower*. Not that he had the slightest idea what to do with it. He looked at Amanda. 'What now?'

'I guess we go back to the base and blow it up,' Amanda said. 'We'll certainly have the element of surprise on our side. Stars don't usually show up at their press conferences with weapons.'

Perry gazed intently at this relentlessly surprising woman.

'Are you really up for this? Are we really going to kill Marty? And Vermy? And *Elvis*?'

She shrugged. 'It's the only way to stop them from ending Earth, right?'

'I thought you didn't believe in killing. That Edenites don't murder each other.'

'We don't,' Amanda said. She didn't meet his gaze – she was busy examining her discharger. 'It's not something I'm comfortable with. I mean, I've never even *seen* one of these things before. But I know the people in that base and how they feel about us.' Perry had never heard her group the two of them together before, which made him feel good despite the direness of their situation. 'I know their attitude towards the talent. The only reason we haven't died already is because we've helped the ratings. So why should we hesitate when our only hope of having a decent life is to kill them?'

She shook her head, clearly amazed at the words coming out of her mouth. 'I'm obviously seeing this quite differently now that I'm on the other side of the camera.'

Perry frowned, unconvinced. 'Leslie Satan said they'll just come back and do it later. It might even jack up the ratings of the eventual finale – raised stakes and all that. You know—' He adopted an announcer's voice: '*This* time, it's PERSONAL!'

'True,' Amanda said. 'But what else can we do?'

Perry didn't have any response to this, so they walked back towards Base Station Blue, dischargers in hand. As they navigated the rim of the crater, Amanda took Perry's gloved hand in hers and he felt an irrational surge of hope. Then he tripped on a rock and fell, accidentally firing off his discharger. A shaky blue beam shot out of the end of the metal tube and vaporised the palace-sized boulder in a puff of white dust.

Perry lay on his side, watching the silent cloud where the boulder had been. 'Whoa.'

Amanda helped him to his feet. 'Are you OK?'

He could hear the sound of his breathing in his helmet intercom. 'Yeah.' Then, after a moment, he shook his head. 'No, I'm not.' Something deep down was bothering him, but he found it almost impossible to articulate. After a few more breaths, he tried. 'This isn't how it's supposed to end.'

Amanda frowned. 'What?'

'It just isn't right.' Perry regarded the long silver tube that still lay on the ground. He bent down, picked it up and, with a sudden jerk of his arms, flung it into the crater.

Amanda stared at him in shock. 'What are you doing?'

'I told you. This isn't how it's supposed to end.'

'You keep saying that. What are you talking about?'

'The show. As far as I can tell, it's a comedy. Not for me, of course – for me it's been horrific. But everyone watching thinks it's funny. Even that old turd Leslie Satan thinks it's funny.'

Behind the visor of her helmet, Amanda furrowed her brow with concern. 'No one's watching this, Perry. We're on the moon now. This isn't part of any show.'

'I know. But you said it yourself – there's something going on here. It may not be fate or destiny, but it's definitely some kind of story, right? And I just don't believe it has this kind of ending. Think of what's happened since you walked into my classroom. My being mistaken for a prophet and a terrorist. Our thing in the van. You getting pregnant. Noah Overton actually getting a chance to save the world. Would any of that have happened in a drama? No. They're all plot points in a comedy.' Perry paced back and forth on the rim of the crater. 'Now, I don't write comedies, but I do teach them. And a comedy would not end with us walking into a press conference on the moon and killing everyone.'

Amanda took this in. 'OK,' she said. She considered the discharger in her hands, and, in one economical movement, pitched it off the cliff. They watched it spin slowly as it fell from view. Seconds later, a shaky blue beam shot up from the crater's floor and struck the cliff.

Perry and Amanda fell in slow motion, the ground beneath them inextricably tugged by the moon's weak gravity into the mouth of the crater. Like cartoon coyotes momentarily suspended in mid-air, they flailed their bodies away from the disappearing ground, diving with outstretched arms for solid terrain until they dangled from the new rim of the crater, clinging to moon rocks as their legs swung free.

Amanda pulled herself up first and helped Perry to his feet. They crouched forward, gloved hands on the knees of their spacesuits, panting for several seconds before they could speak.

'See?' Perry wheezed. 'Comedy.'

'So tell me,' Amanda said. 'How does it end?'

CHANNEL 36

THE WAY IT WAS SUPPOSED TO END

On the stage between the Stool of Truth and the real-time image of Earth, Perry and Amanda sat facing members of the galactic media. The journalists' attention was focused on screens around the auditorium, which played a selection of 'highlights' from *Bunt to the Rescue*: Perry getting punched by gang members, chased by a bag lady, tear-gassed by police, pummelled by Del Waddle, drowned by the Gardener. Perry wasn't sure which annoyed him most: the polite chuckling of the assembled journalists or the roaring guffaws of Marty Firth, who sat next to him, throwing his head back in hysteria, Vermy swinging from his right ear. It was probably his imagination, but Perry thought he saw amusement in the eyes of Marty's brain parasite as well.

Finally, the clips ended. Before the lights rose, Amanda squeezed Perry's hand, stood and slipped out. Moments earlier, while sitting in their dressing room, they had agreed this would be the perfect moment for her to leave so as not to draw undue attention to herself or delay the start of the press conference. This was just after Perry had told her the inspiration that had come to him as he was going to the bathroom.

Entering the bathroom, Perry had been in a state of panic. The press conference was five minutes away and he had no idea how to stop the destruction of Earth scheduled for its end. He walked across the tiled room to a metal vessel affixed to the wall that he decided must be the urinal.

He peered into the mirror on the wall and saw a terrified man, the terror made oddly comic by the make-up on his face. Marty Firth had insisted that Perry, in addition to shaving, wear make-up to counteract his genetically unaltered complexion. 'We received complaints from the viewers about your pasty appearance on my show,' Marty had told him. 'I don't mind your whole crazy-eyed "What the hell am I doing here?" look. There's nothing we can do about that. But we can make you look less anaemic. This press conference is going out live to billions of viewers, so we need you to look your very best.' Perry, distracted as he was by the fate of Earth and his inability to come up with a plan to save it, was unable to mount an argument. Now, looking into the mirror, he wished that he had: he looked utterly ridiculous, a grim, balding drag queen in a white suit.

At least no one he knew would be among the billions watching.

With shaking hands, Perry unzipped his fly. Why was his mind such a terrible blank? It wasn't as if he was sitting in his crappy apartment by himself, unable to come up with a satisfying end to a script that no one would read, much less produce. The world was counting on him! Amanda was counting on him! *His unborn child* was counting on him! It's no wonder that when he reached into his fly he couldn't find anything, his genitals having attempted escape by nearly shrivelling up inside themselves. Whatever the opposite of an erection was, Perry had one.

He yanked down his pants, grabbed the reluctant discharger and pointed it into the vessel. As he did so, he noticed that his pubic hair was growing back after being vaporised on his first trip to the moon. Interesting, he thought, that they hadn't seen fit to burn it off this time.

And then he had it. The ending.

'Why are you urinating in the sink?' Amanda said, standing in the doorway.

'Never mind.' Perry pulled up his pants. 'I need the razor and the make-up kit.'

Sitting in the press conference, Perry fidgeted in his chair as the sparse applause subsided. He had never succeeded in going to the bathroom, and there would be no relief for a while. The lights rose and Elvis stepped behind a podium next to the stage. He said a few words about how happy everyone was with the new show and how Mr Perry Bunt was poised to become one of the galaxy's biggest stars 'whether he's trying to save Earth or anything else'. Perry noted the telling choice of words, but maintained his nervous smile. 'He's such an exciting performer,' Elvis continued, 'it seems that he's fooled some of you into thinking he's something more than a product of fornication. Well, we're going to put that issue to rest right off. Mr Bunt, would you take a seat on the Stool of Truth?'

Perry remained in his chair, as if he hadn't heard. 'Mr Bunt?' Elvis prompted. Perry nodded at Elvis. He took a deep breath, stood and stepped over to the stool. He began to lower himself down onto it, then hesitated. Marty reached over and rested his hand on Perry's shoulder.

'It's quite all right, Mr Bunt,' he said. 'Go on ahead.' When Perry continued standing over the stool, Marty pushed down on his shoulder. Perry deftly twisted away, shrugging off Marty's hand, reached out and plucked Vermy from the host's ear. The parasite was longer than Perry had expected. While he tugged at its head, its tail snapped out of Marty's right ear and wound around Perry's wrist like a bullwhip.

As Amanda had predicted, Marty was completely para-
lysed by this action. What she hadn't planned on, however,
was what happened next: Vermy blinked once, lunged
forward, and burrowed its head into Perry's ear. Before Perry
could react, Vermy was deep inside his head, doing what
every parasite does: changing its environment to better suit
its needs. When confronted with the environment known as
Perry Bunt's brain, Vermy immediately began altering it by
giving it a vision of the future Vermy now wanted for Perry.
In this vision, Perry sat on the Stool of Truth, was confirmed
as a product of fornication and, after the Earth was destroyed,
was whisked with Amanda to a different planetainment for
another triumphant season of *Bunt to the Rescue*. Perry and
Amanda quickly became so famous and rich they no longer
needed to entertain. Instead, they gallivanted from one solar
system to another in their luxury spacecraft when they weren't
relaxing on their own planet, a stunning ecosystem of jungles
and oceans where they could lie on an untouched beach in
each other's arms for days on end while being served drinks
and snacks by telepathic dolphin-like creatures.

Perry jolted out of the narcotic fog of this parasite-induced
vision and found himself back on the stage in the press
conference, a stunned Marty Firth in front of him, the tail
of the *Vermis solium* entwined around his wrist. The future
had taken less than a second. Summoning his will, he yanked
his arm away from his body, jerking Vermy out of his head,
then hurled the brain parasite over the heads of the journalists to the back of the conference room. Marty Firth screamed
like a Sicilian widow and launched himself into the audience.

Now alone on the stage, Perry turned to Elvis. 'I'm sorry,
I can't go through with it. You did it, but I can't. I'm sick
of the lies.'

Elvis gaped at Perry from behind the podium, completely baffled. Perry took advantage of his bewilderment to address the galaxy's media. 'I'm not a POF. I'm a producer for Channel Blue.' He slid up the cuff of his jacket, revealing a blue fly tattoo on his wrist. Even though she'd been under considerable time pressure, Amanda had done an excellent job drawing the insect with nothing more than mascara and blue eye shadow. After it had dried, she'd even smeared a little foundation over it, giving the appearance that Perry was wearing make-up to conceal the tattoo.

The journalists seemed to catch their breaths simultaneously. The King smiled and shook his great head. 'I'm not sure what the Earthle's up to, but he's lying. I mean, this is exactly what POFs do, right? They lie their fool heads off. Perry Bunt is the biggest damn POF I ever met. You couldn't get a more mixed-up set of DNA if you had your genes programmed by a blind monkey.'

'He knows the truth, he just doesn't want *you* to know it!' Perry shouted. 'I'm an Edenite! If you don't believe it, look for yourselves.' In a single, dramatic gesture, Perry yanked down the waistband of his pants, revealing, in addition to every bit of Perry, a complete absence of body hair. The pièce de résistance, however, was just north of this area, where Amanda, with an eyebrow pencil, had drawn a quite credible shunt.

Up to this point, the collected journalists had watched dumbstruck. But when Perry pulled down his pants, it was as if a bomb had gone off. The journalists howled and roared; Perry thought he even heard the gnashing of teeth. He yanked up his pants, suddenly concerned about the sudden near-riot he'd created. The next part of the plan was the most crucial. He and Amanda had concluded that the only way to save

Earth was to make *not* destroying the planet more cost-effective than destroying it. The only way to do this, they had agreed, was to get viewers to turn off Channel Blue before the finale began. They knew that Gerald O. Davidoff was ultimately a businessman. If there were no ratings to be gained from blowing up Earth, there'd be no reason to spend any additional money doing so. Perry took a deep breath and shouted over the crowd.

'Listen to me!'

The members of the media fell silent, their sweaty, incredulous faces turned up to Perry. 'You call yourselves journalists. You don't know anything about what's going on down there! Earth is nothing but a giant fake. Everything you've seen on Channel Blue has been scripted and produced. Everyone down there is an actor. We've been hired to act like idiots and entertain you. But we're sick of it, and sick of the lies!'

By now, Elvis had lost any semblance of his usual easy-going demeanour. 'Don't listen to him!' he shouted. 'We'll get him to sit down on the damn stool, then you'll see what the truth is!'

'Did you really think human beings could be that selfish and insane?' Perry continued, edging away from Elvis and the two copbots who had stepped onto the stage. 'All these years you thought you were watching fools, but the only fools have been *you*!' The copbots charged towards Perry, who dived from the stage into the sea of journalists. He hurdled over them, sprinted up an aisle, and out of the nearest door, the copbots in close pursuit. Before the members of the media could stand, the copbots carried Perry back into the room. He seemed to have lost his taste for struggle and lay limply in their arms.

'Put him on the stool!' Elvis shouted. The copbots complied, dragging Perry back onto the stage and hoisting him onto the Stool of Truth.

'Product of fornication,' the soothing woman's voice declared.

Elvis turned to the members of the media with a wide smile of relief. 'You see that? All that ruckus for nothing—'

'Normal,' the soothing woman's voice interrupted. Elvis gaped at Perry and the stool. 'Product of fornication,' the voice said. 'Normal.' 'Product of fornication.' The voice seemed to speed up, growing flustered. 'Product of fornication. Normal. Product of fornication. Unable to read. Unable to read. Unable to read.' The voice subsided and the device gave off a pronounced hum, followed by a few clicking noises, then silence. It had shut itself off.

Elvis stepped up to Perry, who seemed to be enjoying all of this, and grabbed him by the front of his jacket. 'Who are you?' he demanded. 'Where—' But before he could utter another syllable, Perry transformed himself into a winged monkey and took flight from the stage, squawking loudly and flapping around the room while flinging its excrement at the journalists below, inciting havoc among them.

Elvis turned to the copbots. 'That's a facsimilon,' he growled. 'Where's the real Perry Bunt?'

At that moment, he was travelling rapidly in a hovercar away from the conference room, speeding down a hallway to the bank of thirty elevators that serviced Earth. He saw Amanda waiting in front of the last elevator, but had forgotten how to stop the hovercar and, in a panic, flung himself from the vehicle, rolling to a stop at her feet.

'Get in,' she said.

Perry threw himself into the elevator, the doors closed, and Amanda pushed the button numbered 1. The elevator sprang to life and silently slid into dark space, quickly leaving behind the lunar surface. As it slipped around the moon, Perry, pulling himself up to his feet, saw other elevators in orbit ahead of them. 'You hit them all?'

Amanda nodded. Since leaving the press conference, she had managed to call all the elevators and dispatch them towards Los Angeles. This, as she explained earlier to Perry, would force Galaxy's security to follow every car to the surface and buy them more time to escape undetected. While Galaxy Entertainment had filled Earth with cameras, they hadn't bothered putting any in their own elevators.

'How'd the press conference go?'

Perry struggled to catch his breath. 'I think they believed me.'

'Jeff make it?'

Perry nodded. 'It was weird running into the hallway and seeing myself.'

'He told me he'd buy us a few minutes. Hopefully that'll be enough.'

'How'd you get him to do it?'

Amanda smiled. 'Are you kidding? He loves playing Earthles. He always says, "The funnier looking, the better."' Perry frowned. 'He also loved the idea of making executives look bad,' she added quickly.

'Will he be OK?'

'They won't be able to catch him. And even if they did, facsimilons are rarely held accountable for their actions. Pretending to be someone else is just what they do.'

They watched as the Earth grew before them, afraid to speak as if it would jinx their luck. As the blue planet filled the dark space all around them, Perry felt a sudden awe for it. *I'm going home*, he thought. And for the first time in his life, he felt a kinship with the people with whom he shared his home. It was true that they were terribly flawed, that they were all fated to want things they could never have, which made them crazy and in some instances dangerous. But most of them were dreaming of something better, and for this reason alone they were more alive than the Edenites, with the secrets of the universe at their fingertips, would ever be.

When swirls of clouds surrounded them, Amanda exhaled. 'We're going to make it,' she said. 'Now comes the tricky part.'

'What?' Perry said. 'None of that back there was tricky?'

Amanda didn't answer. Her eyes were fixed on the California coastline surging towards them. Perry could now make out the cancer-like sprawl of buildings and roadways that was Los Angeles, as well as the Santa Monica Mountains to the west and a thin yellow strip of beach bordering the deep blue of the Pacific Ocean. Without warning, Amanda reached over to the elevator's control panel and flipped the red switch marked Emergency Shut-Off. The elevator, which had been travelling through the Earth's upper atmosphere at a slight angle, shuddered, lurched and began dropping straight down at an even greater speed. Perry felt the skin on his face tugged towards the floor as he grabbed onto the metal railing.

'What the hell are you doing?' he managed to yell.

'We can't let it take us back to the station – they'll be waiting for us. We have to do a manual stop.'

'We're going to be flattened!'

'It won't let us crash.'

Despite this assurance, Perry watched with growing terror as the coastline hurtled towards them.

'Uh oh,' Amanda said.

'Please tell me you didn't just say *Uh oh*.'

'We're still too far out over the ocean. Lean against this

side.' Amanda pushed her body against one glass wall of the elevator.

Perry just stared. 'You can't be serious.'

'Lean with me or we're going to hit the water!'

Perry rushed to the wall and splayed his body next to Amanda's. The elevator wobbled slightly as it continued plummeting. All Perry could see now was ocean. He squeezed his eyes shut anticipating impact. Then he heard a gentle 'bing' and the sound of the doors sliding open. A gull cried. Perry opened his eyes. A beach stretched out before them. He turned to Amanda. She smiled and flipped the Emergency Shut-Off switch back. They stepped out of the car and Perry could hear the elevator's doors close behind him, even though when he turned, he couldn't see anything there at all. If anyone had been watching, they would have seen Perry and Amanda emerge from thin air. But there hadn't been anyone watching.

The only human inhabitants of the beach were a surfer bobbing out on the waves, a woman bent over the sand in a yoga pose, and two teenagers absorbed in throwing a red disk to each other, all oblivious to the man and woman dressed in white. If you were an alien from outer space and had landed on the beach at that moment, you might have interpreted these activities as some sort of religious observation celebrating the elements of water, ground and air that comprise Earth. You might have felt that these beings, with their primitive yet poetic approaches to honouring their surroundings, were worth saving.

Or you might have just felt what Perry and Amanda felt, which was grateful.

EPILOGUE

It worked.

The nuclear crisis in the Middle East passed and was replaced by the usual everyday bombings and killings, to the great relief of everyone. Except for the leadership of the young religion called Buddyism, which had placed so much importance on the imminent end of the world that it had no contingency plan for the Earth's survival. Its leader, Brother Ralph, went into hiding. He was last seen in front of a convenience store in Southern California.

The air became strangely free of flies.

President Grebner received an anonymous letter. The author claimed to have been sequestered and tortured in a secret prison located in the caverns beneath Drummond Nash's hunting lodge. The letter told the President that he must close all of the United States' secret prisons or risk exposure of their existence.

The letter closed with the words, 'What would Jesus ask you to do?'

Shortly thereafter, an investigation into the activities of a rogue counter-terrorism unit within the CIA was initiated in the US Senate. The secret prison in the Colorado Rockies was discovered and most of the prisoners freed.

One of these detainees, Alistair Alexander, was repatriated to England, where he promptly abandoned his study of literature at Cambridge. After his harrowing experience, the books he once loved seemed hollow to him; he decided that stories had never held any answers for him and never would. He sought out a conservative Muslim cleric with a reputation for anti-Western rhetoric and confided the realisation he'd come to during his incarceration in Colorado: that Drummond Nash was right. Alistair actually was the kind of person who wanted to kill someone like Drummond Nash or, for that matter, anyone vaguely like him. He was, by definition, a terrorist. 'It took them quite some time to convince me, but in the end, they did it.' The cleric put Alistair in touch with a fringe group that arranged for his passage to Pakistan, where he entered into a new field of postgraduate study.

As chance would have it, one of his teachers was Ali al-Zander. He never did see the Rockettes.

Since most of his work was considered secret for reasons of national security, Drummond Nash himself was never obligated to answer questions before the senate investigation. His new hunting lodge was rumoured to be in Idaho.

The President, meanwhile, took a three-week 'leave of absence', citing unspecified medical problems. Even in his medicated dreams he saw the face of Perry Bunt burning in the wreckage of a helicopter. He prayed daily and fervently for relief.

Galaxy Entertainment surprised Wall Street analysts by dissolving and selling all of its assets to another cable company. The offices on Ventura Boulevard were boarded up and eventually, after some major remodelling, converted into an International House of Pancakes.

On some Saturday mornings, Perry Bunt and Amanda Mundo could be found there having breakfast with their baby boy, Milo. Milo had been born with a full head of dark hair on a windy spring night that became, without portent or pretence, the greatest night of his parents' lives. Perry and Amanda chose the restaurant not so much for the pancakes as for the location. But as far as Milo was concerned, it was all about the pancakes. He ate them in large messy handfuls, his ringlets inevitably coated in sticky syrup.

Perry resumed teaching screenwriting at Encino Community College. The administration had accepted the far-fetched excuse for his disappearance (he told them he'd hit his head on a dryer door at a laundromat and contracted temporary amnesia), which he suspected had more to do with the lack of people willing to teach screenwriting at a community college than anything else. To his surprise, he discovered a new love for his job. In a universe of infinite, unfathomable dimensions, he found that there was something deeply therapeutic about immersing oneself in finite imaginary worlds.

Amanda found employment in reality TV and quickly became one of its most sought-after producers. She actually enjoyed working and living among Earthles, despite their, well, *earthiness* – there really was no other way to describe it. Mostly she found their obtuseness comic, and she and Perry spent many nights after Milo was asleep drinking wine and laughing about their fellow products of fornication.

She missed her friends and parents in Eden, but knew she would see them all again. She'd managed to rewire a laptop and a satellite dish to communicate with her mother and father, and they promised to save up for a holiday on Earth.

She no longer saw any conspiracy involved in the events that brought her to Perry, no unavoidable fate or destiny that had somehow influenced her life's events. In this sense, her Edenite sense of rationality was stronger than ever – with a major exception: Milo. In her mind, there was no explanation for Milo other than a miracle. When she watched him sleep, late at night, she felt as if she were turning her back on millennia of knowledge and staring into some unfathomable secret of the universe that was written in the swirl of his hair, the curl of his ears and the tiny saucers of his toenails.

The Earth, of course, continued to be a mess – even without anyone to watch it – its violent and toxic inhabitants seemingly hell-bent on finishing the job Galaxy Entertainment chose not to complete. Perry still couldn't bring himself to read a newspaper, though once a week he would drive over to St Jude's and volunteer with Noah Overton, serving meals at the soup kitchen. While recognising that he'd never be able to match Noah's zeal for helping people, Perry had come to appreciate it. Every once in a while one of the diners would stare across the steam table, a look of nascent recognition on their faces, but fortunately none ever connected Perry to the martyred leader of a religious movement. Noah, meanwhile, had placed his adventures with Perry and Amanda in the category of 'helping friends through a difficult time'. He was happy to see the couple seemingly liberated from the delusions that had turned the ill-fated trip to Washington into such a nightmare.

He had not hallucinated Gandhi or anyone else again, which he credited to his new vegan diet.

No one knew, of course, that Perry and Amanda had saved the Earth; few even knew the Earth was on the verge of being destroyed. And certainly no one knew that Perry Bunt, through guile, determination and luck, had lifted the yoke of entertainment colonialism from the world and its inhabitants. This was actually OK with Perry. Now that he had Amanda and Milo to share his life with, he didn't care about being a hero. He no longer felt the tidal pull of destiny, the need to achieve greatness. His experience tangling with an advanced civilisation had given him a keen appreciation for mere contentment. He sat at the kitchen table with Amanda and Milo, a mug of coffee in his hand, and thought to himself, *What more could anyone want?*

Well, success, for one thing. But Perry didn't waste hours pining for this – which was good, because he didn't have any. Despite the death of Del Waddle, his script *Dead Tweet* remained moribund, as did the rest of his unproduced oeuvre. And after he showed a willingness to return her calls, GALL agent Dana Fulcher promptly stopped returning his. *The Last Day of School* remained an unfinished monument to mediocrity; no longer did Perry hear the siren call of the Big Idea.

He began writing something about his remarkable experience in the guise of fiction, but quickly gave up on the project. Once written down, the adventure read as far too ludicrous and unbelievable, even for a fringe science-fiction audience. He realised that he was content to live the story of his life without having to claim authorship.

Amanda's producing pay cheque paid for a nicer apartment, on the hill just above where Perry used to live. One evening, when Perry was giving Milo a bath, he impulsively decided to wash his son's hair. While carefully wetting it with a washcloth, he noticed something he'd never seen before. 'Amanda,' he called.

'Yes?'

'Come here and look at this.'

Amanda walked into the bathroom. 'What is it?' Perry pointed to Milo's scalp, where a birthmark was now clearly visible beneath his son's wet hair: a small star.

In the bathroom in Los Angeles, on the western edge of the North American continent, in the Western Hemisphere of Earth, which orbited a Class 2 star on the far edge of the

Milky Way Galaxy, which swirled near the centre of the fifty closely bound galaxies that comprise half of the Virgo Supercluster, Perry and Amanda exchanged a stunned look that was watched with great enjoyment by life forms gazing down from a universe away. These beings appeared nothing like Perry and Amanda and, in fact, were composed of different material entirely; they were immense and had many more dimensions to their corporeal forms. But they enjoyed what they were seeing nonetheless. They conveyed their intense enjoyment to each other by clicking loudly.

The clicks roughly translated as: 'This was all worth it.'

ACKNOWLEDGEMENTS

The creation of Channel Blue would have been as unlikely as that of its fictional counterpart if not for the efforts of Katie Roberts, Peggy Orenstein and Louis Theroux. Ian Roberts and John Martel provided crucial and invaluable feedback throughout the process. Georgina Capel took on the unenviable task of finding an audience for it with astonishing gusto, intrepidly searching the known galaxy for readers. And finally I would be remiss in not acknowledging the support of my fellow cast-members: my mother, Ann, and my sister Melissa, as well my closest co-stars, Sarah, Cleo and Julian; our ratings may go up and down, but no one can deny our chemistry.